Sweet Revenge

Sweet Revenge

Robert Lockwood

Library of Congress Control Number:		2011961478
ISBN:	Hardcover	978-1-4653-1080-4
	Softcover	978-1-4653-1079-8
	Ebook	978-1-4653-1081-1

This is a work of fiction. Names, characters, places and incidents either are the product of the author's imagination or are used fictitiously, and any resemblance to any actual persons, living or dead, events, or locales is entirely coincidental.

This book was printed in the United States of America.

To order additional copies of this book, contact:
Xlibris Corporation
1-888-795-4274
www.Xlibris.com
Orders@Xlibris.com
107692

Contents

BOOKS BY ROBERT LOCKWOOD

NONFICTION

NUCLEAR POLICY, GAULLIST STYLE

MILITARY UNIONS

LEGISLATIVE ANALYSIS

FICTION

A CULTURE OF DECEPTION

POLITICAL DUCKS: LUCKY, LAME & DEAD

AU REVOIR, ISRAEL

SWEET REVENGE

A GLOBAL PRESIDENCY? (in progress)

ACKNOWLEDGMENTS

THIS STORY MADE great demand on friendships acquired over a professional lifetime. I am very grateful to associates from my Senate interaction with the committees on labor, finance, and, especially, judiciary, where I served as counsel for ten years. I have also drawn heavily on contacts formed during my lobbying career. All selflessly provided updated policy amendments and materials as well as critical attention to the presentation of the parts of the story related to their assistance.

An advantage of fiction writing is assured anonymity, and fiction writing is the chosen method I've employed to reveal the guile of our political system. It is yet another form of voice allowed to those who share my views.

CAST OF CHARACTERS

Eastwood, Earl H. – President of the United States

OTHERS (IN ALPHABETICAL ORDER)

Baldwin, Mark – Former senator (R-VA), resigned in scandal; CEO, Brent-UK

Baptiste, Henri – Swiss banker and board member of Lucas Holdings, Brent Trading, and Belmont

Bago, Jean-Claude – President of the Ivory Coast

Bago, Robert – Son of Jean-Claude

Castignani, Bob – Former senator (D-ME), lost seat in 2010; lobbyist for Swiss companies

Cohen, Sue – Chief of staff to the president

Davidson, Marge – Senior administrative assistant and personal secretary to the president

Di Nardo, Jeannie – Senior paralegal at the law firm of Castignani, Tranh, and Ochs

Dubin, Louis – Secretary of treasury

Edwards, Kenny – Assistant to the president and White House communications director (press secretary)

Ford, David – Former representative (D-NY), resigned in scandal; executive VP, Brent

Gomez, Al – Mayor (R) of Hartford, Connecticut

Gorgens, Lutz – CEO, Belmont Confections of Vevey, Switzerland

Gregoire, Jane – Wife of Mark and counsel at Lucas of Chamby, Switzerland

Gregoire, Marc – Former representative (D-LA), resigned in scandal; senior managing director, Lucas

Guillermo, Domenic – Former governor (D-CT); ambassador to the Vatican; board member of Lucas, Brent, and Belmont; CEO of Swiss-American Confections Corporation (SACC)

Hammond, Jack – Attorney general of the United States

Holmes, Audrey – Representative (R-TX), lived for three years in the White House with the president

Howard, Monica – Secretary of health, education, and welfare; MD; confidante extraordinaire to the president

Kallias, Sophia – Governor (R-CT)

Koerner, Mark – Former representative (D-NJ), resigned in scandal; Brent VP and counsel

Lehman, Nancy – Former senator (D-CA), resigned in scandal; executive VP, Lucas

McMahon, Kyle – CEO, Havens of Massachusetts; later, department secretary of commerce

Matthey, Chantal – Swiss Justice councillor

Maurer, Ruth – President of the Swiss Confederation

Mourgos, George – Representative (R-CT), Rose Confections located in his congressional district

Ochs, Ben – Former Senate staffer, now law partner of Bob Castignani

O'Meara, Kevin – Senator (D-MA); chairman, Senate Armed Services Committee

Provenzano, Tony – Representative (D-RI), ranking member of the House Armed Services Committee

Rallis, Nikos – Former Greek finance minister, CEO and chairman of Lucas Holdings, and senior board member of Brent and Belmont

Rathbone, Anne – Former representative (D-DE), resigned in scandal; CFO, Lucas

Rodman, Jarrett – Former representative (D-MI), resigned in scandal; CEO, Brent-Canada

Sachs, Liz – Executive assistant to CEO Domenic Guillermo of Swiss-American Confections Corporation

Sawicki, Tim – CEO, Rose Confections of Connecticut; later, US ambassador to Switzerland

Scharfman, Jeff – Former senator (D-NJ), resigned in scandal; president, Lucas Holdings

Schlesinger, Sam – Former senator-elect (D-CT), resigned in scandal before taking office; CEO, Brent-USA

Scott, Henry – Secretary of state, former legal scholar at University of Virginia Law School

Seaton, Charles – Treasury secretary in previous presidential administration, caught up in scandal; president, Brent in Chamby, Switzerland

Smit, Marc – President, Belmont of Vevey, Switzerland

Stehlin, Karl – Swiss Foreign Affairs councillor

Stokes, Bill – Former Yale professor, Connecticut Democratic Party official, national security adviser

Tagro, Emile – Ivory Coast prime minister who won presidential election from Jean-Claude Bago

Tantillo, Andrew – Former senator (D-NJ), resigned in scandal, convicted and served sentence in federal prison; senior managing director, Lucas

Thompson, Bennie – Former representative (D-MS), resigned in scandal; executive VP, Brent

Tranh, Don – Former senior Senate staffer, law partner of Castignani and Ochs

von Schlossen, Paul – CEO, Brent Commodity Trading Company of Chamby, Switzerland

Wooley, Mary Rossotti – Representative (D-MD), former Speaker of the House, then majority leader in the 112th Congress.

CHAPTER 1

REWARD, NOT REVENGE

THE MOOD INSIDE THE OLD TOWN, ALEXANDRIA, RESIDENCE OF FORMER SENATOR BOB CASTIGNANI WAS NO LESS SOMBER THAN THE CLOUDY, BITTERLY COLD DAY ON DECEMBER 9, 2010. The Maine Democrat, chairman of the Senate Foreign Relations Committee in the 111th Congress, lost his seat to a Tea Party candidate. The so-called Tea Party movement was a wrenching minirevolution for the Democrats. The far-right wing of the Republican Party managed to ally itself with enough independent voters to secure eighty-two seats in the House of Representatives and majority control of the body. The movement changed the composition of the United States Senate, taking six seats from the Democratic lineup, one of which was Castignani's, ending his twenty-four-year career in the upper house.

Several of Castignani's former congressional colleagues trickled into the unusually contemporary town house at South Royal and Wilkes Streets, a glaring oddity among the eighteenth-century residences in the popular and pre-Revolutionary Washington suburb. They had also lost their seats and their reputations, but for different reasons; several had even served short prison terms.

"It's been damn hell, I tell ya, Bob," said Andy Tantillo.

", Damn right, I can't even show my face in my own hometown. I was once a celebrity there. Among my friends, I was the only one who served in Vietnam. That helped abate my the sentence, I think," said Jeff Scharfman, who, like Tantillo, had been a senator from New Jersey.

"Unfortunately, Andy, you were the only one of us from the Senate who got real time," commented Sam Schlesinger, who had been appointed by the governor of Connecticut to the Senate seat abandoned by Earl Eastwood, now president of the United States.

The foursome made room for Nancy Lehman, who gingerly moved into the group, wineglass in her hand. Lehman, the former senator from California and chairwoman of the Senate Select Committee on Intelligence, looked her age at sixty-two, the stress of the past year having taken a bitter toll. Her gait was unsteady; her face haggard and showing the wrinkles common to many beach-loving Californians as they age. Her appearance caused Castignani to wince unnoticeably as he recalled her dramatic good looks, shapely figure, and modish attire, features that in the past had turned heads whenever she moved about on the Senate floor.

"Any room for a fellow felon?" she said, the cynicism in her humor straightening the postures of the four men.

The overhead lights in the room seemed to accentuate the aging signs on her face, her eyes sunken, and the skin on her neck like a crinoline shadowed by her chin. As she spoke, creases popped up at the corners of her mouth. But the four men greeted her warmly, their smiles stiffened and somewhat forced as they sensed the agony that she had shared with them.

"Who else is coming?" she asked Castignani.

"Just about everyone who was involved. Mark should be here a little later, and the seven House members are on their way," he replied, referring to former senator Mark Baldwin and the former House representatives who were also entangled in the affair. Baldwin's lawyers had managed to get his case dismissed with the well-documented plea that he was an innocent investor in the scheme that had scandalized Congress in late 2008 and early 2009. Baldwin was the only Senate Republican in the investment scheme, although one of the seven House investors was also a Republican.

"I don't begrudge Mark because he was exonerated. The rest of us had reason to figure out what the hell was going on, but we were blinded by ambition and the chance to make some real money," said Scharfman.

"I wish I could say I'm offended by that remark," added Lehman, her typically dark humor stirring light laughter.

The doorbell rang. Castignani signaled to Ben Ochs and Don Tranh, two former senior Senate staffers invited to the meeting. They opened the door, warmly greeting the huddled six men and one woman entering. Their coats barely off, the newcomers stretched out their ungloved hands, shaking and backslapping with their colleagues who rushed to greet them. Ochs and Tranh, the rank-and-order sensitivities of their years on congressional staffs emerging, quietly withdrew, taking coats and attempting to get drink orders.

The decibel level in the foyer rising, Castignani asserted in his command voice, developed during his midshipman days at the US Naval Academy and, again, as chairman over the sometimes unruly proceedings of his Senate committee, "Let's go into the living room." He added, "I've got a fire going."

All turned, talking and overtalking vigorously among them as the blast of warm air from the wood-burning fireplace welcomed them into the larger room.

"Nice digs you've got here, Bob. When did you move from Watergate?" asked Mark Koerner, a former New Jersey Democratic representative who was one of two House members who had served a short prison sentence. A third member of the group, former secretary of treasury in the administration of former president Bob Davids, also served ninety days as did one Democratic senator.

"I bought the place in the summer of 2010 as Mary Ann's cancer was consuming her. I needed more room and had to get out of Washington. Also, I was right in the middle of the campaign. As you know, she died on me in September. Frankly, I lost my enthusiasm for campaigning, which I'm sure didn't make it any easier for my opponent to win. But she was generous and sympathetic, which I appreciated, and I congratulated her with equal respect for the tough but clean race that she ran."

"I'm really sorry about Mary Ann. She was a great woman," Koerner replied.

"I'm broken, Mark. Thirty years of incredible marriage. You know, we got married when I was in the navy. As a young officer, I was at sea constantly. She managed everything, raised our two kids through four years of that hell until I got out. After that, she worked at Mass General as a night nurse while I was in law school, and continued at a hospital in Portland while I got my law career under way and entered state politics."

Castignani's grief became apparent as he spoke. Koerner patted him on the shoulder, saying,

"Bob, I'm glad she was spared the campaign loss. I know she loved Washington and the political scene."

*   *   *

The polybabble that prevails at all Washington gatherings of any number more than one quickly swept over the crowd, now rubbing hands and shoulders near the fire. The drinks were being efficiently dispersed by Ben Ochs and Don Tranh, the two former Senate staffers who appeared quite accustomed, if not satisfied, with their seemingly menial roles.

As talk and bodies warmed, the doorbell again rang, then the door opened without more than a second or two between the last chime. In walked the ex-senator from Virginia, Mark Baldwin, along with David Ford, who had been a New York representative. Last in the door was Nikos Rallis, a Greek national and minister of finance, who departed from his position and Greece following the scandal that marked most everyone in the room.

A new buzz swept over the group. The former House members were especially resentful of Baldwin, whose case had been dismissed. They attributed it to his personal wealth, which allowed him to buy the best legal assistance available, and, of course, to his standing as a senator, something that always put reputational distance between any assemblages of "congressionals."

The murmurs hardly bothered Baldwin. He and Ford were the only Republican members of Congress among the crowd. The third Republican present was former treasury secretary Charles Seaton, or Chuck as he preferred to be called.

Castignani, sensing the new layer of tension in the air, excused himself from Koerner and raised his six-foot-four-inch frame and chesty voice to get everyone's attention. *I need to get this thing under way before they start killing each other,* he thought to himself.

"Folks, let's grab a seat. We should have enough of them. Ben, bring in one of the dining room chairs, if you would, buddy," he shouted to Ochs, who raced toward the attached dining room.

It took several minutes for all to find seats convenient to their choices of seating partners and viewing and listening positions. There was the usual fumbling, drinks tottering on side tables, the floor, and even the fireplace mantel, where some of the abandoned half-full glasses now stood. The noise and group settled down.

"I'm gonna skip the roll call votes, but that doesn't mean you can leave the floor," he said to the laughter of all. The reference was to voting procedures requiring the presence of members of the floor of the House or Senate. Without a roll call vote, members would generally feel free to engage in other activities off the floor, knowing their Blackberries or aides would alert them back into the chamber.

Castignani continued. "This is the first time we've all been together since the court actions. And we're delighted that Chuck, Andy, Mark, and Marc survived their short and unfortunate terms. There were a lot of injustices at play here, and I sympathize with the disappointment and disgust that still stalk some of you."

With that comment, there was a new buzz among those present. Much hand and body language and motion accompanied the chatting, which gradually died down.

"Jeff asked for this meeting, and I was pleased to accommodate him. This is a great place for us to assemble since we're out of sight of the media and away from others who'd probably like to be flies on the wall. Old Town has many Republicans and Democrats living here as you know. Hopefully, most are at work, or those who are capable, engaged in 'other' matinee activities," he added to low chuckles. All knew only too well why they were there.

*   *   *

The 2008 presidential campaign brought to office the first African American president, Earl Harry Eastwood. Eastwood, then the senator from Connecticut and Senate minority leader in the 110th Congress, was the vice presidential candidate on the ticket with Lisa Macon Lewis, the former Virginia governor. Lewis's cancer, which ultimately took her life, forced her to resign before inauguration, passing the mantle of leadership to Eastwood, who entered the White House with strong Democratic majorities in both the House and Senate.

Among the dominant foreign policy issues of that moment was the nuclear saber rattling of Iran's president, Mahmoud Ahmadinejad. Policy wonks and pundits widely assumed Israel would attack the Iranian nuclear facilities threatening the country. Ahmadinejad himself had promised as much. Eastwood and Lisa Macon Lewis both assured Israel and most American Jewish organizations that they would stand by Israel regardless.

In the House and Senate, some members were unsteadied by the thought of US support for an Israeli initiative that could enflame the easily ignitable Islamic states in the region. Eastwood, after becoming the president-elect and then the inaugurated chief executive, was irritated and surprised by eroded backing in the Congress. Some Jewish members were unusually vocal in their demands for diplomatic alternatives to the traditional military response. It was a situation for which few, if any, real solutions could be identified.

In the meantime, Washington lobbyists for a Greek-based investment company called Club Lucas had penetrated deep into both executive and legislative branch officialdom. They offered substantial investment opportunities. Some included interest payments for mere pledges of monies by congressional members. Club Lucas was promoting the development of the Greek island of Santorini into a colossal resort. Cruise ships would be given berths for two-day stay overs with waivers of tariffs and other preferential treatments made for American purchases of products and services at the site. The investors found their pledges paying handsome returns as the shares of the private company grew in value. For many congressionals, the investment was proving to be a very satisfying appendage to their retirement planning.

It soon occurred to the congressional investors that regional stability was critical to the success of the Lucas project and their own interests. But they were also patriots and, for the most part, reasonably responsible and dedicated representatives and senators. However, for some, the Lucas influence did shade their reasoning regarding US foreign policy toward Israel.

It would have been tempting to assume that throwing a blanket over Israel's fired-up militancy was driven by greed. But there were other motives, especially among the Jewish members of Congress involved in the investment scheme. They strongly resented the undercurrent of presumptions that their Jewishness compelled a commitment to Israel regardless. This group felt their political independence eclipsed and even their patriotism as Americans tainted. For them, the investment advantages were distant, if not negligible, influences on their official actions toward Israel.

Club Lucas sponsored a visit to the project in the Mediterranean on a private yacht, the *Athena*, in November 2008, after the election and just before Thanksgiving

Day in the United States. Aboard were the congressional investors as well as several other American officials, including the then secretaries of state and treasury. While moored off the Greek island of Santorini, the American navy's Fifth Fleet commander was alerted to an apparent attack by sea originating in Lebanon. The US Mediterranean fleet prepared its defenses and dispatched a frigate to protect the congressional and other official members on the *Athena*.

The threat was identified as a Hezbollah cigarette boat traveling at high speed, and loaded with explosives, toward *Athena*. This was according to communication intercepts made by intelligence gathered from both French and Spanish warships operating in the same area. Ultimately, the US Navy warship protecting the *Athena* engaged and destroyed the terrorist boat. The *Athena* was escorted to the Athens port at Pireaus, and the passengers were safely evacuated to the American Air Force base in Ramstein, Germany.

Among the passengers – all investors – there were broad differences of culpability, with some even blaming Israel for having "set up" the scheme to ensure support for their attack on Iran, which occurred simultaneously with the attempted assault on *Athena*. Gradually, a consensus was formed precisely along those lines, hardening still further resistance to a US bailout of Israel's provocation, which now led to a threatened counterattack against Israel by Iran.

Soon after he was inaugurated, President Eastwood had learned that Club Lucas had benefited greatly from Iranian investments and that the "earnings" on the congressionals' pledge investments came from the Iranian treasury. Moreover, the earnings were deposited in foreign bank accounts in Athens, Paris, and Zurich, with some funds going to a New York City branch of the foreign banks. Some members failed to report their withdrawals as income received on their individual federal and state tax returns, with many ignoring federal laws requiring disclosure of the existence of foreign bank accounts. The Eastwood Justice Department prosecuted most of the investors on various charges including tax evasion and fraud, conflict of interest, and criminal conspiracy.

Several of the investors and officials on board *Athena*, including Bob Castignani, had fully complied with the law. Castignani, a strong supporter of Israel and leader of the congressional delegation, or CODEL, had assumed a commanding role during the crisis and was widely commended for his "comportment under fire" by the president.

*　　*　　*

The list of persons present this day at Castignani's Old Town, Alexandria, home would have read like a lobbyist's list of dream targets, especially considering their former positions in Congress and the government.

Listed below are former senators, their positions before prosecution, charges against them, and outcomes:

Jeff Scharfman (D-NJ), chairman, Defense Subcommittee, Senate Appropriations Committee. Charged and convicted of tax evasion, failure to report foreign bank accounts, conflict of interest; resigned with $25,000 fine and one-year suspended sentence.

Nancy Lehman (D-CA), chairwoman, Senate Select Committee on Intelligence. The senator was charged as above with the same outcome.

Sam Schlesinger (D-CT), member, Senate Homeland Security Committee. The senator was charged as above with the same outcome.

Andrew Tantillo (D-NJ), chairman, Subcommittee on European Affairs, Senate Foreign Relations Committee. Tantillo was charged and convicted of tax fraud, criminal conspiracy, and conflict of interest; he resigned and then paid a $50,000 fine and served six months in federal prison.

Mark Baldwin (R-VA), member, Senate Select Committee on Ethics. The federal district court found Baldwin to be an innocent investor. Nevertheless, the adverse publicity all but doomed an uncertain reelection campaign in a state now drifting Democratic, motivating him to resign his seat in the Senate.

All the senators had been investigated by the Senate's ethics panel, which turned over its evidence and recommendations to the Senate Legal Counsel, who further coordinated the subsequent Justice Department prosecutions and other actions by the US attorney for the District of Columbia.

Below are former members of the US House of Representatives involved in the scandal with their charges and the outcomes:

David Ford (R-NY), ranking Republican member of the House Homeland Security Committee; he was charged and convicted of tax evasion, failure to report foreign bank accounts, and conflict of interest. He resigned his seat in the House, paid a $15,000 civil fine, and was given a six-month suspended sentence. Ford had reported the income earned and deposited in a New York City bank but not the income earned and deposited in the bank's home office in Athens.

Jarrett Rodman (D-NY), chairman, House Foreign Affairs Committee; he was charged and convicted of tax evasion, failure to report foreign bank accounts, and conflict of interest. He resigned his seat in the House, paid a $25,000 fine, and was given a one-year suspended sentence.

Anne Rathbone (D-DE), chairwoman, Subcommittee on Defense, House Appropriations Committee; she was charged and convicted of tax evasion, failure to report foreign bank accounts, and conflict of interest. She resigned her seat in the House, paid a $15,000 fine, and was given a six-month suspended sentence.

Bennie Thompson (D-MS), chairman of the House Homeland Security Committee and chairman of the powerful Congressional Black Caucus. He was charged and convicted of tax evasion, failure to report foreign bank accounts, and conflict of interest. He resigned his seat in the House, paid a $25,000 fine, and was given a one-year suspended sentence.

Mark Koerner (D-NJ), chairman, Subcommittee on the Middle East and South Asia, House Foreign Affairs Committee. He was charged and convicted of tax fraud, criminal conspiracy, and conflict of interest; he resigned, paid a $50,000 fine, and served six months in federal prison.

Marc Gregoire (D-LA), chairman, Readiness Subcommittee, House Armed Services Committee. Like Koerner, Gregoire was charged and convicted of tax fraud, criminal conspiracy, and conflict of interest; he resigned and then paid a $50,000 fine and served six months in federal prison.

Investigative procedures in the House differ from those in the Senate. In January 2009, the House Office of Congressional Ethics (OCE) was created as an independent entity to examine allegations of misconduct of members, employees, and officers of the lower legislative chamber. OCE, which has jurisdiction only in the lower chamber, may refer its findings to the House Committee on Standards of Official Conduct. Only the latter committee can take disciplinary action against the offenders. OCE is somewhat like the Senate Select Committee on Ethics in that it will consider complaints regarding misconduct from any public source. But once more, only the House Committee on Standards of Official Conduct and the Senate Committee on Ethics can coordinate actions with the Justice Department where appropriate.

Tantillo, Koerner, and Gregoire suffered higher fines and imprisonment as both the investigating committees in the Senate and the House, as well as the district court where all three had been tried, determined that they knowingly and corruptly failed to comply with various provisions of the Lobbying Disclosure Act and were therefore liable for added fines and imprisonment under title 18 of the United States Code.

Two others in the room were also involved.

Charles "Chuck" Seaton, secretary of treasury in the outgoing Republican administration, was also fined $50,000 and imprisoned for six months under the same conditions and for the same reasons that applied to Tantillo, Gregoire, and Koerner.

Nikos Rallis, the former Greek minister of finance, was not charged or convicted either in Greece or the United States. Rallis was the president of Club Lucas, the Athens-based organization that allegedly conjured up the investment scheme that embroiled so many US officials. However, acquiring evidence from multiple global sources as to the Rallis's personal role and any possible wrongdoing became virtually impossible for US investigators.

In summary, the group at Castignani's house numbered fifteen: six former senators including Castignani, six former House members, a former treasury secretary, a former Greek finance minister, and the two former senior staff members, Ben Ochs and Don Tranh. Collectively, it was within this somewhat rancorous setting that Jeff Scharfman would ignite excited minds to cobble together a plan for retribution, revenge, and reward.

*   *   *

"Jeff, it's your show," said Castignani to Scharfman.

"Thanks, Bob. We've all been to hell and back, especially Andy and Mark and Marc. I asked Bob to pull us all together to see where we go from here. We're all hurting. And let's not do any finger-pointing within this group. We were screwed and, for us Democrats, by our own party leader," Scharfman said, the anger in his voice steadily rising as he made blatant reference to Earl Eastwood, now sitting in the White House.

"Hold on, Jeff." The voice was that of Nancy Lehman. "Look, we followed your lead once before. I'm not so sure we want to go there again. My advice to you is to separate yourself from the deep personal angst you have for the president and use a bit more reason and reserve."

"I have to endorse that remark, Jeff. Nancy's right. We're not gonna let your vendetta get in the way of our needs to rehabilitate our reputations, and our psyches," said Andy Tantillo. "And I say that as one who has suffered more than most from the debacle."

There was casual nodding and body movements supporting the comments of Lehman and Tantillo. Scharfman was quick to sense his misstep.

I came on too strong. It was counterproductive. It's no way to find a way out of this mess, at least not if I hope to be able to lead the way, Scharfman thought.

"I guess I can't deny either of the criticisms. I'm still stuck in the grimy outcome and the effects they've had on all of us. But this is why I wanted to get together. And it's why I asked Niko to join us," Scharfman added, referring to the dapper Greek, Nikos Rallis. The name Nikos would be spelled with or without the *s*, which was dropped by friends who preferred the less formal version.

"Niko understands the way we all feel. He approached me with some thoughts for restitution. We need ideas, and I think Niko may help in that regard," Scharfman concluded.

*   *   *

Nikos Rallis was himself a story. The heir of a substantial shipping fortune, he darted into politics, rising in his party through the ranks of regional elected offices to the Hellenic parliament. His performance in Syntagma Square, the site of Parliament House, was notable for his youthful wisdom, especially on the critical matters of foreign trade, a lifeline for the Greek economy. He was elected deputy speaker after two four-year terms in the unicameral legislature, an unprecedented sprint to the crest of Greek political power and one that caught the eye of his party's prime minister; he was made minister of finance, a position he held until 2010, when he resigned to "pursue private interests." Greek laws are substantially vaguer than those in the United States when it comes to collateral business activity while serving in public office. Rallis was therefore involved in any number of investment schemes, as well as his family's trading and shipping business during his elected terms.

His overseas education was yet another source of Rallis's leadership strength. He was educated at an international school in Greece from an early age, his parents having decided to send him to the United States for higher education. He spent two years at St. Paul's School in Concord, New Hampshire. The two-thousand-acre campus and small student body of 524 provided the political testing grounds that gave Niko the self-confidence needed to elevate him on to future stages. Surrounded either by students from well-established wealth or by those who, with lesser birthrights, were rewarded with substantial financial assistance at the elite boarding school where annual costs easily reached into the $60,000 range, Niko's instincts and intuition for making the "right" friends would serve him equally well for years to come.

After St. Paul's, Niko went to Trinity College in Hartford, Connecticut, a lesser distinguished member of the "small Ivy League" that also included Amherst, Williams, and Wesleyan. Once more, he operated smoothly and carefully among the student body, joining St. Anthony's Hall, a somewhat pretentious moniker for the Delta Psi fraternity, its Greek designation. Niko smiled inwardly at the way he could manipulate the brotherhood, even inviting to Greece each summer every member of the fraternity for a two-week bacchanalian eruption that demanded no less concealment than the membership oaths at Yale's Skull and Bones.

Niko graduated with summa honors from Trinity; then he entered the Wharton School's MBA program. The admissions department gave little attention to their usual insistence on prior business experience, fully recognizing that the great wealth and global influence of the Rallis family carried its own future rewards. Again, Niko skimmed off the best of the school for invitations to Greece, which included internships for the invitees in the family's business offices in Athens. Several professors would be included in the delegation and given remarkable access to family business operations that merited case study development for classroom use – yet another way of promoting the Rallis family's Attica Lines.

Always well dressed, physically fit, and gracious, Rallis started to speak in his near-perfect, American-accented English. "Thanks, Bob, for your kind hospitality. I hope I can put an overlay of encouragement on the exchange that just occurred. It's not all that bad, you know. All of you still have substantial wealth residing in your original investments in Club Lucas," Rallis said to the apparent astonishment of many in the room.

Sam Schlesinger spoke up, "Wait a minute, Niko. I thought the Greek government turned the funds over to the Internal Revenue Service. At least, that's what my lawyer led me to believe. I had to pay legal and court costs, as well as the fines and penalties from my own savings. As did most others here, I believe."

"Yeah, that's what we were told too," added Mark Koerner, one of the three who paid the stiffest fines.

Rallis reentered the conversation. Some in the room were now standing so as to hear and see better.

"I can assure you that your investments are secured in Banque Credit d'Helvetia in Geneva. The funds, as you know, were originally managed through the Banque de Moyen Orient in Paris, with deposits made in its Athens branch. Those of you who took withdrawals received them through BDMO's New York office. The fines and other penalties levied by the courts were based on your behavior and your perceived gains. Neither the courts nor the US Treasury Department made any attempt to seize the assets in your accounts. You paid only the taxes and penalties due on the *earnings* in those accounts to the Greek government and the IRS under the standing tax treaty between the two countries. I repeat, the money is yours, and legitimately so. I have here a list of your holdings," Rallis said, removing a file folder from his elegant Longchamp briefcase.

He passed the papers among the crowd, adding, "I've disclosed everything and everyone's holdings so we all know where each of us stands."

All were reaching for the form, then turning either away or to a neighbor as they glanced first at their own accounts, then those of others.

The residual holdings in Club Lucas in Swiss francs and noted as CHF, meaning Confederation of Helvetia Francs, were as follows:

Jeffrey Scharfman: CHF 2.3 million	David Ford: CHF 6.8 million
Nancy Lehman: CHF 4.2 million	Jarrett Rodman: CHF 2.5 million
Andrew Tantillo: CHF 1.4 million	Mark Koerner: CHF 3.9 million
David Baldwin: CHF 2.3 million	Marc Gregoire: CHF 0.7 million
Sam Schlesinger: CHF0.3 million	Anne Rathbone: CHF 3.5 million
Charles Seaton: CHF 7.1 million	Bennie Thompson: CHF 1.6 million

There were a few quiet whistles and sighs as the list was carefully examined.

"Damn, I wish to hell I hadn't taken some of that money out to buy my kids a house in DC," lamented Bennie Thompson.

"Hey, you're okay," said Jarrett Rodman, who was standing next to him. "What's the exchange rate, Niko?" he asked.

"The Swiss franc is equal to $0.93, or about 7 percent more than the dollar," came Rallis's response. "And the rate doesn't change that much. The Swiss franc is appreciating, so you may be better off leaving the money there, in Swiss francs, that is, unless you really need it."

Rallis continued. "The funds have been transferred to the Lucas Investment Trust at the Banque Credit d'Helvetia. The bank will act as the corporate trustee, more of which I will discuss at another time. Your share of ownership and beneficial entitlement in LIT – the Lucas Investment Trust – is obviously based on your financial holding, which is further related to your residual monies in the original

Lucas operation. For example, Jeff, with 2.3 million invested in the trust, owns 6.28 percent and is entitled to that same percentage of earnings from Lucas business enterprises. The total value of the trust is CHF 36.6 million or about 35.2 million US dollars."

"I'll tell you, the way my life has gone and with this cash lode in Swiss francs, I may be better off living in Switzerland," said Jeff Scharfman.

"Interesting that you raise that point, Jeff. That's one of the things I wanted to talk to all of you about," Rallis said.

The room grew suddenly silent; eyes and thoughts were fixed on Rallis.

"Club Lucas has relocated to the area of Montreux, a beautiful city in a location known as the Swiss Riviera. We've redesignated the company as Lucas Holdings, now chartered under Swiss law and acquiring, merging, and investing in a number of companies. I'd like to invite and encourage any of you who may be interested to take a peek at what we're doing and plan to do."

Silence remained; minds and eyes alert, the group went into suspension mode, something highly unusual for any gathering of politicos, even those in the "after market" category.

The former treasury secretary, Chuck Seaton, spoke up, "Niko, I believe there's Iranian money in Lucas, is there not? And secondly, American citizens are barred from dealing with the government of Iran, which is under US as well as UN sanctions."

"No, Chuck, that's not entirely correct. There is Iranian money in Lucas' treasury, but it's private not governmental. Most of it is flight capital. You know, wealthy Iranians who fear for their lives and fortunes with Ahmadinejad at the helm. Many of our investors are Iranian Jews, most now living abroad, including many of them as well as other Iranians now residing in Switzerland as well as here in the US. But most remain in Iran and cautiously move their capital out when they can."

"Wait a minute. Has that always been the case?" Mark Koerner asked.

"Let me say definitively that there has never been Iranian government money invested in Club Lucas, nor is there any such money in Lucas Holdings now," Rallis said with added affirmation and emphasis.

The room erupted into bedlam; so many talking over that nothing comprehensible could be made from the clatter.

"Goddamn it," shouted the irascible Scharfman. "Do you realize Eastwood screwed us? He threatened to go public with our links to Lucas and the Iranian government money that underwrote it unless we resigned from Congress. The president did a job on us!"

Seaton started to speak again, "Wait, Niko . . . there's no government money, it's all private?" The former treasury secretary barely got his question out, and Rallis tried to answer.

But the level of chatter dominated. Above the bedlam came Scharfman's shouts. "Wait, hold on. Let me talk . . .

"Let him talk" and other comments and attempts toward quiet and calmness were heard.

But Scharfman was not exactly a calming voice.

He began. "What I'm sayin' is that we were entrapped. Our arms were twisted into resigning our seats and forcing pleas during the trials that we could have avoided. Our defense guys could have exonerated us. All of this was because the president threatened to disclose the Iranian funding in Club Lucas. That was the deal, remember that: resign, plead guilty, and there would be nothing said about the Iranian money that was *allegedly*, as we now know, paying the dividends and interest on our investments in Lucas.

"We even thought it was some type of Ponzi scheme, with new investments rather than earnings paying us." Scharfman seemed to get angrier as he spoke.

Finally, Seaton was able to get a word in. "Look, I was the damn treasury secretary, I *know* better than anyone here what the hell the statutes and regulations are. The Iranian sanctions were under my cabinet-level jurisdiction. It was my guys who wrote, amended, executed, and enforced them.

"I welcome Jeff's comments, and we all know – some of us here even share – Jeff's tendency to rationalize his deep dislike of Israeli leaders, whoever they might be, I would add," Seaton said to the muffled laughter in the room. He was, of course, referring to the resentment that Scharfman and several other Jewish members of Congress felt in being automatically identified with whatever quirky diplomatic or military move the Israelis undertook in just about any situation.

"But let's get real on this one, folks." He then attempted an explanation and interpretation of the Iranian sanctions.

"I know what the damn law says, and this is how it's been interpreted by the federal courts as well as the administrative law judges, or referees, or whatever the hell they call themselves these days."

Seaton's last comment regarding the regulatory process and the core of US administrative or quasi-judicial proceedings that enforce and interpret them was a cynical reference to the so-called administrative law judges. Formerly called referees in the federal system, the group was upgraded to the title of administrative law *judges* even though they neither are judges nor serve on courts established under the Constitution. Many political appointees as well as members of congressional committees overseeing the regulatory agencies object to treating and paying the administrative law judges as if they were equals to the federal and state counterparts properly created under constitutional authority to interpret and enforce statutes. To their opponents, the "admin" judges were little more than adjudicators and hearing officers regarding government programs and other government matters on which they render decisions. Much of the criticism is misplaced. Most administrative law judges have legal training, render decisions that can be appealed in the regularly constituted courts of equity and law, and are paid at levels well below those who sit on the benches of the courts of law.

Seaton continued. "The Iranian sanctions at play here were enacted by Clinton's executive order in 1997. The key phrase that potentially applied to us forbids, and I quote, 'all trade and investment with Iran by US persons, wherever located, are prohibited.' The rule is referred to as the ITR, or Iranian Transaction Regulation. The ITR was enforced by my Office of Foreign Assets Control, part of the treasury department. The language pertains to exports, imports, and financial dealings between US natural persons and Iran, meaning both the government as well as private Iranians.

"As you know, I was asked to rule on Club Lucas during the crisis. I found no conflict between investments in the organization and the official duties of those of us here. It was an innocent mistake on my part as the courts established in my trial, and I paid the price for my mistake, both financially and with time in prison." Seaton grimaced as he reflected on the outcome of his trial.

"Now, as regards Niko's revelation. The Iranian monies in Club Lucas – now Lucas Holdings SA, the Swiss-chartered successor to Club Lucas – are reposed there by private citizens of Iran. Most of them have left Iran or are keeping their heads down if still in the country, are in Iranian detention centers as political prisoners, or are deceased with their investments under the control of their estates or trusts. In other words, their investments are largely flight money, although that is not the issue here. What matters is the status of the Iranian investments and the investors. Here the Iranian sanction rules are silent. In other words, *we have not violated the sanctions law.*

"But, my friends, we were never charged with that. There were the other charges successfully pursued against us, all but Mark Baldwin, I might add, who didn't seem to know what the hell he was putting his money into," said Seaton, hesitating to allow venting murmurs from those who thought Baldwin simply had a better legal defense. Baldwin sheepishly looked down.

"Look, nearly all of us have had legal training, some even practiced for years before coming to Congress. We knew what the deal was. I'm a Republican and former cabinet member. I'm not the type to waste time defending a Democratic president. But in this particular case, Eastwood had us by the gonads, and the court confirmed he was right."

"Let me add something to what Chuck has said." It was the voice of Bennie Thompson, the former representative from Mississippi and only African American in the group. Thompson – slick, well-spoken, a male clotheshorse with an incomparably stylish wardrobe – was the chairman of the Congressional Black Caucus.

Thompson, fifty-one, was the descendant of slaves; his mother was a schoolteacher in Jackson, Mississippi, where he was born, and his father ran a small artesian well drilling company. Bennie was a bright boy. At the insistence of his aggressive mother, he took the test for admission to the elite Jackson Academy and did well. Catching the attention of an enlightened headmaster, he entered the school at age thirteen, one year ahead of his class; at the same age, he was also over six feet and well on his way to his ultimate altitude of six feet, five inches. He excelled at everything, including basketball, where he led the Raiders to league mastery for four years. He won a basketball scholarship to Davidson, one of the nation's top-notch small colleges, where, again, his athletic prowess brought national recognition to the small school. Rejecting professional offers after graduation, he matriculated at Harvard Law, emerging with a degree and a job with the Office of the Mississippi Attorney General. In 1990, he lost his first stab at a seat in Congress but captured it two years later in the Democratic sweep of the White House and Congress.

Thompson continued speaking. "There ain't no court in this country that's gonna take a case along the lines Jeff is thinkin' and the rest of you are hopin'. Let's get real. We knew what we were doing. I'm not sayin' this because as a black man I'm suckin' up to my black president. Hell, to put it in the language of the brothers, he 'dissed' me."

Thompson's exaggerated vernacular and use of the idiom helped make his point. "I, for one, am not going after the president. He did the right thing, and we did the opposite."

These were meaningful words for a man who, during his caucus leadership role, routinely agitated some of the other caucus members by repeatedly suggesting that the black community needed to pull up the zipper on its pants as well as its bootstraps – to become more family conscious, to become more serious about education, and to look to black leaders like President Earl Eastwood and not to professional athletes whose behavior, which he knew well, kept the black community captive in its own body.

Rallis stood up; he had taken a seat as the exchange became heated over his disclosure of the nature of the Iranian monies. *I need to get back into this,* the wily Greek thought.

"Please, let me add a word here . . . ," he pleaded as the room settled down.

"I'll put it this way," he started, using American-style English. "I'm suggesting reward, not revenge. I've demonstrated that you're all entitled to what you've earned in the original investment program and that there are opportunities to restore your reputations while improving your financial status very considerably."

"Niko, if I read you correctly, you're suggesting that we sign on to one or several of the business entities held by Lucas, is that right?" asked former Delaware representative Anne Rathbone.

"In one word, yes," came Rallis's reply.

"But the organization is in Switzerland. Is that where the jobs are?" she continued.

"Again, trying to keep it simple, yes and no. There are opportunities at our locations in Switzerland, but there are plans for expansion, especially in the United States."

"Please, hear me out." It was Scharfman. "I appreciate Niko's offer, and I am settled down a bit. I apologize for my zealousness, but you all know how I feel, and I think I understand the feelings of many others in this room. But I believe we can have both: reward and, to put a slight twist on Niko's suggestion that we avoid revenge, restitution. After all, we have suffered. We were stupidly innocent in some instances and on some of the charges.

"What I'm suggesting is that we approach the president. Not necessarily as a group, norindividually. We can have a surrogate or representative speak for us. I believe restitution is in order, and while we may not get damages or other financial compensation for time served, I do think we have a shot at getting the president to pardon us."

There was movement in the room. The suggestion was ponderous. Reputations would be restored; some could even stand for public office again, or they could pursue business opportunities more freely.

"Now that idea does appeal to me. But what leverage do we have? Why should the president even listen to us? Politically, he may be better off just ignoring us, even turning us down with a little media attention brought to bear on the 'correctness' of rejecting pardons," said Mark Koerner, the former New Jersey representative who had served time.

"I, for one, think we're dreamin'. This president won't bargain that way," added Bennie Thompson.

"I think Bennie is right," said Chuck Seaton. "But we have nothing to lose. I'm willing to meet with him. I know the laws, served a sentence, like Mark, and was a cabinet-level officer in the prior administration."

"This is a matter of politics that I know little about," said Rallis, still standing. "However, on the issue of leverage, I have a suggestion. Domenic Guillermo, the former Connecticut governor and later US ambassador to the Vatican, has joined Lucas Holdings as vice chairman. He also serves on the boards of many of the companies in which Lucas is invested. I think he would take the assignment, and I believe he would find several forms of encouragement that might grab the president's attention."

"Not a bad idea," said Sam Schlesinger, the former Connecticut senator. "Guillermo appointed Eastwood to the Senate when the incumbent, Bill Rice, had been assassinated in Washington. But there is some bad blood between the two. Guillermo had hoped Eastwood, once in the Senate, would promote Guillermo's aspiration to be the vice president on the next Democratic presidential ticket. As we know, Eastwood's Senate career became so prominent that he landed on the ticket, and Guillermo thinks Eastwood shafted him. But things may have changed. I think it's worth a try."

Throughout the room, there were favorable nods. And true to form, an "executive committee" formed to develop the plan.

Castignani laid out the concept. "My sense is that we need some leadership for us, the 'fussin' dozen.'" This was what the group laughingly referred themselves as. "Chuck is the guru on the relevant laws and has 'standing' as one who had been prosecuted. Sam knows Eastwood well, having served in Connecticut politics with him, and Niko needs to provide guidance in developing leverage to motivate the president to act in our behalf. Unless there's an objection, I'll coordinate the group since I'm without prejudice on the matter. But we're all bound by the lobbying statutes and can't make direct contact with either the executive or legislative branches for two years."

Sam Schlesinger, the former Connecticut senator, spoke up, "Bob, Dom Guillermo's restriction period has expired, I'm quite sure. Also, he is closer to the president than I am. I'd urge that we add him to the committee."

Rallis added his endorsement, and there were favorable comments around the room.

"One more thing," Schlesinger said. "The former House members have a one-year ban on lobbying. Only the Senate is bound for two. I think we need to put Bennie on the committee."

"Yeah, I'll buy that. The president doesn't much like the race card, but I do have a good working relationship with Kenny Edwards, his press guy, who the president listens to," said ex-representative Bennie Thompson.

"Good. I'll contact Dom and happily add Bennie. We'll come back here as soon as we can to get things rolling. By the way, is Guillermo still in Rome or back in the US? Does anyone know?" Castignani asked.

"He's been commuting between his home in West Hartford and the Lucas Holdings office near Montreux, where he also has a residence," Rallis added. "As you know, his wife died shortly after he relocated to Rome, which forced him to resign his ambassadorship to the Vatican."

"Okay, it's settled. Thanks, folks, for coming over. We have a good approach and need to get started," Castignani said, concluding the meeting.

Ex-senator Bob Castignani – the only former congressional member in the group who was neither charged nor forced to resign but lost his seat in the November 2010 election – then closed the meeting, thinking, *I hope to hell I'm not in over my head here. I can handle the lobbying activity on behalf of Rallis's companies by directing my staff where to go, who to see, and what to say. But on the pardon issue, I can't see Earl Eastwood buying the arguments we've been considering here. He's a straight shooter, always has been.*

CHAPTER 2

POLITICS OF REMOVAL

T HE SO-CALLED EXECUTIVE COMMITTEE OF THE FUSSIN' DOZEN, as they laughingly referred to themselves, represented the eleven congressional members and one former cabinet officer who were charged during the investigation in the summer of 2009. This smaller panel gathered again at ex-senator Bob Castignani's Old Town, Alexandria, residence on South Royal Street on Thursday, December 16, 2010.

Former Connecticut governor Domenic Guillermo, Lucas Holdings CEO and chairman Niko Rallis, and Castignani joined three of the twelve indicted in the scandal – former treasury secretary Chuck Seaton, ex-senator Sam Schlesinger, and ex-representative Bennie Thompson. The six men accepted the task of developing a persuasive argument urging the president to pardon the eleven who were actually fined or, in three cases, imprisoned and to remove the scar of accusation from the reputation of the one member who was exonerated.

"The first order of business is to figure out the pardoning process and how we formulate our petition," Castignani said. "I called around town for some help on this and dispatched Ben and Don to the Justice Department's Office of the Pardoning Attorney for some guidance and documentation," he continued, referring to Ben Ochs and Don Tranh, two former senior Senate staffers who were now joined in the newly chartered law firm of Castignani, Ochs, and Tranh. "By the way, we should be established in our new offices in Watergate. They're doing some reconfiguration of the place which has slowed down our move."

He continued. "Next, we'll have to figure out how we approach the president, and I have some ideas on that score as I'm sure Dom will since he knows him better than any of us.

"The law is clear on presidential authority, which derives from Article II, Section 2 of the Constitution. He alone has the pardoning power, and the Supreme Court has endorsed it in any number of cases. But we've encountered a problem, so let me ask Don to review the process," Castignani said, turning to Don Tranh.

Tranh was yet another glance at America as a land of opportunity. Born in Saigon, his physician father and translator mother were evacuated in 1975 as the North Vietnamese Army overran the South. They were settled in San Francisco by a Jesuit-sponsored relief organization. Don learned English easily, while his grammar was perfected under his mother's demanding regime. Along with his two younger brothers, he attended St. Ignatius, then matriculated to Stanford. Financed by an ROTC scholarship, he served three years in the army's Military Intelligence branch, incurring a seven-year reserve obligation as reserve captain; earnings from his reserve meetings helped cover costs at Stanford Law School from where he graduated in 2000. The next two years were spent as deputy counsel to the US Senate Appropriations Committee's Subcommittee on Defense. From 2002 to 2010, he served in various committee positions rising to the lead job as staff director while assuming related roles on investigating panels, where he got to know US Senate minority leader Earl Eastwood. Tranh was part of the congressional delegation aboard the *Athena*. Like his friend and former staff partner, Ben Ochs, he left Senate employment to join Castignani's law and lobbying firm after the latter lost his seat. He married a non-Vietnamese woman, Jesse, a very savvy spokeswoman at the National Geographic Society. They have twin sons born in 2004 and live in the Hollin Hills section of Alexandria, Virginia, approximately one mile from Ben Ochs.

"Thanks. As Bob implied, Ben and I had a stormy meeting with the pardon attorney at Justice. This woman, Remy Stratton, moved from the DOD general counsel's office, where she was director of hearings and appeals. She made it clear to us that she knew her job well and pretty much tried to dismiss the value of the inquiries we had made before we went to see her. The two big obstacles, in her words, was Chuck's lobbying restriction and, more importantly, the rule that pardon petitions had to be filed five years from the date of conviction. It made no difference to her that I recited the pardoning history and concept, back to *The Federalist Papers*, as well as the appropriate case law from the Supreme Court. At this point, Ben had to leave, so I was left to deal with her myself.

"Somewhat frustrated, I said, rather asserted, the president's absolute decisional authority, as well as the rights of petition, was covered under the Constitution. She then said, if you can believe this, that the waiting period was not something the president could set aside and it was her recommendation that would always prevail. We had a momentary stare down at that point. But I blinked first, thanked her for her time, and left.

"What it means is that we have to get to the AG or get the White House's ear on this. There are no appeals from or hearings on the pardon process, including the right and eligibility to file a petition. We have a bit of an edge with Democrats running the show in Justice. But we still have the lobbying issue, which is only a problem in the mind of the pardoning attorney. We can manage that since I believe it is mooted by the right to file the pardoning petition at any time. But this Stratton woman can be a stumbling block for us if, as she says, her recommendations carry the day."

"What a load of crap! How the hell could this Goddamn paranoiac freak have a job like that?" said Seaton, obviously enraged. "Challenging the president's constitutional authority. What's she, nuts? What the hell is her background?"

"As I mentioned, she was a Republican political appointee over at DOD and somehow managed to slip into Justice when we took the White House. I think that says a lot," Tranh responded, the "we" referring to the election of the Democratic president, which, of course, led to party control over cabinet positions.

"We need to relax a bit and tread lightly here. I can talk to Jack," said the calming voice of Castignani. "We may need Republican help, and she probably has some heavyweight supporters somewhere, which is the only way she could have landed on her feet in a major appointee job at Justice, especially after the Democrats cleaned house after the election."

"We need to do it now, Bob," said Domenic Guillermo. "This is something we ought to resolve right away. Everyone wants a presidential pardon. That list is endless. I faced it when I was governor. The state and federal pardoning powers for the chief executives at both levels are about the same. The important thing is to go in to see the president with as uncomplicated a request as possible. We need to settle this, not tell the president that he has to."

Guillermo was someone people listened to. He was known as the optimizer, one who was politically adept at bringing opposite sides together. Born in New Haven, Connecticut, in 1942, he was the son of Sergio and Maria Guillermo. Sergio had been a highly educated senior bureaucrat in the Mussolini fascist headquarters in Florence. Sergio fled to the United States in 1937 as the Italian government became increasingly autocratic. A classical Machiavellian, he threaded easily into local politics, his fluency in English making him a powerful intermediary between the rapidly growing and politically active Italian community and the established Yankee-dominated government in Connecticut. Sergio used his connections to foster Domenic's career.

Domenic was already a hulk of a kid at fifteen and a state-level football star at New Haven's Hillhouse High School. From there, he matriculated at Yale, again using his athletic abilities to gain both scholarship money and recognition. He joined the Connecticut National Guard while at Yale, avoiding the nettlesome draft issues of the period and facilitating his move to the law school after getting his bachelor's degree in 1966. After graduating with an LLB, he clerked on the state supreme court, running for office at several state and local levels while in private practice afterward. By 2006, he was the president pro tem of the state senate, a position that catapulted him into the governor's seat after the incumbent governor and lieutenant governor were convicted and imprisoned on bribery charges.

In 2007, Guillermo resigned as governor, citing the health needs of his dying wife, but surprised all by accepting an appointment from the Republican president Bob Davids as US ambassador to the Holy See at the Vatican. Several months later, his wife having died from lung cancer in a Roman medical center, he resigned again and took a position in Rome with an Italian aviation company peddling military and civilian helicopters in the United States. More recently, he left Italy, moving to Switzerland, where he joined Nikos Rallis's Lucas Holdings SA as vice chairman, as well as becoming a director of several companies in which Lucas was a major stakeholder.

Castignani had endorsed Guillermo's recommendation, gave him the private number for the attorney general, and stood by as Guillermo was on the line. Jack Hammond would come to the phone momentarily, his chief of staff told the former governor.

Although there was a full eighteen years age difference between the two, Hammond was a Nutmegger, born in Windsor Locks, Connecticut, and was a high school day hop at the prominent Loomis School. It was an easy path to Yale College from Loomis, then to the law school. He had practiced law with the Stamford firm of Smith, Rogers, and Berlin, ultimately becoming the resident partner of the firm's Washington office, where his party activity led to designation as a deputy assistant attorney general in the Justice Department's Antitrust Division. In 2009, Eastwood had designated him as acting attorney general after Harry Scott, the original AG, was selected as secretary of state.

*   *   *

"Good afternoon, Ambassador, or do I say Governor?" came the voice from Justice.

"Hey, Jack, it's the same old Dom. How the devil are you? Your star keeps rising so fast in this town that I need to know who your astrologer is," came Guillermo's somewhat lame effort to humor him.

"I'll tell you, if I had a good astrologer, he would have told me to get a real job."

"Oh, c'mon, you shouldn't even be paid for having so much fun," Guillermo said.

"Just between us girls, Dom, I'm *not* getting paid, and with three kids in private colleges, I've got two years of tax returns to prove it."

"Hey, you're at the top of the executive service pay scale," replied Guillermo, making a knowingly jocular reference to the modest salaries paid to cabinet members, especially when compared to the typical earnings of senior partners in the capital's prominent law and lobbying firms. Cabinet members are paid at Executive

Level V, which at the time was about $186,000 annually. All other persons in the federal executive branch, excepting the president and vice president, are paid at levels not to exceed the pay level of a US senator, which was about $168,000, or Executive Level IV.

"Well, something tells me, Dom, that I'm about to earn every penny of it after I hear the purpose of your phone call," Hammond replied with a light chuckle.

"Aha, I see that your astrologer has some merit after all." The light banter set the mood for Guillermo's next comments.

"Jack, you know much about the outcome of the Geek investment case. I'm tryin' to help these folks, in particular, Chuck Seaton. I know he's a Republican, but the president, both Earl and Bob Davids, and most members of Congress always held him in high regard. In fewer words, Chuck wants to file a petition for pardon."

There was a short silence before Hammond replied with a typical lawyerly and slightly bureaucratic response.

"That's certainly his right, Dom. He's got the Constitution and a lot of case law that says he can do exactly that. What's his argument, if you don't mind my asking? He certainly knows his rights as well as I do."

"That's sort of the problem, Jack. You see, your pardon attorney says he has to wait five years from the date of conviction, that he can't lobby for two years from the time he left office, and this is what really throws me, that the president, in her words, cannot set aside the five-year rule."

"Remy Stratton told you this?" Hammond asked.

"Indirectly, Jack. She actually spoke to Bob Castignani's partner, Don Tranh."

"Sure, I know Tranh. He's a smart guy. We once tried to recruit him to Smith Rogers, but he wanted a few more years in government before breaking out. Remy's also a smart woman. She came over from DOD, where she handled appeals and hearings, or something along those lines. I'm a little shaky on the details. She's a Republican, right?"

"Right, but she obviously has someone backing her that encouraged you folks to accept her," Guillermo added.

"Actually, she came over when Harry Scott was the designee. As I recall, someone on the Senate Judiciary Committee pushed the appointment. You know, we'll pay attention to Republican recommendations from Judiciary. They exercise oversight on us, and we try to keep our borders pacified. But I'm more concerned about the counsel she provided Tranh. The five-year rule is a regulatory process. It's not intended to be any particular point in time as far as the president's constitutional authority is concerned," added Hammond, his tone deeply serious.

"Yeah, I'm afraid she's starting at the finish line, so to speak, and ignoring the rest of the process, including presidential authority. I'm just tryin' to work this out between us. I'm not pushin' to have her removed or anything like that. Moreover, politically, since she's from the other side of the aisle, she could leak that as something amounting to preferential treatment."

"I hear what you're sayin' and agree," Hammond said, cautiously avoiding statements that could come back to haunt him. "She must have thought that Tranh was seeking redress or commutation for Seaton only when, I assume, the pardon requests will extend to all others as well."

Guillermo was relieved. *Jack's smart as a whip. He got the point right away. Thank God we have some political wisdom among the guys in these top jobs*, he thought.

"Let me suggest this." It was Hammond again. "I'll call you back in a few minutes. I'll find out who her sponsor was on the Judiciary Committee. We'll have him – or her – call Stratton and remind her of the president's absolute authority on this issue and the indisputable right that anyone who has been convicted of an offense has to petition for pardon. Even if there are lobbying term restraints, they're subordinated to the higher right of petition, I'm pretty sure. Besides, aren't these guys just about beyond the one – or two-year lobbying ban?"

"They're either there or very close, Jack. Frankly, I never got around to asking the question since the fundamental right of petition was the greater issue here. But thanks, Jack, I'll await your call." Guillermo concluded the call after giving Hammond his cell phone number.

The group was moving on to other matters, including fashioning the arguments to present in the application for petition, when the call from the attorney general came. Guillermo took the call, stepping into the quieter area of the foyer in Castignani's residence to take down the information. His head jerked back as he penciled down the information. "Okay, Jack, many thanks," he said, hanging up.

"You're not gonna believe this," Guillermo said to Castignani. "This Stratton woman is a buddy of Connecticut governor Sophia Kallias, who succeeded me. And she apparently had Zbigniew Krakowski, who Kallias appointed to take Earl Eastwood's seat in the Senate after he became president. I know them both very well, of course, and have always had good relations with them. I can clear this up, I think. I can't see either the governor or Zbig creating a problem for Earl even though they're Republicans. The president's popularity in Connecticut is not something they can fight, and they both know if they give me a hard time, the president will be on their case, which is something they definitely don't want. They'd be put in a position to deny the president's pardoning authority, which no case in Supreme Court history has ever seriously challenged. They're both relative novices in politics, but they're smart enough to see what's happened here. I'll call Sophia directly."

Within a few minutes, Guillermo, now seated in Castignani's second-floor office, was on the line with the governor of Connecticut, the lithesome but sometimes politically lethal Sophia Kallias.

At age thirty-seven in 2008, Kallias had pulled off one of the most remarkable election upsets in New England's raucous history. Her deft campaign outflanked every move and countermove made by the veteran campaigner Guillermo himself. She and her lieutenant governor candidate on the ticket, Zbigniew Krakowski, both Republicans with only a few terms in the state legislature, usurped the nomination by self-financing a campaign that the Republican Party's drained coffers could never have sustained. The Republican leadership in the state, believing that none could beat the well-entrenched Guillermo machine, welcomed *any* candidate under those conditions.

Sophia Kallias, of Jewish-Greek origins, was the daughter of parents who survived Greek collaboration with the Nazis by fleeing to a zone in the country occupied by friendlier Italians. Her father, Dmitri, died in the coastal city of Woodbridge, Connecticut, where his wholesale clothing business prospered under defense contracts dating back to the immediate post–World War II era. Krakowski's own Polish immigrant parents had also made it big as entrepreneurs. The two used their inherited wealth, mixed ethnic backgrounds, and savvy to rally the scattered clusters of largely second – and third-generation Americans into a polycentric political force. The core Republican strength in the state, now annexed with a remarkably diverse accumulation of independent voters and former Democrats, grew with such speed that Guillermo, clearly seeing the end in sight, one worsened by his disappointing performance in debates with Kallias, ultimately resigned, claiming that his wife's advancing cancer necessitated his full attention.

In fact, then president Bob Davids, a Republican, stepped in offering Guillermo the ambassadorship to the Holy See; this was quickly accepted. Kallias won the election as the weaker lieutenant governor on the Democratic ticket, Sam Schlesinger, took the fall for his party.

"Good to hear from you, Dom. I am still deeply grieved over Mary Ann's death. She was such a wonderful person and always a good friend. I hope you are doing well," said Governor Sophia Kallias of Connecticut in opening the conversation.

"Thanks for those gracious words, Sophia. I sometimes feared that you would get Mary Anne's vote in our race," came Guillermo's reply, followed by light laughter on both sides.

Both realized that the scar tissue of the fierce electoral fight was now barely noticeable.

"Well, you know I'm always glad to hear from you and welcome your counsel on any state matter. You did much for Connecticut as I am routinely reminded by my friends on both sides of the legislature's aisles. We're in some rough times. Our state pension system has been very generous and our health-care costs are soaring along with our growing retiree numbers. We simply need more jobs. Even the pharmaceutical sector along the coast is hurting."

It was the perfect cue for Guillermo's reentry into the conversation. "You know, Sophia, I'm active on the board of several companies in Switzerland, where I'm now living most of the time."

As he awaited her reply, a thought occurred to him. The chocolate sector – Swiss prices are driven to a noncompetitive level by the incredibly high wage and other production costs in Switzerland. He found himself pondering the prospects of moving production to Connecticut and linking that offer to the pardon issue.

Excited by the sudden revelation, he struggled to sound controlled. The thought was too impulsive, and he worried that his enthusiasm might be premature.

"Yes, I knew a little about your new endeavors," the governor replied.

"My work there is part of the reason for my call. We may have to get together to talk it out, but let me give you the gist of it. You're obviously familiar with the mass resignations of the many members of Congress, including Sam Schlesinger, over the Greek investment plan," he said rhetorically.

"Yes, of course. As you may recall, I have been very active in supporting the museum on Jewish history in Greece in the city of Thessaloniki. The museum sits on the site of an ancient synagogue that has been a Mediterranean center for the study of the torah. I follow Greek affairs very closely. I know Nikos Rallis. I was two years behind him at Trinity. We dated a couple of times and even went to Hartford Hellenic society events together."

"Well, Niko and I work together on many boards. He's a great guy and a very strong supporter of you . . ." *This will make my offer easier,* Guillermo quickly realized.

"I wish he were a US citizen, I could certainly use *his* financial backing," she said jokingly.

"In an indirect way, Niko and I may be able to help the state. You see, Niko's chairman and CEO of Lucas Holdings SA, a Swiss company, where I serve as vice chairman. One of our holdings, Belmont Confections, has been searching for a production site in the US. As you may know, Belmont is a private company, and we are by far the largest shareholder after the Swiss government itself, with 20 percent of it. But our interest in Belmont is actually about the same as that of the Swiss government since another of our holdings, Brent SA, a commodity trading firm, has a 20 percent share of Belmont, and we, Lucas Holdings, own 29 percent of Brent. Belmont, as you know, is the world's largest chocolate specialty company."

"How does that sit with Rose Confections in Bridgeport?" Kallias asked solicitously, uncertain as to what Guillermo was up to.

"Sophia, I helped bring Rose to Bridgeport after the Maryland company split into two following the antitrust actions, which I had also urged when I was in the state legislature and later as governor."

She really is a novice and doesn't remember that activity at all, he thought.

"To be honest, I had forgotten the origins of Rose," Kallias replied, not meekly but with assertive self-confidence. "But my question remains, what's the impact on our own chocolate industry in the state?"

"I think I can bring investment and expansion . . . to put it simply."

"Oh, you devil, Dom, you get my attention in so eloquently," she facetiously purred to their mutual laughter. *There's more to this. Dom has never been known to be too generous when it comes to his political interests.* "So what's the deal?"

"The first step is to get our business houses in order. The US expansion plans require skilled staffing, especially in the area of government relations. We've hired the twelve former members involved in the Greek incident. You won't be surprised to know that it was Rallis's decision." Guillermo hesitated; he had sensed that Kallias had good feelings about Niko Rallis.

"I'm not at all surprised. He's a very considerate fellow, always has been," Kallias replied.

"Right. They've been living on the edge of society. Niko has pulled them back. They're grateful, and they'll do a good job for us."

"Remind me again, Dom. Who are the players?" she asked.

"Sure. First, on the Senate side, Bob Castignani, the former Maine Democrat . . . They're all Dems except for David Ford and Chuck Seaton. Bob, of course, was not indicted but lost his seat in the election and has organized a law and lobbying firm with two of his former top Senate staffers."

"I've always liked Castignani. We've done several New England projects, earmarks really, with his help," Kallias commented.

"And Sam Schlesinger, I know he was your opponent and my former running mate."

"Delightful, Dom, you keep him in Switzerland so I don't have to worry about him running for my job here," she said, then laughed.

"That thought hadn't crossed my mind, Sophia," Guillermo added sardonically. Again, they laughed.

He continued. "The others are New Jersey's Jeff Scharfman and Andy Tantillo, and Nancy Lehman from California."

"Of course, I've spoken to her a few times regarding defense issues. We've coordinated Air Force contract efforts," Kallias added.

"The three Republicans, two of which I mentioned, are Chuck Seaton and David Ford, former representative from New York, and Mark Baldwin of Virginia, who was totally exonerated by the courts. Also on the House side, Jarrett Rodman of Michigan, Mark Koerner of New Jersey, Marc Gregoire of Louisiana, Bennie Thompson of Mississippi, and Anne Rathbone of Delaware."

"What wasted talents. I know and have even spoken to or communicated with all of them at one time or another," she said.

"You can see what Rallis is thinking – exactly that. They're low-lying and overripe fruit needing to be pruned and put to better use."

"But there are still appearances, Dom. The media has dropped their sorry saga, but what makes you think they won't be back in the headlines?" she asked quizzically.

"They will be, Sophia. We intend to petition for presidential pardons," he said with a tone of casual confidence in his voice, as if it would be a rather routine undertaking.

Kallias was not known as the young wonder woman of politics for nothing. *Ay, there's the rub,* she thought, her subconscious conjuring up the Hamlet soliloquy. *I'm expected to push Earl into granting them pardons so as to get Connecticut jobs. Nice move, Dom, you are as shrewd as ever. I better get right on top of this.*

"I love you too, Dom, but I'm worried that sticking my neck out for these guys might be a not-so-subtle invitation to political extinction." She chuckled with deliberate irony in her voice and words.

I guess I expected that, Guillermo thought. "Sorry, I can see why that occurred to you. But that's not the case at all."

C'mon, Dom. You're slick as hell, but you're also a straight shooter. Tell me what you're up to, she thought, adding, "I'm having trouble figuring out your motives, Dom, to be somewhat direct with you."

"I *do* need your help, but not that way. Here's the problem. We approached the Justice Department's pardoning attorney, Remy Stratton, who is your friend, I'm told." He hesitated, sensing her stomach muscles tightening and her brow creasing.

"Remy's a problem?" she asked. "I know her from law school. She was with a DC law firm but never made partner. So I helped her get a job with DOD, working through party channels with the Davids administration. Her family lives somewhere in Fairfield County, Norwalk, area, I think. They have always been supportive of my campaigns." She was referring also to the outgoing Republican presidential administration of Bob Davids.

"I knew that, Sophia."

"And when the Eastwood administration designated a Democrat for the DOD job, I asked Zbig, who's on the Senate Judiciary Committee, to find something for her at Justice," she added, mentioning Zbigniew Krakowski, now the senator from Connecticut. "As you know, very few Republicans survived the house cleaning after Earl took office. And it works the other way around, I guess. I removed most of your appointees when I became governor."

"That's a privilege of incumbency. Getting back to Stratton, in the meeting with Castignani's partners who were seeking her counsel for Seaton's pardon petition, she told them that Chuck Seaton, as a former cabinet official, was barred by the Federal Lobbying Disclosure Act from, in her words, 'lobbying' for a pardon. Worse, and this really stumps me, she said that her department's *regulations* require that he wait five years from the time of conviction to submit his application for pardon and that the president lacked authority to change the rule." Guillermo awaited Kallias's response.

Kallias was also surprised. *How could Remy be so stupid! The executive powers are glaringly evident in both the state and federal constitutions. I seem to recall that she once taught constitutional law at the undergraduate level, somewhere.* "I cannot for the life of me understand why she would have said something like that. She's a smart woman, she anchored her class at UConn Law, but she got through it. She had some trouble with the bar exams, took them a couple of times. But that's no disgrace. A lot of smart people have trouble with bar exams."

"We need to be careful. She may have a predisposition to being overzealous to avoid any impressions that she's giving favorable treatment to either party's petitioners," Guillermo suggested.

"Yeah, I see. Seaton's a Republican, and he's the lead petitioner, isn't that what you were saying?" she queried.

"I didn't say that exactly, but it was in Seaton's behalf that the meeting with her took place. And yes, she may have felt that the Democratic administration would think she was accommodating a *Republican* pardon helped along by her, a Republican appointment in a Democratic justice department."

"I agree that caution is the rule. I'm assuming that you want to keep this from the president and to bypass her, even replace her. Let me suggest this. You call Sue Cohen, the president's chief of staff. I'll talk to Zbig. You tell Sue about the pardon petitions coming forth in the near future, mentioning the Stratton incident. Sue will react, I'm sure. She's a very savvy politician as well as lawyer. I'll tell Zbig to advise Remy to resign and that I have a job for her in the state AG's office. Zbig will also have to tell her that the White House objects to her interpretation of the pardon process and could make her life miserable if she hangs on there." Kallias awaited Guillermo's response.

"Perfect, Sophia. Sue will appreciate our taking care of the problem and alert the president to what's coming his way. It's not going to affect his decision one way or the other. But he'll know that you're cooperating," Guillermo said, then was interrupted by the acutely attentive Kallias.

"And he'll also think that I'm indirectly encouraging the pardon to get Connecticut jobs, you sly dog, Domenic!"

As they laughed, Guillermo decided to provide his own provocative but well-intended jocular jab. "Oh, I think he'd be more interested in your relationship with Zbig. What is the status there?" he asked, knowing the two had been companions just short of living together.

"I have no idea what you're talking about," Kallias replied laughingly. "He lives in Washington, and I live in Hartford, doesn't that say something?" The sharp-witted Kallias again had the last word.

"It says a whole lot to my mind, Sophia honey!" The two laughed heartily.

*   *   *

Guillermo's next call was to the Office of the Chief of Staff to the President of the United States, Sue Cohen. The value of inserting Guillermo into the process was increasingly obvious. The former governor and state senate leader of the small state, where the political airwaves of most state – and national-level officeholders intersected regularly throughout their active careers, knew everyone and was known by all. He could have the president's ear if he chose but wisely knew that he too had only so many so-called political chips to play, and he would husband these assets until they would produce gains for him first.

He dialed 202-456-6798, the direct line to the most important member of the White House staff, the number being highly privileged information available to very few persons.

Sue Cohen – thirty-seven, a Connecticut native and graduate of Connecticut College in New London – received her law degree from Yale in 1999 and immediately headed to Washington, where she worked with the firm of Sherman and Stuckey. The young woman dabbled on the edges of politics, gradually assuming many lobbying functions, which took her into like company, as well as many executive branch and congressional offices. Male members like dealing with smart, attractive, and preferably younger woman lobbyists. As targets for special attention from favor-seeking lobbyists, they would be treated like demigods, legends in their own minds, some would add. And there was always the chance of a romantic liaison, an outcome for some straying members that could prove to be a better bet than their reelection, especially if the relationship created marital difficulties, which was often the case as well.

Sue fell into a few of those outcomes. However, she was more interested in an open and honest relationship, the type that wife cheaters eschewed. Her scruples in this regard might have accounted for her status as an aging yet single and still very attractive woman. Serving as Senator Earl Eastwood's counsel and chief of staff, she moved with him through the campaign and into the White House. As the chief presidential adviser, her opportunities for suitors improved in quality but waned in number as the cheater variety dare not tamper with one of the most powerful women in Washington.

She answered her own phone with the simple greeting "Sue, here," and seeing the caller ID, she fell into a more casual mood. "Domenic, we talk about you all the time. Where have you been? Why haven't you called?"

She sounds real. Is that possible? My last contact with Earl was not exactly the stuff that long-term friendships are made of. "Sue," he almost hissed, having been surprised with her greeting, and then caught himself. "Great to talk with you again. How are you?"

"I'm fine, but we'll all be a lot better now that we've heard from you. The president had a few feelers out looking for you. I'm sure he'd like to see you. Last we heard, after dear Mary Anne's death, was that you had decided to spend most of your time in Rome or somewhere else in Europe, but the US embassy in Rome had no record of you after you left the Holy See." She rattled off this history as if it were her top priority, deeply impressing Guillermo.

Guillermo brought her up to date on his activities, ending the brief review with a reference to his work in Switzerland. "Which is what I want to talk to you about," he concluded.

"Sure, but is this something that Earl needs to attend to as well?" she asked.

Guillermo carefully thought out his next words. "It is a matter that only he can act upon, but there's some preliminary housekeeping that will make that easier. You see, I'm helping the folks caught up in the Greek resort case petition for pardons."

Nothing Dom asks for is ever easy. He picked a real challenge this time, she thought to herself. "I'm all for making his decision easier, Dom. Tell me what I need to do," she said, sitting back in her chair, checking on the recording equipment to ensure the accuracy of the call. *I need to keep this one away from the president until the decision is reviewed thoroughly over at Justice,* she had already concluded in her mind.

"In a few words, the pardoning attorney at Justice told our attorneys that there's a five-year waiting rule to file the application and that the president himself, she added, can't change that. Moreover, she also claims that Seaton specifically is ineligible to file since he would be lobbying and he is covered by the statute barring lobbying for a period of two years by former high-level officials," Guillermo said.

Sue started taking notes to supplement the record. "Who is the pardon attorney, and have you spoken to Jack, the AG?"

"Yes, he says she's dead wrong. And that's yet another complexity. You see, Remy Stratton, the pardoning attorney, is a Republican appointee who was transferred from DOD. We all agree that reprimanding or even firing her could be a greater problem."

"Yes, I can see that. So what's your thinking?" she said, mixing metaphors as has become colloquially acceptable in the usage of American English.

"Stratton is a friend of Governor Kallias who had Senator Krakowski influence the transfer. Sophia will offer Stratton a job in Connecticut and will have Zbig encourage her to accept it. But it would be easier all the way around, we all believe, if we could say that the White House supports the attorney general."

I'll settle this now and just let Earl know what I've done. No harm in expressing support for Jack Hammond, she thought. "I think that's a good move. Let's do it exactly that way. I don't have a lot of background on pardon issues, although we're already getting quite a few applications. At least that's what I'm told by White House counsel, who's been working with Justice. That astonishes me even more since she, Stratton, knows or must know well that the president's authority is pretty well anchored in Article II," she said, referencing the Constitution.

"Terrific, Sue. I'll coordinate the pardon details with Justice."

There's something else here. I need to find out what he's really up to. "Dom, it would be better if you come in, alone, and explain these cases to the president. Can you do that?" Sue asked.

I better be up-front with her. There's too much at risk, reasoned Guillermo, whose political career in Connecticut bestowed on him the moniker of the optimizer. He could fashion compromise from even the most polarized conditions, and both parties would walk away feeling they had thoroughly outmaneuvered the other.

"That would be terrific. Let me add that I will be presenting our case, but I am not necessarily an advocate. That's the job of Bob Castignani. However, there are some good outcomes that the president will understand."

Just as I thought. We better fathom this thing as early as possible. I can't deny Dom access to the president, nor would Earl want to. He's reliable, and he's much too savvy to abuse the privilege of a conversation with the president. "Let's look at some dates, Dom. Do you have any preferences?"

"How about Thursday, December 16?"

"That looks okay, make it early, say, 10:00 a.m. Congress is headed for recess, and Earl and Audrey are thinking of going to Camp David for the holidays," she said, referring to Representative Audrey Holmes, the president's companion and also the only black Republican woman in Congress. "Also, I want to brief the president and get a memo from the AG. Maybe I should contact Harry Scott too. The president seems to like having Harry second the AG's opinion on many things," she added, referring to Harry Scott, who was to have been the attorney general before Eastwood shifted him to the state department."

They hung up. Guillermo sat back in the desk chair in Castignani's home office. He pondered the details of the call. It was just too easy; she was too agreeable. But everything she said and did must fit with her profound understanding of Earl's interests.

Sue is smart, smart enough to have a hidden agenda. The question is, would she behave that way with me, and if so, why? And Harry Scott's involvement, he's too smart, like Earl. He'll wonder why I'm involved and start nosing around the Swiss deals . . . But we're okay there. Everything's kosher.

*   *   *

Negotiating the staircase as fast as his now fleshy frame would allow, Guillermo, the former Yale All-Ivy running back, took Castignani and Rallis aside, advising them that the White House would support Stratton's removal. All was on track, and that major planning was now in order to develop the petitioners' arguments along with the Swiss scheme for integrating the former members into Lucas Holdings' business operations.

He returned to the upstairs office, his mind afire with the next steps in the process. *Hammond, I've got to get that side moving as well.* He was on the phone with the US attorney general in minutes.

"How's it goin', Dom?" came Hammond's greeting.

"It's pretty much done. I spoke to Sue. She said the White House fully supports you, the attorney general. Furthermore, Kallias will tell Zbig that there's a job for Stratton in the Connecticut AG's office and that she, Stratton, needs to resign *e rapidemente* [quickly]," he rattled off in perfect Italian.

"I don't speak Italian, but I get the picture," said an elated Hammond.

*   *   *

During the same time frame, Republican governor Sophia Kallias was on the phone with Senator Zbigniew Krakowski, whom she appointed to the Senate seat occupied by President Earl Eastwood before he entered the White House.

Kallias and Krakowski became involved romantically during their tenures in the Connecticut legislature barely two years earlier. Kallias's pending divorce, only recently completed, demanded as much discretion as possible in their encounters. Even though they lived in the same building, they would ensure they never arrived or left together and depended on middle-of-the-night hallway sprints when hormonal spirits were aligned. The two lovers grieved the decision to part, with Krakowski in Washington and Kallias in Hartford. But in other ways, it made matters easier since the availability of the Connecticut Air National Guard's Citation X executive jet allowed for quick trips to Washington to consult with Connecticut's "favorite son," now the president of the United States, and the state's congressional delegation. The abundance of political heavies in Washington blurred Kallias's private and official time with Krakowski, whether in public or at his residence, a town house that he owned on Third Street, Northeast, barely three blocks from his Senate office.

Zbigniew Krakowski's background was not unlike that of Kallias. Other children of immigrants, Krakowski's father fled Krakow as Nazi influence penetrated and destroyed university faculties. A devout Catholic, he harbored and aided his Jewish colleagues as they struggled to avoid the many persecutions befalling them until his activities made him a Nazi target. Already a distinguished physicist, he was recruited to the faculty of the New School, a New York City university expressly structured to accommodate scholars by Nazism. Ultimately, he made his was to Boston University, then retiring to managing a highly successfully research and development laboratory in the picturesque village of Windham, Connecticut.

Young Krakowski acquired his father's scientific aptitude. Graduating from Wesleyan in 1997, where his large-boned but muscular six-foot-two-inch frame made him a squash court menace and star, he entered the Massachusetts Institute of Technology. He finished a doctorate in nuclear physics in a record three years, his dissertation on the subject of quantum mechanics having been directly related to working hypotheses that he had pursued in his father's labs since the age of fifteen. The ever-curious-minded Krakowski worked in MIT's labs while he was at Northeastern Law, which he finished in 2004. He was elected to the state house of delegates one year later.

Appointed to the Senate's Judiciary Committee, he was the junior member on the panel's technology subcommittee, where, however, he served as ranking member, or senior Republican. In the Senate, the ranking member can be junior to others members who may hold other positions on one or more committees that would make them ineligible for leadership positions on a particular panel. For example, a senator who chairs a major committee, like appropriations, might be on a judiciary subcommittee where, because of his chairmanship of another major committee, he would be denied seniority on the subcommittee. The rule hinders the aggrandizement of too much power by any single senator.

Kallias's voice was noticeably more tender when speaking to Krakowski. "I miss you terribly, Zbig. I was an idiot to send you there."

Krakowski, never the romantic type, tended to make light of such talk. "C'mon, Soph. We've never had it easier. Down here the media couldn't care less about a small state governor and even less about some mysterious escapade a single junior senator might be engaged in."

"It's the frequency, Zbig. I need more of you."

"Well, you may get that. If I don't get on a decent workout schedule, you're gonna get a whole lot more of me," he said to his own light laugh, one not echoed at the other end of the line.

"We have to talk business, damn it. This should be pillow talk, like other normal couples," she added.

"Sophia, believe me, the way the federal snooping policies are headed, even that type of conversation may be admissible in evidence," he joked again, realizing he was not being funny in her mind.

"Let me get to the point: Remy Stratton."

"Oh, yeah, a bit of a pain. She's called me a couple of times, you know. She wants to take me to lunch or come over here so all can see she's influential enough to be in the Senate dining room. That's what most status seekers do, I've learned," Krakowski responded.

"Well, you're about to lessen her status. You got to call her and tell her to resign," said Kallias, her voice turning serious in a way that made appointed-senator Zbig Krakowski realize the boss was speaking.

No more joshing. She's not on that airwave at the moment, Krakowski realized, and then asked,

"What happened? I never had the impression that she was screwing up."

"She has screwed up okay. Enough so that she told some influential people that they would have to wait five years before petitioning for a presidential pardon and that the petitioners, in this case, couldn't petition right now because they were barred from lobbying under the disclosure statutes."

"You're kidding. That's pretty basic stuff. She told me she taught constitutional law, some undergraduate institution, I can't remember which one. But even at the undergraduate level, the delineated presidential authorities in the constitution are well covered, I'm sure."

Kallias continued. "Domenic Guillermo is representing the former Greek resort scandal folks. He's working with Bob Castignani's law firm, who will present the petitions on behalf of the group. Castignani's guys met with Remy, who gave them the terms I just mentioned. In the meantime, Guillermo spoke to the AG, Jack Hammond. Both agreed she had to go but in a way that doesn't send her marching to the media or some publishing house to manage her memoirs in a way that would be embarrassing to Democrats and Republicans."

"She would do that, from what I've seen of her. She's very ambitious, and equally insecure," Krakowski responded.

"It gets worse. Guillermo spoke to Sue Cohen. Sue agreed with Hammond, making it clear that the White House would stand behind the AG. So you need to tell Remy that, first, I have a job for her here in the state AG's office. Second, tell her that her counsel to Castignani's firm was wrong and is contrary to the opinion of the US attorney general and the White House. You might want to add that the Judiciary Committee's membership agrees with the AG. In other words, we don't want any escape hatches left open. She has to go, okay . . . honey?" Kallias's voice suddenly softened.

"It's a done deal, even without the 'honey,'" he replied to their joint laughter.

*　　*　　*

Krakowski lost little time in calling the Office of the Pardon Attorney. Remy Stratton, having lunch at her desk and advised by her assistant that Senator Krakowski was on the line, swallowed a morsel, cleared her throat, and spoke. "Hi, Senator, how are you?"

"Okay, Remy. I have to call you on an errand that I've done a total of zero times before," he said in deliberately awkward language, hoping to muster whatever lightness he could. "You're going to have to resign," he said in the simple and direct language of Zbig the engineer, a character quite different from the fuzzier legal Zbig. He paused to let the message register with her.

Stratton's face went hard, her lips quivering, tears welling in her eyes. Finally, words trembled out of her mouth into the phone. "What . . . what is the problem?" She caught her sob, covering the mouthpiece with her hand, thinking, *I can't lose control. He'll think I'm unprofessional.*

"Remy, I'd be surprised if you didn't immediately recognize the problem. I'm referring to the counsel you provided to the attorneys for Chuck Seaton's pardon petition."

"Oh, yes, I do remember meeting them. They were very rude to me, made me feel as if they knew more than I did on the subject. I am the pardoning attorney, you know. It's my job to understand the law," she responded, her voice becoming more firm as her emotional state improved.

"There's some disagreement on that, Remy, and it begins with your boss, the AG, as well as the White House." Krakowski's voice was equally firm.

Stratton was taken aback; she knew she was cornered. She was not a novice in government and political cabals, having participated in a few herself when she was at DOD as well as now at the Justice Department. Her words, barely audible now, eased out. "The . . . White House, what have they got to do with this? They don't get involved until I make my recommendations over there."

Incredible, she still doesn't acknowledge the absolute authority of the president on this matter, including his discretion as to intervene whenever and wherever he chooses in the process, he thought. In a voice slightly modulated for emphasis, he said, "Remy, I want you to prepare your letter of resignation and fax or e-mail a copy of it to me at the Judiciary Committee. And, by the way, you have no support in the Senate, especially on my committee."

Stratton was actually getting angry. "I have rights, you know, Senator. I want to talk to the president. I'm a political appointee."

"Remy, settle down, and get serious. You are under the cabinet-level supervision of Jack Hammond, the AG. And your boss is an assistant AG. You'll send your letter to your boss, not the AG and not the president. You serve at the pleasure of the president as a political appointee, and he delegates your supervision to the AG who further delegates it many layers down to your boss. You have no legal, regulatory, or even customary rights of appeal on the matter. You are not a career civil servant, you know."

"But I can sue or even go to the media, so I do have rights, you know." *I'm not going to let him or anyone else destroy me this way,* Stratton thought.

"Good God, Remy, have you lost your mind? What media? Fox News, the *Washington Times* online, someone's blog?" Krakowski asked, adding, "And sue on what grounds? Where in case law do you find even a hint of a precedent? You're a smart woman, and the governor knows that. In fact, she wants you in the state AG's office."

"What . . . Sophia wants me in Hartford? If I agree to this, can I stay in Washington? I have friends here, an apartment lease, and like the town," she added, a frenetic tone in her voice.

She's softening, getting some damn sense. "Look, now you're getting the picture, Remy. Take the job in Hartford and do it well. Then work your way back. Maybe run for office, join a Washington firm with heavy Connecticut links. There are lots of possibilities. You can come back for more money and with more prestige. And this incident will be a thing of the past that no one else will know about or remember, or even care. This is Washington. These things disappear in the political fog that always hangs over the place."

I'm trapped, but he's given me an alternative. It's not a bad one. I have lots of influence in the state through my family and friends. The AG's office there puts me in contact with hundreds of different firms and other contacts, possible clients. I could even go out on my own if I have to, Stratton reasoned. "I'll accept the offer and do the letter," she conceded finally.

A major obstacle to the pardon plan eliminated, Castignani rallied his colleagues to prepare the pardon petitions and their related arguments for a meeting with the president.

CHAPTER 3

A SELF-ENRICHING APPEAL

For the next two weeks leading up to the meeting with the president, the executive committee of the dozen convened at Castignani's residence. Washington is a town where politicians move about relatively anonymously. However, egos being what they are, members engaged in celebrity events or preferring to be less visible to their constituents harbor expectations that a media mite could be lingering in the shadows of their presence. On the contrary, when a cabinet secretary takes a position that infuriates, say, public unions, gay rights advocates, or other groups bent on protesting, media coverage becomes both assured and very obvious. TV vans, reporters, filming crews, and rubbernecks can sweep over neighborhood lawns and sidewalks and block streets for days. Communities have on rare occasion objected to the presence of government agencies or even courts or certain politicians living in their midst. For example, in Old Town, Alexandria, enraged locals successfully fought against the trials of 9/11 terrorist accomplices being held at the federal district court venue located there.

At ten on Monday, December 13, 2010, after a busy weekend, the group met to finalize the arguments they would present to the president, along with what they considered sufficient leverage in the form of creating new employment opportunities to motivate his strong commitment to improving the jobs picture as the recession continued.

Castignani opened the discussion, the other executive committee members being Domenic Guillermo, Chuck Seaton, Niko Rallis, Sam Schlesinger, and Bennie Thompson. All sipped their coffee, some still rubbing hands and gathering near the comforting wood-burning fireplace, still shaking off the bitter December cold in Washington. The other persons involved in the process would be there for a catered lunch at noon. The purpose of this preliminary session was to ensure the agenda materials were in order before presenting them to the entire group and getting as much of a consensus as possible.

"I'm wonderin' if we've lost our cotton-pickin' minds. Life in Switzerland? Talk about cold, the temperature in *Montroo*, or however you pronounce that place, was minus-ten degrees Celsius, that's about fifteen degrees Fahrenheit!" said Bennie Thompson, troubled like most with the pronunciation of Montreux (*moan-***trhur***), the capital of the so-called Swiss Riviera, where Lucas Holdings and its commodity trading subsidiary, Brent SA, were headquartered.

Rallis and Guillermo, now residing in the Montreux area, laughed, with Guillermo commenting, "Not to worry, Bennie, it's only bad when you go outside."

The rest joined in the laughter, signaling the upbeat mood. The pardon petition was ready for review, and all the members involved in the scandal had landed substantial positions within Rallis's many-layered business scheme.

"Ben, lay it out for us, please." Castignani was addressing Ben Ochs, who, with Don Tranh, had done much of the research and drafting of the pardon plan.

Ochs began. "We will remind the president of the boilerplate in Article II, referring to his absolute authority to grant as well as manage the pardoning or commutation process. This opener should immediately dismiss the objections raised by the pardoning attorney at Justice who, I understand, has already resigned and is moving to Hartford to work in the Connecticut AG's office. We have Dom to thank for working that out."

There was light applause and backslapping; Guillermo modestly and graciously nodded.

Ochs continued. "Our informal plea will emphasize to the president that the petitioners were misled and even entrapped into believing that they were receiving Iranian government money that had been underwriting their investment program. In advising the president that he had been misinformed by his official sources, including the intelligence community of the outgoing Republican administration, we will assert that the president, while acting appropriately, did so on the strength of factually wrong information since all Iranian monies were from private, not official, sources.

"It follows, we'll tell him, that the outgoing Republican administration's key agencies involved in this matter were led by political appointees who had apparent motives to embarrass the largely Democratic investors and petitioners. Indeed, we will add, the president himself may have been hoodwinked into becoming an unwitting accomplice to the Republican plan.

"If this is the case, the harm done is far-reaching. Eight Democrats resigned from the House and Senate, of which six were replaced by Republicans, distorting the most basic of all democratic traditions in our polity, the electoral process.

"We will leave with the president a one-paragraph letter, the text and body of which will read as follows:

"The petitioners for pardons, therefore, hereby appeal and request the restitution and restoration of their valued reputations by undoing the harm they have endured through accusations, fines, penalties, and even imprisonment, premised on deliberately false information and the continuing injustices they will face over and beyond the lifetimes of the petitioners."

"Why doesn't the letter delineate our arguments?" Ochs asked rhetorically. "Traditionally, the reason for pardon is not disclosed, nor is the president under any obligation to do so. Moreover, claims under the Freedom of Information Act do not lie on pardon cases, so there is little chance the media will learn of the substantive nature of our request."

"This, by the way, is one of the many reasons we had to remove Remy Stratton, the pardoning attorney. When Don met with her, he gave her a glimpse but by no means a complete picture of our case. It would have been very different if she were in that job when we submitted our pardon application, where we might have been pressured, by her, to make a stronger plea," Castignani added, referring to Don Tranh.

"But the letter left with the president is not our pardon application," said Chuck Seaton.

"That's right. It's just a courtesy summary of our appeal awaiting the textual substance that will be included in the formal application," Castignani added.

There was general consensus that this phase of the proposed meeting with Eastwood was sound.

"Dom and Niko will brief the entire on the second part of our request at lunch. That involves everyone since we will discuss the proposed roles of all members in Niko's business organization and the advantages the pardons will bring to the president's job development program," Castignani added in concluding the short session and awaiting the arrival of the other members.

*   *   *

By twelve thirty, the other member of the dozen gang, those charged with offenses, were seated at the stretched-out dining room table, a valued Duncan Phyfe treasure bought by Castignani's late wife when the couple resided in Maine. The 1920s three-pedestal mahogany table, with three leaves, stretched to a length of eight feet. Attached was a second Duncan Phyfe of the same height with one leaf, providing another four feet of seating space, easily accommodating all seventeen persons present, including the more recent arrivals: former senators Jeff Scharfman, Nancy Lehman, Andy Tantillo, and Mark Baldwin and former representatives David Ford, Jarrett Rodman, Mark Koerner, Marc Gregoire, and Anne Rathbone. The executive committee members – Guillermo, Rallis, Seaton, Thompson, Schlesinger, and Castignani – rounded out the fifteen former officials who were joined by Ochs and Tranh.

Lunch was served by Capitol Catering, an organization formed by retired members of the Capitol Police Force. The catering group was highly popular among House and Senate members; while its culinary offerings could lack the quality to which many had become accustomed, the information and behavior at meetings and other events could be reliably protected.

Ochs and Tranh hurried through their lunch, their briefing papers in hand, conferring with Rallis and Guillermo as they ate and talked among themselves. After about twenty minutes, Castignani interrupted the chatter.

"Folks, let's get on with the purpose of today's meeting. Niko and Dom will cover the Swiss plan after Ben Ochs summarizes the pardon information for the meeting with the president on Thursday."

The session moved quickly. Ochs reviewed the pardon plan and the arguments to be made in the Oval Office meeting. Castignani asked for a show of hands of those in favor; it was unanimously adopted.

The next order of business would not move either as quickly or as smoothly. The offer of lucrative employment had raised hopes, almost all of which would be satisfied. However, the operational plan would prove challenging to many, few of which had had any experience in the financial markets, commodity trading pits, or even, in a few cases, the private sector.

The occupational profile of the US Congress has changed dramatically in the past twenty years. In 1991–1992, the period of the 102nd Congress, the 435 House members and 100 senators, taken as a group, were overwhelmingly men over fifty and white. By 2011, the 112th Congress, there were ninety-two women in both houses, an increase of nearly 200 percent, along with forty-four African Americans, a 67 percent increase. This diversity was matched occupationally. Whereas in the 102nd Congress 45 percent of the body came from legal backgrounds, the dominant occupational background by the 112th Congress of 54 percent were from jobs in public service including education, with lawyerly careers diminishing to 37 percent.

These changes affected congressional retirement plans, whether the member left voluntarily or was defeated electorally. Law firms used to be available only to licensed lawyers or those with legal backgrounds but unlicensed in the District of Columbia or neighboring states of Virginia or Maryland. Today, many former members and staffers lacking law degrees but having substantive policy-related knowledge routinely find employment with law firms where lobbying-related revenue provides a healthy share of earnings. The local bar associations and state corporate affairs authorities have not yet allowed nonlicensed persons to actually practice law in their respective jurisdictions, but there is movement toward partnership arrangements in law firms favoring nonlawyers.

The membership profile changes in Congress, as mentioned here, were reflected in the way that Niko Rallis, Domenic Guillermo, and Bob Castignani decided to organize the group for functions related to the plan to expand Rallis's business operations to the United States. They would target an industrial sector in selected states and localities that would assure the support of their mutually related political interests.

Guillermo began. "Niko is a genius on these things. The business plan that he's composed whittles away at my brain."

Rallis interrupted, "Let's not forget that it was Dom here who conjured up the idea of the chocolate industry in Connecticut and Massachusetts."

"Yeah, that was the easy part," Guillermo added. "Developing the operational plan and process and the means of its execution was beyond anything I could ever have conceived."

The group was becoming both wearisome but anxious over the self-congratulatory fawning; eyes began to roll and shifting in the chairs more obvious, especially as the group was being served their dessert and what appeared to taste like supercharged coffee.

Castignani sensed the change of mood. "Guys, I think we need to get into the plan."

"You're right. I wanna get all of us involved in this love affair," Guillermo said, nodding to Rallis. "Okay, Niko, it's your show."

"Ben," Rallis motioned to Ben Ochs. "Could you please pass out the documents?"

Ochs and Tranh distributed several pages of a document laying out the information all were awaiting.

LUCAS HOLDINGS S.A.
Corporate Headquarters:
Route de Villard, Chamby, Haut Montreux
Montreux, Canton de Vaud
Switzerland CH-1820
Tel : +41-21-962-1200

Executive Memorandum 2010.12.3

FROM: Niko Rallis
TO: Corporate staffs: Lucas Holdings S.A. and Brent S.A.
DATE: 14 December 2010
SUBJECT: Corporate Structuring and Organization [**HIGHLY CONFIDENTIAL**]

PURPOSE: This communication outlines the reorganized management structures of Lucas Holdings S.A. ["Lucas"], Brent S.A. ["Brent"], and Belmont Confections S.A. ["Belmont"]. The three privately held corporations remain chartered in the Confederation of Helvetia [Switzerland].

- Lucas' principal business focus is on the development of luxury recreational facilities in Greece with ancillary investment and other holdings in commercial operations that fulfill the chartered purpose of the company. It is headquartered in Chamby, CH.
- Brent, a principal holding of Lucas, is a commodity trading company with global operations. The company is coheadquartered with Lucas in Chamby.
- Belmont, a Lucas holding, is a food-producing company specializing in chocolate-base confections. The company's global market is substantial, with nearly 30 percent dominance in specified chocolate products. Belmont is planning a major expansion into the United States of America [US]. The company is headquartered in Vevey with various operations of the production facility and administration overlapping into nearby villages.

PRINCIPAL STAFF POSITIONS AND COMPENSATION:

LUCAS

Board of Directors:

   Chairman and Chief Executive Officer (CEO): Mr. Nikos Rallis, GR [Salary: CHF 2M plus bonus]
   Vice Chairman: Hon. (Amb.) Domenic S. Guillermo, US [Compensation: CHF 200K]

Director: Hon. (Frau) Urs Hochdorf, SW, Deputy Minister of Finance, Government of Switzerland [1] [Compensation: CHF 50K]
Director: Mon. Henri Baptiste, SW, President, Banque Credit d'Helvetia (Corporate Trustee, Lucas Investment Trust and Persian Investment Trust)[2] [Compensation: CHF 50K]

Management:

CEO: Mr. Nikos Rallis, GR
President: Hon. (Sen.) Jeffrey Scharfman, US [Salary: CHF 1.7M plus bonus]
Executive Vice President: Hon. (Ms.) (Sen.) Nancy Lehman, US [Salary: CHF 1.2M plus bonus]
General Counsel (International): Mme. Marcia Beauvais, SW [Salary: CHF 600K]
General Counsel (Domestic-US): Mrs. Jane Gregoire, US [Salary: CHF 400K]

Senior Managing Director and Chairman, Europe, Middle East, and Africa (position vacant)

Senior Managing Director and Chairman, North America: Hon. (Rep.) Marc Gregoire, US [Salary: CHF 800K plus bonus]

Senior Managing Director / Chief Risk Officer: Hon. (Sen.) Andrew Tantillo, US [Salary: CHF 600K plus bonus]

Chief Financial Officer: Hon. (Rep.) Anne Rathbone, US [Salary: CHF 500K plus bonus]

Ownership:

Government of Switzerland (GOS) (19 percent share)
Lucas Investment Trust (LIT) (25 percent share)
Persian Investment Trust (PIT) (25 percent share)
Niko Rallis (25 percent share)
Domenic S. Guillermo (6 percent share)

---

[1]   The Government of Switzerland (GOS or GCH) is an investing party in Lucas with a 19 percent interest.
[2]   The Persian Investment Trust (PIT) includes holdings of private Iranian citizens while the Lucas Investment Trust (LIT) manages the holdings of expatriates and funds of American citizens employed by Lucas Holdings.

DISTRIBUTION TO LUCAS HOLDINGS' OWNERSHIP

Gross Revenues (2009) [Swiss Francs (CHF)][3]

Source	Total	GOS %	GOS AMT	LIT %	LIT AMT	PIT %	PIT AMT	Rallis %	Rallis AMT	Guillermo %	Guillermo AMT
Brent	CHF 2.5B	19	475M	25	625M	25	625M	25	625M	6	15M
Belmont	3.0B	19	570M	25	750M	25	750M	25	750M	6	18M
Club Lucas[4]	200M	19	8M	25	50M	25	50M	25	50M	6	12M
TOTALS	5.7B		1.083B		2.508B		2.508B		2.508B		45M
Net Earnings[5]	1.14B		216M[6]		502M		502M		502M		9M

BRENT

Board of Directors:

Chairman and CEO: Herr (Dr.) Paul von Schlossen, SW [Compensation: CHF 4.0M plus bonus]

Vice Chairman: Mr. Nikos Rallis, GR [Compensation: CHF 200K]

Director: Hon. (Amb.) Domenic S. Guillermo, US [Compensation: CHF 100K]

Director: Hon. (Treas. Secy.) Charles Seaton, US, President, Brent S.A. [Compensation: CHF 100K]

---

[3]   Lucas Holdings received 29 percent or CHF 2.5B from Brent's gross revenues of CHF 8.62B and 20 percent of Belmont's CHF 15B gross revenues. Both receipts were based on Lucas Holdings' ownership share. These figures do not include special bonuses awarded for specific nonrecurring market operations, such as the cornering of the cocoa bean market in April 2011.

[4]   Club Lucas operations in Santorini, Greece, generating modest revenue from nascent recreational activities.

[5]   Net earnings for all revenue sources calculated after eliminating corporate taxes, including Swiss profit tax (8.5 percent) and other operating expenses, a 70 percent claim on gross revenues amounting to CHF 4.56 billion, resulting in distributable earnings of CHF 1.14 billion.

[6]   Swiss Government does not pay taxes to itself but reduces its share through deductible operating costs incurred by the taxpaying entity in which the government holds a material interest.

Director: Hon. (Frau) Urs Hochdorf, SW, Deputy Minister of Finance, Government of Switzerland [7] [Compensation: CHF 50K]
Director: Mon. Henri Baptiste, SW, President, Banque Credit d'Helvetia Corporate Trustee, Lucas and Persian Investment Trusts [Compensation: CHF 50K]

Management:

Chief Executive Officer: Herr (Dr.) Paul von Schlossen, SW [Salary: CHF 4.0M plus bonus]
President: Hon. Charles Seaton, US, President, Brent S.A. [Salary: CHF 2.5M plus bonus]
Principal Executive Vice President and Zone Director (US, Canada, Latin America, and the
Caribbean): Mon. Jean-Louis Bujon, SW, President, Brent S.A. [Salary: CHF 1.2M plus bonus]
Executive Vice President for Africa, Asia, Oceana, and the Middle East: Hon. (Rep.) Bennie Thompson, US [Compensation: CHF 1.0M plus bonus]
Executive Vice President (Commodity Futures): Hon. (Rep.) David Ford, US [Compensation: CHF 1.0M plus bonus]
Vice President and Counsel (Domestic-US, Canada): Hon. (Rep.) Mark Koerner, US [Compensation: CHF 900K plus bonus]
Vice President and Counsel (International): Henri du Puy, SW-US [Compensation: CHF 800K plus bonus]

Offices:

Global Headquarters: Route de Villard, Chamby, Canton de Vaud, Switzerland
Brent-USA Headquarters:

>**Brent-USA CEO:** Hon. (Sen.) Samuel Schlesinger, US
>[Compensation: US$1.0M + bonus]
>One Rockefeller Plaza, Suite 1510
>New York, NY 10020

Trading Offices:
World Financial Center, Suite 3500
One North End Ave.
New York, NY 10282

Brent-UK Headquarters:

>**Brent-UK CEO:** Hon. (Sen.) Mark Baldwin, US

---

[7]   The Government of Switzerland (GOS or GCH) is an investing party in Brent with a 25 percent interest.

[Compensation: US$1.2M + bonus]
Canary Wharf Towers, Suite 4800
One Canada Square
London, UK E14-5DY

Brent-Canada Headquarters:
Brent-CA CEO: Hon. (Rep.) Jarrett Rodman
[Compensation: US$800K + bonus]
The Exchange Tower, Suite 460
130 King Street
Toronto, Ontario M5X 1J2

Brent Ownership:

Lucas Holdings S.A.[8] (LH) (29 percent)
Government of Switzerland (GOS) (25 percent)
Institutions[9] (Inst.) (20 percent)
Private Bond Holders [10](Bond) (26 percent)

BELMONT

Board of Directors:
Chairman and CEO: Herr Lutz Gorgens, SW [Compensation: CHF 5.0M plus bonus]
Vice Chair: Hon. (Sen.) Mark Baldwin, US [Compensation: CHF 100K]
Director: Herr Marc Smit, SW, President, Belmont Confections S.A. [Compensation: CHF 90K]
Director: Mr. Nikos Rallis, GR, Chairman and CEO, Lucas Holdings S.A. [Compensation: CHF 90K]
Director: Hon. (Amb.) Domenic S. Guillermo, US, Director, Brent S.A. [Compensation: CHF 90K]

---

[8]   The 29 percent share of Brent held by Lucas Holdings, of course, was further split according to the investor shares in Lucas itself, which were the Swiss government (19 percent), Lucas Investment Trust (25 percent), Persian Investment Trust (25 percent), Rallis (25 percent), and Guillermo (6 percent).

[9]   Institutional investors in Brent consisted of numerous Swiss banks, insurance companies, private equities, and hedge funds, none holding a share of greater than 1 percent.

[10]   The three private bond holders and their respective shares were directors von Schlossen (10 percent), Rallis (8 percent), and Guillermo (8 percent).

Director: Hon. (Sen.) Jeffery Scharfman, US, President, Lucas Holdings S.A. [Compensation: CHF 90K]
Director: Hon. (Frau) Urs Hochdorf, SW, Deputy Minister of Finance, Government of Switzerland [11] [Compensation: CHF 50K]
Director: Mon. Henri Baptiste, SW, President, Banque Credit d'Helvetia Corporate Trustee, Lucas and Persian Investment Trusts [Compensation: CHF 50K]

Management:

Chief Executive Officer: Herr Lutz Gorgens, SW [Compensation: CHF 5.0M plus bonus]
President: Herr Marc Smit, SW [Compensation: CHF 4.0M plus bonus]

Offices:

Executive Offices and Headquarters, Global Operations:
Belmont Confections S.A.
Château Belmont
Quai Ernest-Ansermet
1800 Vevey Switzerland
Tel. +41-21-962-54-38
Fax +41-21-962-54-37
www.belmont.ch

Production Facilities:
Gospic, Croatia
Kladno, Czech Republic
Bratislava, Slovakia
Krakow, Poland

Belmont Ownership:
Government of Switzerland (GOS) (25 percent)
Brent S.A. (20 percent)
Lucas Holdings S.A. (LH) (20 percent)
Private Bond Holders[12] (Bonds) (35 percent)

---

[11] The Government of Switzerland (GOS or GCH) is an investing party in Brent with a 25 percent interest.

[12] The private bond holders and board members are Gorgens (8 percent), Smit (7 percent), Baldwin (5 percent), Rallis (5 percent), Guillermo (5 percent), and Scharfman (5 percent), amounting to 35 percent.

*   *   *

The group was mulling over the memorandum, chatting among themselves. Castignani spoke up. "Folks, before we get into the memo, which is obviously critical to both your future as well as the Eastwood meeting, let me ask for a consensus on the pardon arguments to be presented to the president. As Ben detailed earlier, we have three critical, main talking points.

"First, reminding the president of the Article II language and his own Justice Department pardoning attorney's attempt to corrupt his authority."

"Just a minute, please. I've been thinking about that." It was the voice of Jeff Scharfman, the generally acclaimed leader of the congressional members in the last Congress who objected strongly to their presumptive support of Israel because they were Jewish.

"This Stratton woman, the pardoning attorney, remember, she was a Republican appointee. We're finding now that there may have been a deliberate attempt to feed erroneous information regarding Iranian investment in the original Club Lucas project. Let's not forget it was the assumption that Iranian government money was invested in Lucas that the president used to force our resignations. Even Eastwood was blindsided, *we think*!

"Maybe the same Republicans who conjured up the false Iranian money scheme were also behind getting her a job in the Democratic Justice Department," Scharfman asserted to the doubting heads of many.

This guy never quits. Talk about noodle-headed conspiracy nuts in the right wing! Castignani thought to himself.

But not surprisingly, at least one other member in the group was agitated by the thought. Andy Tantillo, the other former senator from Scharfman's same state of New Jersey, elbowed Nancy Lehman, the former California senator. "Damn it, he has a point there," he muttered to her.

"Let it go, Andy. That's just one of Jeff's speculative fantasies," she muttered back, shifting her weight away from the side on which Tantillo sat, crossing her legs in the same direction.

Tantillo was too agitated. He had been imprisoned and was desperate to resuscitate his reputation and especially his ego in any possible way. He spoke up. "Jeff is right. We need to know more about this."

Guillermo looked at Castignani, who caught the glance and rolled his eyes. He gestured with his hand for Guillermo to enter the fray.

"That's a bit of a reach, Jeff. I know Eastwood better than anyone else in this room. Also, I tracked the nomination of this woman, Stratton, to the Connecticut governor. She wouldn't BS me. It was a sympathy move on the part of Sophia Kallias, the governor, to find a job for Stratton. Neither she nor her appointed replacement for Earl in the Senate, Zbig Krakowski, would dare to cross the president, himself a former Connecticut senator and, certainly, the most popular living political figure from Connecticut.

"The thought that they would try to beguile a powerful leader like Eastwood with some type of petty scheme like this makes absolutely no political sense. Besides, we all know Earl Eastwood. First, he's much too smart not to see through a charade like this, and second, he's too much a straight arrow to ever go along with it. We've all worked with him and watch him in action. You don't deceive this guy!" Guillermo ended his retort, adding, "Bob, let's get on with this," looking in the direction of Bob Castignani.

We need to bring everyone together. There doesn't seem to be much interest in Scharfman's theory from the look on faces here. But I need to rescue Scharfman from himself, Castignani thought, then acknowledged Guillermo's suggestion.

"I agree with Dom. Let's move on. But in deference to Jeff and Andy, let me add that we have agreed that there may have been some distortion of the intelligence information the Republicans in the intelligence community gave to both outgoing president Bob Davids and to Earl Eastwood as his successor. We'll raise this in the meeting with the president."

"I agree, Bob," Nancy Lehman added, the emphatic tone in her voice implying the issue was settled.

Perfect, it worked, Castignani realized. He continued.

"The second argument is that the parties, those of you charged in the Lucas incident, were entrapped into believing that their earnings on the investments were funded by the Iranian government, and that the pressure brought to encourage their resignations was therefore premised on false grounds.

"Finally, we will plead the pardon as restitution. Any further discussion, comments?"

There were none, and sensing the eagerness of all present to get on with the review of the memo, Castignani then said, "Okay, Niko and Dom will explain the business plan."

Niko Rallis and Domenic Guillermo moved to the front of the room, where a large sixty-three-inch plasma screen was set on a table, intended to display the pages of the memo, copies of which were in the hands of all.

The presence of the two captured a sociological slice of the contemporary American polity. Rallis – a Greek, educated at the best institutions in America, including the highly prestigious Wharton School at Penn – spoke unaccented American English. His glib speech, businesslike approach to issues, and conservative attire made him appear as any other executive likely to be encountered in a setting like this. Guillermo – a first-generation, Ivy-educated, remarkably successful politician from the heavily Italian enclave of New Haven – rounded out the portrait of unbounded opportunity in America, where merit and ambition can trump ethnic origins.

Domenic Guillermo was to speak first; he would set the stage for Rallis. *There's still a lot of distrust with Rallis,* he thought, reminding himself that it was Rallis who had created Club Lucas and the Mediterranean investment scheme that brought the nightmares to most in the room. *On the other hand, it was Niko who disclosed that the Iranian investment in Club Lucas was not government but private money,* he then reasoned.

Because the president had pressed for their resignations while promising not to disclose the Iranian connection, the members themselves were unaware of the private nature of Iranian money in Lucas. *But now, that revelation is what the entire pardon request is now hinged to,* Guillermo had this settled in his mind before speaking. *I need to set the stage for Rallis just in case there's some lingering hostility to him.*

Finally, Guillermo started to speak. "As I said earlier, getting the idea implanted in Kallias's head that we can help the Connecticut economy was the easy part. It was Niko here who is making it happen. Niko, could you brief us on the memo?"

"Sure, Dom, thanks," Rallis responded.

"I'm going to do this a little backward," he started, "which is to say, I'll discuss structure and organization before getting into the business strategy.

"I've talked to each of you separately over the past few days. I didn't have anything close to the offers I'm making now because the deal that Dom has worked out didn't even cross my cranial plateau. Keep that in mind as you review your position and I explain your roles.

"Our business strategy can lead to a dominant position in the US confections market whether that means as partners with or owners of the two leading US competitors, Rose Confections of Connecticut and Havens of Massachusetts."

"Question, Niko," asked Sam Schlesinger, the former Connecticut senator. "I thought the Guillermo plan called for expanding the existing US confection leaders, Rose and Havens?"

"Let me answer that," remarked Domenic Guillermo.

"Sam, we're entering a squirrelly situation here with the president. We need some leverage. What if he rejects the pardon request? Our deal is we expand the US confection industry and he delivers the pardons because the folks gathered here, like you, Sam, are critical to the operational plan to do that. You'll notice, Sam, that Niko puts you in charge of Brent's US operations for which, I might add, you are more handsomely paid than anything close to what you've ever made in your professional lifetime."

Schlesinger was somewhat offended by the remark, thinking, *Screw you, Guillermo. I'm not slipping back into one of Rallis's greed fantasies for any price.* He could see expressions of identical concern from the faces around him.

"What I'm sayin', Dom . . . and Niko," Schlesinger added with unmistakable and controlled assertiveness, "is that I'm not goin' down for a final ten-count knockout for any price, and I'm not sellin' out *our* state's economic well-being," he said, stressing the mutuality of the two men's Connecticut origins.

I insulted Sam. I'd better back off, it occurred to Guillermo, realizing the meaning of his verbal jab. Guillermo, known in politics as an optimizer, had surprised himself;

he was eager to pacify the noticeable uneasiness in the room that accompanied Schlesinger's reaction.

"Yeah, a bad choice of words on my part, Sam. I apologize and will explain. What I intended to say is that we need a fallback position for ourselves. If the pardons don't materialize, what do we do? Can we even undertake the merger with the US confection leaders without government approval? There are antitrust implications on both sides of the Atlantic that will be in play, and they will remain a risk whether we merge or buy out the US competitors. But, Sam, if you accept the offer, like it or not, my good friend, you are working for a competitor."

"Dom, we're enthusiastic, for the most part, talking to some others here. And we realize we're putting ourselves in a competitive position with the US companies. But like Sam, some of us are also thinking that there should be a little more transparency," added Andy Tantillo, the former senator from New Jersey.

"Please, allow me a comment on that." It was the voice of former New York representative David Ford. "What we have here is a difference between government and business perspectives, and most here are Democrats, not great supporters of business, at least in your public lives. I come from a Wall Street background and," he started to say, nodding briefly to Rallis and Guillermo, "I'm sure the position you've put me in as the commodity futures manager for Brent took that into consideration.

"Transparency can be a pitfall in business. This is why we have laws protecting trade secrets. It's neither prudent nor necessary to disclose business objectives, and the courts have rarely veered from that position. But Sam is arguing with the business objective, Andy is promoting disclosure. We can talk about Sam's concerns. But, Andy, if you sign on, you have, ipso facto, accepted the purpose of the business and the obligation to protect its methods, provided they're legal, of course."

"That's exactly my grievance, guys," inserted Schlesinger. "I don't want to be seen doing things which can be construed as downright traitorous to Connecticut's interests. Besides, many will think we're acting in vengeance. That could bring the whole house of cards down on us. The president doesn't have a whole hell of a lot of power on commercial issues without the support of Congress, we all know that. We can tie his hands, and we've done precisely that quite routinely," he added to light laughter, grins, and nods.

"This is good. We needed this discussion." It was Guillermo again.

Rallis stood by, listening closely. He understood Americans and recognized that morality is often little more than self-righteousness. Rallis was also a politician; in fact, he had served in the Greek legislature and as minister of finance. The parliamentary form of government usually requires ministerial members of the prime minister's cabinet to be serving members of the national legislature. This practice would amount to a conflict of interest in the American presidential system, where the Founding Fathers intentionally sought to avoid the perils of parliamentary government by hitching the American political culture to the doctrine of separation of powers.

Guillermo began speaking. "Sam, Andy, we're not concealing anything illegally. We're all in business now. Our objectives are to please our shareholders first, to create wealth, and at the same time to offer quality products and services to the marketplace. Moreover, you'll notice, Lucas and its principal holdings, Brent and Belmont, are all *private*, not *public*, companies. Sam may have missed that," he said, glancing at Schlesinger.

Schlesinger, furiously scanning the document, replied, "Yeah, I didn't see that. It's clear from the ownership profiles that all are private firms."

"And, Andy, if we go public – and I'm not opposed to that, nor is Niko, I believe – we will fully comply with the disclosure requirements imposed by the SEC or Swiss FINMA," said Guillermo, referring to the US Securities and Exchange Commission and its Swiss counterpart, the Financial Market Authority.

"Yes, in fact, we may very well pursue an IPO," Rallis added, referring to an initial public offering of the company's stock and other equities for public purchase. "But that will depend on how the initial business strategy unfolds. Let me try to get us back on track and finish with the structural matters before talking briefly about our strategy."

The room settled down. Several persons rose, filling their cups with coffee or taking other beverages; there was light chatter, even smiles. Rallis sensed the change in mood following the discussion, which, however caustic at times, had resolved a few prominent questions.

"Dave had commented on what he perceived to be the reason for his role selection in one of the companies. He's right. Looking at the professional, public, and private backgrounds of each of you and especially the work you had done in Congress or the administration, as in Chuck's case," Rallis said, looking at Chuck Seaton, a former secretary of the US Treasury Department, "I made offers accordingly. Your backgrounds will be entirely appropriate to the functions in the jobs assigned. You'll not be the frontline traders for those of you with Brent. Those are technical jobs for which the company is amply staffed in the trading pits and on the digitized global trading floors where cocoa beans are traded. More about cocoa beans later.

"Your jobs are supervisory, managerial really. You are team leaders, working to ensure that the policies that implement our strategies are effectively executed and that the obstacles that will inevitably arise can be overcome. This last requirement is especially directed at you. For example, in the US, we will encounter commodity trading rules that will have to be negotiated with Congress and the regulatory agencies that enforce them. The vast body of foreign trade laws under the World Trade Organization will come into play. Since the trade laws are subject to sovereign negotiation, talks in the dispute settlement tribunes will require good relationships with, for example, the US Trade Representative's office. There are no rights of private action in trade negotiations, so we will have to make sure our arguments are carried into the settlement process by creating a reliable source of information for government officials."

They're getting the picture. They can see that they're going to earn their keep, Rallis thought, glancing at Guillermo, who smiled approvingly.

"Lastly, let's talk about housing. Living in Switzerland is expensive. In lieu of a housing allowance, Lucas has leased half of Palais Montreux, which is among the top three hotels in Switzerland and among the top twenty in Europe.

"Housing together at the Palais Montreux is, of course, optional. But it's in the interest of all of us that we get settled and get right to work, 'hit the ground running,' as we like to say in the US. Eventually, you might want to find other quarters better suited to your own personal interests. But our recommendation is that you get into the job before making alternative housing commitments that can be undone."

"You mean like getting fired?" asked Nancy Lehman with just enough sarcasm to elicit a chuckle or two.

"Anything's possible," responded Rallis to light but nervous laughter in the group. "I'm not thinking that way. We're all highly *incentivized* . . . Now there's one word that has no real roots in Greek. One great thing about the US is everything is open to entrepreneurial treatment, including the language.

"Getting back to the topic, this is extraordinary housing. You'll be a guest in the hotel as far as the amenities are concerned but have all the privacy that you would in a condominium situation."

Palais Montreux was certain to meet with everyone's satisfaction, which became evident as the wall-mounted plasma monitor lit up with its images. The massive château-like structure faced the lake with the French and southeastern Swiss Alps beyond. The structure's green window awnings reflected its belle epoque legacy. Balconies fronted the master bedrooms and *grands salons* of each apartment. The next image showed the typical room layouts. Each unit would have three bedrooms and a separate room to be used as a home office, each appropriately cabled for high-speed digital transmissions under secure conditions.

There was obvious interest in this important part of the relocation. Rallis continued to speak. "Transportation couldn't be more ideal. You're less than eight kilometers from the Brent and Lucas joint headquarters in Chamby and about three kilometers from the Belmont plant. Of course, there's a hotel garage and a health club that's among the best I've ever seen, anywhere. It includes two indoor pools and an outdoor pool as well as a spa which, even in spa-crazed Switzerland, is exceptional. One final feature, the restaurants and bars are as you would expect, all among the country's best, with liberal operating hours, great food and drink, and convenient for any type of activity, social or business."

Rallis was satisfied with the general acceptance of his plan; he wanted to keep them as closely grouped as possible, like the overseas embassies, which often housed its delegations in compounds. The Palais Montreux would be the corporate compound of sort, offering every convenience and, in Rallis's mind, enticing even the most reluctant spouses and whatever ménage the individual members would have to accommodate. Meetings could be arranged at any time of the day or, if necessary, night without dragging the members out onto the treacherous Swiss roads during the winter.

Noticing some movement among members as they took notes on the living arrangements, which could lengthen the meeting, Guillermo intervened, "I know you have many questions on housing. Most of us are empty nesters, but we have spouses to please, and most of us would like to accommodate the certainty of family visits. The hotel living arrangement, in my judgment, couldn't be better for those of us in the stage of our lives. But let's move on and reserve the more individualized questions for later.

"Next, and finally, we want to lay out a synopsis of the business strategy. Please, keep in mind that the details will be forthcoming and aligned with each of your job descriptions and their related missions and functions.

"Niko, would you start, please?" Guillermo concluded as the group once more settled down with increased coffee consumption.

Rallis, playing with the keyboard on his laptop and checking cable to the wall-mounted plasma monitor, brought up three talking points. "In a few words," he started, "this is our strategy. Our objective is to expand into the US confections market. Our strategy is as follows:

"First, we will get control of the cocoa bean market. The cocoa bean is the critical element in the production of the chocolate-base products that generate more than 90 percent of Belmont's earnings. And of course, it is the single most important component of our competitors' production as well as total business model.

"No simplicity or simplemindedness intended, if it works the way we hope, the rest will fall into place. There is one overarching, large producer of cocoa beans, the Ivory Coast, which produces 40 percent of the world supply. The rest is portioned in small slices among nearly twenty countries. The country is a political cesspool at the moment. That might work to our advantage. We can either play with the current government, the head of which lost reelection and refuses to quit, or the opposition, at the moment quiescent because the in-place illicit regime controls the real rule of power in much of Africa: might makes right.

"We will seek to buy the two-year crop, enough capacity to give us the time we need to achieve substantial enough domination of the market and to weaken our competition. By that I mean the following: Belmont already gets 50 percent of the cocoa bean production coming to the EU from the second-largest source, Ghana, which produces 21 percent of the world supply. *If we* capture the Ivory Coast, which provides 88 percent of its cocoa crop to the US, it wraps up the market for us.

"Second, as we move toward optimal control, we will stabilize the market to avoid 'circuit breakers' and to provide plausible availability of the commodity to other user sources. As commodity markets shift toward apparent buyer dominance, evidenced by excessively high trading, trading can be suspended in a manner similar to the stock markets. If this happens, media and regulator attention would turn to the buyers – or sellers – depending on which way the market is headed. In our case, it would not be too difficult to discover that Brent was attempting to corner the cocoa bean market. Moreover, we will continue, while we buy, to sell market futures at gradually raised prices. The spread between the current and future commodity price will be maintained carefully enough to create an impression that, while a short supply of the commodity appears to be developing, it could be related to events in the producer countries, but there is still *availability*.

"Finally, once we determine to have optimal control of the commodity, we will continue to raise the selling price to a level where our US competitors would find their earnings and, especially, their profit margins diminishing at a dangerous and unsustainable rate. This is where we would make our move. We will make a merger or acquisition offer, almost certainly including, de minimis, Belmont products for manufacture and sale by our US competitors, and our merger or acquisition targets, under a licensing agreement. That would probably be a first step."

There were many questions as immediately obvious from the movement of feet, chairs, and torsos. Several hands were in the air. Rallis decided to select David Ford's question; Ford had been a Wall Street trader and, later, an investment banker. Rallis therefore expected the question to be sophisticated enough to cover many of the other likely questions.

"Let me Dave's question first," Rallis said.

"Niko, the plan sounds, if you'll excuse my use of *your* word, 'plausible.' But what's to keep the speculators from mucking things up? I don't have a lot of experience in the commodity markets, except that I do know the speculators always have an important presence in every transaction."

"Right, on the second part, we can't avoid speculators, nor do we want to. We can actually use them to support our strategy."

"I'm lost here, Niko," came the query from former senator Nancy Lehman, speaking out. "Aren't we the speculators?"

"No, Nancy. We are the 'hedgers' and very different from speculators. Speculators trade for money. They raise risk and make money from it. They're our opposites. We seek control of the commodity so as to ensure a price beneficial to our interest or the interests of the buyers of our contracts," Rallis responded.

"But the speculators are buying your hedge contracts, aren't they?" asked ex-representative Anne Rathbone, herself a former and very shrewd corporate finance officer of a number of corporations in her home state of Delaware.

"Yes, Anne, speculators do buy our contracts, and we are always very happy to take their money," Rallis answered to the laughter of some, including those who weren't sure why they were laughing.

Rallis continued. "It works this way. We sell a contract to a speculator at, say, a high price. The speculator expects the price to go higher still. The hedger expects it to go lower. In our case, our company, Brent, is the hedger and knows the price can go lower since we will have controlled the cocoa bean market. So we transfer our risk that it will not go higher to the speculator."

"That doesn't make sense, Niko," said Rathbone again. "Why would we lower the price?"

"Very clever, Anne. You see, it depends on who's with you on the dance floor. You'll recall our second strategy point, *availability*. We will be selling some of the commodity, even as we're buying immense amounts of it, to stabilize the market. Making it available, but at steady, slightly climbing prices with a small spread from the last futures sales price, will diminish the prospect, in the minds of the regulators and speculators, that we're intent on capturing the market. We will carefully calibrate the gains from our availability sales to our hedge customers with the gains, or modest losses, from contract sales to the speculators to ensure that we have a favorable marginal gain. This will be the job of Brent's traders and technicians who engage in these types of contracts and other sales and trades every day."

"And it is this strategy, if executed properly, that will achieve our goal of gaining a major share of the US confections market," Guillermo added. "In other words, the interaction between hedger and speculator is what makes for efficiencies in the futures market. Brent is one of the world's shrewdest commodity trading firms. As a holding of Lucas, Brent becomes a conduit through which we raise the value of Belmont, also a Lucas holding, while lessening the profitability of our US competitors, opening them to our offer to merge with or sell to us."

"I have to ask this question, Dom." It was Bennie Thompson. "I've accepted the position as Brent's executive vice president for Africa, Asia, Oceana, and the Middle East. I know the president of Ivory Coast pretty well. I visited the country many times as chairman of the Africa subcommittee in the House. Jean Bago is desperate. His prime minister, Emile Tagro, who won the election, has his own following in the South, where he was once a rebel leader. The US state department and most of Africa support Tagro. I have to deal with Bago since he's gonna be there a while. Do we want to oppose our own state department, and president?"

Guillermo had anticipated the question. "I know it's a tough one for you, Bennie. And we both know that Joe Jefferson of Louisiana was a close friend of yours."

"Yup, and there's still that stigma in Africa. He was a Harvard Law black guy, like me. But he bribed his way to self-aggrandizement in a way that I won't," Thompson responded.

William "Joe" Jefferson, the former House member from Louisiana's second congressional district was convicted and sentenced to thirteen years in prison for bribery and other corrupt practices in 2009. Jefferson, known for having concealed

$90,000 in bribery money in the freezer trays of his refrigerator, had accepted bribes from sources in Nigeria, Ghana, Cameroons, and other African countries in exchange for promises to influence Congress in their favor.

Guillermo continued. "There's a very great difference here, Bennie. Joe was charged with abusing his public office for personal gain. His solicitation and acceptance of bribes constituted the conflict of interest that resided at the base of his wrongdoing. And I am aware that many Africans were both surprised and offended that, first of all, he had committed an offense that would have been an acceptable yet illegal practice in their countries. Secondly, they had expected an educated black, like many of them, to be smarter and certainly to know and understand the differences in the ways laws are enforced or not enforced in his own country.

"Bennie, you are neither indulging in anything even remotely illegal nor any behavior that violates our kickback or related bribery laws as they relate to the conduct of all US citizens doing business abroad. Secondly, you're a senior management officer of Brent, a highly reputable Swiss trading company that has been doing business in the Ivory Coast for twenty-plus years. Your job – and correct me, Niko, if I miss something – is to encourage the appropriate power yielders in the Ivory Coast to sell us their crop rather than market it through other commodity brokers to the various world exchanges on which it is bought and sold."

"It's a tough job, Bennie," Rallis added. "But we're giving you all the discretionary freedom needed to figure it out, not to mention a substantial bonus."

Thompson stood, pensively staring at the two men fielding his question. He blinked, smiled, and then sat down, thinking, *I can do this, and I'll do it in the right way, in a way that even the president will understand. My role is a hell of a lot more critical than I ever realized, but there are a lot of restorative palliatives here as far as my tattered reputation is concerned.*

CHAPTER 4

PARDON ME, MR. PRESIDENT

A T NINE THIRTY ON THURSDAY, DECEMBER 16, 2010, FORMER CONNECTICUT GOVERNOR AND, OF LATE, US AMBASSADOR TO THE HOLY SEE DOMENIC S. GUILLERMO, left the Hay Adams Hotel across Pennsylvania Avenue from the White House. He would arrive early for his 10:00 a.m. appointment with his former protégé, Earl Eastwood, now president of the United States.

It won't take much to screw this one up, realized Guillermo, deep in thought. Then catching his senses, he carefully negotiated across several icy patches on Pennsylvania Avenue, now open to traffic having been recently and temporarily closed down for various repairs, security, and other reasons. He headed toward the West Gate of the eighteen-acre compound, which together with the fifty-two-acre elliptical spread behind it was known as President's Park.

The uniformed Secret Service officer at the gate kiosk recognized him from afar, his monitor zooming in on his profile captured by one of the several remote cameras surrounding the front fence. With a touch on his keyboard, he matched the photo on his monitor with that provided from his data bank, confirming the appearance of the expected distinguished visitor.

"Good morning, Governor Guillermo," the officer said, stepping out onto the well-cleared sidewalk after a night of dusting snow. Guillermo extended his ungloved right hand, ever the politician, greeting the officer as if his vote was critical to his electoral survival.

"Good to see ya," Guillermo said, placing his glove in his coat pocket and removing the other from his left hand.

"Please, sir, follow me. The president's chief of staff is waiting in the corridor."

They moved through the pedestrian gate. Guillermo was unaware of the concealed sensor equipment discretely mounted on the gate pillars. The sensors included new-technology, forward-looking infrared, or FLIR, devices, which provided thermal images in all conditions of darkness and light. FLIR equipment, in use on army intelligence and observation fixed-wing aircraft and helicopters for over thirty years, was now being adapted to body inspections at certain government facilities. Together with the collection of other cameras and sensors, every aspect of Guillermo's clothing as well as briefcase contents would be imaged on the kiosk monitor and was being observed by another Secret Service officer in the post.

They walked up the driveway toward the front columned entrance, Guillermo asking the officer about his origins and making other small talk.

"I'm from New England, Ambassador," he said. "Ipswich, Massachusetts, ever heard of it?"

"You bet, it's just south of Marblehead. It was always a stop on our summer vacation list when we traveled as a family, years ago, of course. We used to stay at the Ipswich Inn . . . I'll never forget those McMorley sandwiches and the so-called Irish Bennie, a type of eggs Benedict that was the house specialty. And, as I recall, it has the oldest cemetery in the US, dating back to 1630, or somewhere around there. My late wife was a pediatrician, but her real interest was colonial history."

The chatter continued as they reached the front porch of the White House. Sue Cohen, the presidential chief of staff, darted out onto the landing as they approached, her hands deep into her coat pockets. They emerged as she reached out to Guillermo, her arms opened to hug him. Guillermo returned the warm greeting, his free right arm around her back, just below her well-enclosed shoulder blade.

"I'm just so glad to see you, Dom," Sue said with obvious sincerity.

"It is a bit of a homecoming in a way, isn't it?" Guillermo replied.

"Well, we *do* call this place the people's house, you know," she replied through a cold-stiffened grin.

They laughed as Guillermo turned to thank the escorting officer, then he followed Sue into the White House corridor. She removed her coat, handing it to another uniformed female Secret Service officer who also helped Guillermo with his wrap. "Would you mind taking my briefcase as well?" he asked.

"I'm happy to, Governor. They'll be available at this position when you leave the White House," she replied.

Together, they stepped into the Blue Room, formerly the main reception hall in many past administrations. The Christmas tree stood in the center, under the nineteenth century French crystal chandeliers; it dominated the French Empire–style furnishings in the room.

"Always breathtaking, isn't it?" Sue said, referring to the room now accented with the tree. "It's actually my favorite spot in the White House. My thoughts become clearer, and I feel almost as if feng shui is squeezing out the Western existentialism in my brain."

Guillermo laughed politely at the cultural comparisons. "You sound like my old buddies at the Vatican fretting the influence of tai chi, yoga, and other mysticisms. My unuttered response was always, 'My friends, you're only contrasting one set of mysteries with your own.'" They both laughed.

Guillermo and Sue continued down the corridor, its vaulted ceiling and indirect lighting on this dank day creating an impression of a catacomb visit despite the cheerful blue carpeting and other contemporary decor that softened it.

"Earl is eager to see you, Dom. It's been almost two years since you two have had a moment together," Sue offered.

"Well, our last encounter was memorable, but not a happy one, as you know," Guillermo replied.

The two men last spoke in 2009. Eastwood was then a US senator appointed to the seat by then governor Guillermo to replace an assassinated predecessor. Guillermo was seeking reelection, facing Sophia Kallias, his Republican opponent. Realizing that defeat was imminent, Republican president Bob Davids stepped into the race to rescue Guillermo from humiliation and, of course, to secure the gubernatorial seat for a Republican by offering Guillermo the Holy See ambassadorial position as his presidential term came to a close. Davids also coyly expected the Republican governor to appoint a Republican to the seat being abandoned by Eastwood, who was the vice presidential candidate on the presidential ticket headed by the late Lisa Macon Lewis, who was elected but died prior to inauguration.

Eastwood was annoyed that Guillermo accepted the Davids appointment, abandoning the state's Democratic Party. Eastwood had campaigned hard for Guillermo. Moreover, Davids had arranged for him to go to work for an Italian aviation company, which was competing for the presidential helicopter upgrade, after he left his ambassadorial appointment. The Italian firm was in direct competition with Connecticut's Sikorsky Aircraft, one of the state's longest, largest, and most honored industrial giants. To Eastwood's mind, the entire arrangement was a clear conflict of interest and one that threatened the very state in which Guillermo's political fortunes had been made.

"Time heals, Dom," Sue replied.

Two plain-clothed Secret Service agents joined the two as they approached the Oval Office. "I'll be right out," Sue said as she entered the door, closing it while Guillermo stood with the two agents, both gregarious middle-aged men looking very fit even through their two-piece suits.

The door opened in less than a minute. President Earl Eastwood, America's first African American chief executive, walked out, hand extended and smiling with Sue Cohen in tow.

"Hey, Dom, great to see you," he said with sincerity ringing in his voice while throwing his left arm onto Guillermo's broad right shoulder. "C'mon in," he added without even a glance at the Secret Service agents, who fanned out to the two outside positions of the office door.

Sue moved past them with a slight twitter of the fingers in her waving arms. "See you, Dom," she said as she walked away.

"Thanks, Sue," Guillermo replied, awkwardly turning his head to the right over Eastwood's left arm on his shoulder.

"It's about time I heard from you. I got a report from Sue about your new life, and you know how sorry I am about Mary Anne. I loved that woman, Dom," Eastwood added, his voice firm but sympathetic.

"Everyone did. She was saintly, in her professional life as well as in everything else that she did. She's my guardian angel. I pray to God every day and through my intercessory prayer to the Blessed Mary that Mary Anne be embraced in their heavenly presence as one who lived the exemplar Catholic life," Guillermo responded.

"I could use her at this very moment," Eastwood added. "Our health-care agenda is a nightmare. Just getting people to acknowledge the need for children's health, you can't believe how many parents will put money into a new car or even home improvements rather than buy health insurance. I spent years in the Senate, I know everyone over there. Even my Republican friends tell me that it's a parental decision. The government has no business directing families how to live. It's not that they don't care, they do, and as much as I do. But they see future governments expanding the mandate into other parts of family life, even limiting the size of families, crazy stuff. Someone like Mary Anne, who practiced medicine in New Haven for years, could tell them the facts."

"And she'd have loved to have done it, Earl – excuse me," Guillermo added hastily, "Mr. President."

"Oh, yeah, that." They laughed together, but it did not escape Guillermo that Eastwood did not invite him to refer to him by his first name. *Must be that West Point training. Once a general, it becomes your first name*, he thought.

They moved across the massive presidential seal sewn into the carpeting to a conversational pit preferred by Eastwood. Rather than sitting in his usual wooden-framed fauteuil with the red cushion padding, he motioned Guillermo to a comfortable stuffed chair opposite the beige sofa on which he planted himself.

Standing up, the president said to Guillermo, "Dom, you look in pretty good shape, help me adjust this sofa a bit, I want to keep an eye on *Squawk on the Street*. The labor report went out this morning, pretty dismal. I need to learn what the impact on the markets is likely to be." Eastwood was referring to the CNBC business channel playing out on the sixty-two-inch LED TV monitor mounted on the wall to the left of the presidential desk. Despite the incongruity of this information technology system with the prevailing office decor, it had become a bow to necessity.

Guillermo easily lifted his brawn from the chair into which he had sunk. "Sure, even at sixty-nine I've still a good back." The two men, the president of the United States and the former Connecticut governor and emissary to the Holy See, transformed themselves into the honey-do furniture rotators common to most family situations.

Earl Harry Eastwood was born in Bridgeport, Connecticut, in 1965. He grew up in the Stratfield village enclave between Fairfield and Bridgeport, an upper-class area. His father, Harry, was an aeronautical engineer and senior executive at Chance Vought Aircraft and later at Sikorsky Aircraft. They were the only black family in the reclusive community for many years. Earl attended Catholic grammar schools and, later, Fairfield University College Preparatory School, a Jesuit institution, for two years. He transferred to the new Roger Ward High School in town. The loss of their best football running back, and one of the few black students and top academic performers, shattered the Jesuits. But Harry wanted young Earl immersed in a public high school where, he believed, his son would be better exposed to the real tempo of the culture in which he would work as an adult.

Earl accepted an appointment to West Point above the objections of his father who still harbored thoughts of the US Army as a southern subculture. Earl prospered at the US Military Academy, serving six years on active duty following graduation, including a combat tour during the Gulf War in which he distinguished himself. As a captain and engineer company commander with the Eighty-Second Airborne Division, he conceived and executed a plan to destroy the entrenched Iraqi army blocking the avenues of attack into Iraq by leading a stream of armored bulldozers the length of the trenches, burying alive their defenders. He was awarded a Silver Star and Legion of Merit with a *V* device, for valor, attached to it. Steeped in the West Point ethic of integrity and personal honor, these attributes would underscore his behavior for the rest of his life.

Eastwood graduated from Yale's law school following military service. He served an important clerkship with an influential judge on the Fairfield County Superior Court in the county seat of Bridgeport, and from there he joined the staff of the US Senate Subcommittee on Military Readiness in Washington as counsel. Committee member Tom Felice, then senator from Connecticut, brought him into his personal office as chief of staff. Felice slipped into corrupt behavior and later died after having been investigated and encouraged to resign by his Senate peers. Eastwood never forgave Felice for his shortcomings.

Eastwood, untainted by the scandal affecting his boss, was brought back to Connecticut by then governor Guillermo and appointed as the state attorney general *pro tem* following the resignation of the incumbent. As the gubernatorial election approached, Guillermo recognized Eastwood's strong constituency among the state's substantial minority clusters. He had climbed the political ladder with a persistent shove from his own ethnic community and knew the advantages that Eastwood could marshal for his own electoral enclave; he put him on the ticket as his running mate.

The campaign plan was stalemated by the assassination of US senator Bill Rice of Connecticut. Guillermo was ratcheted between his own political aspirations, which included a White House bid down the road, and the steady clamor from Democratic Party leaders in Washington to fill the Senate seat, lest Republican initiatives dominate the legislative calendar. In Connecticut, the state's Democratic heavies wanted a viable gubernatorial ticket, which, to them, took priority over the gripes of their Washington counterparts. But Guillermo reasoned that he would need many national endorsements for his future presidential campaign; he couldn't short the Washington crowd.

Accordingly, he appointed Eastwood to Rice's seat and, to satisfy the local Democrats, picked Sam Schlesinger, the former mayor of Waterbury and a current state senator, as his running mate for the lieutenant governor position. Ironically, Schlesinger would be elected to the Senate intended to be vacated by the senior Connecticut senator Roger Evarts. When Schlesinger resigned before being sworn in, yet another casualty of the Lucas scandal, Evarts decided to return to his Senate seat with the help of the Republican governor Sophia Kallias.

Eastwood's service as a former senior staff member on Senate committees and as a personal staff facilitated his easy slide into his new role. He fashioned working relationships with the Republican president Bob Davids, who acknowledged that his own political legacy would be badly written. He would use Eastwood as a sluice through the feckless and stumbling executive branch investigations of the terrorist attack that involved Rice's assassination. The diversion worked; Eastwood, enlisting the assistance of Israeli intelligence, identified the terrorists.

Eastwood's performance and ability to work across the Senate's battle lines, as well as with the adversarial White House, brought him a reward with few precedents: as an appointed, unelected, freshman member of the Senate, he was made minority leader. These new responsibilities limited his ability to campaign for Guillermo back in Connecticut. Guillermo, recognizing defeat, ultimately resigned from the race, accepting the Republican president's appointment as ambassador to the Vatican. Almost simultaneously, the leading Democratic presidential aspirant and Virginia governor, Lisa Macon Lewis, put Eastwood on her ticket as the vice presidential running mate.

Guillermo turned bitter, voicing to many at the state and national level his judgment that Eastwood had betrayed him. He believed that Eastwood withheld more active support of his gubernatorial campaign to remove him from the political front pages. That having been done, Eastwood's presence on the presidential ticket, according to Guillermo's analysis, was premeditated and ensured by removing the former governor as a possible competitor.

Over the past two years, Guillermo's nostrils had lost their flare. The death of his beloved wife, his deep spiritual commitments lifted by his appointment to the Holy See, and his accrual of substantial wealth and prestige in his business endeavors softened his ire. In that frame of mind, he was on this day at ease with himself and had forgiven Eastwood.

Eastwood had navigated his way through a lifetime of prejudice; he could read body language, faces, expressions, and gestures with this acquired skill. He too forgave easily, but he did not forget and treated his adversaries accordingly. His preferred tactics: confrontation and resolution. He had learned from his combat experience that disagreement could be managed under even the worse conditions, and success could be yanked from the impotence that controversy can create, especially when survival was at stake.

Dom's made the transition, Eastwood sensed. He's at ease, no lingering angst, anxious to get on with it. They made a good choice in electing him as their advocate, he reasoned, with reference to the group of appellants. Attorney General Jack Hammond had prebriefed the president, at the request of Chief of Staff Sue Cohen.

"Well, Dom, I'm glad you came in. I don't yet know if I can be of much help. I've asked the AG to research the situation in depth. My first instinct, to be right up-front with you, is to reject the request for pardons."

Guillermo smiled inwardly. It was classic Eastwood. *Always the debater, the moot court star since his law school days,* he thought, *he lays out the proposition and lets his opponent rebut it.*

"I understand that," Guillermo replied. "We're connected at the ankle as Democrats and can't stray too far from core principles. This is basically a tax issue. We're a spending party, and revenues count. Tax offenses among Democrats are especially heretical because we're supposed to be progressives. What the better-off shirk, the lesser fortunate lose in more ways than one."

Good rebuttal, Dom. You're resetting the argument, Eastwood thought.

Guillermo continued. "As you know, your predecessors, Republican Bob Davids pardoned 189 persons, Bill Clinton pardoned 456!"

"And how many tax offenders, Dom?" the president asked.

Damn it! I didn't get those numbers, Guillermo thought, trying to hold to his friendly countenance. "Well, Bush pardoned Dan Rostenkowski, the former House Ways and Means Committee chairman."

"Rosty defrauded the House of Representatives' postal fund, using the monies for gifts instead of such legal purposes as mailings," Eastwood said, always ready with details.

"For heaven's sake, Earl, he *defrauded* his colleagues as well as the taxpayers, putting the entire House in disgrace," retorted Guillermo, amusing Eastwood two ways: first by using his first name, a second time in the short period of this meeting, and then speaking in exclamatory tones and language that differed from the former Domenic Guillermo until recently the US delegate to the Vatican.

Guillermo suddenly realized what he had said. "My apologies, *Mr. President,*" he emphasized.

"Just don't let it happen again," he said in jest to their joint laughter. Actually, the lightness of Earl's criticism lessened the mounting tensions between the two, alerting Earl to identify the right moment to provide a counterargument.

"I'd like to help, if I could, Dom. But you know, the congressional Republicans Dave Baldwin and David Ford were exonerated. Only the Democrats in the group were actually convicted and sentenced. And as you may know, there were three tax evasion cases among the pardons granted by President Bob Davids, and that was after all three had served sentences that, in my judgment, far outweighed the seriousness of their crimes. That was the basis for their presidential pardons."

Guillermo visibly winced with the use of the word "crimes." "Yes, I guess they were crimes," he said, pretending to move toward some type of conclusion and then trying to avoid the use of the same word. "But the *offenses* charged here were much murkier and therefore resulted in a lessened penalty. And if I may say it, Chuck Stratton is a Republican and served a jail sentence."

Two good attempts at rebuttal, Dom. You're on your game today, Eastwood thought, lifting the water glass and filling one for Guillermo and the other for himself from which he took a sip before speaking.

"Thanks," Guillermo added, accepting the glass and bringing it to his lips as Earl watched his hand.

He's steady, no signs of nervousness, Eastwood thought, looking for behavioral changes in his opponent by serving him the water, a tactic Eastwood had used throughout much of his professional lifetime.

"Dom, I think we both agree that Stratton got off easily. He was the secretary of the treasury! He controlled and misdirected the investigation that the president himself had ordered him to pursue, and he did it to divert attention from his own wrongdoing. His defense that he believed the Club Lucas group was an innocent investment opportunity was bought by the jury. But you and I know that there was Iranian money behind Club Lucas and the interest and dividends that the investors, like Stratton and the others, were receiving against their investments."

Okay, my moment at last, Guillermo thought as he carefully put the glass back onto the silver tray on the coffee table between them. Guillermo had planned to save his best argument for last, using it only if everything else failed.

Something's coming, Eastwood thought, watching the deliberate movements of his opponent and longtime friend. *He's too self-confident, almost cocky.*

"Mr. President, there was Iranian money in Club Lucas, but none of it came from the deranged Ahmadinejad regime. It was money invested by private Iranian citizens who either fled the state or were barely hanging on there under great duress," Guillermo replied, his voice calm in tone but unyielding.

A stare down followed, the two men looking into each other's eyes with intensity, the president thinking, *He wouldn't dare BS me. He's too much of a straight shooter. What in hell have we missed here? Is our intelligence that bad?* Then it struck him: *Bob Davids wouldn't do that to me, but the mob he put in the state department's research and intelligence organization would. Davids relied on them more than the other parts of the intelligence community.*

Guillermo could see through Eastwood's demeanor. *He gets it. He believes the Republicans set him up.* "I know what you're thinking, and it's what I figured out also. You forced our guys to resign their seats in Congress on the grounds that they had accepted Iranian money, which could have been contrived as bribes. They all resigned, mostly for that reason. The Iranian issue was never entered in the courtroom either by the prosecutions or the defense. After they resigned, most were replaced by Republicans in both houses. Even your seat went to Zbig Krakowski."

The president's mind was racing. *And Davids took Guillermo out of the gubernatorial race as he appeared to be losing anyway. But then, the resignations followed Sophia Kallias's victory in Connecticut, and she appointed Krakowski to my seat after I was elected. Other Republican governors did the same thing, and the rest of the seats that changed parties took place in elections where the Lucas scandal was very prominent. But is Dom just retaliating here? He may believe this stuff . . . But it may be true!*

At last, the president spoke. "Dom, that could be, it is plausible, I admit. And I'll get to the bottom of it. But there are indisputable facts at play here that need acknowledgment, the most important of which is that the appellants did break the law. They were convicted and sentenced. The tax evasion issues remain prominent, and it's on those grounds that, for the moment, I can't agree to a pardon."

He's weakening. It's a start. I think he'll come around eventually, Guillermo thought, then said, "Just one more part of our plea. These folks have had their careers and reputations damaged." He was interrupted by Eastwood.

"But by their own doing, Dom. I repeat, they committed crimes."

"Yes, sir," Guillermo politely retorted, reluctant still to use the word "crime." "Once more, if I may, sir," he continued with decided formality, as if he were in court and addressing the presiding judge as Your Honor. "Allow me to add that these men and women now hold responsible positions in several companies that are endeavoring to bring jobs to the US, to New England."

"Sue mentioned that, as did Governor Kallias. I told the governor that I am always committed to improving the nation's employment picture, especially through the creation of production-type, well-paying jobs in all regions of the US. But you know as well as I do, Dom, I'm dedicated to all states, not just Connecticut or New England, and I won't let that prospect influence my decision.

"There is new information here," Eastwood continued. "And I did act on the basis of it. But we still face the reality that laws have been broken, and the appearance, politically, of pardoning a bunch of Democrats who evaded taxes at a time when the economy is in a slump is not something I can ignore.

"So that's where we stand, Dom."

The two men parted; there were good feelings on the part of both. Guillermo believed he had awakened the president to a plot into which he had inadvertently slipped, and which harmed his ability to work with a House that had now been taken over by the other party.

But Eastwood, for the moment, seemed adamant. In his own way, he would reason a solution, he thought.

CHAPTER 5

FEE, FLEE, OR ME

AT 0900 HOURS ON MONDAY, JANUARY 3, 2011, BRENT'S COR-PORATE JET, THE FALCON 900LX, cruised at five hundred miles per hour over Dakar, the capital city of Senegal. At thirty thousand feet, the climatic demarcation lines between the desert heat and the humid mass of jungle air confronted each other in complex cloud formations. The Falcon 900LX, the flagship of Dassault Aviation, headed southwest toward the Felix Houphouet-Boigny International Airport in Abidjan, Ivory Coast, skimming the clouds as it continued its flight path over Guinea. In mere minutes, it reached the Atlantic coastline, breaking out of the cirrus cloud formations just minutes beyond the capital of Conakry.

Settling down to eighteen thousand feet and into a cumulus-and-nimbus-cloud mix with rain now beating the windows, the aircraft rocked and on occasion dropped as vacuum-like air pockets separated the changing cloud formations. They continued eastward, descending farther until they were out of the rain and turbulence. The aircraft would swing wide over the ocean, then resume its eastward approach to Abidjan, now twenty minutes from touchdown.

Aboard the jet were three Brent executives, Swiss Chairman Paul von Schlossen, Vice Chairman Domenic Guillermo, and the executive vice president for Africa, Asia, Oceana, and the Middle East, former Mississippi congressman Bennie Thompson. The rough flight had made the men tense, but they talked quietly and calmly in the heavily insulated silence of the three-engine small jet, known for its business suitability in terms of both mobility and the posh circumstances surrounding the effort to get anywhere.

Their discussion was broken by the pilot's announcement in clipped American English: "Gentlemen, we're about thirty minutes from touchdown. My apologies for the turbulence over the landmass. I'm afraid that's the way Africa is." The pilot and copilot, both retired US Air Force colonels, had spent more than twenty years and thousands of hours in the cockpits of large aircraft – such as the C-5, C-17, and even the B-52 eight-engine giants – in their earlier careers. Brent sought and paid for the best pilots it could find; training and flying experience in the US Air Force or Navy almost always produced the best of the best.

"It was not too bad, do you agree, Domenic?" asked von Schlossen, a Swiss whose English was grammatically perfect but studded with idioms and other word and phrase usages that often caused Americans to listen exceptionally closely to his comments.

"I barely noticed it. When I was at the Vatican, I flew back and forth for consultations in Washington several times a year, sometimes two to three flights a month," replied Domenic Guillermo, the former Connecticut governor and later a US ambassador to the Holy See. He skirted the question; flights in the region, known as the weather-making sector of the southern hemisphere, were rarely comfortable, and Guillermo was as much ill at ease as the others.

Bennie Thompson had been napping off and on but was awakened by the turbulence as the aircraft left the landmass over West Africa. He was seated behind the other two. "Yeah, I felt it. Those clouds over Africa are always like that at this time of year," he added. Thompson moved up to the four-place seating arrangement, facing the other two over a table laden with a bowl of fruit, numerous file folders, two open laptops, and an activated iPad, the latter belonging to Thompson. He quickly scrambled the interactive screen bringing up the European Geostationary Navigation Overlay Service, a satellite application referred to as EGNOS. The pilots had authorized the space-based augmentation System information to be transferred to the passenger monitors; along with a navigation aid called localizer performance with vertical guidance, or LPV, they could follow almost all aspects of the flight plan filed with the various air traffic control authorities.

"Yup, right on target, and on time," added the fifty-one-year-old Harvard law graduate with a flair for information technology gadgetry.

"Bennie, you can probably fly this thing from that iPad," said Guillermo to the smile of von Schlossen.

"Believe me, you wouldn't want me at the controls. I don't have a strong enough stomach for some of the weather that these guys routinely encounter," Thompson replied.

"What is the weather in Abidjan, Bennie?" asked von Schlossen.

Thompson pressed a few more keys on the interactive screen. "Overcast with occasional sunshine . . . Oh, yes, and ninety-eight degrees Fahrenheit with 90 percent humidity," he commented to the burrowed frowns of his two colleagues. "Hey, it's just like home. If you've ever been in Gulfport, Mississippi, in August, you'd know what I mean."

The American "expats," as they were now referred to, routinely interacted with their Swiss counterparts as this trip evidenced. The entire group, except for Bob Castignani, had relocated to the Swiss housing in the Montreux Palace Hotel immediately after the December 16 meetings, when the job assignments were announced. Some had even spent the Christmas holidays in Switzerland. Their finances had been in shambles following the court trials, and money was tight; many were anxious to get on the payrolls as soon as possible therefore. Castignani and his law partners, Ben Ochs and Don Tranh, would remain in Washington as the counsel to and representatives for Lucas Holdings, Brent, and Belmont. But the visit to Ivory Coast was the first major step in implementing the strategy that involved direct cooperation between the integrated American and Swiss executives.

"Seat belts, gentlemen, and please shut down all electronic devices. We're beginning our approach to Abidjan," came the pilot's firm-voiced guidance.

"We have a lot riding on this visit. I've never met President Bago, but I've read just about everything we could find on the guy," said Guillermo, referring to the embattled Ivory Coast president.

The country had been in civil disorder since Jean Bago had refused to step down after losing reelection. Rebel groups had popped up and were amassing arms and supporters although the former prime minister, Emile Tagro, himself a revolutionary in past years, had refused to take to the streets and jungles with them.

Tagro was determined to enter office with as little bloodshed as possible. The Organization of African States and even the United Nations Security Council had issued warnings urging Bago to step down. Some OAS officials and even President Eastwood had joined the push for a new election monitored by independent observers.

As the aircraft slipped beneath the ten-thousand-foot ceiling, the moisture density of the air became more visible. Steam seemed to emanate from the vegetation and drifted eastward across the open jungle and farmlands, toward the interior of the country.

"Two minutes from touchdown, gentlemen," came the copilot's voice. The braking air flaps were deployed, causing vapor entrails to race across the wings' surfaces; the landing gear smoothly moved earthward.

The conversation among the passengers continued even as they looked out the windows.

"I have met with President Bago several times," said von Schlossen. "The country has always been our major source of cocoa. He's not very honest, always has his hand out. He has substantial deposits in our banks. That fact has always made him sympathetic to the Swiss."

"Hopefully, it'll help us in this negotiation," chimed in Guillermo. "He's gonna want a big reward for what we're asking of him."

"And we've a lot to offer him, a secure haven above all else, I believe," added von Schlossen.

The aircraft eased onto the runway with barely a thump as its three engines reversed their output to slow the aircraft down.

"Yup, this is Abidjan," added Thompson. "The airport has been kept fairly modern. The French have seen to that and have been hired by the Ivory Coast to maintain it since their independence in the early 1960s."

The scene out the aircraft windows confirmed the slight touch of cynicism in Thompson's voice. The aircraft were all from foreign carriers; the ground crews were mostly white Europeans. Alongside the impressive terminal stood logistics support facilities with a steady flow of small vehicles trafficking around them. It reminded one of an airport in a medium-size French city, like Dijon or Brest.

The Brent Falcon taxied to a smaller terminal some distance from the main passenger depot. From the window on the port side of the aircraft, Thompson could see two tall Africans in civil attire accompanied by a French-made Panhard military scout vehicle that seemed to be an escort to the large black Renault. Manning the machine gun emplacement on the military vehicles were two French Foreign Legionnaires. To the rear of the convoy was a Renault-made Sherpa, a light armored vehicle with a 12.7 millimeter machine gun mounted and manned on the roof. The vehicle usually carried four or more soldiers as well as a crew of two or three.

*   *   *

The Brent delegation had rehearsed the expected meeting with the Ivory Coast president several times while in Switzerland as well as in Washington. Guillermo would be the lead speaker, his Vatican background expected to have some meaning in this relatively Catholic country, in which was located the Notre Dame de la Paix, the largest Christian church in the world. Its footprint was more than twice that of St. Peter's Basilica in Rome. Yet its twenty-one million people were one-third Catholic, one-third Muslim, and the balance distributed among believers in indigenous mysteries and nonbelievers. The country's leadership was traditionally from the Catholic segment.

The Falcon arrived at the terminal annex, which obviously was a military facility less glamorous than the main terminal, a source of pride in the small country. Von Schlossen, squinting through the small window, spoke, "Aha, it's Robert Bago here to greet us, the president's son."

Thompson quickly pulled up information on the son on his iPad, which he had preloaded with background material on the various personalities that they would be expected to encounter. "Yeah, that looks like him," he added, looking out the window from his seat. "Good background, educated at UCA – that's the University of Abidjan at Cocody. It's their elite institution. He then spent a year at the London School of Economics, must be pretty sharp. But he doesn't hold any official position. I guess that isn't necessary if you're the son of an autocratic president!"

They all laughed as the jet taxied to its open-apron position in front of the small terminal. A wheeled staircase was already in motion as the engines were shut down and the Brent Falcon's port-side passenger door was unlocked by a crew member.

It was ten in the morning, but the blast of hot, muggy air singed away the air-conditioned comfort the instant the plane's door was opened.

"Wow, do you feel that?" Guillermo gasped.

"Not to mention that awful smell," added von Schlossen.

"That's Africa," Thompson commented. "It has its own scents, sort of like Asia. You get off a plane anywhere in Asia – Japan, China, Thailand, Vietnam – the cooking smells grab your nostrils."

The taller of the two Ivorian men stood at the bottom of the staircase; they were now joined by a white French army officer, a captain, von Schlossen noted, pointing to the three brass loops on his shoulder straps. The captain stood to the rear of the two Ivorians.

"*Bienvenue, mes amis. Abidjan vous salue avec grand plaisir.* [Welcome, my friends. Abidjan greets you with great pleasure.]" said the Ivorian. It was Robert Bago, the president's son, speaking Parisian-accented French that differed substantially from the harmonic tones of French commonly found among native African speakers.

First down the staircase was von Schlossen, whose Swiss French was slightly tinged with his use of the conventional German spoken in his native Zurich. "*Nous sommes bien content etre a terre* [we're very happy to be on the ground]," von Schlossen said with a smile, extending his hand to greet the younger Bago.

"Ah, yes," Bago replied in perfect British-accented English, "flying into West Africa at this time of year is never very pleasant. And then you are greeted with our humidity. This is not exactly Switzerland," he said to the general laughter of the other Africans as well as Guillermo and Thompson, who were now with von Schlossen at the base of the staircase.

"Please, let me introduce the foreign minister, Patrice Alassane," Bago said as the others in the Brent party shook hands with Alassane, stating their names.

"And this is Capitaine Gillon, French army, who commands the legionnaire detachment which our friends, the French government, have provided to protect our airport," Bago said as the French captain stepped forward, saying "*Enchante,* pleased" as he shook each hand.

As young Robert Bago escorted the three Brent executives to the waiting convoy, to which was added a second large black Renault limousine, Guillermo suggested that von Schlossen ride with Bago while he and Bennie Thompson would ride with the foreign minister.

"*Ca suffit, come vous voulez.* That's fine, as you wish," added Bago. "These vehicles are a bit tight anyway."

The group quickly got in the cars, and the convoy drove off. En route, Guillermo tried to engage the foreign minister in a conversation. But the official seemed cautiously reticent. *He may not be entirely on board with the president's effort to hold his seat after losing it in the election,* Guillermo thought to himself.

"Mr. Minister," Bennie Thompson asked, "exactly whose side are the French on? I thought they were supporting Emile Tagro?"

The foreign minister was clearly disconcerted by the question, shifting uneasily around front his front passenger seat, attempting to look at Thompson. "They are neutral at the moment, monsieur. Like the United Nations peacekeepers here in Côte d'Ivoire, they will help us keep order until the electoral returns have been reconciled. That is why you see the French army here."

The perfect answer, Thompson thought. *He's suggesting that a ballot recount is under way and that the French, like the UN, could go either way depending on the outcome.*

"But these are French legionnaires. Are they the real French army?" Thompson continued.

The minister chuckled. "You are very perceptive, monsieur. Actually, they are considered to be a division of the French army, but as you may have noticed, they are mostly of non-French *origines,*" he added, accidentally slipping in the French word for "origins."

"Their officers seem to be French?" Thompson queried rhetorically.

"Yes, that is always the case in the legion. Also, these days, the French rarely send regular army troops on missions in Africa or to other destinations outside of France. As in the Gulf War, which America fought in the era of the first president Bush, most of the French army fighting there consisted of legionnaires."

"I'm sure that keeps peace at home. The casualties are usually non-French," Thompson added wryly. "*Exactement, monsieur.* Exactly, sir," came the minister's reply along with a light laugh.

The convoy traveled along the Route de l'Aeroport, arriving at a traffic circle that would redirect them on to Boulevard Valery d'Estaing and then crossing a bridge across the Bay de Cocody. The bay and its several lagoons were dark with the chemical and human pollution that festered in its waters.

The convoy picked up speed as the boulevard swung west, passing through the heavily Muslim section of the "numbered avenues," where several mosques dominated the ideological formation of the population. In Abidjan, Christians and Muslims were about equally numbered as in the rest of the Ivory Coast. The Christian factions dominated the south while the Muslims were more prevalent in the north. The winner of the now-contested election, Emile Tagro, represented the Muslim north from which area came most of the growing militias determined to force Bago out of office.

Guillermo noticed that the legionnaires manning the machine guns atop the convoy's lead and rear vehicles had slipped back inside.

Finally, the convoy reached the Pont de Houphouet-Boigny, then crossing the Lagune d'Ebrie. The convoy slowed as it reached the other bank, and the gunners reappeared to their positions atop the two military vehicles.

"I gather this is a more friendly part of town," Guillermo commented to the foreign minister.

"Yes, as you can see, there are several embassies along the route," he said, pointing to the flags just east of their direction of travel, signaling the presence of African delegations from Egypt, Cameroons, and other countries of so-called Afrique Noir, or Black Africa.

Finally, after negotiating around yet another traffic circle, the convoy reached the military encampment at the entrance of the compound for the presidential palace. At this juncture, a squad from an Ivorian army platoon consisting of two Panhard military vehicles relieved the legionnaire escort, taking the convoy to the entrance of President Jean Bago's official workplace in Abidjan. Although the capital of the country is at Yamoussoukro to the north, where the country's administrative offices are located, most of the political and policy decision-making is done in the more cosmopolitan Abidjan.

The palace looked as if a siege was intended. Sandbagged gun emplacements were positioned at the corners of the thin-faced white concrete structure with two wings looking like college dormitories. As the convoy pulled up in front, two soldiers greeted the first car with Robert Bago and von Schlossen aboard. The two men got out and headed to the entrance as the second Renault discharged its passengers.

As Thompson, Guillermo, and the foreign minister approached the entrance, Robert Bago turned, signaling with a nod of his head to the foreign minister, who then did an abrupt about-turn, leaving the others without even a farewell word or gesture.

"What the hell was all that about?" Thompson asked Guillermo quietly.

In a near whisper, without looking at Thompson, Guillermo replied, "I don't think he's in their favor at the moment. The president has a number of defectors from his team. I wouldn't be surprised if this guy will soon be in their ranks. He seemed pretty circumspect."

"Messieurs," said Robert Bago, "I will leave you with the president and arrange for your departure after the meeting, which I hope goes well." Bago bowed his head slightly to the three visitors, then turned and walked away.

Once inside, they encountered dingy hallways, only barely lighted and wreaking body odors no doubt related to the troops camped inside around the clock. At the end of the hallway, they turned into an alcove with a ragged red carpet covering a marble-tiled floor. Cobwebs were noticeable at the edges of its vault-like ceiling of the rotunda room. At the far end stood the president, Jean Bago, awaiting them.

"Welcome, *mon ami*," said Bago to von Schlossen, who was the first in the door; equally warm welcomes were extended to Guillermo and Bennie Thompson. But it was Thompson whom Bago seemed most interested in.

Speaking in decent English, with the usual fusion of French and harmonic African accents, Bago put his arm on Thompson's shoulder, guiding him to the middle of the three stiff chairs with cushioned seats in which presidential guests planted themselves.

"Bennie," the Ivorian president said, "I was very sorry to learn of your problems. I hope that things have worked out for you."

"Thank you, Mr. President. Yes, we are appealing not only for a presidential pardon but my life as well, and that of the others involved in the problem. In the meantime, we have become gainfully employed in the confection industry, as you know."

"*Tres bien*, but you have always been a faithful friend to me and my people, I am eager to be of any assistance that I can," Bago added, motioning Thompson and the others into their seats as Bago himself sat facing them on a small cushioned sofa with a sturdy-looking rattan frame.

The office was modestly air-conditioned, with four large-paddled fans whirring overhead. Large windows looked out on broad-leafed tropical plantings, now resplendent green from the morning sunlight. The room was studded with colorful cushions and draperies, which were offset by the darker furnishings made from various bamboo-family wood products as well as several massive rosewood and mahogany pieces. Portraits lined the walls, including several of the line of presidents since the country's independence from the French in 1962. The largest portrait was that of Felix Houphouet-Boigny, the country's first and longest president in office, who fostered a postindependence economic miracle. Ivory Coast's ports and forest, agriculture, and mining products led the economic revolution that had brought much prosperity to the former French West African colony.

"Ambassador," Bago began, "I have not had the pleasure of knowing you as I have Bennie and Herr von Schlossen. But I know you by reputation as I am a very devout Catholic and follow Vatican developments very closely. A full third of Ivorians are Catholics, and we are very proud of our cathedral, Notre Dame de la Paix, which is the largest Christian church in the world, as you may already know."

The three visitors acknowledged affirmatively with the movement of their heads.

"But I am eager to know how I can help you. Herr von Schlossen and I have been close friends for many years, and we pride our business relationship with Brent," Bago added.

The three visitors remained almost stone-faced. Guillermo's thinking seemed to radiate their thoughts. *It's almost as if Bago believes things are okay outside his gates. There's nothing in his behavior or voice that suggests serious concern for the disorder that keeps him bottled up here. This might be his strategy. Make things appear normal so as to encourage some type of deal in his favor. I need to get the reins here*, Guillermo thought, then spoke, "Mr. President, as you may know, I am very close to President Eastwood, who I had the honor of visiting just several days ago in his office."

Bago's lips widened in a polite smile, saying, "He is a very fine man. I regret that I have not met him, but our ambassador in Washington has reported the great support that he enjoys among the American people."

"I, as governor of Connecticut at the time, appointed him to the United States Senate when a former senator was assassinated. He proved himself well in that position and was put on the presidential ticket as vice president, then succeeding the president-elect, who died of cancer," Guillermo said.

"Yes, yes, of course. I know the history well," Bago said politely but with a sense of managed urgency; he seemed eager to get through the formalities.

Thompson sensed the sudden change of temperament, thinking, *Don't drag it out, Dom. Move to the point.*

Guillermo also read into the interstices of the president's comment. *Good, he's more anxious than I had first realized.* He continued. "I mention this because official America is not on your side. I believe our state department would tolerate a recount, but only if it happened very quickly."

"I have agreed to a recount, Ambassador. But you are talking about a country divided into many tribal regions with very poor communications and a federal-system-type of administration. I cannot depend on my cantonal or communal party leaders, especially those in the opposition, to honestly engage in a recount. Nor can this be done quickly," Bago replied.

I need to concede slightly, Guillermo thought, ever the compromiser that rocketed him to escalating successes while in political office. "That, regrettably, Mr. President, is something the West doesn't understand when it comes to dealing with developing states."

"*Vous avez raison, justement* [you are very right]," Bago replied in French with a graceful nod.

"Nonetheless, both the European Union and the US are contemplating sanctions against Ivory Coast unless you resign or move very quickly to settle once and for all the electoral dispute.

"And you know what the sanctions will bring, Mr. President. The ports will be closed, your access to the world's financial and commodity markets will be curtailed, and, in both the EU and US, your assets will be frozen, whether they are financial or material, such as residences, boats, and even embassy properties."

Oops, better correct that, Guillermo thought, then added, "Excuse me, embassy properties are protected under the Vienna Convention. I had forgotten that although the treaty was signed in 1961, before your independence, the Ivory Coast had since acceded to it."

"*C'est vrai, nous sommes signataires* [that's right, we are signatories]. And have been very active in amending negotiations," the president replied, again speaking in

French. "But I understand what you are saying. And I assume that you are here to do business, not as a representative of your government."

He's getting it, Thompson thought. *Better get into it, Dom.*

He is getting it, was the identical thought of Guillermo.

"We do have a business proposal, Mr. President," Guillermo added to the slight nod of Bago's head and an accompanying smile. *I have his attention, that's for sure,* it occurred to Guillermo.

"We are offering to buy this year's harvested cocoa bean crop and that which awaits harvest, two years of the crop for the current market price less 20 percent," Guillermo said.

The president sat back in his chair. Highly educated and a legendary math whiz at his lycée in his youth, he said, "Well, the current market price in the US for cocoa is $3,352 a ton. Your offer would take the price back to November, just before the election here, when the price was $2,800 per ton, which, I assume, is how you calculated the 20 percent discount. Now why would I agree to that, Ambassador?"

He's definitely on his game, Thompson thought, admiring the quick mental move of the president. *I need to get in here.*

"Excuse me, Mr. President, Dom," Thompson started. "I am Brent's manager for African markets. You are correct. We did take the price back to November. We did that because if we're to be able to intervene with US officials to delay the sanctions, it would be helpful, for the sake of appearances, for us to be able to argue that you are acknowledging the importance of the electoral dispute in our relations, intend to do something about it as soon as is practicably possible, and have *even agreed to forgo the higher profit margin created by the electoral crisis,*" Thompson emphasized.

"I see," Bago replied.

Guillermo resumed his discussion of the offer. "It is also important to realize that the US is only a part of the picture. But to the US, Ivory Coast is important because you supply 88 percent of US-imported cocoa, which is about 38 percent of your exported crop. And you export 57 percent of your crop to the EU. The EU will not necessarily follow the US lead on this matter and can still shut you down.

"Let me elaborate on this point. Your opponent, Tagro, is very close to the French president. For the moment, the French legionnaires are neutral. What is to keep the French from supporting Tagro?"

"I am very aware of all this, *bien entendu,* of course," the president replied. "And I expect that Tagro will ultimately need the cocoa revenues to underwrite his rebellion. It follows logically that he will make a deal with the French, possibly giving them yet a lower price than your offer in exchange for their military intervention to get me out of this office."

"If I may add something, Mr. President," Thompson spoke up. "There are two contingencies here that need to be added to your decision. First, the Economic Community of West Africa, dominated by the French, opposes your clinging to office. They are joined by the African Union and the United Nations. In other words, you have virtually no allies against this massive international coalition.

"And my last point, you cannot assure that the crop in the ground awaiting harvest can be delivered. Our 20 percent discount was, in part, a hedge against the futures contract that we are offering."

"Bennie makes important points, Mr. President," Guillermo added on the heels of Thompson's remarks. "We will find it very difficult to keep the US from agreeing to the use of force if the French decide to support Tagro in an aggressive manner.

"The US has always been predisposed to the use of force over negotiation. We do this, repeatedly, regardless of who's in the White House. Reagan chose that route in Beirut, Clinton in Kosovo, and, I suspect, Eastwood will act accordingly if Libya's leadership doesn't step down in time. Allow me to remind you that on Kosovo, Secretary of State Madeleine Albright, realizing her diplomacy was going nowhere, argued with then chairman of the Joint Chiefs of Staff Colin Powell that he was always praising US military forces but always reluctant to use them."

"Logically, I am troubled by your thinking. You are offering me a price for my bean crop and now telling me that my days in office are numbered. Isn't that both a tautology and a contradiction?" the president asked.

Guillermo was quick to sense the opening in the argument. "It is indeed, Mr. President, because we have not completed our offer. Paul will cover this aspect," he said, referring to the Brent chairman, Paul von Schlossen.

"You see, Mr. President, Switzerland is not a member of the EU, and we are among your largest consumers of the cocoa crop. We also act independently of the EU as a Swiss company, Brent, in purchasing the commodity. EU manufacturers and consumers care little about where the cocoa comes from as long as it's there, and Brent makes it available through our exchange purchases and sales in our foreign commodity contract business, as you know so well.

"We are convinced that your resignation, if that happens, does not mean that you cannot benefit from the years of good work that you have done as president."

"I'm not sure I'm following what you say, Herr von Schlossen," the president added. "I have had offers of asylum from several countries, like Cameroon, Togo, and even South Africa."

The hell he doesn't. This guy is as coy as they come, Thompson thought to himself.

"That is understandable, Mr. President," von Schlossen added with great deference. "Your family's assets are held largely in Swiss banks, including one such bank that holds a substantial interest in Brent, and in this proposed transaction that we are discussing here. The Swiss government is also an interested financial party in Brent's ownership.

"I am sure you see the intersecting interests. Brent, the bank, and the Swiss government all have an interest in protecting you while ensuring the US and Swiss companies that we sell cocoa to through our exchange operations get the commodities they need to prosper."

"*Tiens*, really, I was unaware of Brent's ownership profile. But the larger question provokes me. How do I survive whatever time I have left here in a way that I can assure delivery of my crop to you?" the president asked, then answered his own question in part, "I could, I suppose, nationalize the production and marketing operations, now conducted by British and Brazilian companies, and in fact have largely done that already. My plan is to put those activities under the control of my son, Robert."

That's it. There's the move we need, thought Thompson excitedly as he interjected a few words. "Mr. President, there is, I believe, a somewhat unconventional solution to this problem. Please hear us out."

"*Certainement, mon frère,* of course, my brother," replied the president.

Thompson, moving to the edge of his seat and looking directly into the president's eyes, spoke. "We will negotiate with Tagro. I have met him in the past when I was here on congressional delegations. As you know, our state department usually arranges for meetings with the legitimated opposition in many countries. I will offer him a share of proceeds from Brent's sales of Ivory Coast cocoa in the EU and the US. In return, he must cooperate in ensuring the harvest and shipment of the crop.

"And, Mr. President, all sides, especially yourself in my respectful judgment, would benefit from your resignation."

Guillermo and von Schlossen were pleasantly surprised but controlled any signs of it in their behavior or body language, trying to give the impression that it was planned this way.

For his part, Bago's face was gravely serious; this might be the answer he was looking for. But there were, in his mind, obstacles.

"How can you be sure that Tagro will go along with this? He could destroy the crop, even remove Robert or kill him after I've left," Bago asked.

"It would not be in his interest to do either of those. The crop is his greatest source of personal revenue as well as that of the Ivory Coast. He will need both the crop's revenues and the support of your party in his coalition government, which ensures Robert's continuance as the responsible person for marketing the crop to Brent."

"*D'accord,* a deal, let's do exactly that. I will ask the French commander to escort you to see Tagro before you leave."

*　　*　　*

Robert Bago escorted Guillermo, von Schlossen, and Thompson to the waiting convoy at the entrance to the presidential palace's compound. There, the younger Bago departed, instructing French Capitaine Gillon to take the threesome to meet with Emile Tagro, held under house detention by the Bago forces in the Hotel du Golf, located in the more upscale Riviera section of Abidjan.

Bago's driver carefully kept his Renault limousine in line with the convoy as it maneuvered past the several roadblocks and checkpoints to the hotel. Von Schlossen, seated in the front passenger seat alongside the driver, was unable to comfortably turn his head to the rear to engage the other two in conversation, which made him feel somewhat uncomfortable. He did not like the direction in which the talks had been proceeding. There were too many pitfalls for Brent, not the least of which was the forthcoming meeting with Emile Tagro, the successful presidential candidate in the November election. Here it was, January, and there was no real likelihood that Bago would give up his seat or that Tagro had the forces behind him to overcome Bago's resistance to the electoral outcomes.

These Americans, von Schlossen thought, they are all so impetuous. *They try to force outcomes that could happen with the mere passage of time.* He then had second thoughts. *But if this works, Brent will do very well. We will wrap up the cocoa bean market and control more than half the futures contracts written against the commodity for years to come. On the other hand, if Tagro hesitates or if he succeeds, he may not want to do business with us. After all, there are many of our French competitors entrenched here, and Tagro is very close to the French prime minister. If he goes along with our deal, we will have to pay him handsomely.*

In the backseat, the mood was very different as Guillermo and Thompson discussed the impending meeting with Tagro.

"That was a brilliant move, Bennie," Guillermo said quietly. "We're now positioned to be the real mediator not only for the commodity but in working out the resolution of the standoff between Bago and Tagro."

"Ya know, Dom, for a guy like me, who's spent my professional lifetime in politics and public service, this is a real revelation. Imagine having this type of decision-making freedom in politics. Everything has to be coordinated. Even if you're a cabinet secretary, there's always a political cast of characters at the White House who're breathing down your neck. Here we are, as you just suggested, really influencing the outcome in the fate of this country's leadership and making these decisions on the run." Thompson was reflective. *Damn, I've finally found my real calling!*

The convoy pulled up to the modernistic Hotel du Golf, its simple lines flanked by towers clearly reflective of traditional African structures found on the edges of such Sahara communities as Mali and Burkina Faso, both to the north of Ivory Coast. Three Ivorian soldiers met the convoy, exchanging what seemed to be friendly greetings and words, then motioned to the Renault driver to discharge his passengers.

"*On peut sortir, Messieurs, s'il vous plaît.* You can get out, sirs, if you please," the driver said as the three men quickly dismounted. They were greeted by a young lieutenant who said, "*Suivez-moi, s'il vous plaît,*" then lead them into the hotel. There they were met by two fit-looking Africans. The taller of the two, in English, said, "Please, gentlemen, follow me to the pool area. We will be meeting with the president outside."

The two escorts and the three visitors from Brent walked through the dingy-looking hotel lobby, emerging out onto a massive pool deck overlooking a lagoon. The deck was arrayed with healthy, well-groomed palms, which surrounded a meandering pool system complete with footbridges crossing it in places, along with slides and waterfalls. Several African children frolicked in the water while the adult crowd, both white and black, mostly lounged about on modernistic well-cushioned chaises.

They arrived at a large thatch-roofed gathering area situated at the edge of the deck, on the lagoon. The hut's windows were unshuttered and without screens, adding to the comfortable ambience enhanced by cooling breeze from the water.

Emile Tagro stood up to meet them as they approached him. Dressed in a Western-style suit with a fashionable shirt and solid maroon tie, he looked like a prize fighter who had changed into his mufti. Solidly built with broad shoulders, he was every bit the former guerrilla fighter who had pacified himself into the politician who had now won the presidency through the legitimacy of the democratic process.

"Good morning, gentlemen," Tagro said as he extended his hand, first to Bennie Thompson, whose eye he had caught, suggesting some type of past encounter of which he was not sure.

Thompson quickly took the lead. "Mr. *President*, it is good to see you again," he said with some emphasis to the delight of Tagro and the two escorts who had guided the threesome to him. "Allow me to present my colleagues, Herr Paul von Schlossen, chairman and CEO, and Ambassador Domenic Guillermo, vice chairman of Brent."

"Pleased," said Tagro as he shook hands all around. "I very much welcome your visit to me. I have not had the pleasure of meeting Brent officials before when I was prime minister, but I know your company well." Tagro invited them to sit at a table on which sat several bottles of water and a tray of tropical fruits. "I regret that I am not greeting you at the presidential palace, but hopefully, that too will happen in time."

The perfect opening, thought Thompson. "That is a big part of our purpose in meeting with you, Mr. President," Thompson added as Tagro's eyes widened in surprise.

"*Ca m'interesse, evidement.* I'm interested, obviously," Tagro replied. "I understand you have met with Jean Bago."

"Yes, there are some new developments which may interest you, Mr. President," Thompson said.

Tagro nodded with a slight forward bend from the waist.

"Brent's interest is, as you no doubt know, sir, in securing cocoa for its clients and ensuring a stable price and market for its continual flow to producers and other users of the commodity. Accordingly, Mr. Bago appears willing to step down if you will cooperate with him in selling to Brent your entire harvested cocoa crop, now in storage in Abidjan, and the next year's crop, which is awaiting harvest."

"And why would Bago want such an agreement?" Tagro asked suspiciously.

"Brent would buy the crop at the current market price less 20 percent and pay him a commission, as well as offer him and his wife a safe haven in Switzerland. The second condition is that his son, Robert Bago, would assume control of the country's production of cocoa and manage its continuing sale and shipment to destinations designated by Brent," Thompson said, deciding to get right to the pulp of the matter.

Tagro seemed agitated. "You see, gentlemen, *I* am the elected president of Ivory Coast. Jean Bago has no constitutional or other legitimate authority to do anything affecting this country's future, its economy, or any of its official policies. You are asking me to delegate the authority and confidence the people of this country have vested in me through the electoral process to a man who is a rogue usurper of the public power."

"Mr. President, if you please," said Guillermo. "Your retort is indisputable. You are no doubt the legitimated president of this republic. But you do not have the power in your hands and, at the moment, face odds that militate against that happening any time soon. This is the unfortunate reality of your predicament. And to transform this reality into the legitimacy that you and the people of this country demand, there are only two routes to that objective. The first, a bloody civil war, one already under way, or a bloodless arrangement that allows Bago to exit."

"Yes, Ambassador, you are correct. I recognize the realities of my predicament. But the bloodletting is already afoot. Indeed, as we speak, my intelligence sources tell me that Bago forces are moving on the town of Douekoue to the northeast of here. This is one of my strongholds, the source of much of my Young Patriots movement of several years back. The town is mostly Muslim. Bago intends a massacre. You see, I have no choice but to defend the town, and must rally militias."

"Mr. President, if you can come into agreement with the plan we're laying out here, it can be implemented quickly, and the massacre you speak of averted."

Tagro sat back into his chair; the statement caught his attention. He stared at Thompson, then said, "I will need resources, funds, if I am to demobilize my militias and restart the country's productive engines."

Von Schlossen immediately grasped the inferences; he had worked in Africa before, and he worried that Guillermo or Thompson might not have caught the real drift of Tagro's words. The monies to "demobilize" the militias would go into Tagro's pocket. *I have to get involved here*, he thought finally.

"We understand, Mr. President. The militia members have no doubt sacrificed jobs and their well-being to come to your support. They will need to be compensated. Part of the revenues that we will provide for the purchase of your crop can be allotted to the maintenance of peace. That is your decision, of course, as president.

For our part, we are pleased to make the payments in whatever format you choose, to include separate accounts to manage your several policy needs."

Good work, Paul. I would have missed that, Thompson thought, noticing the same light coming on in Guillermo's mind as he glanced at him with his peripheral vision.

"And Robert Bago as your export authority? Is that condition satisfactory?" Thompson asked.

"*Certainement*, sure, I know Robert well. He will cooperate with us, and he will be paid accordingly as an official on my presidential team. But I do not see a place for him after this transaction of which you speak is concluded." Tagro then thought, *Robert will be no problem. Bago supporters are already too dissatisfied with the Bagos. They're not going to stir up an armed or even a disorderly resistance. Besides, the French are on my side. They're just reluctant to get involved too soon because of their past colonial image. And they don't want others to think I'm in their pocket. This arrangement with the Swiss and Americans will help me avoid any commitment to the French in the future.*

"That is entirely your decision, Mr. President," Thompson said, thinking, *I hope to hell Robert's as smart as Tagro seems to think he is and knows enough to get out of town when the job is done. On the other hand, there are still Bago supporters in this country. Robert may become their titular leader. If that happens, I'm sure Tagro will make short work of him. Hey, that's not my problem.*

"*Alors, nous sommes d'accord, mes amis.* Okay, we're in agreement, my friends. Kindly convey my agreement to Bago," Tagro said, extending his hand to Thompson, von Schlossen, and Guillermo in that order.

CHAPTER 6

WASHINGTON AWHIRL

T WO DAYS AFTER THE BRENT EXECUTIVES MET WITH EMILE TAGRO, THE SUCCESSION WAS VIRTUALLY A FAIT ACCOMPLI, and the media lost no time in getting out the word. The late-news edition of televised France 2 at 11:00 p.m. on Thursday, January 6, 2011, was first to proclaim the change of regime in Abidjan.

"*Messieurs, mesdames, la Côte d'Ivoire, s'est libéré!* Ladies and gentlemen, Ivory Coast has freed itself!" resonated the speaker, providing the first report that was heard throughout the francophone region of West and North Africa as well as France. The report went on to say that Jean Bago had left the presidential palace and had actually exchanged living arrangements with his elected successor, Emile Tagro, now occupying the palace. The transition was surprisingly fast and friendly, read the newscaster, while Ivorian troops supportive of the outgoing president had stood down, pledging their loyalty to the new leader. Tagro, for his part, had granted amnesty to the military forces, including the independent militias that had been warring on both sides.

Operating in the same time zone, US ambassador Michael Jackson, the Eastwood envoy to Abidjan, was on the phone with his CIA station chief within minutes after the TV report began. The call was brief. Jackson, who as ambassador was the country chief, was highly critical that he had been blindsided by his inept intelligence support staff. The station chief was unapologetic, insisting that his sources were reliable, so much so that he doubted the accuracy of the French report. Jackson, realizing that further arguments were getting him nowhere, ended the conversation. He then called the deputy national security adviser, Bill Stokes, still in his office at the White House.

"Bill, we've got both a crisis and a noncrisis here," Jackson said.

Michael Jackson, an African American, was born in Norwalk, Connecticut. His mother had been a housemaid to a very prominent and affluent old-money family living in New Canaan. The family took a liking to her and recognized young Michael's intelligence and good character. They generously bought the single mother a small house in Norwalk and financed Michael's education in private schools through his higher education at Amherst and graduate school at Tufts. Michael became a career foreign service officer with extensive postings in West Africa and state department headquarters in Washington. He had also spent three years on the National Security Council during the Clinton era. Like Stokes, he was also an African American with an equivalent pedigree of successes in key political positions in Connecticut. The two were part of the black political elite in Connecticut, a small community from which President Earl Eastwood himself had emerged. The chain that tightened trust between the members of this group had no weak links.

"Give me the bad side first, Mike," responded Stokes.

"We were outflanked . . . Bago has resigned, and Tagro has taken the presidency."

"Isn't that all good news?" Stokes asked.

"No, Bill. We have no idea how the hell it happened. We've been expecting continued fighting, maybe even the assassination of Tagro. There have been no indicators that a transition like this was in the making. Our intelligence was telling us just the opposite."

"What does the station chief have to say about all this?"

"He's just damn unbelievable, giving me this crap that it's probably erroneous information, which, by the way, I heard just minutes ago on France 2. That's the French state-owned television station. They don't make mistakes like this, believe me. I've been tuned to that channel for the seven years I've served in West Africa and always watched it when I was at state and with the council."

There was a brief silence; finally, Stokes spoke. "The president and Audrey are at Camp David, but he should be back early tomorrow for the intel briefing. I'm gonna call Harry. You know, Mike, you probably should have called him first. He might be a bit peeved."

"Normally, that's my channel, of course. But in an urgent situation like this and knowing that you always coordinate well, I wanted to get this info to you. Besides, there's an intelligence issue here. I asked for a substantial increase in my country intel budget and got it. They've staffed up the station here with some pretty smart people, except for the station chief. He's an old-timer whose usefulness has passed.

But I'm looking like a jerk, as is Harry who strongly endorsed the need for the budget increase."

"That'll help in my call to Harry, Mike. I'm not gonna tell you to cover your rear end because that's not your MO. I hope Harry will recognize that," Stokes said.

They hung up as Stokes flashed Scott.

Harry Scott, the former University of Virginia law professor and scion of one of the state's oldest and most prominent families, had bought a weekend residence in the Ford's Colony community of Williamsburg soon after becoming the secretary of state. Always looking ahead, he anticipated that he could become president of the academically prominent but small College of William and Mary after his political service. With several years of teaching experience at UVa, he knew that William and Mary was a jewel needing a bit of burnishing, especially in its international affairs program and at its law and business schools, a challenge that he felt he could readily manage. After all, the school had so few distinguished graduates that it still lived on the fame of Thomas Jefferson, who had graduated nearly 250 years earlier.

Scott was in his study, scanning the *New York Times* and watching several die-hard golfers play through the growing darkness and cold on the treacherous thirteenth fairway of the Blue Heron golf course. As he watched a failed fairway shot fall into the partially iced pond, he both grimaced and chuckled as his official phone flashed. *Not good!* he thought. *Congress out of town, the president at Camp David, all quiet on all fronts . . . Worse, Harriett's made reservations at the club.*

"Scott here," he said into the receiver.

"It's Bill Stokes, sir. We've a minor situation that you need to be aware of."

"Bill, I've never known you to have anything but *minor* situations on your plate. Is anything ever a major problem?"

They both laughed.

"It's not altogether bad, but it's newsworthy. Ivory Coast has undergone a peaceful regime change, and the bloodbath there has stopped."

"Hey, outcomes like that are good by my standards. But tell me what the so-called situation's all about."

"I was called by your ambassador there, Mike Jackson. He tells me we've had a major intel failure, his station chief disbelieves the change. All this on top of a massive increase in the intel budget which he requested and you signed off on."

"Yeah, I sure as hell did. The highest intel budget in Africa for a country of only twenty million, no less. The Senate wanted my head on that one, and the Republican house was completely unsupportive."

"You're not upset that Mike called me first?" Stokes asked.

"Hey, you're at work, and I'm boondoggling in my Williamsburg paradise. Mike doesn't screw around, he gets to the guy who's at the helm and ready to make things happen, which is obviously what he did here. That's why I solidly endorsed the president's selection of him for the job. But we've got to get this to the president before tomorrow's intel brief. They'll make it sound like everything went well. I'll call him at Camp David. Where's Thayer, by the way?" Scott asked, referring to Stoke's boss, retired navy admiral Thayer Eaton.

"He's in the air with a congressional delegation due back tonight. I can't safely convey this type of information to him in flight. The president approved the temporary designation of me as the acting national security adviser pending his return."

"Okay. Thanks, Bill. I'll call the president."

Within a few minutes, Secretary of State Harry Scott was on the phone with Sue Cohen, the president's chief of staff, who was with him at Camp David. He explained the hurried call from Bill Stokes, the acting national security adviser.

"This sounds like something I should know more about," Cohen said, thinking, *Dom Guillermo! Ivory Coast is the world's largest cocoa producer. Dom's plan was to bring Swiss investment into Connecticut and Massachusetts. To do that, he'd have to raise the prospect of substantial returns for his Swiss firm, Brent. That's a commodity trading house, and they, as well as the Swiss government, are big shareholders in Belmont, which would be the investment vehicle for the US deal.*

"I'm not following you, Sue," Scott replied.

"You'll recall the president's meeting with Guillermo. He asked you, the AG, and Lou Dubin to get some background on Brent," she started, referring to Eastwood's meeting with Guillermo on December 16, barely three weeks earlier. Sue had asked the attorney general, Jack Hammond, and the treasury secretary, Louis Dubin, to ensure as best they could from available information and intelligence if the Swiss companies were legitimate and that Guillermo was exercising the authorities available to him as officer or board member in each of the three companies – Brent, Belmont, and their financial overseer, Lucas Holdings.

Cohen continued, "As I recall, all reports showed nothing shady. Your guys in Bern found the Swiss companies to be legitimate and reputable and that they included Swiss banking and even government officials on their boards. Jack, for his part, felt that Guillermo did us all a favor in getting rid of our pardoning attorney, who seemed to have her own agenda at play in suggesting her powers were superior to those granted under the constitutional to the president."

They laughed.

"I'll go through this with the president, who's out on the pistol range here with a couple of Secret Service guys. But, Harry, it probably would be very helpful if you could attend tomorrow's intel brief. I'll call Jack and Lou and make sure they're here too."

"Sure, I'll leave in a couple of hours and spend the night at our house in Old Town."

"See you then. Give my love to Harriett," Cohen said, hanging up.

*   *   *

At 0645 military time on Friday, January 7, 2011, Marine One landed on the southwest White House lawn. En route from Camp David, Sue briefed the president on the several issues he would be confronted with during what was to be a busy day. The Ivory Coast issue was not high on Sue's agenda; the country figured very slightly into the president's foreign policy or his African initiatives, most taken to please his constituents as well as growing business interests in Africa's vast and largely untapped mineral resources. The major players in the US-Africa game book were Nigeria, the nation's third-largest oil supplier; South Africa, a major trading partner; Zaire for its copper and diamond mines; Kenya, where the attack on the US embassy in the 1990s tightened assistance links; and the Sudan, where Muslim-dominated regimes were slaughtering many of its own citizens.

By eight, the president was seated in the White House situation room. At his right was acting national security adviser Bill Stokes. On his left was Secretary of State Harry Scott, and running down the table on the right was Jack Hammond, attorney general; on the left next to Scott was Admiral Horace Bain, the director of National Intelligence. Treasury Secretary Louis Dubin entered the room as they were about to start, glancing his apologies for being somewhat late to the president, who smiled forgivingly. Dubin took a seat next to Hammond rather than alongside the secretary of state as precedence would suggest. But seeing Bain in that position, and knowing it was an intel show, Dubin wisely decided to make as much room as possible for the briefer, who from time to time would have an aide slipping information during his presentation.

As the intel brief got under way, priorities went to operations in Afghanistan, old business in Iraq, and the uprisings in the Middle East, with focus on Egypt and Tunisia at the moment. Bain then skipped Africa south of the Sahara, shifting to developments in China, where citizen unrest over working conditions and worker mobility were irritating the regime. Finally, Bain concluded his presentation with the situation in the Ivory Coast.

"We've buttressed up our intel assets there, Mr. President, thanks to your approval of our request. My station chief reports that there are rumors regarding the resignation of Jean Bago, who lost the election to his prime minister, Emile Tagro, and that Tagro has formally succeeded him, de facto, assuming control of the government and occupying the presidential palace. We are still without formal confirmation that all this has happened."

"Horace, there's some confusion here. Bill Stokes and State have a different report," Eastwood said.

"I'm aware of that, sir. My station chief said that Ambassador Mike Jackson is convinced the regime change has occurred."

"Well, who's right, and what are the consequences for us?" asked Eastwood, controlling his annoyance.

"My sense, sir, is to await confirmation," Bain replied, ever the cautious person.

"And when will we know?" asked Eastwood.

"I would hope by Monday morning. I had asked the station chief the same question."

Has Bain finally gone over to the intel side? Eastwood wondered. *These guys get entrenched in their bureaucracies, and they forget they're political appointees working for me. I have to deal with this myself.*

"Horace, the Ivory Coast is not prominent on my policy radar. But the smooth operation and coordination of intelligence within and between the agencies of this branch are. I expect the intelligence community to coordinate the potential consequences of a major situation with the other agencies which could be impacted. The IC does not operate only for its own purposes.

"We have a treasury attaché in nearby Dakar. What are the consequences for our trade interests if the regime change has occurred or for our antiterrorism efforts in Nigeria with Tagro in office? These are matters that I should be raising in a national security meeting in the White House, like this one. This is the time and place that I'm supposed to be getting recommendations, answers."

Eastwood's annoyance was beginning to show.

"There are some major military and foreign policy consequences as well. I'm sure the French know exactly what has happened. Bill tells me that the ambassador got his information from the late evening's French television news. The French are always worried about our competition in their Communaute francaise d'Afrique Noir, French Community of Black Africa as they call it," said Eastwood in excellent French. "It's intended to be an economic union, but it keeps an official French hand on the state's steering mechanism."

"In fact, they have troops in Ivory Coast right now. They're supposed to be neutral, to provide security for the thousands of French citizens living there. But no one's fooled by that posturing," Scott added. "The ambassador said they were supporting Tagro. They may have pulled off a quiet coup. I don't think that'll hurt us."

"I'm not so sure, Harry," added Treasury Secretary Louis Dubin. "Abidjan is a major trading port for exports and imports. An unfriendly government there can hinder our trade in the entire region. The French may see us a serious trade rival in certain sectors and encourage their guy in the presidential palace to make life a little more complicated for us. They did this to us years ago, drove our financial and trade interests out of Mali, Senegal, and even Guinea."

"What I want all of you to realize is this," Eastwood said. "There are basically three forms of foreign policy initiative and management in this new world of ours. And the new world that I speak of is one where the dollar is no longer a real reserve currency or the safest on the globe for that matter, at least any more. Let's not be naive enough to think otherwise.

"Since the time of Woodrow Wilson, we've demonstrated that a moral dimension drives our foreign policy. JFK's Berlin speech was the pinnacle of that commitment. And it's been morality that justified the use of force when diplomacy has failed, and that has been too many times. Reagan's quick retreat from Beirut and Clinton's hightailing it out of Somalia after the battle of Mogadishu in 1993, when a sudden surge of casualties occurred, established the limits on moral crusades.

"Now, the world sees our involvement in the Gulf War, Iraq, and elsewhere in the Middle East as something much less forgivable and over something that is now much less available: oil! At the same time, in the eyes of some of our own allies, we've simply joined their camps. Think of de Gaulle, who once said when he demanded US forces leave French soil and after ending his participation in NATO's military missions, 'France has no friends, only interests' when it comes to foreign policy."

I'm philosophizing too much, Eastwood thought. *Time to get to the point.* "What I'm saying is that we have interests even in obscure places like Ivory Coast, although, and thanks Lou, our distinguished treasury secretary rightfully sees potentially harmful consequences even there from an unfriendly regime.

"And these interests are to be identified and monitored by our embassy there, where the country team chief, as long as I am in this job, is and will always be the ambassador himself or herself. So, Horace, I don't want to get intel from your station chiefs that is not seen and commented on by the ambassador. And, Harry, where we have political appointees in ambassadorial slots, I want a chop on the report from the deputy chief of mission. Please make sure you get this word out to all of our ambassadors. Any of them who have a problem with this rule are invited to call me directly.

"The IC should be humiliated that they were scooped by the French media in a place like Ivory Coast. You can be sure that the Congress will be all over my case because we tripled the intel budget to raise the level of our resources there.

"Now, let's get down to the grit. Why do I know that some American executives of several Swiss companies were in Ivory Coast earlier this week? And that their departure coincided almost perfectly with the regime change?" Eastwood asked rhetorically.

"I know this because I met with one of them and informed almost everyone in this room of the meeting, asking for your inputs prior to and afterward. In other words, you were alerted to their presence."

"Excuse me, Mr. President, but we did know they were there," Bain said.

"But, Horace, your guys on the ground ought to have had some question as to their purpose, especially since there was *presidential interest* in their presence in the country.

"Let me give you my take and get back to my opening comment. Today, besides military and diplomacy as the key instruments of foreign policy, there enters a third stimulant: commercial interests. Economics, xenophobia, and egos have always driven foreign policy. God only knows we've seen enough Hitlers, Japanese-style economic zones, and Soviet empires. But today relatively ordinary business people can exert heavy influence on foreign regimes that affect our foreign policy objectives. Wall Street influence on China's purchases of US debt is one example. China owns a third of our foreign debt at a time when we're in double jeopardy. Sixteen percent of my budget goes to service on our debt, and yet one-third of this year's budget is a deficit for which we have to borrow yet more. What leverage do we have over China? You can guess the answer to that one.

"When we see companies bellying up to sovereign leaders, we should get concerned fast and find out what they're up to. Applying this to the Ivory Coast, there's too much propinquity here. I want to know what transpired between the Swiss companies and Bago and Tagro because I personally believe that a deal was struck that, more than anything else, led to the regime change."

With that comment, the meeting broke up. The assembled cabinet and cabinet-level officers started for the door; Eastwood nodded to Admiral Horace Bain, the national director of intelligence. As the room cleared, Eastwood motioned to Bain to be seated.

Bain seemed to anticipate what was to follow.

"Horace, the time has come for you to resign. You've served two administrations with brilliance, loyalty, and distinction, not to mention nearly forty years of naval service."

"I understand, sir," Bain, now sixty-six, replied.

The two men discussed in a friendly way the reasons for the president's decision, which largely rotated around the changing causes and effects of foreign policy decisions. Military service was no longer a sine qua non to understanding the roots of change. Bain would be replaced by his deputy, former Colorado senator Jim Douglas, a Democrat and onetime deputy minority leader of the US Senate.

The next day, in the same manner, Eastwood would dismiss National Security Adviser Admiral Thayer Eaton, replacing him with Bill Stokes, the Yale PhD and former professor who was a master of the evolving American political scene and its altered role on the globe.

CHAPTER 7

PICKLING CONGRESS

BOB CASTIGNANI, THE FOR-MER CHAIRMAN OF THE SENATE FOREIGN RELATIONS COMMITTEE, LOST HIS SEAT IN THE NOVEMBER 2010 ELECTION. NOW OPERATING AS SENIOR PARTNER IN A LAW AND LOBBYING FIRM – CASTIGNANI, OCHS, AND TRANH, LLP – he was on retainer with Lucas Holdings SA as their Washington attorney and lobbyist.

After more than four terms in the Senate, Castignani knew that his contacts, privileged access to all parts of the Capitol, including the Senate floor, and his knowledge and prestige as a former major committee chairman would greatly benefit his clients. His former colleagues would take his telephone calls, and for all practical purposes, their staffs could be made available to him for limited uses if they benefited their boss.

Guillermo had called Castignani after the Brent corporate jet returned to Switzerland and the group had been lifted by helicopter to Montreux and from there driven to Brent's global office in Chamby, several miles up the treacherous Alpine roads to the headquarters location in the heights of Montreux, also known as Haut Montreux. The three men, exhausted after the meetings, had chatted briefly, then slept for most of the six-hour flight that took them over the Sahara, Mediterranean, and up the Italian peninsula to Geneva.

It was around midnight Swiss time, Monday, January 7, 2011,when Domenic Guillermo reached Bob Castignani to report on the meeting with the Ivory Coast principals, outgoing president Jean Bago and his successor, Emile Tagro. Castignani had left his new Watergate office early and was at his Old Town, Alexandria, residence, wrestling with the options before him for dinner, usually meaning a decision as to which restaurant to dine in and whether to find a dining companion or go alone. He had been a widower for almost a year now. He had a few female friends, mostly social companions, but like many men, he was slightly uneasy with the appearance of a male dining mate. He had decided he would go to the Warehouse and sit at the bar, where food could be served. It was a convenient walk to King Street, just a few blocks away, even on a cold night. The Warehouse displayed pen-and-ink caricatures of its distinguished clientele on its walls, which now sported one of Castignani, a rower's oar in one hand and a champagne glass in another, a scene from a surprise birthday party at the restaurant several years ago planned by his late wife. A strong dose of sadness and nostalgia used to overtake him each time he glanced at it, but now, he seemed to just smile, even chuckle quietly to himself.

It was just about 6:15 p.m. when Guillermo's call came through on Castignani's Blackberry.

"Hello, Dom," Castignani said as he spotted Guillermo's name on his caller ID. "How'd the meeting go? You've gotta be exhausted. What the hell time is it there?" Castignani asked, knowing they had returned to Switzerland.

"It's around midnight, and yup, I am tired, but we all napped for about four hours on the plane back. The meeting went well, I think. But there are some unexpected outcomes that may complicate your role," Guillermo reported.

"Hey, that's what I'm paid for. I used to solve other people's big-time problems for the pay of a senator, so lay it on me, I'm ready to earn my keep."

"You'll earn it here, Bob, believe me," Guillermo replied. He then explained that the first element of the business strategy was now in place, which is to say, the world's major producer of cocoa had turned over its crop to Brent for two years. This, he went on to say, meant that Brent, and Lucas Holdings, now controlled the most important component of chocolate production.

"But there's a high price attached, and I'm not talking only about money," Guillermo continued. He related the difficult negotiations, resulting in Bennie Thompson's successful and ingenious mediation of a deal between the warring politicians, leading to Bago's departure and Tagro's succession. "This," Guillermo said, his voice strengthening, "is sure to upset President Eastwood, as well as some in Congress, as it all happened without their participation or even awareness."

Castignani listened very carefully, thinking as Guillermo spoke, *I hope to hell there are no bribes or kickbacks or even the appearances of unlawful enticements. But the deal with Bago and Tagro does give somewhat of an appearance of conflicts of interest.*

Finally, Castignani was able to get a question in. "Dom . . . is Bago getting a fee of some type?"

"I think it could be characterized that way," Guillermo answered.

"That can be done, I believe, with two conditions," Castignani said. "First, that any formal or informal agreements are entered into and the actual commencement of payments begin after he's left office and is a private citizen and, second, that the Ivory Coast government agrees to the payment of the fee to the former president."

"That should be easy to arrange," Guillermo said.

"The other deal with Tagro may be more complicated. You said that he wants to unwind the many militias that supported his fight against Bago and that some of the revenues would have to cover that cost as well. I think Paul's answer was partially appropriate, namely that Brent is simply buying the crop for an agreed-upon price. However, the government decide to use the revenues is their privilege. But Tagro wants payment for the disbanding of his militias to go into a separate account, presumably his own pocket. That could be a problem for us.

"It would be better that Tagro arrange for the separate account within the structure of his own government. Obviously, he's not gonna do that because his personal gain would be too obvious. There are several perspectives on this type of issue.

"First, as regards the US, the Foreign Corrupt Practices Act makes it a crime for an American company to bribe a foreign official or to engage in behavior amounting to this type of influence. Brent, Lucas, and Belmont are not US companies, but Belmont does seek to take a position in the two largest US confectioners, Havens and Rose. The Justice Department, Federal Trade Commission, and other departments and agencies will examine Belmont's offer to ensure there are no antitrust implications as well as other factors. Although Belmont is partially owned by several other entities, Lucas, Brent, a Swiss bank, even the Swiss government, someone doing due diligence could discover the deal with Tagro. Great political pressure, if not legal authority, could be applied to block the acquisition, if you see what I mean?"

"But aren't there loopholes, like so-called grease payments?" Guillermo asked.

"Of course, and the argument could be made that the payments to Tagro were exactly that: he was keeping the militias from destroying the cocoa bean crop, the source of the commodity trade, provided that the militias could be reasonably shown to have targeted the crop to cut off revenues to the Bago regime," Castignani reasoned. Grease payments are generally defined as monies to ensure the trade transaction expedites smoothly, without obstructions.

"I think we can plead that, Bob. Good reasoning," Guillermo replied. "Any other US rules that we should worry about?"

"Well, in the trade statutes, the Tariff Act of 1930 could apply. It could be interpreted to suggest that the payment of monies into Tagro's nonofficial account was an unfair trade practice in the sense that it influenced a sale to a Swiss company, thereby potentially injuring a competitive US company, which would find its bid rejected. The US could rule on that as a sovereign matter, or it could go to the World Trade Organization's dispute settlement panels in Geneva for relief. But here, we, that is Lucas or Brent, would have a defense. First, there was no illicit payment, as we discussed a second ago, and secondly, if the objective were to benefit a US company, since the attempt to hedge on cocoa bean prices would ultimately benefit a merger or acquisition with a US company, Havens and or Rose, it would be hard for the government to argue injury to a US company, especially where the US entity was aware of the proposed merger or acquisition," Castignani said in ending his long reply.

"And at the international level, what should we worry about?" Guillermo asked.

"As regards the Bago and Tagro payments, not a lot," he replied. "The WTO continues to make many different efforts to control corruption, especially in developing countries like the Ivory Coast, which, by the way, was an early signatory to the WTO agreement in 1995. In the last Doha Round meeting of the WTO, a group called the Civil Society Organization urged a resolution that the WTO see attempts at corruption as nontariff barriers to free trade. But most nations see it as an internal problem, and it's therefore unlikely to entrust major controls to a global trade panel like that of the WTO's dispute settlement facilities. Once more, trade treaties are no different than other international agreements, like NATO, the European Union and the United Nations. National sovereignty allows the member state to decide ultimately what's best for itself. When the WTO's dispute settlement panels rule against a country, the country itself still retains its right to accept or reject the ruling. Of course, there may be sanctions, but they pale in the face of a loss of sovereign independence of action.

"Let me add, Dom, this is not to say we don't have problems. I'm going to have to explain the deal that Brent cut with the two Ivory Coast officials as something that was not intended to interfere with US foreign policy. I'll start by chatting with Paul Rienzi. He's the New Hampshire Democrat who succeeded me as chairman of the Senate Foreign Relations Committee," Castignani added.

"I don't know him. But I'm hoping the New England delegation can support us," Guillermo added.

"That's my lobbying strategy, Dom."

*   *   *

On Monday, January 17, Congress had begun circulating back from its long recess. The new committee and party leaders in the House resumed its business under new Republican management. The Senate, which had not changed hands in the November election, retained most of its leadership profile, which benefited Castignani, of course. But Castignani, still under a two-year ban on lobbying his former Senate colleagues on matters in which he played lead role, needed to emphasize that this would be a friendly meeting, one allowable under the lobbying statute, as well as the protected by the constitutional right to petition Congress.

At 10:00 a.m., Castignani was being escorted into his former office in the Dirksen Senate Office Building – Dirksen SOB, as it was known – now occupied by Senator Paul Rienzi, a Rhode Island Democrat.

"Good to see you, Bob. You're looking good. Maybe losing the seat wasn't the end of the world after all," Rienzi, fifty-three, said, one hand on the shoulder of the taller Castignani.

"Ya know, the best period of my professional life was when I made little money, serving in the Senate. Back in practice, of course, I'm makin' one hell of a lot more. But there's not that personal fulfillment that comes from public service. If you do it right, keep straight, and focus on the issues, service in the Senate is like the priesthood," Castignani said thoughtfully.

Rienzi – like Castignani, practicing Catholicism, now the dominant religion in the Senate, as well as in the nation's Supreme Court – was quick to respond, "Yeah, that may be so, but every once in a while you need to abort some wacko idea while it's in the embryonic stage."

Both men laughed.

"So you're reinvigorating your law practice. We haven't had much of a chance to talk. I'm presuming this to be friendly call since you're covered by the statute," Rienzi said, referring to the Lobbying Disclosure Act as well as various other lobbying restrictions, some of which were part of the US criminal code at Title 18. Senators often made such statements to ensure that, in a possible investigation, they could avoid perjuring or otherwise incriminating themselves by being able to say that they were aware of the appropriate law and recognized it at some point in an encounter with a lobbyist.

"I sure am, and this is indeed a friendly meeting. As you may know, some of my clients are the folks who were caught up in the Greek resort fiasco. As their attorney, I can, of course, represent them in petitioning for pardons. Since Congress has no role in the pardoning process, which is the constitutional domain of the executive, there's no lobbying interest in Congress, but I can tell you that the petition process is under way," Castignani said, carefully choosing his words.

"Right, I was in the Rhode Island AG's office as a young lawyer. The state-level pardoning process pretty much mirrors the federal guidelines. What are the chances of success?" Rienzi asked.

"Dom Guillermo is hauling the load on that and has met with the president. He's optimistic, and there are grounds for that mood," Castignani replied.

"Like what?" Rienzi asked.

"It's all a matter of public record, the opinion's slip copies pretty much detailed the arguments on both sides, except for one crucial fact. The president, then president-elect, urged the members involved to resign on grounds that Iranian money had been invested in the Greek project and that the dividends earned by the members included payments from those Iranian funds. There *was* Iranian money involved. However, it was *private* investor money from Iranian dissidents seeking a safe haven for their flight capital, something the intelligence folks didn't know, nor of course did the president," Castignani replied.

"That's major stuff, Bob."

"I'll say. The president could be embarrassed. But you know Earl Eastwood, he's not budging, still insisting that they did offend the basic conflict-of-interest restrictions at law and in congressional rule books. In the meantime, all of the members involved in the Greek projects who gave up their seats are seeing some restitution. They've been hired by Swiss companies and are involved in various trade and foreign investment projects for which I'm also their Washington attorney. So those things I can't discuss," Castignani said, adding, "However, Don Tranh and Ben Ochs, my partners, are eligible to see you and other members of Congress on the matter."

"Sure, I see," Rienzi replied. There was no wink and nod. The understanding was much deeper.

Changing the subject, Castignani asked about Rienzi's family.

"My two sons, the twins, are at Providence College, so Dianne has elected to spend most of the time at our house in Providence to be closer to them. You can be sure that's the last thing they want!" he said to mutual laughter.

I've said enough. I could be crossing lines here, getting into lobbying matters. I need to stop to protect Paul as well as myself, Castignani thought.

Rienzi caught the drift. "Listen, let's try to do something social sometime. We're going into the February recess. I'll be staying in Washington rather than going back to the state, and Dianne will be back next week. She knows many good-lookin' single women around here, so we'll set you up!" he said half jokingly.

I need to keep the social bond, Castignani thought. *That always helps.* He then said, "That'd be great. I'm not looking for anyone, but I do like female companionship. But please Catholic widows only, no social or family baggage, and over sixty but under seventy, and fit," he said laughingly.

They parted. As Castignani moved down the corridor, occasionally nodding to several staffers who recognized him, he thought, *That went nowhere. I need to get Don and Ben up to speed. They're gonna have to carry the lobbying load, unless I can get real creative and find a loophole around the restrictions on my lobbying. I need to get out on the water and think this thing through.* Castignani found that he did much of his best thinking always rowing on the Potomac.

Despite the chilly weather, he headed for the Thompson Boat Center, shoehorned into the Potomac riverbank at the foot of New Hampshire Avenue. He changed quickly into his winter rowing suit, consisting of a polar waterproof jacket over a fleece vest and polar fleece leggings. The third layer was a typical Gore-Tex ski skin capable of wicking out sweat-generated moisture and heat at a fast enough rate to avoid the hypothermia that occurs when wet garments stick and absorb body heat. Castignani had been a Naval Academy star rower and never abandoned the physically demanding sport. He would be out on the water in most weather, except for heavy precipitation.

Muscling his twenty-six-foot Olympic Rowing Scull into the water, he climbed aboard and with four vigorous heaves on his oars was moving toward the center of the river, a riparian boundary between Virginia and the District of Columbia. There was no traffic on the water as the noon hour approached, and the wind was mild in the forty-degree cold. Castignani breathed deeply and systematically with each heave of his oars, his well-developed deltoid, triceps, and latissimus dorsi muscle groups overcoming joint, spine, and other skeletal strains. He was moving with the current, now headed south toward the Kennedy Center on his left, as he began thinking through the new obstacles encountered during the morning's meeting with Senator Paul Rienzi, his replacement as chairman of the Senate Foreign Relations Committee.

I'm too close to breaking the lobbying laws. I'm not gonna do that. Ben and Don can't handle this alone. They're smart guys, but members want to talk to prestigious folks, who have money. I need to get the attention of the New England delegation. I can't use the New England Congressional Caucus, and the New England Council is all over the map, covering too many topics to get too concerned about industrial issues. That's it, by damn. I'll set up a New England industrial council, society, association, whatever. It'll be independent. We'll recruit some major companies in the region, like aviation and pharma folks, and register it as a nonprofit providing education on New England investment opportunities. The purpose will focus on the Swiss money going to the two chocolate manufacturers, but I can get some support from the New England state's economic development organizations to keep things looking legit.

Excited over the decision, Castignani finished a short workout and rowed back to the boathouse. Wiping down the craft and showering and changing, he was at his Watergate office within an hour.

"Jeannie, I'd like to get together in the conference room. Please round up Ben and Don," Castignani said in passing the office of his newly hired chief of staff, Jeannie Di Nardo. A former member of his Senate committee staff, the twenty-nine-year-old was a recent graduate of George Washington University Law School, which she attended in the evenings while working in the Senate.

It was 2:00 p.m.; Ben Ochs and Don Tranh, like their senior partner, Bob Castignani, were heavily attuned to fitness after years of service in the Senate, where stress, long working hours, and missed meals substituted for working out. They used the services of the Watergate Health Club, situated in the former hotel building, which was now undergoing renovation. Along with Jeannie Di Nardo, they took their places at the table, looking out onto the grayish Potomac laboring under an equally dismal-looking sky.

Castignani reviewed his meeting with the Senate chairman of the Senate Foreign Relations Committee. "I found myself skirting the lobbying law, right on the edge, too much risk for me and for us. So here's my thought. We'll set up a 501(c)(3) organization under the IRS code. Tentatively, I'm thinking of a name like the New England Industrial Association . . . I was thinking of the word 'committee,' but it would be an association, and I want to distinguish it from the New England Congressional Caucus, the Hill group, and the private New England Council.

"Our foremost purpose, of course, is to get the attention of the New England congressional members, whose help we're gonna need to promote the Lucas plan, especially as it relates to the Brent and Belmont operations. Through this type of conduit, we can contact and talk to members of Congress directly since our charter is to educate them on industrial development activities in the region. In fact, members, elected officials, could even join the association, although that's not an objective. But we would be fully exempt from coverage under sections 3(15) and 3(10) of the Lobbying Disclosure Act," Castignani added, looking down at his handwritten notes on a small yellow pad.

"If we hire a lobbyist, which we will, of course, the lobbyist would register and report his or her lobbying activities as required by the law. But the framework of the idea is to allow us to talk to elected members provided we avoid overt attempts to influence them in any way. We all know well how to do that since in our Senate careers we've dealt routinely with many medical, social, academic, and other groups, also 501 organizations subject to the same restrictions facing our new organization."

"Bob, how do we staff this thing, and what's the revenue flow?" asked Ben Ochs.

"For the time being, we'll set up an office adjacent to us, here in the Watergate. There are two suites that are empty at the end of the hall, we'll negotiate for them. I thought we'd make Don the executive director and Ben as the general counsel. We'll fund it initially from Lucas and Brent fees, adding the cost as a business expense to them and reportable under their Swiss tax regimes."

"Bob, you're not worried that the association could be seen as a deliberate evasion of the lobbying restrictions?" Jeannie asked.

"I am, Jeannie, very much so, which is why we have to be extremely careful in the language we use with members. But you, Ben and Don, are all eligible to lobby. You, Jeannie, have been out of public service for almost three years, and Don and Ben were in private practice for the past year before signing on with me. Your one-year ban on lobbying has now expired."

The four went into more detail, brought out copies of the relevant laws, pouring over them together, before deciding that the idea was sound, legally sufficient, and useful to the firm's objectives in promoting Lucas' interests in the United States. Ochs would draw up the charter and application for IRS tax exempt status, while Jeannie and Don would contact the Watergate Management Company regarding the new office space.

*   *   *

During the next few weeks, Castignani would amend the lobbying strategy in light of the need to form the New England Industrial Association, which he believed to be a legitimate loophole allowing direct contact with his former colleagues in Congress but within the guidelines of the lobbying laws.

The Castignani lineup included all the major congressional players from the New England delegations. On February 3, 2011, a private luncheon, catered by the Senate dining services, was organized in the antechamber of the Senate Judiciary Committee in room 224 of the Senate Dirksen Building. Attending were the principal congressional members of the various New England delegations, who would be introduced to the New England Industrial Association and the project that the association had adopted.

The group included the following from the US Senate:

Mike Lampert, R-ME, Ranking Minority of the Senate Finance Committee
Paul Rienzi, D-RI, Chairman, Senate Foreign Relations Committee
Kevin O'Meara, D-MA, Chairman, Senate Armed Services Committee
Roger Evarts, R-CT, RM, Senate Commerce Committee
Zbigniew Krakowski, R-CT, Senate Finance and Senate Judiciary Committees
From the US House of Representatives, the following were included:
Tony Provenzano, D-RI, Ranking Minority, House Armed Services Committee
Brendan McNeal, R-NH, Chairman, House Foreign Affairs Committee
George Mourgos, D-CT, RM, House Rules Committee
Frank Pole, R-ME, Chairman, House Ways and Means
From the White House, the following were included:
Sue Cohen, Assistant to the President and Chief of Staff

Guillermo was in Washington for the meeting and was joined by Castignani and his partners, Ben Ochs and Don Tranh.

Castignani opened the meeting after everyone gathered in the room, quickly taking seats.

"I want to thank everyone for coming over. This is our first formal meeting. The association has been formed to adopt and promote special projects that will benefit ultimately all or most of the New England states. Absent today is someone from the Vermont delegation, which I invited. However, they felt that there was no real state interest in the project, but as a matter of comity, they would stand with us on any vote where the region would benefit."

Castignani quickly moved through the formalities surrounding the establishment of the association, giving special attention to its restricted behavior under the terms of the IRS code regarding the so-called 501-c tax-exempt organizations.

"The function of the association, NEIA," he said, "is to *educate* or to inform the congressional delegations on economic and industrial development." He reiterated this several times.

All present knew exactly what NEIA intended. It was yet another convenient loophole in the lobbying statutes. While the organization could not form a political action committee or make contributions, it could hire lobbyists, provided they were covered by the terms found in the lobbying statutes. The members' interest was nonetheless piqued, knowing that the association could provide valuable insights on emerging job-creating projects that would make good campaign grist and provide an advantage over any rival candidates.

"Let me ask Dom Guillermo to take it from here. I believe you all know Dom, former Connecticut governor and later ambassador to the Holy See," Castignani concluded, remaining seated as did Guillermo as he started to speak.

"I know most of you from my past jobs and am very happy to be back in Washington in my new business capacity. It is good to see everyone again," Guillermo began.

"Obviously, I harbor strong feelings for our region, especially my own state. I have talked to Sophia Kallias several times about this project and other state developments. As vice chairman of two very large Swiss companies, Brent SA, a commodity trading firm, and Belmont Confections, the third-largest chocolate manufacturing company in the world and one what has over 60 percent of the European market, we are proposing a major investment in Rose Confections of Bridgeport and Havens, headquartered in Newton Highlands, Massachusetts.

"Belmont is eager to expand its market share either through production here as well as the licensing and production of some of its Swiss product line. The company wants a bigger US presence. For their part, both Rose and Havens have unused production capacity. Between the two companies of approximately the same size, they've laid off nearly three thousand workers since 2008."

Attention became invited on Guillermo at the mention of jobs with hopes that they knew what would follow.

"We want to restore those jobs and then add some," said Guillermo, his simply worded proposition quite sufficient to keep their attention. He continued speaking with no notes, slides, or charts. The intent was to allow folks to digest their lunch, get a provocative message, and leave knowing what was expected of them.

"How do we plan to go about this?" Guillermo asked rhetorically. "In a single word, our best strategy is price related. This means controlling production costs since the market is very competitive with many excellent brands out there.

"Belmont is partially owned by Brent, the commodity trading company. We are in the process of acquiring through futures contracts and direct crop purchases as much of the cocoa bean crop as is possible and practical, subject of course to monopoly and antitrust restraints. We essentially will create a private commodity exchange for cocoa beans, encouraging customers, including some of our rivals, to buy through us because of our price competitiveness.

"Belmont's holistic picture is one of a global operation feeding product, production components, like the cocoa beans, and investment cash to its US partners, Rose and Havens. There is much market reciprocity in this deal, with Rose and Havens' products entering the EU through the retail and wholesale marketing facilities of Belmont.

"Our estimates show that leading Rose and Havens' product sales in the EU alone could restore as many as 90 percent of the layoff jobs in Massachusetts and Connecticut. The added cash investment from Belmont will provide the start-up, or should I say 'start-back,' funding needed for both this aspect of the jobs-and-earnings restoration effort but also allow for local manufacture in these states of Belmont products licensed to the two US firms. Our sales surveys show that the licensing-manufacturing element of this deal could add 50 percent more, or nearly 1,500 jobs."

Guillermo, seeing body motions suggesting questions and with a few hands already at half-mast, decided to take their inquiries.

"Dom, I'm sure we have a few folks from Maine who've worked in Newton for Havens, but do you have any figures on that?" asked Republican senator Mike Lampert of Maine, who was also the ranking minority member of the very important Senate Finance Committee, which has jurisdiction over foreign trade.

Just what I wanted, Castignani thought. *They all need to see that the relatively short driving distances in the region could bring jobs within their reach.*

Guillermo's own thoughts were along the same line.

"I don't have good data, Mike, except to say that when layoffs and early retirements were offered back in 2008, Havens found that those driving the longest distances were often at the front of the line. But you know, I think it's only about seventy miles to Havens from Kennebunkport, and there is now good train service as well as an MTA quick link from Boston to Newton Highlands."

"Terrific, let me know what I can do," the crafty Maine senator replied, thinking, *Damn, this is great. I've a lot of my folks working in the Boston area. "Jobs" is the name of the game in this economy. With the February recess coming up and my campaign just eight months away, this is gonna be a big part of my reelection stump speech.*

As the hour-long luncheon drew to a close, with members facing the usual Thursday rush to deal with a cascade of votes before getting out of town, this group of savvy politicians saw concrete advantages for assisting the effort, not being entirely sure what would be asked of them. They adjourned, each shaking hands with Castignani, Guillermo, Ochs, Tranh, and, especially, Sue Cohen. All were pleased to see her there, a signal that there would be White House interest and support from New England's first president in eighty-two years, dating back to Calvin Coolidge of Vermont, the thirtieth president who left office in 1929.

Sue lingered a while. *Too many "ifs" here: regulators, foreign exchange trading of the cocoa bean, not to mention the trade and antitrust laws. Congress is not likely to accept Swiss dominance of the US chocolate sector, not with the lobbying clout of the two giants, Rose and Havens,* she thought. *Unless the two US companies see some benefit in the deal.*

"Thanks for coming, Sue," Bob Castignani said, walking over to Sue, who now stood alone after chatting briefly with Roger Evarts, the senator from Connecticut. The two knew each other well despite the cast age differences and parties, Evarts being a Republican. Sue's parents and other members of her Stamford family were heavy contributors to many Democratic causes in Fairfield County. She had been surprised that he was very supportive of the plan. Evarts had decided to resign from the Senate, and his seat was assigned to Sam Schlesinger by Guillermo before leaving the governor's office. Schlesinger rushed to Washington, involved himself in activities even before being sworn in. He managed to get himself wrapped up in the Lucas Club scandal. When Schlesinger withdrew because of it, Evarts successfully regained his seat.

"It's an interesting deal. I still think you'll face some antitrust complications," she said. All knew she had been a former antitrust lawyer with a Washington law firm before coming to the Senate as a senior staffer.

"You mean market domination by one or both US companies?" Castignani asked. "Isn't that already the case, Sue?"

He really doesn't get it, she thought.

"No, Bob, that's not the primary or only issue. Of course, with Belmont as a partner, the two dominant companies could logically be expected to get more market share. But the bigger issue is the monopsony created by Belmont's linkages to Brent. I can't image the Justice Department ignoring that," she added, recognizing the quizzical look on the faces of Castignani and Guillermo, who had walked over to join them. It was evident the two men, although lawyers, had little knowledge or recollection of this particularly complex area of economics.

"Would you mind elaborating on that issue, Sue?" Guillermo asked.

"Sure, the monopsonist, unlike the monopolist, is a buyer, not a seller. If he can reduce demand for a product, he can buy at a lower price. The Belmont-Brent objective is to control the cocoa market, raising the price to chocolate sellers and thereby lowering demand. That's assuming that chocolate has enough inelasticity so that price influences demand, which I assume it does."

"I think people will search for substitutes if chocolate prices rise, don't you?" Castignani asked.

"I have no idea. I would, but I'm not a chocoholic, or whatever that term is and means," Sue replied to their friendly smiles.

"But that's not my immediate point," she continued. "How do we know that the Swiss consortium won't force higher prices on the US companies by selling beans at prohibitively high prices, suppressing competition with Belmont in the

US as well as other markets? Then having gutted competition, Belmont buys out the two US companies?"

"The two US companies have *invited* Belmont as a potential partner, and even if that was Belmont's objective, the two US companies would have to agree to it," Guillermo answered.

"But, Dom, their agreement could be seen as something made under the duress of unfair competition, that being the behavior of the monopsonist who had deliberately driven their prices up, forcing them to sell out," Sue countered. "And there is the pesky issue of market manipulation. Neither the US nor the European Union will just stand by. They and we may force the companies to break up."

"Belmont and Brent are Swiss companies, and Switzerland is not part of the EU although, of course, they operate in the market jurisdictions of both the US and EU. But Belmont has a very small market share in the US confections sector," Castignani offered.

"Yes, Bob, but here you have a potentially monopsonistic move by a Swiss company in the US marketplace. Justice's antitrust division will invoke the Sherman Act, which addresses buyer cartels, like the Belmont-Brent combination. Secondly, the case law is pretty broad, if not vague. It basically forbids any type of contract, combination, or conspiracy that restrains trade. Look, I'm just telling you what the law says as I'm sure you will be told or maybe have been by your own attorneys.

"Obviously, the president is very interested in this and is a friend of both of you. He just wants everything to work out in the favor of US interests, which is something I know doesn't surprise either one of you at all," Sue concluded with a firm voice.

"Sue, there's no reason to think that we're not determined to benefit the two US companies. Why else would we be explaining this to the delegations of the two states where they're located and to the president and you?" Guillermo said.

I may have gone too far, maybe even scared them. I don't want to interfere with a good business deal, but I'm not yet convinced that's what this one is, she thought. *There's already too much Swiss involvement. They have government interests in Lucas, Belmont, and Brent. And with the government change in the Ivory Coast, there has to be some connection. I'll bet Bago is going to live there and has stashed his cash in Swiss banks or other financial institutions.*

"Well, I've gotta run," she said finally, noticing that her Secret Service escort was nodding to her at the door of the room. "But I want to congratulate you for forming the New England Industrial Association, if I have the name right," she added as the two men moved their heads affirmatively. "This was a good opportunity to learn about and discuss the plan. As you can see, my security detail wants to get me back to the White House before traffic picks up. People hate us when we tie things up."

She embraced both of them with friendly brushes of her lips on each man's cheek, then departed.

Minutes later, the two men sat down at the table, each with a glass of water. "As she spoke, it occurred to me that we may have a little too much transparency on our plan, and transparency on issues that you and I may not fully understand," Castignani said to Guillermo.

"You mean the Swiss, what their hidden agenda might be?" Guillermo responded. "I worry about that too. They could pull the rug out from under us, you know. I don't mean to be too prosaic, but they could turn the whole plan upside down, decide to grab and hold the entire confections gig once the capture of the cocoa bean market is complete. But would they do that?" he asked rhetorically, adding, "I'd be surprised. I can't see them taking on the US . . ." He paused, then said, "Unless they have some pretty heavy artillery to call up."

"Like the EU," Castignani inserted.

"Yeah," Guillermo responded thoughtfully, his eyes squinting a bit.

CHAPTER 8

SCHUSSING THE MOGULS

IT WAS IMMEDIATELY CLEAR THAT THE FEW OBSTACLES IDENTIFIED BY THE WASHINGTON AND IVORY COAST MEETINGS WOULD NOT LESSEN THE SPEED AT WHICH THE STRATEGY TO SEIZE THE COCOA BEAN MARKET WOULD BE IMPLEMENTED. A general meeting of the key corporate players from Lucas, Brent, and Belmont would be convened at Belmont's conference center, located down the road from its main plant in Vevey, Switzerland.

On Sunday, February 13, 2011, Domenic Guillermo, Bob Castignani, and his partners, Don Tranh and Ben Ochs, and Nikos Rallis departed Dulles International Airport, located in the Virginia countryside outside of Washington. It was 4:10 p.m. as Brent's Falcon 900 LX executive jet lifted off the runway for the seven-hour flight. Normally fitted to accommodate twelve to sixteen passengers, the aircraft was reconfigured so as to provide minisuites for the five passengers. They reviewed their meeting agenda and notes for about an hour before retiring. The flight was smooth. Castignani was restless in his "air cave" and rolled to one side, looking out the port at the near-full moon.

Strange, it's a bit early in the month for a moon like this, he thought, his early naval training as a navigator having instilled a lifelong sensitivity to the positions of the moon, sun, and stars. He stretched his neck closer to the port-like window. *And Sirius, my favorite navigation aide, too angled to the east. Aahh, I've other things to worry about. I sure as hell am not gonna change the heavens. But I'm gonna have some rough times ahead. Sue Cohen, her questions were right on target. How reliable are these Swiss? Nikos seems comfortable with them. And Dom does too. But that's because he trusts Rallis,* he reasoned, responding to his self-interrogation. He muddled through several lobbying scenarios. Satisfied that he and his associates could handle the political side of the strategy, he drifted off to sleep to the steady whirring of the Falcon's three Honeywell TFE731-60 turbofan engines.

Castignani awoke about 5:30 a.m. Washington time as the pilot alerted the five men that they were within an hour from Geneva, having been delayed somewhat by military operations off the Bay of Biscay in Southwestern France. Castignani knew the region well from his six-year stint in the navy and at a time when friendly US-French relations called for common exercises. The copilot, now in the passenger compartment, was talking to Guillermo and Rallis as Castignani walked over.

"There were two French Rafaele fighters in the air as we entered French airspace from the Atlantic. They reported that they were monitoring the airspace since the naval base at Bayonne, near the Spanish border, was testing several missiles. They were courteous, even inviting us to divert to and land at the Rochefort-Saint Agnant Air Base if the diversion would cause a fuel issue. This aircraft's range was sufficient to carry us to our destination at Geneva, I reported."

"My own take is that they're exercising for something else. The French don't usually operate that way. They use the missile test as a cover for something else. It may be an operation in Libya, Algeria, or maybe even Ivory Coast. Things are popping up there, as you probably know," Castignani explained. "I did some service in this area when I was in the navy. Later, as chairman of the Senate Foreign Relations Committee, I routinely complained to the state department that they needed to intervene to ensure our navy's port visits to places like La Rochelle. DOD complained that our military flights over this sector in France as well as the port visits were often cancelled over some flimsy excuse that an exercise was planned or under way. It seemed like a lot of harassment to me, and I thought all that had changed."

"So you think they may be reacting to developments in Ivory Coast. All that was a month ago," Rallis added.

"Yeah, but Bago hasn't yet turned over the presidency to Tagro, and Tagro is a good buddy of the French president," Castignani replied. "I just hope that the French don't muck up our deal over the cocoa bean crop."

"We may need to *encourage* Bago to get out of the country, the sooner the better," Guillermo added.

"We can do that," Rallis added. "After all, no go, no dough," he said to the laughter of all while the copilot pretended innocence. "I'll get von Schlossen on it. I don't want Tagro to think we're, in any way, tampering with his rule."

The copilot returned to the flight deck. Minutes later, the pilot announced that they would begin their approach to Geneva.

The aircraft glided gently to its touchdown at Cointrin, the Geneva international airport, then taxied to La Citadelle, a section to the northwest of the main runway. The area was populated with numerous corporate helicopters, including that of Belmont, which stood out in the fleet. The sleek Agusta AW139 was designed for the Italian aircraft manufacturer by Paninfarina, the hugely popular automobile architect. The helicopter's body resembled that of the jet from which the passengers had just disembarked.

Climbing aboard, even Nikos Rallis, accustomed to high luxury and grand living, was somewhat awed by the aircraft's interior. Walnut-veneered paneling framed the passenger compartment with two set of seats facing each other and separated by consoles with networked televisions and computer monitors. The white kid-glove leather seats emitted a welcoming odor that overwhelmed even the stench of fuel and other mechanical fluids common to aircraft holding areas.

The five men were now seated as the crew chief slid the doors shut; the two Pratt-Whitney Canada PT6C-67C high-thrust engines whirred. Within five minutes, the aircraft lifted from the ground, nosed down slightly, and climbed to its departure altitude of two hundred feet while moving eastward over the tarmac toward Lake Geneva. As the helicopter climbed to its assigned cruising altitude of seven thousand feet, the monitors on the consoles facing the two sets of parties came to life. The face of Belmont president Marc Smit suddenly had a voice. "Welcome, gentlemen. I look forward to seeing you at the landing pad. Hope the flight went well. You're in good hands now. Jurgen and Hans love that helicopter more than their own wives and children," Smit said in German-accented yet grammatically perfect, even idiomatic, English, referring to the pilots.

The chopper cruised gently through the brisk air over Lake Geneva, passing such landmarks as the lakeside vineyards dating back to Roman times, now a UNESCO World Heritage site. The Romans established camps along the lake region, where troops rested and trained for their farther trek into Northern Europe.

"We haven't heard much from Marc Smit before," Guillermo said, referring to the somewhat erudite Belmont president.

"He's certainly key to our plans," Rallis responded. "He'll be briefing us on the cocoa bean genome project, about which little has been said."

"You mean genome as in DNA?" Thompson asked.

"Right, as you know, we're all scared as hell of the fungal plight that has wiped out so many trees. The hope has been that we could find a clue to an antibiotic within the genome sequence," Rallis said. "Belmont sent Marc to the Sloan School of Management at MIT for the executive MBA program, which he finished somewhere around 1999. Belmont has invested in an MIT corporate research program that is looking for solutions to the disease problem. Also, Marc was planted there to keep an eye on Havens, which is in Newton Highlands and which has been working with the Harvard biological labs on a genome project."

"So this issue affects all chocolate producers?" Castignani asked.

"Yes," Rallis responded. "Our strategy is to get control of the crop before the disease strangles supply as well as existing inventories. Getting it stored in the right places in the EU and US is also important. The New York City and Swiss storage sites are probably the safest and best managed in the world. Most importantly, we've got to get it out of Africa, where they lose substantial tonnage soon after harvesting for many reasons – disease, rot, theft, and limited shelf life among them."

The forty-minute flight passed quickly as the chopper approached the landing pad, now in sight as the aircraft turned north, heading toward the Alpine region, the snowcapped brownish-green mountains dead ahead of them. The pilot announced the imminence of touchdown as all checked their seat belts.

As the nose of the chopper lifted upward, the aircraft, resembling a praying mantis suspended in air, slowly descended onto the X-marked landing pad alongside the principal Belmont factory on the Avenue de Savoie. Looking out the door windows, Guillermo could see Belmont CEO Lutz Gorgens and his corporate president, Marc Smit, both holding their hats with one hand while the other grasped the lapels of their business overcoats. The aircraft touched down with barely a thump while the rotors immediately went limp. The crew chief leapt from his position in the forward cabin, opening the doors as the two Belmont executives walked to greet them.

"Welcome to Belmont," said the affable CEO as both he and the president, Marc Smit, extended their hands, which were shaken by the five newcomers as they walked south. "We're going to walk to the château, which is our conference center," Gorgens said. "I'm sure that you want to get those legs moving after sitting in airplanes for so long. The luggage will be placed in your rooms at the château."

The wind off the lake was surprisingly mild. Guillermo and Thompson, now residing less than three miles away at the nearby Montreux Palace Hotel, had become accustomed to the Swiss winter on what is called the Swiss Riviera because of the normally warm and more pleasing climate at the eastern end of Lake Geneva. The American expats were now living in Montreux as part of their new jobs with Lucas and Brent, the Swiss holding and commodity trading companies, respectively. But they had spent little time at Belmont, except for former senator Mark Baldwin, who was now Belmont's vice chairman, and Guillermo and former senator Jeff Scharfman, both of whom had been added to Belmont's board because of Lucas' substantial investment in the company.

*   *   *

Château de Belmont was the formal headquarters of Belmont. A few steps from the plant, the facility was used as a conference center for major corporate meetings and included several rooms and suites available to important out-of-town visitors and customers. This was easily one of the prize private properties on the lake, the former residence of a remnant of the once-great Savoy family, Prince Donald Belmont von Rieben Savoy, who held reign over his empty principality until a decade ago, when he abandoned Switzerland to retire in New Providence, New Jersey. He was educated in the United States and, by coincidence, at Trinity College, the school from which both Connecticut governor Sophie Kallias and Nikos Rallis. Prince Donald's American mother saddled him with a very prosaic first name that widened the eyes of his fellow royals on the continent. The Savoys had owned the entire waterfront on which sat Belmont, the food confection company founded in 1850. The Savoy homestead was a reserved enclave on the property with a deed that compelled its surrender to the Belmont corporation upon the demise of its singular owner, now Prince Donald, or his election to dispose of the property, which was completed with his departure for New Jersey.

Grecian revival architecture framed the stately facade of the thirty-thousand-square-foot structure with four columns supporting a balcony off the ballroom, now the corporate conference room, on the second floor. Florentine Renaissance etages were integrated into the Grecian frame, their alternating Romanesque and Gothic windows contrasting elegantly with the scrolled capitals atop the columns. Many of the château's sixteen bedrooms were now offices, and the original twenty-two bathrooms were modernized and reconfigured with showers and even saunas in a few cases.

Positioned at the edge of Lake Geneva, a private marina could be seen over the scalloped shrubs of the formal gardens, in the center of which was placed an outdoor swimming pool, one rarely used except by the most durable visitors willing to forgo the properly heated indoor pool.

The group entered the conference room, now populated with the full complement of officials from Belmont's principal investor, Lucas Holdings, and Brent SA, now Belmont's commodity trading source and investor. The large room was centered on its round forty-seat conference table, which easily accommodated the approximately twenty-five persons gathered for the session. On three walls were installed thirty-six-square-foot plasma screens to monitor project presentation and other display materials.

*   *   *

This would be the first full plenary meeting of the three companies. Seated at head of the table, looking over the table toward the lake, were the hosting officials, Belmont's CEO, Lutz Gorgens, and his president, Marc Smit. Former Virginia senator Mark Baldwin, director of Brent's UK operations, and a vice chairman of Belmont was also at the head section. Guillermo sat to the right of Smit while Rallis to the left of Gorgens.

"Ladies and gentlemen, welcome to Château de Belmont. I recognize that many of you have been at the Belmont plant before, and some have been in this headquarters from time to time, so I know that you have some sense of the history of this structure, which we are very fortunate to have as our global operations center.

"Belmont continues to thrive. Our revenues for the 2010 capital budgeting year closed at $10 billion. Of this amount, 30 percent came from the European Union and 20 percent from the United States market. The rest of our revenues came just about evenly from Asia and Africa and other destinations.

"Our partnering with Lucas Holdings and, through them, with Brent has been premised on the reasoned and calculated expectations that we can raise our US share very substantially. The US confections market is valued by the United Nations at $20 billion . . . All figures are in US dollars by the way. The EU confections market is valued some 25 percent less at $15 billion. Belmont holds 10 percent of the current US confections market, which accounts for only $2 billion compared to the $3 billion earned from sales to the EU. However, the big difference here is that value of the per capita consumption of chocolate and confections in the US is $63, compared to only $30 in the EU, or 83 percent higher. Also, the US population is estimated at 317 million compared to 220 million in the EU. Average per capita consumption is less than $15 in the rest of the world, which we will not concern ourselves with for the moment."

The numbers flashed around the three walls' monitors. Gorgens poured water from a carafe into a glass, sipping it.

He continued. "Our short-term objective is to raise our US market share to 25 percent. This would give us a $5 billion revenue stream, adding 30 percent to our current revenues. But we believe that with the licensing of some of our Swiss products as well as new product lines now under development, we can eventually tap into as much as 50 percent of the US market over the long term, or ten years, increasing our revenues by 130 percent in a decade. I know that many of our US partners are thinking of competition, and rightfully so. There are more than four hundred manufacturers of chocolate and confections in the US, which constitute over 90 percent of that market. But there are only two that constitute nearly 60 percent of it, and they are Rose Confections of Connecticut and Havens of Massachusetts.

"Now, we remain a private company. Some of our competitors, as well as other companies, see the public financing market, which is to say essentially the stock and bond markets, as the best sources of revenue. We're a bit different here and in many ways more Swiss, if our US partners will permit me to say."

There were friendly nods and smiles around the table.

"The so-called Swiss way is to sell more. This gives us a relatively unfettered, less regulated, less volatile, and much more reliable source as long as we remain competitive. Therefore, we are considering the partnering and limited acquisition or merger with some current US confectioners, which collectively control as much as 60 percent of the US market.

"This is not to say that we will never be a public company either here or in the US or EU. But for the time being, our business strategy is headed in a direction that suggests we can do better by expanding through our marketing efforts than through the stock markets. The current state of the economies in Europe and the US as well as the wildly fluctuating stock markets in Germany, France, the UK, and the US suggest that our thinking on this point is quite sound.

"How we accomplish this is why we have brought our US partners to this table. And I turn the meeting over to my good friend and colleague Nikos Rallis to explain the strategy for enlarging our US market share. Before we get into the exacting details of the next phase, I'm told that our bladders are demanding a pause. That we will do for thirty minutes."

*　　*　　*

The coffee and bathroom break was timely. Small coteries gathered in the corners of the room, bathrooms, and even out on the balcony overlooking the river. One thing was on the minds of all, but it was most dominant in those of the US members of the Lucas-Brent-Belmont coalition. Anne Rathbone, now the Lucas chief financial officer, caucused with former Louisiana representative Marc Gregoire, now chairman of Lucas-USA, and Bennie Thompson and David Ford, both former members of the US House of Representatives and now serving as executive vice presidents at Brent. Her HP business calculator in hand, standing in the refreshingly brisk air on the château balcony, Rathbone started talking numbers.

"Just a quick calculation, guys, but if this thing pans out, we're going to be in very good financial shape," she said.

"You mean individually," Gregoire added.

"Right. Look, we, the dozen of us involved in the consortium, own 25 percent of Lucas, which will get 20 percent of Belmont's after-tax earnings. Total earnings, according to what Gorgens just said, should be about $1 billion by the year 2021. Allocating that amount to our individual shares after an estimated 20 percent Swiss taxes, and considering the future value of money, gives our ownership group in Lucas – the so-called Lucas Investment Trust group, LIT as we call it – about $200 million for that year alone. If we further apportion the $200 million to the seventeen members of LIT, including Rallis, Guillermo, and Castignani, we're talkin' about $11–12 million each by the year 2021. I've scaled that down to our start-up year, 2011, and worked a compensation ladder back to the end year, giving each an estimated $65 million in pre-US taxable income for the decade. Listen, these are just back-of-the-envelope estimates, guys. But even if I'm as much as 20 percent off and, after all, everything is contingent upon markets and a successful workout of the strategic plan, we're still in pretty good shape."

"I'm feelin' goose bumps, and it ain't the cold air out here," Thompson added to the laughter of all.

"Look, after the screw job that Eastwood did on me, I'm not about to let this opportunity pass. I've uprooted my family, relocated almost entirely to Switzerland, and lost anything even resembling a political or business career option back in the States. Fortunately, Jane has the necessary skills herself to be on the Lucas legal staff," said Gregoire, referring to his wife as well.

Former New York representative David Ford, the only Republican involved in the original Lucas scandal and who, along with Castignani, were the only investors totally exonerated by the courts, spoke up.

"Boy, I don't think I could have done as well as this if I went back to Wall Street," Ford, the former investment banker, said. "That's assuming I could get into the financial sector, and even that was doubtful since I had become so controversial."

"My only real option was lobbying," said former Delaware representative Anne Rathbone. "I'm tainted too. The few clients I managed to get over the past year paid badly and were not reliable engagements for any appreciable period of time. Besides, there are over 1,200 of us former congressionals out there humpin' for business. That's a lot of competition, and being a woman doesn't help."

Clearly, the earning potential was dazzling for any former House member. For most House members, their congressional salary, about $160,000 at that time, was more money than they had ever made before. Increasing numbers of new members in the US House of Representatives come from public service levels at all levels of government. For many of the others, their compensation from small-business ownerships, lower-level corporate management jobs, and struggling law practices drove their attention to politics in the first place as a way either to secure new clients and customers or to buttress their income. The desire to serve the public was largely vague as became increasingly evident from their determination to get reelected once in office. The situation is slightly different in the Senate, where 55 percent have had legal training and several benefit from substantial family or acquired fortunes, a trend ironically more prevalent among Democrats.

"Welcome back, all," Nikos started. "We needed that break. Today, for the first time, we will cover in open session between the three partnering companies the implementation of our strategy, a major tactic of which, I am happy to report, has already been put in place. First, I want to ask Ambassador Guillermo to review the history and status of our operations to this moment in time."

"Thanks, Nikos," Guillermo said. "I will provide a quick backdrop to how we've arrived at this point."

Mindful of the presence of the Swiss managers in the room, Guillermo would temper and tweak his remarks to avoid disclosing too much regarding the Washington political scene and the details of sensitive meetings with the president and others.

"Our Swiss colleagues are aware that their American partners, as original investors in the Lucas recreational and hospitality projects in the Greek islands, were wrongfully charged with having interests that conflicted with their high-level elected offices. Those charges, it now appears, were subject to newly uncovered information that promises to mitigate them. I refer to the pressure brought on the Lucas investors by the president of the United States, who had been provided false evidence that Lucas investors included the government of Iran. It turned out that while Lucas did indeed have Iranian investors, they were private citizens trying to secure safe havens for their monies outside of Iran and monies from Iranians who had escaped the harsh regime of Ahmadinejad. That information has led to appeals by the members for pardons, a process that continues.

"Over the past year, we had met several times with Niko, trying to develop a business opportunity that could aggregate the substantial skills of the members. Niko's concept to form the consortium that brings us all here today was the outcome. And as you heard from Herr Gorgens, we are on track to realize exactly that. The project envisioned and developed between the partners is a highly legitimate, enlightened, and rewarding opportunity. The members are not driven by revenge. They will have justice in the end. Rather, this endeavor, however challenging, invites everyone's enthusiasm for the reasons so eloquently expressed by Herr Gorgens.

"I have met with President Eastwood, and I have discussed the importance of our members' participation in this project, one that offers more jobs and greater prosperity to the New England region of the US. In honesty, the president is not yet on board with us. He is studying the pardon application, or I should say his staff at the Justice Department is reviewing it, and I feel confident he will approve it. I am also confident that he will see the benefits of our efforts to assist the US economy at a time when it is reeling from a near meltdown of the financial sector and in the midst of a debt crisis. The US budget deficit-to-national-debt ratio is second only to that of Greece at the moment. The US is poised for only the second time in the country's relatively short history to risk default on its national debt, half of which is in foreign hands, largely those of the Chinese and Japanese, in that order. The president's need for this type of foreign investment in the US economy is obvious.

"Moving on, we have met with Ivory Coast president Jean Bago and his successor, Emile Tagro. Thanks to the negotiation skill of Brent's new executive vice president for Africa, Bennie Thompson, we believe our offer will help avoid further bloodshed and civil strife in the country. Bago has been offered residency in Switzerland and a small but earned compensation from cocoa crop sales, now managed by his son, Robert. Bennie's former role on the House Foreign Affairs Committee was instrumental. He knew the players, they had confidence in him, and they welcomed his role as a senior management official of Brent.

"While it would seem that we were all winners from Bennie's arrangement, there is one important source that does not quite see things that way – the Eastwood administration," Guillermo said to light laughter in the room. "They are not entirely pleased that we, a legitimate commodity trading business, could accomplish what feckless diplomats could not. I do not use that word cynically. I am, after all, one of them myself, or was for a short while in my role as US ambassador to the Holy See. The problem is that political bodies don't often appreciate the importance of business interests in foreign-policy making. I saw this on a recurring basis in the state department. The US is a nation dependent on tax-based revenues from businesses to finance extraordinarily wasteful agencies and to engage in shams."

Guillermo paused, sipping water, then continued. "Speaking of waste, one such sleight-of-hand technique is the so-called earmark, which sidesteps the meritorious selection process mandated to agencies by Congress, the very source that ignores them. But without digressing further, let me continue. The president appears to be offended because he was denied the political gain that could have been achieved through an Ivory Coast settlement done by his state department. The situation is not unlike the endless Israeli-Palestinian crisis. We in this room all know well that the economic tool is locked away in the diplomat's kit bag. The president was so incensed that the Ivory Coast crisis was settled outside of his involvement that he fired his intelligence director. This move tells me that we will be under close scrutiny.

"My point is that we might even expect to find government obstacles interfering with our progress. To avert them, we rely upon our distinguished former senator Bob Castignani, who is our legal and lobbying representative in Washington. Bob has established a nonprofit organization called the New England Industrial Association, which is chartered to inform lawmakers on our interests. The group has already met with key lawmakers at a Washington luncheon sponsored by NEIA and has received, without soliciting them, the support gestures of many members of Congress who are critically important to our project. The president sent his chief of staff to our meeting, by the way. She raised many issues, which reinforces my suspicion that official Washington will be watching us.

"I believe our strategic plan to be solidly reliable and will turn the meeting over to Niko, who will provide more information on our tactics," Guillermo concluded with a nod to Nikos Rallis, the chairman of Lucas Holdings.

"This won't be a long or unnecessary rehash of the material we covered at our meeting on December 14 back in Alexandria," Rallis said, sensing some ennui among the group after Guillermo's lengthy presentation. "But I do want to go over a few important details since we're here with our Swiss partners this time.

"Dom pointed out that the Ivory Coast phase worked out for us, and we now have the country's cocoa crop within our reach. However, in executing its capture without roiling the commodity exchange markets, we need to take very careful steps. This level of caution results from Washington's dissatisfaction with the way we settled the conflict in Ivory Coast. We expect the US regulators to be watching us even though we're offshore and out of their jurisdiction.

"The US and other exchanges will be expecting product – cocoa bean offers and contract futures. And speculators will have quickly realized that efforts are being made to control the commodity. Unless we make gradual and token releases to the markets in the US, UK, and Canada, speculators will drive the price up and even trigger the market circuit breakers, which could shut down trading and cause the exchange authorities – and the regulators – to investigate the causes. That is the last thing we want to do. It would not take long to discover Brent's fingerprints on the trigger.

"Coordination within Brent and between Brent and Belmont must be constant and timely. In New York, where Sam will watch the price spreads between current and futures contracts from his perch in the Battery section of Manhattan, he will have to assure his traders and market partners in other commodity houses that Brent's holdings of the commodity is for purposes of the usual trading advantage only and not an attempt to corner the market," Rallis emphasized, referring to former Connecticut senator Sam Schlesinger, now CEO of Brent-USA with headquarters in Manhattan's financial district.

"Question, Niko," said Mark Koerner, the former New Jersey representative, now CEO of Brent-Canada, operating from the Exchange Tower on Toronto's King Street. "I'm getting orders from a few Canadian hedgers or users of the product, but I'm also getting even more orders from speculators, all this in the course of events at present, where the commodity is trading quite normally. Most of the speculation money is coming from Asia, places like Hong Kong, Singapore, a little from Japan. I can accommodate the hedgers, but the speculators will go to the Indonesian cocoa markets if I can't give them a decent price. Do we want that?"

"Niko, I can answer that," said Paul von Schlossen, the Swiss chairman and CEO of Brent and a savvy, longtime commodity trader in his own right.

"The answer is yes, Sam. By shifting demand to the Asian exchanges trading the cocoa commodity, they will raise prices there. Remember, the reason you're getting more and more Asian interest is the fear that China, already a major and competing manufacturer of chocolate products, is squeezing the supply lines available to the rest of the world. As the Chinese prosper, they're demanding the same luxury discretionary products as the developed world enjoys. I hope that helps," von Schlossen concluded.

"It does indeed. Thank you," Koerner replied.

"And" – Rallis was back – "Mark, you have two major functions in Toronto. First, to make modest amounts available so as to appease the very limited Canadian demand while keeping the US regulator watchdogs calm as they routinely observe the Toronto Futures Exchange, where you'll be operating.

"Secondly, you are trading with the UK as well as the Chicago Mercantile Exchange, the CME, and NYMEX, the New York Mercantile Exchange on the CME Globex system. The futures trades are highly automated, as you now know, and occur almost instantaneously. Both the speculators and hedgers have rooms of people watching them minute by minute. You need to ensure that there are as few peaks and valleys in the prices as possible. TFE, the Toronto Futures Exchange, in my judgment, could become a key precursor in that regard, alerting folks to a supply issue even before it's noticeable on the larger NYMEX, the New York Board of Trade's Intercontinental Exchange, ICE, CME, or on the London International Financial Futures and Commodities Exchange. When the big exchanges run short, they turn to the little guys, like Toronto, to bail them out. You, Mark, will be their first signal that the noose is tightening!"

"Niko, much of the futures in agricultural trading for Europe is done at my post in London. I'm constantly trading with my continental counterpart, Euronext, to smooth out demands from the UK as well as Belgium, France, Holland, and Portugal, as well as other EU countries. As the supply from Ivory Coast begins to diminish, won't they start wondering?" asked former Virginia senator Mark Baldwin.

"Paul, perhaps you can answer that," Rallis said, turning to Paul von Schlossen, Brent's chairman and CEO.

"Of course. Mark, you asked the right question. As we all know, Côte d'Ivoire is a former French colony and member of the French Economic Community. The French believe they still own the place, which must have disturbed them greatly when we worked out the presidential succession crisis there. But the French chocolate manufacturers have long since hedged their cocoa needs on many exchanges, Euronext included. These exchanges, for the EU at least, receive most cocoa from Ghana, the second-largest bean producer. In my judgment as a trader, the EU will be the least worried about what will seem like a short-term loss of cocoa from the Ivory Coast. They will probably relate it to the civil strife there," von Schlossen said.

"I believe we've managed the questions for now. At this juncture and before we adjourn and return to our respective destinations to get back to work, I'd like to ask Belmont's president, Marc Smit, to talk about another development that we need to be mindful of," Rallis said, gesturing to Smit.

Marc Smit held the second-top job at Belmont as president. Paired with CEO Gorgens, who was two years his senior, the two balanced perfectly: Gorgens, the shrewd lawyer, and Smit, the technical maestro who orchestrated the entire production process. But Smit's expertise was far-reaching. A graduate of the distinguished ETH, short for the Eidgenossiche Technische Hochschule Zurich, the Swiss federal institute of technology, Smit held an undergraduate degree in biochemistry and a master's degree in process engineering. In 1997, Belmont sent him to the Massachusetts Institute of Technology's Sloan School of Management, where he earned his MBA. It was immediately clear even then that he was being groomed for higher responsibilities, including chairman and CEO as Gorgens's successor.

While in Cambridge, Smit managed to involve himself in the MIT corporate research program in which Belmont had invested $5 million for the privilege of fostering and benefitting from laboratory-level research on the cocoa genome database. Equally important was the participation of Havens in the MIT research program. A rival US confectioner, Havens was headquartered in nearby Newton Highlands with a plant situated on the Charles River. Smit befriended a number of Havens employees, some working at MIT and others at the Newton facility, which he had been invited to visit a number of times.

Therefore, it was not entirely by coincidence that today, fourteen years later, Belmont would be considering a partnering arrangement with Havens and, possibly, even a buyout, a thought that never left the minds of the Swiss company's leadership and board.

"Thank you, Niko, and welcome again to our US partners both in Belmont and those in our major investor-owners, Brent and Lucas Holdings. Very briefly, I will say a few things about the work being done here and in the US regarding the cocoa bean genome. At the moment, the principal focus of this work is crop protection. There are some six million farmers of cocoa bean worldwide, but quite obviously, many are inefficient and subject to massive losses from the common fungal diseases that often destroy crops before harvest.

"In the US, the lead investigators in this scientific effort are at the MIT laboratories, where US Department of Agriculture funds, along with smaller contributions from Havens and from Belmont, underwrite most of the research. And I add that as this objective goes, the research is progressing quite nicely. Today, we have analyzed more than four hundred million parts of the cocoa genome, much of it intended for the Ivory Coast and other growers in Africa, who produce 70 percent of the world's cocoa.

"Please forgive my use of technical language, which I will be happy to explain, if necessary. Right now, we continue sequencing the genotype for cocoa. The genotype is the structure of a specific cell, or a type of gene. Another way to think of it is to designate it as the genotype of the specimen plant. The cocoa genome by the way is many times more complicated than even the human genome. But at the moment, we have released information on sequenced genotype Matina 1-6, which covers 92 percent of the genome and about thirty-five thousand genes.

"The relevance of this research to our business is immediately obvious, and we support it, of course. But think about it for a second. The emphasis is on prevention of fungal diseases that destroy the plant. We at Belmont want to take this research much, much further. We believe we can *reproduce the cocoa bean, synthetically,*" Smit said as the large room became starkly quiet, enough so that individual breathing could be heard.

Former New Jersey senator Jeff Scharfman, now president of Lucas under the leadership of CEO Nikos Rallis and a board member of Belmont, raised his hand, then spoke without awaiting Smit's acknowledgment of it. He had heard Smit's explanation of the synthetic bean genome that had been presented to the Belmont board several weeks earlier. "Marc, I think it's important for all to know that this is our ultimate backup plan from a strategic standpoint."

Rallis intervened. "Allow me, please, Marc, to address that comment. What Jeff is saying is that our bargaining strategy in effecting the partnership with Rose and Havens in the US, and ultimately expanding Belmont's market there, could depend on the availability of a synthetic bean, provided it has the scientific properties that would allow for Belmont to operate even if the organic cocoa bean crop is diminished or even lost entirely. Moreover, of course, the quality of the synthetic substitute is important, especially when it comes to the attributes, such as end-product taste pleasing to the consumer."

"And we must be able to use the synthetic substitute in the production process," Smit added, "which is to say that chemically, the molecular structure of the substitute must be amenable to our current production processes. The synthetic substitute's properties important to us in this regard are temperature and physical transformations regarding solids, liquids, and even gasses, for example. Also, we have to consider what type of changes would have to be made to our production equipment and whether the comparative cost of those changes would justify use of the substitute.

"Therefore, we are following closely the research done on the disease repellant because the millions of parts of the genome that are being discovered in that effort will include those that are critical to our synthesis. The synthetic research will probably be done in Switzerland at ETH but with the cooperation of an American partner, if we can be assured of confidentiality." Smit concluded, nodding to Rallis that he had finished.

"Exactly. This information is highly confidential and important enough to be covered by the nondisclosure clauses in each our employment contracts, including my own," Rallis said to the scattered pockets of laughter at the large table.

"This concludes the first of what will be several plenary sessions over the next year as the strategic plan is being implemented," Rallis said.

There was an upbeat mood evident throughout the room. Smiles, handshakes, and pats on the shoulders and backs were everywhere as the assembled parties fractioned off in twos and threes, walking toward the door or standing apart from the table. Rallis, Castignani, and Guillermo joined the several Swiss attendees while Thompson seemed to be the pivot point for many US members of the several companies.

*   *   *

At the lunch that followed, there were animated discussions of compensation, competition, the genome issue, and even living conditions in Switzerland, which the Americans were finding to be much better than anticipated. But as the talking drifted to the next step, control over the trading of cocoa on the several global commodity exchanges, the conversations became more serious.

Paul von Schlossen, the chairman and CEO of Brent – the company that would be the linchpin in maintaining the complex cocoa market capture – had signaled earlier to Belmont's Gorgens and Smit that he wished a private meeting. Gathered in Gorgens's elaborately furnished office just above the conference room, the three men sat facing one another in a semicircle with a coffee table in front of them.

"*Die habe ich nicht gekauft* [I don't buy it]," said Lutz Gorgens, the Belmont chairman and CEO. The three German-speaking Swiss executives then switched to English, an increasingly common occurrence in European business circles.

"Belmont's taking the larger part of the risk. The entire company could be in jeopardy if this effort fails. Yet for this level of exposure, the rewards, in my judgment, are not sufficient," Gorgens added.

"*Haben sie den Brief geschrieben?* [Have you written the letter?]" asked von Schlossen, speaking in German for purposes of emphasizing his opening comment.

"If you mean the letter to the finance ministry, the answer is no. I wanted to discuss this further before taking that step," Gorgens replied.

"When we spoke last in the conference call, we decided we would ask the government if the Swiss chocolate industry is a so-called protected legacy of our culture," Gorgens continued, referring to a method used by some countries to lessen competition with some of their historically important, or "legacy," industries. The Japanese have protected rice and the French certain agricultural products from trade competition, claiming potentially ruinous results. The World Trade Organization (WTO) rules allow for some exceptions.

"My fear is that just asking the question, especially in writing, poses some risk for us. The ministry folks will wonder why we're asking the question and what we're up to," Gorgens said.

"But we have the deputy finance minister, Frau Hochdorf, on our board of directors," replied von Schlossen. "If we raise the issue at a board meeting, we disclose the same risk to the American board member at Brent. Frau Hochdorf is also on the boards of Lucas Holdings and your own company, Lutz. As the Swiss government's board member, the letter to the ministry would almost certainly be referred to her anyway."

"But you see, we're creating a board within a board here with the Swiss members acting on a potentially different agenda and one that the American members may not like," Gorgens said.

"Rallis has told me several times that the Americans want two things, a presidential pardon and the wealth that we're creating for them. If they don't get the pardon, they're not going to care much about what happens to the two US chocolate companies. In fact, Rallis has said that Guillermo fully understands that Belmont's investment in Rose and Havens may ultimately result in full acquisition. He also understands that the two US companies must perform, and if they don't, they risk the same consequences as any other business, to include bankruptcy," von Schlossen said.

"*Es ist wahr* [it is true], Paul, but that is not our scheme. My plan for Belmont is to dominate the US market, to replace the market power of both Rose and Havens. We are not going to *await* poor performance by our competitors. We are going to make it happen," Gorgens said emphatically.

"*Wir selbst warden dies machen. Ich habe beide manner gesehen* [we ourselves are going to make this happen, I have seen both men], Guillermo and Rallis," Gorgens said, again speaking in German to punctuate his remarks. "They told me that if the president fails to grant the pardon, this may be the outcome. Don't you see? The Americans are using us to avenge these others who were wrapped up in the Lucas scandal regarding that project on Santorini."

"If I may, Herr Chairman?" Marc Smit, the Belmont president, asked.

"*Bitte* [please], Marc," Gorgens replied, encouraging his subordinate to speak.

"We believe that, either way, we hold the trump card. Our products are superior to anything made in the US, and we can produce it there or in our factories in Eastern Europe at competitive prices, made even more so with the help of Brent in successfully controlling the availability of cocoa. Moreover, we are much more advanced in cocoa bean research at a time when the conventional bean is more exposed than ever to feverish fungal diseases.

"It is another way of saying that time is on our side. Even if the pardon fails, the Americans on our staffs are being well compensated. They're just not likely to abandon us, I believe, especially when their reputations in the US continue to be rather questionable," Smit concluded.

"Marc makes good sense. He has lived in the US and understands the American mentality well," von Schlossen replied.

"What I do know, gentlemen, is that Americans do not generally sell their country short. I know that here in Switzerland we see much the opposite with many Americans in our financial sector shorting the dollar, as well as many on Wall Street and elsewhere shorting industries in a way that hastens their demise in some cases. I'm thinking of the banking crisis back in 2008, when everyone shorted Bear Stearns and Lehman Brothers, which made their recovery all but impossible. I see the Americans on our staffs acting the same way. As long as they are compensated well, they will go along with our plans," Smit concluded.

"I don't pretend to have Marc's grasp of the American mentality or the country's financial scene. But I still don't see the Americans on our staffs engaging in destroying their own chocolate industry even out of vengeance. These are men who held high elective offices, one even a former secretary of treasury. They must have a much higher level of patriotism," Gorgens replied.

"Marc's point, Lutz, is that they *will not have had to act out of vengeance* if the takeover of the two US companies and even their demise are legitimate, sensible, and prudent business-based decisions. Moreover, the letter to the Swiss ministry of finance becomes little more than an option for us to remove the Americans from our staffs if they become obstacles to our plans. As a legacy company, we can put in place an entirely Swiss management structure without running afoul of the WTO rules," von Schlossen said with a tone of conclusiveness that seemed to bring a mutually satisfactory end to the meeting. The letter would be sent.

CHAPTER 9

SHAKING UP WASHINGTON

S UE COHEN, CHIEF OF STAFF TO PRESIDENT EARL EASTWOOD, HAD WORKED WITH HIM FOR SEVERAL YEARS, HAVING BEEN THE PRESIDENT'S TOP STAFFER WHEN HE WAS SENATE MINORITY LEADER. She was acknowledged as one of the most powerful women in Washington and not only because of her access to the president, which was certainly the principal source of her influence on the political system. Sue possessed a quick and alert mind, of course. She was personable and inviting and enjoyed a fair social life despite the near impossibility of any real privacy. Now thirty-seven, she was very attractive. But not unlike many other highly successful women, she had built-in safeguards that filtered out suitors who pursued her to get closer to the seat of authority. Regrettably, there were too few of the ones who had the self-confidence, suitability, and even courage to approach her socially.

She had slipped into a few trysts with influential men from the private community and even one from Congress. All were married, making highly suspicious claims of imminent separation from their wives that Sue was wise enough to doubt. She found little compensatory comfort in her work, too often too intense to even allow time to think of her personal interests. But she did find herself increasingly sensitive to witnessing the pleasure of women, some like herself, coupled in relationships of many varieties. On weekends, or late at night, she would find herself relatively secluded, isolated really, apart from what she knew she strongly desired when momentary lulls in her busy life brought out such basic instincts.

Her substantial power, influence, and authority, the three fundamental sources of eminence in politics were not enough, she had begun to realize. They were not substitutes for the simple pleasures of companionship, a loving and caring male partner, even a family, and the threatened maternal instinct that never stopped gnawing at her conscience. *The damnation of the ovary-blessed*, she would occasionally muse to herself.

Her behavior could become parabolic at times in this regard. The job called for a public persona that masked toughness. She would sometimes catch herself drifting toward an unwelcome compromise on an issue when suddenly, although, rarely she could be distracted by a likeable male opponent. More alarmingly, her immediate attention had become spotlighted on the junior Connecticut senator, Zbigniew Krakowski. The two talked frequently on the phone, Krakowski pressing hard for more presidential involvement in the Swiss investment in the two dominant US-based confectioners, Rose of Bridgeport and Havens in Newtown Highlands, Massachusetts. Krakowski was urging changes in regulatory policy that would ultimately diminish possible antitrust obstacles as the Swiss moved into the US market via their large investment in the two US companies. This was the subject of a telephone conversation on Monday, March 21, 2011.

"Sue, I know the banking crisis has heightened public demands for tighter regulation, but it doesn't reach to the issue before us regarding the chocolate industry," Krakowski was saying.

"Zbig, I'm aware of the differences. My point is that, at this moment, there is an appearance of lax government regulation, and that image will become stronger as this integration of the world's largest set of confectioners begins to form in the minds of the public," she replied.

"But that may be good because, as I see it at least," Krakowski said, trying to be very civil, "the public will not be focused on the industries they trust but on the ones they have grown to dislike, namely banks, the pharmaceuticals, and insurance companies. The chocolate industry? C'mon, Sue. As long as the product is desirable, safe, and has a competitive price point, the consumer is not going to see a fantasy that isn't there, like market domination by the Swiss."

"Let me put it another way, Zbig. Connecticut's great industrial strength at the moment is in the sectors of insurance and, more recently, pharmaceuticals as the so-called pharma coast has prospered along Long Island Sound. If the public is angered over a confection dynasty with foreign roots and the demand for tighter controls over that sector extends to pharmaceuticals and insurance, Connecticut, *your* state, Zbig, will suffer more," Sue countered.

"I doubt a scenario like that. It's too structured in our dynamic economic climate. Let's be realistic. If Connecticut holds dominant market power in these sectors, like insurance and pharma, and good-paying jobs result, they're not gonna give a hoot. But we're not about to allow any type of Swiss takeover of the US chocolate industry anyway.

"Let me get to the point. If a Swiss takeover were a threat, there is enough political clout in the New England delegation to organize a government rescue – okay, call it a bailout – in much the same way we just rescued the auto industry," Krakowski said with some firmness.

Sue was not easily persuaded. "I can't believe what you're saying, Zbig. The auto industry, technically, had been put in bankruptcy by the government because without the rescue monies, it would have collapsed. Do you want government management of Connecticut companies?"

"Of course not. I'm sayin' that *in the event* that the choice was between a Swiss takeover and bankruptcy, a government loan would avert both. I don't see the bailout as having created a technical bankruptcy," he said emphatically.

"Tell that to the shareholders of Bear Stearns or Lehman. They were the ones who were screwed as were the Citibank shareholders, who lost their dividends when the government took over the bank. Holders of common stock are last in the restitution line," Sue replied.

"Besides," she continued, "what the president is fighting at the moment is the attempt by the liberal wing of the party to convert regulation into domination so that the traditional firewall between applying the basic rules of regulatory policy are replaced by government making business decisions, like control over executive pay that my mindless Democratic colleagues in the House are demanding."

"Well, we both don't want that. I'll tell you what, you and I need to discuss this on our own time, although I'm sure that, for both of us, we don't own any time," Zbig said to Sue's chuckle.

"That's for sure," she added, thinking, *I'd like to see him socially. He's a Republican. That would cause a bit of a stir. But on the other hand, others might see it as a strictly social relationship and take some pressure off both us. He's a smart, good-looking guy. Since he made the offer, I won't worry about his reported relationship with the governor.* Sue reminded herself that Connecticut governor Sophia Kallias and the young senator had been romantically linked for several years.

"You know, that's an offer I'm not going to refuse, and I might add, there are few offers in this place that we don't reject," she said, trying to put a different face on her intentions.

"Listen, it's Monday, a dead day. I don't have any votes tomorrow. Let's get together tonight. How do we do that? Do I pick you up at your place, the White House, or what?" Krakowski asked.

Sue had been through this routine a couple of times. She was a high visibility figure and, like many high-office holders, presumed to be a target of some deranged mind somewhere. The Secret Service provided a security detail that would have to be consulted. It went with the territory, the job.

"The best thing is to have me meet you, wherever, then you can take me home. My security detail monitors everything I do until I get in my apartment."

At seven that evening, Krakowski stood in the doorway of Washington's most expensive and luxurious restaurant, Four Sails, owned by a Swiss businessman living in Bermuda and commuting to Washington. Simon Walters was offered $10 million from several Saudi investors to create the best restaurant in the nation's capital. Walters had much success in the business. A sister Four Sails restaurant was the best in Bermuda, and two other dining establishments owned by him in London were frequent stops for throngs of Arab visitors and residents. Four Sails was in a structure that was designed by McKim, Mead, and White, who dominated the architectural landscape at the turn of the twentieth century. Originally a private residence for a one-term member of Congress from Utah who had made a fortune in mining, the place had fallen into disrepair and was on its last legs as a nightclub when rescued by Walters.

Walters put $2 million of his own funds into the restoration of Four Sails Washington, elevating it to the lead among the upper-end dining establishments in the city. The place was highly attractive to public figures who sought privacy. The downstairs bar was lit dimly, making it impossible without night vision glasses to detect who was sitting with whom at whatever tables. Even the bartender seemed to be a denizen of the dark, a gnomelike pale figure with long fingers that sometimes could be found tapping out popular sing-along tunes on the Wurlitzer piano planted in the corner.

Krakowski watched as the Secret Service GMC drove into the small horseshoe drive to the front door. Spotting Krakowski, Sue sat patiently as the doorman approached the vehicle. He was immediately intercepted by a Secret Service agent, who jumped from the front seat, thanking the doorman, and opened the door for Sue himself. The doorman, quite accustomed to yet another Washington charade, stepped back, his amusement evident, and was rewarded as Sue slipped a five-dollar bill into his hand. Escorting Sue up the short canopy-covered staircase to the front door, the Secret Service agent delivered her to Krakowski, who gave her a quick hug and greeting. The agent positioned himself at a discrete distance after they had settled in the darkened downstairs bar.

Krakowski had performed his own reconnaissance of the bar beforehand and had guided her to a corner table across the room but on the same side as the piano.

"Ya gotta love these guys," Krakowski said, nodding unnoticeably toward the agent, now seated some distance from them. "Must put a cold blanket on your social life," he added with a chuckle.

"I don't know. It's rather nice to realize you're never alone," she said to their mutual laughter.

"I'll opt for loneliness anytime, thank you." They both laughed again.

"It's good to see you, well, I should say to *have seen* you. I can barely see my hand. I'll light the wick on the table light," Krakowski said, picking up the box of matches placed there for that purpose.

As the wick thrived with flame, the faces of the twosome came into better view. Both had much the same thought, finding the other rather refreshingly attractive. Krakowski moved from his place across the table to one at Sue's right elbow, a gesture which she welcomed.

"I've not been here before, but I know now why it's such a big hit, especially down here in the bar. This is a town where egos, especially those of the male variety, sometimes operate best in the dark," she added.

"Hey, keeping things in the dark is what this town's all about," Krakowski wisecracked.

"So getting together here is just a continuation of your busy day of keeping everything in the dark," Sue lamely joked, then said to herself, *Stupid comment. He'll think I'm accusing him of cheating on Sophia.*

It was exactly the way Krakowski interpreted Sue's comment. "If you mean Sophia," he said, "I don't cheat, and I'm not now. First, this is a friendly business meeting, and second, even if it were something else, I have no commitment to Sophia nor she with me that interferes with our separate social lives."

"Actually, that isn't what I meant, but I can see that it was easily misconstrued. Sorry," Sue said, feeling somewhat awkward.

The two returned to their earlier discussion regarding possible antitrust issues pertaining to the chocolate industry. It was a friendly chat through drinks and dinner, lasting over two hours. From time to time, to make a point, Sue would lightly touch his hand, a gesture that Zbig began to return. As the conversation drifted to talk of personalities, the bartender sat down at the piano, turned a small light on above the keyboard, and played light Sinatra favorites. When he started to play "Chicago," Zbig suggested they dance on the small wooden dance platform half an inch above the floor.

"Smooth, Zbig," Sue said as he pulled her along a foxtrot routine with added promenades and twirls. They both seemed to enjoy the "sweetheart" move, entangling their hands and arms in a way that brushed their hips together. Sue found the sensation rather arousing as did Zbig, who was thinking, *She's got a great body and moves fluidly. She must be in great shape.*

"How do you keep yourself so fit in that place?" he asked.

"Oh, I swim every day, either in the Gerald Ford pool in the White House or at the Watergate Health Club, when I can get over there," she replied.

As the piano sounded out the jaunty "New York, New York," the two sang, Zbig dipping her at inflective points in the music as the two laughed.

The music stopped, and the two returned to their table.

"Do you realize we've been here three and one-half hours? It's past ten thirty," Sue said, adding, "But I have to say, I barely noticed the time. I have to get my security detail home."

"Okay, so as I understand it, I'll drive you home," Zbig said.

"Right, if that's okay."

"Sure, what does the security guy do?" he asked.

"He'll follow us to my apartment, then leave."

Sue and Zbig stood up; he paid the bill as they continued making preparations to leave. The Secret Service agent darted to the staircase ahead of them, escorting them to Zbig's car at the rear of the restaurant. The two drove off with the large Secret Service van behind them, moving straight up Connecticut Avenue from the restaurant's location at corner of Connecticut Avenue and Twentieth and R. Streets in the northwest section of Washington.

They pulled into the drive in front of Sue's elegant apartment building, one dating back to the gothic revival period of the early 1900s, the big black SUV behind them adding to the somber, if not funereal, architectural setting.

"Why don't you come up? I'll show you how the other half lives," she offered.

"Will the security guy allow that?" Zbig asked, his brow furrowed.

"Allow *what*?" Sue replied with a grin. They both laughed, hard.

"Talk about misconstrued comments," he added to their continuing laughter.

He parked the car; they dismounted and walked toward the door, the same security agent ahead of them. As they reached the elevator, he turned, saying, "Good night, Senator. I'll see you in the morning at seven, Ms. Cohen. Have a good evening."

The two got in the elevator, riding to the third floor. Sue guided him to her apartment door as they chatted about the corridor's decor and elegance. Entering the apartment, partially lit, Sue turned to him.

"I really had a great time, Zbig. I barely get a chance to do anything like this," she said.

"We need to do it again. We gotta get a rumor mill cranked up. You know, Republican senator seen with president's biggest wig," he said as he leaned down somewhat, his face on his tall frame encountering hers, as he kissed her gently on her welcoming lips.

Sue was electrified by the touch of his lips, her neck softly arching back as the kiss lingered. *How nice, so gentle*, she thought. She made no attempt to ease out of his light embrace, her arms now resting on his shoulders.

"Yes, I'd like to see you again. This town can handle another rumor," she said as they disengaged, and she walked him to the door. They pecked each other once good-bye, and he left.

As she puttered about, preparing for another stressful day, she sensed a certain calmness. *This could work if he feels the same way, and I think he does. I'll need to talk to Earl . . . Well, maybe not yet. I might be a little presumptuous.*

On Tuesday, just before lunch, as Sue was thumbing through the calls on her Blackberry, the number of which she had given Krakowski, she saw that he had called. *I have to run to lunch. I don't have time for a lengthy call . . . But he'll understand. No, I'll call him.*

"Thanks for calling me back," Krakowski said. "Look, no groans, moans, hesitations, apologies, or anything but straightforwardness – I want to see you again. Can we do the same routine tonight?"

Why is he so eager, too soon, to get together again, tonight? Wednesday is a heavy day normally, she thought, but the impulse was too strong.

"Yes, it was nice. I think I can do it, but it might be later. Let me get back to you," she said.

*   *   *

Ultimately, Sue found herself slipping into a closer relationship with Zbigniew Krakowski, four years her junior and a freshman Republican senator from Connecticut. For the next two weeks, they saw each other several times, even passing a weekend engaged in the many daytime activities of the capital area. The romantic dimension grew naturally stronger although they had yet to spend a night together.

March 31 was a busy Thursday with Congress as well as senior administration officials struggling to pass a defense budget while essentially maintaining last year's spending levels as several "continuing resolutions" kept the government functioning in the absence of a fiscal year 2011 federal budget, now an incredible six months overdue. The April Easter recess would start soon, and plans were being made for dozens of congressional visits throughout the globe and a series of foreign trips to be undertaken by President Eastwood.

It was late morning this day when the president was wrapping up an Oval Office meeting; he had asked the secretaries of state and treasury, as well as National Security Adviser Bill Stokes and Attorney General Jack Hammond to linger for a few minutes as the room cleared.

"Jack," President Eastwood started, "what's goin' on with this Swiss 'invasion,' if you'll excuse the term?"

"You mean who's fudging, sir?" Hammond said to the general laughter in the room. "Well, as Sue no doubt reported, the Swiss group, which uses Bob Castignani as their lobbyist, has organized the New England Industrial Association, which has not-for-profit status. Right, Lou?" – he nodded to Treasury Secretary Louis Dubin, who returned an affirmative nod – "And has met with the senior members of the several New England states that could benefit from the promise of jobs to be added to the Massachusetts and Connecticut companies that they want to partner with."

"Has Bob registered as a lobbyist?" the president asked.

Hammond answered, "Yes, but there's an odd twist to this. There are three Swiss companies involved here. They're all private, nonlisted, and therefore traded only on the secondary or private market. They all have substantial Swiss government ownership interest. And that's what makes this interesting. Castignani is registered under the Lobbying Disclosure Act for Lucas Holdings but as a foreign agent for the other two companies, Belmont and Brent. Lucas has less than 20 percent foreign government ownership, but the other two have substantial government interest, 29 percent in Brent and 25 percent in Belmont. As a registrant under the Foreign Agents Registration Act, FARA, Castignani has much more operational latitude than under the lobbying act."

"And I assume it's Belmont that's really our greatest interest?" the president asked.

"Right, sir, but we also want to know more about Brent since they're the commodity traders," Hammond replied. "The two have interlocking directorates, ownerships, and even operations that are not very transparent under these conditions."

"Lou, what's in it for the Swiss government? Is there a tax benefit?" the president asked, turning to his treasury secretary.

"The tax gains for the Swiss are not exceptional. Obviously, the government is an investor expecting a nominal return, but that seems to be more important to them than a tax windfall," Dubin replied. "Moreover, the companies will be liable for taxes on any US-based earnings that are reaped from their partnership arrangements in the US."

"What troubles me is why the Swiss are making what is emerging as a major player in our chocolate market when the gains are not spectacular," Eastwood responded.

"And it bothers me, Mr. President," Hammond added. "Something unusual is also happening. The two US companies, Rose and Havens, have fired their Washington lobbyists. Dom Guillermo mentioned this rather offhandedly in a telephone conversation on a slightly different topic."

"Yeah, I agree. It doesn't make sense. They need representation here more than ever for this deal. There are a lot of complexities, including possible antitrust issues," Eastwood added.

"It's not so much the antitrust issue, at least yet. That picture may come into later focus, however. But they are shaking up this town when they substitute their congressional members for their lobbyists," Hammond said.

Zbig never said a word about that, Sue thought, *and we talked quite a bit about the benefits for Connecticut from the chocolate companies' mergers, or possible merger.*

"How the devil can that work, Jack? Members are not likely to be out peddling the interests of the two chocolate companies . . . Or are they?" Eastwood said after a thoughtful pause.

"I think you see it too, Mr. President. It's a hell of a lot easier for members to get access to administration officials, other members, and even the White House. And if there is an EU issue, they can talk to key parties in Brussels a lot more easily than a typical lobbyist," Hammond replied.

"I see. I also smell something I don't like. The three Swiss companies are loaded with former members of Congress, all making a hell of a lot more than they would by slogging it out in the already-overcrowded, highly competitive lobbyist market in Washington. I knew that would happen. What do we have, over 1,000 former members out there hustling business?" Eastwood asked.

"It's actually over 1,200, and that doesn't include former staff members, who usually have the technical knowledge members depend on. Up until about a decade ago, the staffers became lobbyists, using their former bosses' influence for access and assistance throughout government and the Congress. Some even set up reserve funds and hired their former bosses, paying a hiring bonus from the funds, which was illegal as hell but impossible to enforce. They also hired their wives and other family members in many cases.

"It took a while, but the members finally realized they could make some of this big money and grabbed a lot of business from the staffers, many of whom are back working for their former bosses, but in lobbying offices now," Hammond added.

Hammond continued. "Getting back to this particular situation, Rose and Havens have taken experienced executives from their staffs, put them on paid sabbatical, and placed them in key congressional offices as interns. This provides instant expertise at no cost to the member. Is the member getting some type of promise or even a gratuitous job offer from this arrangement? My off-the-record answer is 'probably.'"

"So these guys think they've found a way to bypass the lobbyists' lobby. Boy, are they in for some heat," the president said with a light laugh.

"It's already happening, Mr. President," Hammond said. "The lobbyists are themselves organized, and their association executive director has called me. He wants us to investigate but to keep the lobbyists' fingerprints far away from the request or the future query. They know they're on very dangerous grounds here since they're attacking the members who are engaging in this ruse."

"And you're not doing anything more than enforcing existing law, is that right, Jack?" the president asked.

"Right, sir. I'm not avoiding a fight. I just don't have anything close to the reliable level of information that I need to even suggest a breach of law," Hammond replied.

Eastwood laughed softly, then said, "You know, I suspect this problem will solve itself. We don't need to point fingers. The lobbyist community will do it for us, and the media will have a story being developed by others for them. Just keep following this closely, Jack. Besides, the lobbyist community may find that even if they succeed in getting a DOJ investigation, they would almost invariably end up indicting themselves. Much of the inquiry would inevitably disclose some of their own shady practices." Most in the room also laughed.

Sue, however, was neither smiling nor laughing. She had not yet told the president about her relationship with Krakowski. *I just don't think Zbig would do this to me. But come to think of it, even though we've been close, there's still no real sex between us, and we've seen each other ten or more times. Is Kallias behind this, a conspiracy between the two of them to get the state's interest better protected at the White House level?* But privately, Sue doubted the governor of Connecticut would sacrifice her solid reputation for integrity and risk losing Zbig, her "former" lover.

CHAPTER 10

ANY PORT IN A STORMY MARKET

THE MAJOR FUTURES CON-TRACTS ON COCOA BEANS WOULD EXPIRE ON THURSDAY, APRIL 14, 2011. THIS WOULD BE D-DAY, THE LONG-AWAITED LAUNCH OF THE MINUTELY PLANNED USURPATION OF THE GLOBAL COCOA SOURCES FEEDING THE US CONFECTIONS INDUSTRY. At 4:00 a.m. in New York and Toronto, and 9:00 a.m. in London, Brent trading staffs were poised to act as the trading begun. The news was now out that the entire cocoa crop of the Ivory Coast would not be traded. The loss of the world's greatest source of cocoa to the trading exchanges had the expected result. The futures contracts, which always traded in US dollars, had been placed at $2,662 per metric ton.

Paul von Schlossen, Niko Rallis, and Domenic Guillermo were glued to the trading monitors at the Brent Swiss headquarters in Chamby, Switzerland. They barely noticed the glorious sunrise over Lake Geneva as the charts on the screens scattered equation-driven curves across their monitors.

"Good grief!" Guillermo exclaimed. "Look at this opening, will you?"

"*Yah, das is gut,*" von Schlossen said smilingly in German. "It is as we planned. As you can see, the price is at $3,600 per ton and climbing rapidly, and it's only less than a half hour of trading." Turning to the closed network screen of activity on the Intercontinental Exchange floors in London, New York, and Toronto, he added, "As you can see, it's bedlam in the pits." Actually, the so-called pits, where traders frenetically scream buy-and-sell offers, barely exist anywhere anymore, having been replaced by quieter and much more efficient big-frame IBM computers that spew millions of trades in seconds. Chicago, however, is somewhat of an exception.

The interoffice screen on the wall came to life. It was the image of former Connecticut senator Sam Schlesinger, now managing Brent's New York commodity trading office in the World Financial Center. Schlesinger had instantaneous contact with Brent traders everywhere on the globe.

"Gentlemen, we are executing well here. The speculators are taking their profits, unwinding their positions, and jumping out of the market."

"What, no shorting contracts or positions, Sam?" von Schlossen asked.

"Not yet anyway. There's too much uncertainty, at least that's what I'm being told by our floor traders. The pits are in turmoil. Speculators can't figure out what the strife in Ivory Coast is doin' to the market, but they know profits when they see them, and they're taking them and running," Schlesinger replied.

"That's okay. We're still gaining, but I always like making money on contract trades too. Sam, I suggest that we moderate prices by tomorrow to encourage the speculators and hedgers to get back in the futures markets. Otherwise, the regulators will get all over us. They may even shut down traders if the circuit breakers kick in," von Schlossen directed.

"That's our plan, Paul. We'll start selling at a lower price, maybe $3,200 per metric ton. Let people know there's availability and hope that the release of these small quantities will excite the hedgers, especially since they need cocoa for their own uses."

"Good morning, Sam," said Guillermo as his image popped up on Schlesinger's screen in New York City. "Our concern is the other thousands of small cocoa users. Altogether, they make up 40 percent of the market compared to the 60 percent market share and demand represented by Rose and Havens. But we don't want them, because of their numbers, to start bugging Congress for more regulations or investigations."

"Right, Dom. I spoke to Bob last night," Schlesinger replied, referring to Castignani, who was already in his Washington office. "He's ready and assured me that with the New England congressional delegation now acting as our lobbyists for Rose and Havens, they can keep the regulators at bay . . . That's something no ordinary lobbyist could have done without arousing a lot of media attention. But he did say that the lobbyist community is mad as hell with the two companies sidestepping the established lobbying routines. That's gonna have political ramifications, that's for sure."

"I agree, but let's not sweat that issue just yet," Guillermo replied.

As they spoke, the image of former Michigan congressman Jarrett Rodman appeared on a companion closed network screen. Rodman, speaking from his office in the Exchange Tower on Toronto's King Street, where he was overseeing Brent's operations at the Intercontinental Exchange offices there, had much the same report.

"Mornin', gentlemen. I saw Sam's report. It's the same deal here. Speculators, especially the big money in South American customer bases like Sao Paolo and Quito, are taking profits like crazy and also holding off on new options. I agree that they want to watch for a while, not being sure if they can risk shorting this market. I'll ensure that we follow Sam's lead in offering lower costs for our future contracts to get the traders back in the game."

The last report to Brent headquarters came in almost simultaneously from Brent's London chief, former Virginia senator Mark Baldwin. "We're cool here, guys, so far anyway. The EU is a little worried about their share of the Ivory Coast crop now that we've cornered it. I'm assuring them that, as we had planned, there would be no change or any amount less than the 376 tons they received from the last seasonal crop. Both my contacts on the London International Futures and Options Exchange and the Paris Exchange have been all over me this morning. I think they're satisfied that they'll have their usual 54 percent of the Ivory Coast crop as well as no interference from us with the 425 tons they traditionally get from Ghana."

"But what are they saying about prices, Mark?" asked von Schlossen.

"They know there's gonna be a premium, and I suggested $3,220 per metric ton after hearing Sam's report. That gives us incredible margins, something like 21 percent, plus our trade commissions and other service costs related to deliveries and storage and distribution," Baldwin replied.

"And all EU deliveries are made to our distribution and storage facilities in Genova and Switzerland. Is that correct, Mark?"

"Yes, right, Paul. Jarrett in Toronto told me several minutes ago that he's also getting much of the Nigerian crop, about 100 tons, being offered through Canada. That's a bonus for us since the smaller US confectioners will look to Toronto next as a source. He's gonna sell it at gradually rising futures costs, aiming at an ultimate price point of as much as $4,000 a ton," Baldwin replied.

"I'll talk to him. That's not a bad target, and I think we can achieve it. But I want to manage the release of that figure very carefully. Once the US chocolatiers get wind of it, they're going to start looking at us, which is to say Belmont, to license our products rather than attempting to compete with their own. Their production costs will just become unmanageable at the $4,000 level. We don't want to cause panic just yet, but there will be US job losses among the smaller producers. That fact could cause some regulatory interest in what we're doing," von Schlossen cautioned.

*   *   *

Perhaps the greatest flaw in the plan would be found in the next step, linked to von Schlossen's order to lower prices by dumping token amounts of cocoa on the market to meet demand. This occurred on Friday, April 15. With the weekend ahead of them, traders rallied driving the price well above the intraday and two-day "moving average," a series of charted points that depict a trend. With the intraday moving average jumping from $2,660 to $3,220 on Thursday morning, then falling on Friday morning to $2,700 as Brent made token amounts available to the markets, the volatility indices fluctuated wildly and ultimately skyrocketed as speculators leapt back into the fray. Futures contracts were "shorted," meaning some hedgers, those who have a need for cocoa, and speculators, those who just want to make profits, were anticipating a fallback from the now-two-day moving average of $4,000 price per metric ton that cocoa had achieved as the markets closed. The cocoa crop price had now climbed 50 percent above the moving average in slightly more than twenty-four hours.

"Dom, Paul, it's insane," screamed the normally reserved Castignani in his conference call with Guillermo and von Schlossen, who were taking the call at 1:00 a.m., Saturday, April 16, from their Swiss residences.

"The CFTC is gonna be all over this thing by tomorrow morning," Castignani said, glancing at his watch; it was now slightly after 8:00 p.m. eastern standard time in the Washington area.

"We need to get Niko on the call, Bob," said Guillermo. "In the meantime, let's talk a bit. What case can the CFTC make?" he asked, referring to the Commodity Futures Exchange Commission, an independent body charged under the CFTC Act of 1974 with regulating trading on the US futures exchanges.

As Castignani went through the legislative mandate and related enforcement powers of the commission, Niko Rallis came up on the conference call. Always calm and well-armed with facts, Rallis posed a question to Castignani.

"Bob, we anticipated the surge somewhat, but I admit it went well beyond our expectations. I attribute that to our buyout of the Ivory Coast crop. But we are making the crop available, isn't that our defense?" Rallis asked.

"In part, Niko. Brent now controls well over half the US cocoa market, and the company is making some available. The problem is that we have been cashing out futures when the price peaked yesterday and then shorted other futures and took profits when the price went back down. The commission may see the release of cocoa by Brent to the market as just another money-making market manipulation," Castignani replied, now much more settled than initially.

"But that's merely speculation and something that is not disallowed, is that not right, Bob?" Rallis asked.

"It is speculation *and* market manipulation, yes. But in the eyes of the commission, it is the manipulation they will focus on," Castignani answered.

"Describe for me, from a legal perspective, what the likely charges against us could be," Rallis asked.

"Sure, I was on the Senate Commerce Committee for years. I understand the commission's routine, and the law, very well. They will invoke provisions of the Commodity Exchange Act that forbid speculation that is linked to or motivated by manipulation. This will be filed in the US District Court for the Southern District of New York against Brent," Castignani started, then was interrupted by Guillermo.

"Bob, Niko, let me help out here since I have some legal experience on these matters. My practice in New Haven dealt with many of the federal regulatory agencies, including the CFTC. I think our defenses are substantial or can be made that way," Guillermo said.

"First, Brent-USA does not have total control over the cocoa crop. It is shared with the firm's operations in the UK and Toronto. Although that in itself is not a defense, the situation or storage of the crop is, and much of it is stored in Europe. I remind you that the CFTC has jurisdiction over US exchanges, although its legal reach can obviously exceed that, especially where there's some hope of foreign cooperation.

"Second, there is no EU objection or threatened action. I can't see them joining a CFTC action. We've covered our EU friends, ensuring them an uninterrupted flow of product.

"Third, and this is a critical point that Niko and I have discussed before, Brent and Belmont are linked at the waist. In both practice and theory, Brent has a legal need for the product and therefore cannot that easily be designated as some type of speculator or even a hedger acting as a speculator.

"Finally, Bob, I also understand the politics involved here, not as well as you, admittedly, but rather *because* of you. What I'm saying is that we need to exploit your idea regarding the purpose of the New England Industrial Association. The New England delegation, the guys who attended our meeting back in February, what day was it, the third?"

"Right, Dom," Castignani interjected.

Guillermo continued. "We need to get those folks back in the game. That was your plan anyway. My thought, and I leave the strategy to you, is to get to the White House first, then the Congress. What'd ya think, Bob?"

There was a pause; Rallis and von Schlossen, speaking from separate locations as the others, murmured agreement that Castignani needed to act.

"Okay, I think we do have some good defenses. I'll talk to the delegation principals, the ones on the key committees," Castignani replied. "We need to stop a CFTC move."

"Bob, I'd recommend talking to Zbig Krakowski," Guillermo said. "I hear he's been squiring Sue Cohen around. In the meantime, I'll call the Connecticut governor. I can call her at the governor's mansion. I'll ask her to put pressure on Eastwood as well. I'm not being naive on this matter. Eastwood is no pussy. He's gonna see what's up and recognize and, where appropriate, even resist pressure from anyone. But he doesn't need a flap like this when the very effort we're making is promising thousands of new jobs at a time when the economy's in the toilet."

"Okay, I'll get on this right away. I'll have Don and Ben track developments at the CFTC, which I'm sure will be taking some action or making some announcement before markets open on Monday," Castignani said, referring also to partners Don Tranh and Ben Ochs, his firm's principal lobbyists for Lucas, Brent, and Belmont.

*   *   *

It was 2:00 p.m., Saturday, April 16, in Montreux, Switzerland, and 9:00 a.m. in Hartford, Connecticut, when Sophia Kallias picked up the phone in the governor's mansion. Guillermo's name lit up on the oversize caller ID screen.

"Dom, this is no surprise. I'm sitting here reading the *Hartford Courant* and Saturday's *Wall Street Journal*, both of which have covered the cocoa market turmoil. So why am I expecting this call?" she asked with obvious sarcasm in her voice.

"Good morning, Governor. I can see that your political antennae are already abuzz," Guillermo replied.

"Yes, as it is, the previous occupant seems to have left behind some type of global listening devices," she replied to their joint laughter at her rather lame reference to Guillermo's presence in the mansion as the former governor. "So what is going on?"

Guillermo would gradually work his way to the real reason for the call. "I just wanted to check on my dogwoods on the mansion lawn. I hope they're in bloom and you're taking care of them."

"Actually, they're right outside the breakfast area, near my kitchen window. They're rather pinkish but radiate in the morning sun, brightening up the whole room. I trust you're also about to make my day even brighter?" she asked, somewhat directly, her voice dripping satirical irony. They laughed.

"I am indeed, Sophia. I wanted to report that our effort to buy much of the cocoa bean crop is proceeding well. We expect that our offer to partner with Rose Confections in the Bridgeport area will progress and that we will, as planned, be moving much of our production from various Central European plants to Connecticut," Guillermo said.

"The media is saying something that makes me wonder about that. The *Wall Street Journal* says that the market fluctuation suggests manipulation or excessive, even unlawful, speculation and that the commodity police are expected to act over the weekend," Kallias added.

"I'm glad you brought that up. We're not too worried about a CFTC inquiry. We've some pretty solid reasons for being in the market. After all, we are joined with Belmont, the Swiss confectioner, as you know. So we have a need for the crop and are not speculators."

"Good answer, even better, a good defense."

"Furthermore, Brent-USA is not the only trading group involved. There are hundreds of other traders in play, including Brent's overseas subsidiaries. The CFTC's jurisdiction extends only to US exchange activities," Guillermo said, anticipating her follow-on comment.

"That doesn't keep the regulators from charging or prosecuting foreign firms or persons. The Justice Department goes into federal courts all the time with cases like this," she added.

"That's right. The CFTC does pursue foreign speculators in our courts. But we're not speculators, domestic or foreign. And that's one of the reasons I'm calling."

As if I didn't know, Kallias thought to herself somewhat sarcastically. *I can't imagine what he wants now.* Kallias was keeping that thought to herself.

"I think it would be helpful if we got the White House and Congress behind us. What I'm saying is that they need to understand where we're going on this," Guillermo added.

"What's my role, Dom?"

"It's a small part, Sophia. I'd suggest you talk to the president, reminding him that we're legitimate in our efforts, that we're cocoa traders as well as cocoa users, and that stabilizing the cocoa futures market is a critical step to our work in expanding the US chocolate production sector and casting it onto the global stage," Guillermo said with a firm voice.

"I have limits, you know, Dom. You've been in this job. I can't tell the president to stop an investigation by regulators because of my state's interests," she replied equally firmly.

"But you *can* insist that he balance the nation's economic well-being with a reckless, unjustified government action taken to impress the media. The CFTC is also being lobbied by a few rival enterprises that wished they had thought of the same plan. He's saddled his administration with liberals who hate markets anyway, especially traders. The CFTC has several of them as commissioners. They don't seem to distinguish between those of us who are in the commodity markets to ensure a flow of production materials that make and sustain jobs and the wild, speculating, or day-trading communities."

"Well, the liberal wing is doing a good job with the banks. That's the prevalent image among the population. Our constituents are screaming for controls on the markets, commodity, and other financial ones. I'll work on your request anyway. You're right. But I'm a Republican. He can't rely on me for support. Otherwise, the *antagonistas* in your party will think he's joined the other side of the aisle," she said with emphatic use of exaggerated Spanish.

"You're still the governor and of a very important state that seems to survive the economic downturn better than most. Besides, he needs House support for anything he does, and the Republicans control things there. They'd welcome your support. Even if it leaked to the media, which we can assume it will, show me the pundit who's gonna smear you for fighting for jobs for the state," Guillermo argued.

"Keep this in mind, Dom. I've got a lot of my supporters in Fairfield County, many from the financial sector, that's why they live in Connecticut. But I have to balance that cohort with my other constituents, the ones of whose votes I depend for my political life. These are the working folks whose 401(K) and other financial plans have been devastated, they're the majority. My Republican ideology isn't shared by the dominant GOP guys in Congress. This is New England, not Arizona or South Carolina. My political brand is very suspect among party stalwarts outside our geographical region. I have to be very careful when I suddenly start working against regulatory reforms that make for more transparency.

"Despite all this, I'll call Earl. He still got that nostalgic nutmeg blood in his veins. I'm just saying something you already know. He's going to do what in his mind is right. It's not that he's impervious to political exigency. He's figured out how to make the system work by being too smart to short circuit it. My friends tell me that he gets away with things because he's black, and the media won't touch him for fear of appearing racist. That's partially true, and we both know it. The difference is that Earl doesn't depend on that type of suit of armor."

The conversation ended pleasantly. Kallias decided she would call Zbigniew Krakowski first. He could follow up either with Sue Cohen or by sending a note to the president through her. She knew that the president liked Zbig despite his Republican affiliation.

And she realized that he was seeing Sue Cohen, the president's chief of staff. To what extent that relationship had progressed, she was unsure. She had ended her longtime relationship with Zbig, which was now one of mere convenience. That is, they got together when time and circumstances permitted. The hormonal nexus, often frenzied, had ended. Yet they harbored strong feelings for each other. It had just become unworkable for them to the point that her appointment of Krakowski to succeed Eastwood evidenced the distance they mutually agreed to put between them.

*   *   *

It was just after 10:00 a.m.; there was no answer at Krakowski's Washington condominium, except for the voice mail on which Kallias left a message urging him to call her. She pondered the wisdom of calling his Blackberry, thinking that he might have spent the night with Sue Cohen. She suspected from her conversations with Krakowski that the relationship was moving along. But calling him while in her presence? That could be difficult, maybe even emotional for Kallias. She made the call.

Kallias had guessed right. Krakowski was with Sue Cohen at her condominium on Connecticut Avenue. They had spent their first night together and were planning their Saturday morning activities. The president and Audrey Holmes, the Republican congresswoman from Texas who "domesticated" with Eastwood in the White House living quarters, were at Camp David. Sue had a reprieve: a rare weekend out of the office. It would be a special one: the first night together with Krakowski. On Saturday, maybe Sunday, they could act normal like any other couple, visiting the East Market for fresh, organic, and whole foods; a jog or walk together along the canal. Dressed in weekend mufti, baseball or golf hats pulled well over the faces covered in part by sunglasses, they would largely escape notice.

Through this much anticipated plan, as they sipped a final cup of coffee with at least four newspapers spread on the floor around the table and on it, a phone rang. Both snapped to a position of alertness.

"Is that yours or mine?" Sue asked as they both laughed and began fumbling for their Blackberries.

"Mine, I think. Sounds like my call tone," Krakowski said as he reached around to a nearby chair on which hung his blazer, placed there the previous night after they had returned late from dinner and a stroll.

"Hello," Krakowski said, then paused.

"Hello, hello . . . Oh, hi. How are you? Good to hear from you. Yes, I'm just finishing breakfast with a friend. No, I'm not home."

Sue wondered, *I should probably give him some privacy. Who would be asking him if he's home, parents, other family? He'll decide if he needs to talk privately.*

It was at that moment that Krakowski signaled just that: he would take the call to the open balcony off the living room. Talking as he walked, he opened the balcony door. Standing there in jeans and a blue-striped dress shirt with rolled-up sleeves, he shivered briefly as he encountered the still-cool morning air.

"I'm sorry to call so early, especially on a Saturday," the governor was saying at the other end. "I won't ask you where you are or what you're doing," she added.

"Nor would I ask you, Sophia," Krakowski deftly replied.

Oh well, it was to be expected. He's probably at Sue's place or with her elsewhere. I'm sure they're sleeping together by now, anyway. I'm not going to let it get to me, she decided.

"Zbig, I just had a call from Dom Guillermo in Switzerland. He needs our help," Kallias started.

"I'm sure he does. Have you seen the reports on the cocoa trade? The commodity market went nuts yesterday. I'm surprised they didn't stop trading. If they had hoped to avoid arousing the regulators, they sure as hell failed," Krakowski replied.

"That's the issue," Kallias replied. "He wants to me to talk to the president. You know, appeal to his Connecticut roots, urge him to consider the job benefits for Connecticut and New England and to call off the liberal hound dogs on the commission."

"I disagree. That's not a good move for you, Sophia. The political and economic impacts from your intervention are a grasp of the obvious. Of course, you don't want any interference with a market trend that benefits Connecticut. You don't need to tell him that, and Earl is certainly smart enough to know both things: that you don't have to remind him of your interest, which makes your call somewhat irrelevant, and that, as a Republican, opposing oppressive regulatory reform is part of your political makeup.

"Besides, you have a congressional state delegation down here, both Republicans and Democrats, that feels the same way you do. Your call almost certainly would get exposure. Someone will leak it out. You could be embarrassed. I think it's better that you say you're in touch with the congressional delegation on the matter. That's innocuous enough politically. Of course, the media will want to know what we talked about. You can manage that answer easily enough."

Good advice. He cares about me personally and politically. That's probably the best I can hope for right now, Kallias thought. "So you'll caucus with the delegation and get a consensus note or statement to the White House?" she asked.

"Something along those lines, Sophia. I haven't figured out what strategy to pursue just yet," he replied, thinking, *Too many divas in the New England delegation. They're all gonna be humpin' for attention on this one. I need to weigh the prospects of success any way. If I can realistically slow or stop regulatory harassment myself, I'll do it alone. This is gonna be awkward . . . dealing with Sue.*

Connecticut governor Sophia Kallias and Senator Zbigniew Krakowski, her former romantic companion, now the state's senator in Washington, ended their call; both had the same internal conflicts.

In her own mind, Kallias weighed the political consequences of a more passive role with her lingering affection for Krakowski. *Does he really care about me still? Or does he see himself as my successor, taking the lead on a state matter, although at federal level that's appropriate? It could be both. If he does succeed me, we're back here, together again. But it could never be the same. It's over.*

Krakowski, of course, was mired in a three-way conundrum with no easy exits for the thirty-three-year-old bachelor. Any political move he made could be seen as exploitive of one of the two women with whom he was or had been involved. Kallias would suspect, he was sure, that his lead role on the issue was motivated politically. He would have to involve Sue; she was the gatekeeper to the president. Worse, he had just spent the night with her. *There she is, sitting at the table waiting for me to come back,* he thought as he shut down his Blackberry, returning into the warm room from the balcony. *I gotta do what's best for number one,* he had decided, adjusting his countenance to his decision.

"Everything okay?" Sue asked as he took his seat opposite her.

"I wish," he said with a slight smile and barely audible laugh.

"It's reciprocal, I'm sure. If it had been my call, I'd probably be reacting the same way," she said.

Ouch, I haven't concealed my concerns too well. She picked it right up. Maybe I should just deal with it, Krakowski thought.

"Earl knows that we're seeing each other, right?" he asked.

"Yes, I didn't tell him before he learned of it. I'm sure it rattled him a bit. Not that he would involve himself in my personal life, but Washington is the biggest fishbowl in the world. I think he resented it a bit . . . that I didn't tell him I was seeing you," she replied. *I know what he's thinking. I'll bring it up to save him the agony. He's a straight guy. He'll explain himself.*

"And let me add, you can be sure that somewhere along the line he expected that we would have our personal and political lives intersect. Is this one of those moments, Zbig?"

"Yes," came Zbig's pithy, terse reply. *Better to work it out. She's much too smart to be misled, and I'm lousy at deception,* Krakowski thought.

In fact, this very attitude had been instrumental in the breakup with Kallias. They were dating before she had been legally separated and ultimately divorced from her husband, a Boston University economics professor who had stolen funds from a trust fund provided to Sophia by her late father. He was a highly successful Greek immigrant who started a defense-related company in Connecticut. It supplied uniforms to the military, and its highly moisture-resistant tropical field suit garnered him a fortune.

Kallias, like Krakowski, was a Connecticut state senator. Both had political ambitions for higher office and ran as a ticket with Kallias as the gubernatorial candidate and Krakowski as the lieutenant governor. They won the primary and nomination quite easily as they agreed to provide their own financing, a welcome respite for the state Republican Party, whose dwindled resources faced extinction from a race against the immensely popular Democratic incumbent, Domenic Guillermo. Ultimately, as fate would have it, Guillermo's dying wife and a sudden appointment opportunity as the ambassador to the Holy See caused him to quit the race. Rumors continued to fester among state pundits that none other than Earl Eastwood, then the US Senate minority leader, had "arranged" the ambassadorial appointment with the Republican president Bob Davids, who had become Eastwood's close friend. Eastwood, as the rumor persisted, was believed to have seen Guillermo as a highly desirable challenger to his own promised position as vice president on the 2008 presidential ticket.

Kallias had insisted that her trysts with Krakowski be secretive and fashioned absurd and even amateurish contrivances to ensure it, such as lovemaking in their cars, dining in the dozens of out-of-the-way country restaurants in the Hartford region, and having ridiculous disguises and even aliases when traveling together. It was more than Krakowski could bear and directly influenced his surging flirtations with other women. For Kallias, his behavior was an offense to her self-respect that trumped her affection for Krakowski, and she initiated a change in their relationship.

So here he was again, faced with the hated hypocrisy and deception that were so much a part of most politicians' lives. This time, he would not tolerate it.

"Sue, I like what we have here. We've only been seeing each other a few months. But it's working, isn't it?"

Damn, I can't go through this again. I like him, I can't go back. My life was meaningless. She grappled with emotion; her toughness had thickened in the White House, but perhaps not enough, which bothered her.

Her eyes started to moisten, but her voice was firm. She rose. "It's a gift, Zbig, a very special one," she said, walking over to him; he hugged her, his Blackberry still in hand. She eased her head beneath his neck, her face turned to her right as they held on to each other, then released themselves.

Zbig stood back, holding her at arm's length with his hands on her shoulders, his Blackberry awkwardly in hand. "This is something serious that we need to talk about," he said as he sat her down in his chair, then pulled hers from the other side of the table so that they could sit facing each other with good and deliberate eye contact.

"That was Sophia," Zbig said. "She wants me to talk to the president about the cocoa market crisis."

"You mean, she wants you to use me to get the message to him whatever it is?"

"Not quite, that's neither her idea nor mine, and it's not what we talked about," he said, feeling refreshingly honest, which was quickly sensed by the highly intuitive Sue Cohen.

"Guillermo called her from Switzerland. He warned her that aggressive regulatory intervention in the cocoa market now could jeopardize the partnership with the two New England chocolate producers. You know, what we talked about at the New England Industries Association meeting with Bob Castignani in February."

"Sure, I remember it well. And I anticipated this type of problem as you'll recall my mentioning it to both Castignani and Guillermo," Sue replied.

"I wasn't part of that conversation, but Guillermo did tell me about it later. But, Sue, I want you to know that when I first asked you out, I did so in consideration of using you as my pipeline to the Oval Office."

"No kidding, yours and just about every other social invitation that I get," Sue replied to their laughter, which lightened the conversation. Sue thought, *I like what's coming next.*

"It's now more than that. What I said last night, in bed, I meant it." He took her hand as he leaned forward.

"My problem is I have a political duty, and there's an appearance that I'm abusing our relationship in performing it."

Sue tightened her grip on his hand. "It's my problem too, Zbig. I don't know if I can recuse myself. My hope is that when I tell Earl, he will accept my explanation, knowing very well that I have always been totally loyal to and honest with him. At the same time, knowing Earl as I do, he may tell me that I too have obligations to him and to the office that I hold. Whether he will allow me to recuse myself from this particular issue is something I can't guess right now. It would depend on how important the matter is to him. He will need reliable counsel, and that's what my job description calls for."

"I can't and won't ask you to put your career in suspension for my sake, Sue."

"To be frank, Zbig, I'm not so sure I would do that as much as I feel so strongly about you."

"We both need to think it through. Let's begin with your explanation to Earl and along the lines we both discussed, which is to say that we have strong affections for each other and both conscientiously want to avoid a conflict of interest."

"I'll do that. For the moment, don't give me anything more on the issue. I want to tell Earl that we did not discuss it in detail. It's not too hard to conjure up what Guillermo wants us to do," Sue concluded.

The two felt liberated; the conversation was open, honest, and heartfelt and gave both a good feeling toward each other, strengthening their growing bond, which quietly pleased them.

* * *

It was late Sunday afternoon, April 17, 2011, when Sue and Zbig finally parted; there had been no further discussion of the cocoa market crisis or even pillow talk on work matters during their second night together. Sue reveled in the temporary release from the persistent stress that underwrote everything she did in life, but she missed it, strangely.

I can't shake it off. I love everything about it. I think I love Zbig. These past few days seem to have cemented us together. We're thinking alike, share many values. There's the religion difference, not an issue for either of us. We both emerged from happily liberalized communities in that regard. He has a future in Congress, maybe beyond even as a Republican. That's a real issue, not an unmanageable one, especially after the administration ends. Then another reality set in as she pondered the consequences of their togetherness. *I'm four years older, thirty-seven, nearing the end of safe childbirth. I want a child. Earl is almost sure to get reelected in 2012. He'd want me to stay. But there are lots of opportunities for me out there, though. Law firms, commissions . . . Many talented women I know take those government jobs to have babies. It's easy work, much flexibility. Right now, Zbig is as good as it's going to get for me. I've been in this town since I graduated from law school. I've met them all. I know the good and the awful. I know I waited too long . . . But it could work. I need to know how he feels.* These were thoughts that began to consume, almost obsess, her.

Zbig's thought process was not much different. *She's not Sophia, better in some ways but lacking Sophia's talents. Then again, her ambitions are very different. Sophia will be in politics for the rest of her working life. I'm not goin' in that direction. Nor is Sue*, it occurred to him suddenly. *Damn it, Zbig. You are thirty-three. You've had more women in your life than any ten friends. Get it together, fella. This may be it.* He sat at the desk in his condominium, looking down onto South St. Asaph Street in Old Town, Alexandria, a few blocks from Bob Castignani's town house. "Late Sunday afternoon" couples walked about; the weather had become balmy, the inklings of spring, the most beautiful season in the Washington area.

Krakowski and Sue had known each other for over a decade; despite the party differences, their political careers in Connecticut and Washington crossed constantly. The difference now was that of intimacy, and it was a big difference in the path the relationship had now taken, but not in the way that they looked at each other substantively. Privately, they had made a decision; dangerous perhaps? Of course, based on such limited intimacy, yet they would pursue each other; living together would be awkward. Marriage was even more complicating in their very separate professional lives.

*   *   *

Sue was talking to the president; he and Audrey Holmes, now living together in the White House, were preparing to depart Camp David for Washington. Typically, President Earl Eastwood wanted to know the lay of the land before he returned; no surprises.

"It's been a welcome break. Lots of running, a short swim in the outdoor pool, and biking with a couple of the Secret Service guys. I'm thinking of forming our own triathlon team," Eastwood mused, then asked for a review of the usual agenda items the two would discuss upon his return.

"I know I've given you some time off, Sue, and I hope it helped. You're killin' yourself for me, and I appreciate it," he said.

"Thank you. It was wonderful, I was with Zbig the whole weekend."

"Hey, sounds good. I won't ask for details," he said lightly.

"And you wouldn't get them if you did," she responded to their mutual laughter. "So here are the priority items for the morning," she added, reviewing a list of about ten topics.

"We're together on the priorities. What's up with the commodity market crisis? Is the media just making another issue, or is it real? I scanned some of the reporting in today's copy of *Barron's*," he said, referring to one of the most prestigious weekly print media on the markets.

I need to be completely open on this, Sue thought before responding. "It affects Connecticut, as you know, and of course, Zbig is right in the middle of it. He received a call from Kallias while we were together on Saturday. We did not discuss it for the obvious reasons. We both realize that our positions and partisanship could poison our personal relationship."

The president's reply was like a knock on her head but with a delicate rose.

"Hey, I live with a Republican, remember? You can handle it. I know you too well, and you know what our relationship depends on. You'll do the right thing, and I'll help you along when necessary. Zbig's a terrific guy. He's good for you, Sue, and I know you like him. Our gig is only temporary. Take a long-term glance and don't cheat yourself. I'm very confident you won't compromise your position, by the way."

"Thank you for saying that. It means much to me. I know that recusals aren't allowed in my job description," Sue said with quiet comfort in her mood and voice.

"There's no need for them, Sue. I've been in that situation in every political job I've ever had, especially after Guillermo appointed me to the Senate. You and I can talk it out without prejudice. You won't let your personal preferences interfere. But if I ask for them . . . well, you'll need to deliver. But that's the way we've always been, and we've been together a long time."

As presidential chief of staff, Sue Cohen held the most important political job in Washington that did not require Senate confirmation. She was the first woman in history to occupy that position, one that had seen such predecessors as Dick Cheney, Howard Baker, Donald Rumsfeld, and others move to cabinet-level jobs. At the federal level, the lifetime use of the title "Honorable" is available only to elected officials and to other persons whose appointments are confirmed by the Senate. But the politically savvy understand well that the prestige and power attached to the chief of staff title overwhelm the honorifics.

* * *

Early Monday morning, April 18, Bob Castignani's partners, Don Tranh and Ben Ochs, were actively pursuing the assignments Castignani had given them following his long conversation with Guillermo.

Tranh would talk to the US Commodity Futures Trading Commission, the CFTC, and Ochs would get out a message to the New England Industrial Association, the specialized interest group formed by Castignani, regarding the state of market play by Brent and its implications to their political jurisdictions, both at the state level and in Congress. The plan would proceed with Tranh's visit to the CFTC followed by an NEIA alert to its congressional members regarding any necessary action to secure the promises of the job surge that the Swiss partnership was to provide.

Thanks to several years of senior staff service in the Senate, Don Tranh was able to use his robust network of former colleagues, many of whom secured chairs of major commissions and other senior executive branch jobs. In this particular case, one of Tranh's former colleagues, and good friend as well as a neighbor in Fairfax County, now chaired the CFTC. Sam Schlichter – thirty-four, a Wharton School graduate who directed the staff of the Senate Agriculture Committee following a four-year stint on Wall Street as a commodity trader – had agreed to see Tranh.

It was eleven that morning when Tranh entered the dismal-looking redbrick building bordering Washington's DuPont Circle. The CFTC headquarters was at one time a rather quiet bureaucratic backwater staffed by dedicated, hardworking elder civil servants who were masters of their trade. The commissioners, by contrast, were too often political appointees with precious little understanding of either the commodities market, its operations, or, even more rarely, the nature of the products being traded. Schlichter was somewhat of an exception, enough so to prevent him from being subjugated to the recommendations by competent staff, which routinely got their way.

After exchanging the usual pleasantries, Tranh got down to business, explaining the purpose of his visit.

"We need to ensure that the markets don't shut down in the face of heavy volume, which is expected at a time when the world is so dependent on just a few sources of cocoa," Tranh said as an opener.

"Don, it's not only the volume we worry about here. It's the way the volume, whatever it is, moves. And at this moment, we're looking at a possible cross-market scheme involving the cocoa trade over the past few days," Schlichter replied.

"Sam, there's no deliberate manipulation of the futures prices. There are speculators, of course, but that's what they do, and it's a healthy and normal way of achieving a fair market value, is it not?"

"Yes and no. Yes, speculation does that. No, when it trends toward manipulation, it creates a ruse, an artifice of a fair price. That's what we're considering right now," Schlichter responded in a matter-of-fact way.

"But I'm talking about hedgers, firms that are users or brokers for product users who need to ensure a continual flow of product for their businesses to operate," Tranh offered by way of counterargument.

"Sometimes, my friend, hedgers can be speculators, and speculators can mask themselves as hedgers, to put it another way. That's what makes us investigate, and that's what may be happening here. There's just too much of a price swing. How can I not act? I've had guys here all weekend. Look at the record," Schlichter said, moving to the white board behind his desk.

Schlichter had always been known as a quant. Even during his time in the Senate, he could reduce arguments to numbers that would make a difference. Staffers rarely have math or technical backgrounds, and Schlichter's canny skills in graphing out predictions easily boosted his leadership and popularity among staff and members. Schlichter, with a Wharton MBA, quickly realized that lawyers, often the largest single human component of committee staffs, were notably weak in math. This gave him an easy leg up in achieving staff leadership jobs.

Schlichter drew an x-axis and a y-axis on the board, assigning values of time to the x-axis and price to the y-axis. "Look," he said, sketching curves across the graph with a black Magic Marker. "On Thursday, the price went to $3,220 a metric ton, up 21 percent. On Friday, cocoa opened at $3,220, but was up to $4,000 at market close, a rise of an incredible 50 percent in slightly more than twenty-four hours." This was a figure Tranh knew from Castignani's talk with von Schlossen and Guillermo in Switzerland. He was prepared with a response.

"How much of that volume passed through speculators, Sam?

"Yeah, you're right. I don't know," Schlichter reluctantly admitted, then continued to speak.

"But that's the point, that's why we're investigating. Our problem is that we've had to end our plan to develop a program that would detect suspicious trading. That's because there's a big-time battle between myself as Republican chairman of

CFTC who wants more technology to do the job, and the majority of the other commissioners, led by a smart Democrat, who wants to increase staff. Of course, I lost, and we had to take $11 million from the technology budget to hire these other guys' buddies as more staff. Six of the seven are lawyers no less. In all due respect, Don," Schlichter said with a grin, "but I've haven't met a lawyer yet on this hundred-person staff that has even a modest aptitude for the technology we need. The other commissioners are giving me this crap that in times of economic downturn and high unemployment, replacing bodies with technology doesn't look good."

Tranh was unsympathetic. The lawyers, not the quants, are always the bigger threats. The mode of investigation causes problems.

"But the mere threat or reality of an investigation causes worsened market volatility. Business operations are disrupted, investors back away, and speculators thrive on this uncertainty, taking wild risks which trigger even bigger price swings. Isn't that so?" Tranh asked.

"Once more, I have to say of course. But, Don, I have to know what's goin' on. I have to answer the 'why' question that the media, consumer groups, investors, bankers, and even members of Congress are asking."

Schlichter put down the Magic Marker, walked back to his desk, and sat down looking serious but with a slight, if not wry, smile. "Look, off the record, Don. We're friends. This gig is no less political than the ones we had on the hill. The difference is we're an independent commission, at least in name. But you know as well as I who puts the puppets – like myself, I regret to say – in action. We still respond to Congress. They make the laws, the ones you and I used to write, and we conceive the regulations to implement and enforce them. I can't change my instructions, which are part of the Code of Federal Regulations, the CFR. I have to act according to them. But if Congress chooses to amend some part of Title 7 that preempts my requirement to act, I don't act!" Schlichter said, referring to Title 7 of the United States Code, where the text of the Commodity Exchange Act is inscribed.

"Yeah, I see. Thanks, Sam. I was afraid it would come to that," Tranh offered.

"Don, I want you to know that I'm not sayin' all this just to kick the can down the road. I'm at my worst when I just do nothin', which is why I love this job. I'm an activist. I'm tellin' you in sincerity that we're heading toward a civil enforcement action. Your clients, Brent, maybe even Belmont, are almost certain to be among the defendants. That's to be expected with all these lawyers hangin' around here. If you can work this out legislatively, that's the way to go. And I know I'm not tellin' you a damn thing you already haven't thought of. Bob Castignani was always one of my favorite senators. He's smart as hell, knows the commodity laws, and has never been known to take on battles that he doesn't at least think he can win. You're partnered with the best of the best."

"Thanks, Sam. If you ever decide to quit all this fun, let me know," Tranh said. It was an unspoken and quite common proffer of future employment made in vague language that could avoid perjurious replies if the situation called for investigations by Congress or other actions in the judicial system.

*   *   *

Upon his return to the office, Tranh reviewed the meeting with his two partners, Bob Castignani and Ben Ochs.

"We've gotta act legislatively. Schlichter admitted that. His hands are tied, they're going to court," Tranh said.

"Can we get him to hold off until we get our congressional guys to act?" Ochs asked.

"Ben, Congress can't act that fast. Schlichter says a court action could be in the works next week. It would take us months to get the bill that's needed here in place," Castignani said.

"I don't know, boss," said Tranh in his typically respectful language when addressing the more senior partner in the firm. "If we get movement, even a draft, we might give Schlichter the ammo he needs to let the CFTC realize that Congress is working on a bill that would nullify their action. Having a court action mooted because of a congressional bill will scare the hell out of them. Most of the appointments to the commission depend on congressional support. They're not gonna bite the proverbial hand."

"I see, that makes more sense, Don," Castignani said pensively. "Ben, let's crank up the New England Industrial Association. Get a notice to the congressional members, include even a draft of the legislation that's needed."

It was ten that evening when the alert message was finalized for dispatch to the congressional targets of the Castignani group. Clearly, it was a lobbying effort, but it was masked, like so many others, as a simple informational notice to the members of the NEIA, the section 501(c) nonprofit organization exempted from certain tax liabilities under the Internal Revenue Code because of its educational or informational functions.

As the congressional adherents to the association filtered back into their offices on Tuesday morning, April 19, 2011, making their way through their e-mails, the alert message from their former colleague Bob Castignani definitely caught their attention.

CONFIDENTIAL

NEW ENGLAND INDUSTRIAL ASSOCIATION
HIGH ALERT

DATE: Tuesday, April 19, 2011   TO: NEIA Members
FROM: *Castignani@neia.org*   202-259-1959

The draft below is commended to your attention following a meeting between NEIA staff director Don Tranh and Sam Schlichter, chairman, CFTC, on Monday, April 18, 2011. Schlichter advised Tranh that the CFTC would embark this week on a civil action against the dozens of hedging and speculating groups engaged in trading during coca market volatility period last Wednesday through Friday and continuing yesterday.

The CFTC litigation would seriously undermine the job-creation progress under way in expanding the New England confection sector by failing to distinguish between legitimate user-based hedging in the commodity markets and the price-distortive effects of speculation-based futures contracts. It is our judgment, therefore, that the draft legislation below, once introduced and assigned to committee, would be sufficient to suspend the CFTC action, PROVIDED that there was evidence of a reasonably quick and certain passage of the draft or language akin to it.

Bill Text
112thCongress (2011-2012)
H.R. 1610

H.R. 1610 – Business Risk Mitigation and Price Stabilization Act of 2011
(Introduced in House – IH)

H.R. 1610 IH

112th Congress

1st Session

H.R. 1610

To provide for end user exemptions from certain provisions of the Commodity Exchange Act and the Securities Exchange Act of 1934 and for other purposes.

IN THE HOUSE OF REPRESENTATIVES

APRIL 19, 2011
Mr. MOURGOS (for himself, Mr. POOLE, Mr. McNEAL, Mr. PROVENZANO) introduced the following bill, which was

referred to the Committee on Commerce and, in addition, to the Committees on Ways and Means, Agriculture, Armed Services, and Foreign Affairs for a period to be determined by the Speaker in each case for considerations of such provisions as fall within the jurisdiction of the committee concerned.

A BILL

To provide end user exemptions from certain provisions of the Commodity Exchange Act and the Securities Exchange Act of 1934 and for other purposes.

FINDINGS. Congress finds that risk mitigation and price stabilization have been subjected to disruptive volatile market swings caused by reckless trades made by certain speculators intent on quick returns at the cost of broader economic benefits for the United States of America. Congress further finds that certain sectors critical to our economic stability as well as our national security risk become regionally disadvantaged, inviting declines in communities on which our national defense depends and which, by extrapolation, affect this country's global leadership.

Be it enacted by the Senate and the House of Representatives of the United States of America in Congress assembled,

SECTION 1. SHORT TITLE.

This Act may be cited as the "Business Risk Mitigation and Price Stabilization Act of 2011."

SECTION 2. TRADING RULES.

Commodity Exchange Act Amendments – The Commodity Exchange Act (7 U.S.C. 1 et seq.) is amended –

In section 1a(33)(A), as added by section 721(a)(6) OF THE Dodd-Frank-Wall Street Reform and Consumer Protection Act, by adding clause(iii) to read as follows:

"(iii) Requirements for the classification of purchases or sales of contracts for future delivery as bona fide hedging under section 1.3(z)(3) of title 17 in the *Code of Federal Regulations* are exempt from this section of the law and any other such sections of this and other current laws that may exist."

APPLICABILITY WITH RESPECT TO COUNTERPARTIES – The trading requirements of this section shall not apply to trades in which such parties are not speculators.

Securities Exchange Act of 1934 Amendments – The Securities Exchange Act of 1934 (15 U.S.C. 78a et seq.) is amended –

In section 3(a)(67)(A), add an amending clause that reads as follows:

"(ii) Speculator losses from security-based debt insurance shall not be eligible for tax relief."

CONFIDENTIAL

The bill was read with great interest and transmitted immediately throughout both houses of Congress. Calls were made to colleagues inviting their participation, emphasizing that the United States had no cocoa bean production domestically and that we were entirely dependent on foreign sources, themselves too often somewhat unstable. Other members were reminded that the United States' reliance on nations like Venezuela, Nigeria, Iraq, Saudi Arabia, and other oil exporters to the United States could call for similar actions for which this bill could become a useful precedent in establishing price stabilization in the global petroleum markets.

Within a day or two, interest in HR 1610 grew substantially, with cosigners of the bill increasing in numbers, which had captured the attention of the CFTC commissioners and staff. In the meantime, Krakowski had sent a copy of the bill to Sue Cohen, who would take it up with the president.

*　　*　　*

What in hell are they doing? Sue thought as she studied the legislative draft. *I was at the December meeting of the New England Industrial Association. The congressional folks there got a glimpse of the plan. I'm sure they went out and bought cocoa futures contracts knowing the strategy: the price would go up as the market tightened. Then they almost certainly shorted them as the market collapsed once Brent released token amounts back into the exchanges. This bill exempts the speculators after the congressional guys made their killing.*

The president was making arrangements to work out as noon approached. He was in the Oval Office's butler pantry, where a shower and changing room had been installed for him, when Sue rang him.

"Can we talk before you go out?" she asked.

"Sure, meet me in the antechamber, I'm in my running gear," Eastwood said as he finished tying his shoes.

Sue walked through the private corridor into the antechamber between the Oval Office and her own. Only the presidential chief of staff had such close proximity to the Oval Office. As she entered, Eastwood was zipping up his running jacket, towel slung around his neck.

"What's up?" he asked.

"I'm going to give you something to think about on your run. Please, take this bill draft. Zbig sent it over to me. In a few words, it's a massive work-around gimmick. The cocoa bean mob is legitimizing their market usurpation by amending the commodities and securities exchange legislation. Worse, I'm guessing they've directly profited from it." Sue tried to control the angst in her voice.

"I'm not surprised. We need to be sure we understand well just what they're trying to walk us into. I'll look at it. It's what, one page?" the president asked.

"It's short, but loaded," she replied, dropping the side of her mouth in a sign of disgust.

Moments later, the presidential convoy was en route to Fort McNair, where the president took occasional runs around the perimeter road of the carefully secured military post. He scanned the document, immediately sensing what the bill intended.

I'll be damned. These guys never stop regardless of party differences. This is just another one of those innocent-looking general amendments that indirectly benefits members.

Congressional rules allow members to invest in financial arrangements on or off the established financial exchanges on the basis of inside information, an act that is illegal under current law. In this particular case, the bill was as Sue had interpreted it, and its purpose immediately evident to her and the president, both of whom had had long stints in the US Senate, Sue as Eastwood's former chief of staff when he served as Senate minority leader. Moreover, as Eastwood also interpreted it, a bill conferring benefits on a broad segment of the population into which members happen to be included is not treated as legislation directly or exclusively, of course, benefiting a specific member.

"Sue, I read this thing," the president said, calling her as the convoy dropped down onto Maine Avenue on the waterfront of the District of Columbia, now less than a mile from the gate at Fort McNair. "What's the market status at the moment?"

"Well, it's getting worse. These CDOs, the collateralized debt obligations, this is the insurance that traders use to avoid heavy losses. The speculators are getting financial haircuts and the market's volatility increases. The banks and other financial institutions holding the CDOs are finding the futures contracts that back them are worth half their original value, all in a few days. We're getting swamped with calls from some Wall Street heavies and big-bank CEOs," Sue replied.

"I need to get Lou Dubin on this. Call him at treasury," the president said, referring to the secretary of the treasury. "I'll call Roger over in the Senate," he added, referring to Republican Roger Evarts, the Connecticut senator who was ranking minority member of the Senate Commerce Committee in the Democratic-controlled Senate.

Equipped with a two-way earpiece, the president dismounted from the presidential limousine and, with a phalanx of Secret Service runners accompanying him, began a slow jog from the front drive-through tunnel beneath the entrance to the National War College.

Senator Evarts was in the Senate dining room when the call to his private android cell phone came through, highlighted with a picture of the president. Sitting with constituents from Connecticut's pharmaceutical community, including two CEOs, he excused himself, retreating into an enclosed telephone booth off the room designed for private calls during lunch.

"Yes, Mr. President, good to hear from you," said the suave fifty-nine-year-old longtime Connecticut colleague of Eastwood. A moderate Republican, Evarts could always be depended upon to cooperate with the other side of the aisle, especially within the past decade as the Democrats increasingly dominated Connecticut politics.

"Problem, Roger," the president began, speaking easily during his jogging pace. "You've seen the draft amendment from Castignani, I'm sure."

"Yes, so who's surprised? Certainly not you." They both laughed. "Obviously, I was not an investor in the coca market. It's too obvious a scam for me. We've been legitimizing wrongful behavior like this for years. You know it's gonna catch up with us."

"Damn right, Roger. You and I have talked about this for many years. It's just downright shameful. Look, I'm in a bond. The last time I tried to inculcate some sense of ethics in these guys, they were forced to resign their seats in Congress. And that's part of the current mess," Eastwood added, referring to the demand for presidential pardon by many of the current players in the Swiss plan to expand the US confection market, located largely in the New England region from which the president himself had come.

"And you're facing the same choices again, Mr. President. If you go after the members who benefited from the market cocoa volatility, they're gonna tell you they broke no laws, and they just won't give a damn about the ethical aspects of their behavior. This time, if you threaten to disclose what they did, they'll just laugh at you, and most of them are from your party.

"And if you veto the amendments, you collapse the Swiss plan, and that will cost several thousand job gains that have been broadcast throughout the media for months now."

As Eastwood listened, his anger and disgust settled into a reality warp. "Yeah, I know, trussing up ethics is easily leeched away by counterarguments like those. Do me a favor, tell the delegations that we spoke and that I'm upset with those who used their official positions for personal gain and the insider information that they acquired as a result of their office. I'm not gonna veto the bill, you can tell them that too.

"But they should know that I can still use my administrative and executive powers, to include my rule-making authority, to slow this thing down, and I can shift the blame to Congress, which has made the regulatory process a nightmare. I'll begin by redesignating those so-called administrative law judges as hearing officers, which is what they are anyway. That'll freak out some of our party who just use the positions and titles to take care of their former staffers."

"I think that's the way to go, Mr. President. We both know that the consensus for the changes we need just isn't that easily available. As long as you set the pace, become the model, you can humiliate some of them. The rest will never change, which is why we legalize bad behavior to keep them from going to jail, where they belong anyway in some cases."

Earl Eastwood, dedicated to bringing change to Washington, like so many before him and as many yet to come, sullenly picked up his running pace, thinking, *Here I am shacking up with Audrey in the White House, or domesticating as we call it now. I'm hardly the best role model.*

CHAPTER 11

A LULL IN THE STORM

PRESIDENTIAL CHIEF OF STAFF SUE COHEN AND CONNECTICUT SENATOR ZBIGNIEW KRAKOWSKI WERE FINDING TIME TO SEE EACH OTHER ON WEEKNIGHTS. LATE DINNERS BECAME MORE COMMON AS THE COUPLE GREW CLOSER. It was ten on Wednesday night as the two sat in Quigley's, a popular pub on upper Foxhall Road; half-price hamburgers were the night's specialty but not part of the couple's individual preferences.

"Who could eat this stuff? They taste like cardboard even when they're done rare," Sue commented.

"I disagree, fusty, yes, cardboard, no – but only because you don't have that moldy, stale aroma that cardboard lacks. Your palate is failing you, Sue," Zbig said to light laughter between the two.

"I'm spending so much damn time in the White House that my palate is beginning to match my gnomic character. You think you're living the pulse beat of the universe and then realize you're really in a cave. People feed us information as if we were caged animals. You never know how valid or verifiable it is," Sue lamented, reaching out to touch Zbig's large hand, wet from the sweating oversize glass of beer that had just been emptied.

Krakowski, wiping his hand on the stained checkered tablecloth, returned the grasp, saying, "Hey, we're away from all that when we're together. Let's leave it for a few hours at least. Is this a night we can spend together?"

"Not a good idea. I have to meet with the president early tomorrow morning. You know, the market crisis along with other economic news," she answered. Then she thought, *Earl's going to ask about Zbig's involvement in the market swings. I don't know if he traded along with the others. The SEC couldn't give us answers. I agree with Earl that we needed to keep the FBI out of it. Having them poke around congressional investing habits is not what Democrats do to each other. Since we're not going to be together tonight, this might be a good time to ask Zbig. If it's bad news, there'll be time to work it out before we get together for the weekend.*

She decided she would raise the issue with him.

"Zbig, I have to ask an awkward question," she said, looking at him affectionately and squeezing his hand again.

"Nope, not married, never have been, not even an engagement or two in my past. No smutty affairs, orgies, or illegitimate children lingering about. I hope you're not disappointed," he joked; they both laughed.

"I'll demur on that question, if you ever get around to asking it. I have scruples you know, but they need to remain 'undercover,'" she said, her sentence loaded with punchy innuendoes that added to their laughter.

I hate to do this. We're having so much fun. I really love this man. I wish to hell my professional covenants didn't have to interfere with my real life. "Well, you know Earl. He wants facts, and he's going to ask questions regarding the New England delegation members who traded cocoa during this week's market frenzy," she said.

"Oh, many of them were trading. All made money, I'm sure," came Krakowski's immediate and stunningly frank reply. There was a smirk on his face; he easily sensed what she was getting at.

Darn him. He read me as if I were a high school debater. He's telling me he wasn't involved in the trading . . . I think. She stared at him, smiling with some embarrassment; she knew he was awaiting her question. *I need another approach.*

"The ethics over there leave much to be desired. During my time on the Hill, I don't think a week went by when something new arose, each event more remarkable than the preceding one. Sex and money, still the two big incentives for wrongdoing. For politicians, add ego.

"This recent Supreme Court case, what is it, *Nevada Commission v. Carrigan*? Some state senator involved in a consulting job, which is allowed under state law for state legislators, refused to recuse himself from a vote on a project related to his moonlighting job. The Nevada Supreme Court said that a legislator's vote was constitutionally protected self-expression," she said.

"C'mon, what crap. Who buys that nonsense?" Zbig inserted.

"The US Supreme Court didn't. Scalia wrote the opinion, which said basically that a legislator is a political representative. His vote, therefore, is not that as an individual but as a political representative acting on behalf of his constituents," Sue responded.

"Damn right, any reasonable, ordinary, and prudent person would see that. And that raises the issue of appearances, which in politics is even more indicting where there's conflict of interest. Except, Sue, the voters really don't care as long as they're taken care of.

"By the way, you never told me what Earl said when you raised the issue of our relationship and whether you might have to recuse yourself from acting on issues affecting my senatorial interests where they matter in the White House," Krakowski said, completely shifting the subtle inquest launched by Sue back into her jurisdiction.

He's not going to answer unless I ask him directly. I just don't know if I can do it, she thought, then turned her attention back to his question. She smiled, saying, "He reminded me that he lived with a Republican."

Krakowski swept back into his seat, letting out a howl of laughter. "Sounds like the Earl I know. The guy's amazing. He can disarm any adversary with the truth. It's one of many remarkable skills that guy has used to put him where he is."

She's agonizing over this thing. I better put her at ease. "Let me answer the question you never asked. Did I make money in trading cocoa? Damn right I did, and a lot. Keep in mind, Rose Confections is one of my constituents. Parts of it have been since I was in the state legislator. They have a plant in my senatorial district. I've been trading commodities for years. You've been in my condo office and seen my computer screens. One is used for my trading, which I generally do a couple times a week at night. But to lift the burden a bit from your shoulders, I had placed my trades long before I got the briefing from Castignani on the takeover scheme. I do long futures contracts and never placed an option, a put or a call, on cocoa *after* getting the inside poop."

Sue closed her eyes, which had begun to well. She was overjoyed. *Thank God! He had me spinning. I was sure he was involved even though he was making the same arguments as I was. Just act as if you knew the answer all along. I need him now more than ever,* she thought.

But Zbig saw through her badly concealed thoughts. *She really doubted me.*

"Listen," Krakowski started, "in your job, you encounter lies and deceptions from every direction. I don't lie and I don't cheat, and that applies to my personal life as well, especially with you. If we can't make something out of this relationship and I feel the need to see others, I'll let you know. I don't cheat or deceive."

"I . . . I just didn't know, and I couldn't bring myself to ask you directly. I should be disappointed in myself," Sue responded somewhat dismally.

"Why, for what, because you put your professional interests ahead of romantic inclination? You think I would have acted any differently? The two are intertwined. Without sounding too hokey, it's all about character. I'm proud of you, Sue. I suspected that you had to ask me the question. But I also know that Earl didn't put you up to it. You did it because *you* understood what he expects of you," Krakowski said quietly, then gently touched her hand, saying, "Let's go. We both have early appointments."

* * *

At six thirty Thursday morning, April 21, 2011, Sue was in her office, earlier than usual. Her spirits had been raised from the late date with Krakowski. She felt, in a very strange way, not simply enamored with him but armored by him. A sense of self-purpose, less the smugness that sometimes comes with the level of self-confidence that feeds it, almost made her quiver. There was noticeable excitement in her thought process, even in her step. She realized what it was: *I'm no longer a captive in this place, or any other. I'm normal again. I can have a life, I can love.*

It was seven when the president buzzed her, asking that she see him.

"Good morning, Sue," the president said as she entered his office. He was bent over from his chair behind the desk, tying a shoe, it seemed to her. He then sat up stiffly.

"Damn running shoes. I've never worn anything but New Balance. Audrey gave me a pair of Nikes, which I appreciate, but they're for flat feet. I have high arches, and now I have plantar fasciitis! I just rolled up a gauze strip and put it under my arches to relieve the pain."

"Why did you run in them in the first place?" Sue asked.

"You don't live with Audrey," Eastwood replied dourly to their joint laughter. "She'll be the loser in the end. The White House doctor told me I shouldn't run for a week. You know how I get when I can't run. Even the usual gym routines don't help my mood. I have to get outside for the real therapeutic benefits."

"Maybe it's time we added a psychiatrist to the medical staff," she said jokingly.

"Yeah right. The media would go nuts over that one, as if they don't have enough trivia on us to muck about now," he said, still chortling.

"I read the intel reports and skipped the briefing this morning. I'm glad I put a little more politics into the National Security Council and the NDI's office," the president said, referring to the appointments of longtime aide Bill Stokes, a former Yale professor who was the political heart of the Connecticut Democratic Party and now the national security adviser, and former Colorado senator Jim Douglas, now the director of National Intelligence.

"A couple of times a week, I can eliminate the morning briefing, scan the reports, and save a hell of a lot of time. More importantly, these new guys can better relate to the political tempo this administration needs."

"I guess I would have a somewhat different view, as sort of a caveat. Reading the reports rather than debating the issues as they're raised in the briefings could leave some gaps," Sue added.

"I'm aware of that, and you're right. In a way, it's like taking one of these crazy online or mail-order academic degree programs. You're listening only to your own arguments. No one else is challenging them, and that worries me. But the value of this new procedure is that they avoid repeating the same old information when there's no update. At the same time, the written reports can provide items that I need to challenge, and that gives me an opportunity to talk directly to someone who knows what's goin' on. Too often, the NDI will refer to an intel issue that's, say, in State's jurisdiction, and they can't elaborate, and there's no State guy in the room, of course. I don't want to have the NDI telling me about Ivory Coast, for example, especially when NDI and State have different opinions.

"Actually, Ivory Coast is one of the things we need to talk about. I'm still troubled over the way Bennie Thompson sideswiped me on that one," Eastwood said, referring to the former congressman, now with Belmont of Switzerland. Thompson had recently negotiated a settlement of the civil war in the West African state by working out an arrangement where the former president and his family and the new president would benefit from the purchase of the country's two-year cocoa crop by Brent and Belmont.

"Of course, that's behind the wild commodity market swings, and now we have this new bill, HR 1610, which I finally read, immunizing some of the parties causing the market problems. Is it plausible that the big trading company, Brent, is not speculating?" he asked. "This bill exempts *hedgers* from regulation, right?"

I'm on the spot on this one. He expects that Zbig and I have discussed it. "I did talk about it with Zbig. And answering the two questions in inverse order, yes, hedgers are exempt in the bill, as I read it and as Zbig understands it. And yes, Zbig and I agree that hedgers can be speculators. But I, not Zbig, can see where a hedger, which is to say, an end user of a commodity, like some company that might be buying copper for its production needs, may speculate on a small segment of the market to secure its position in hedging against ruinous higher prices in the future," Sue replied.

"But how does the bill figure out when and how the hedger is doing that, and how much of the hedging position is based on speculation?" Eastwood asked.

"I did talk with one of the staff authors of the bill. She told me that, first, because if it's a hedger speculating, there's a presumption of moderation. That is, they're not trying to capture the market for a quick turnaround gain. And second, there are trading records. They can be scanned to verify that a small segment of the total futures contracts placed by hedgers are in speculative orders, such as options," Sue said, answering the president's question.

"I doubt that. The CFTC just cut $11 million out of their budget that was designated for technology needed to monitor market operations. What're they gonna do, hire a bunch of lawyers to presume wrongdoing, screw up the markets even more while they're being investigated, and drag on costly delays for years? I want you to coordinate with the House and Senate Commerce Committees and anyone else doing market oversight. Tell them to restore that money even if they have to reduce legal staffs. I know they're gonna remind me that these are so-called independent commissions. But they still depend on congressional funding, and my veto," Eastwood said somewhat threateningly.

"That's a good counterstrategy and good policy. They, Congress, the committees, and Brent and Belmont ought to know that if you're to sign on, the policing mechanisms have to be in place," Sue agreed, taking notes.

Putting a lighter note on the discussion, Eastwood added, "You know, during the BP spill in the Gulf, my left-of-left buddies in the House, most notably Mary Rossotti Wooley, kept pressing me to start building the legal framework for action against BP. 'Send the attorney general,' they were yelling. Finally, as you may recall, I told Mary that I'll send the AG, but I didn't see how that would stem the oil flow unless I stuffed him in the hole. She hasn't pinched my buttocks since," he added to their boisterous laughter, which was loud enough to cause a Secret Service agent standing at the Oval Office entrance to swing the door open.

"We're okay, Frank. I was just telling Sue about the time you slipped and slid into the Potomac when we were running last January," the president said as the agent sported an officious, forced grin and slid back out the door.

"Maybe Mary has found other opportunities," Sue added, still giggling.

"She is one hell of an attractive woman, especially for a sixty-seven-year-old. Audrey said she's sexy as hell, but she knows her limits and is happily married," the president added, referring to the former Speaker of the House, now the House minority leader following the Republican takeover in the 2010 election. Although Audrey Holmes was the only black Republican woman in the US House of Representatives, she was unusually close to the former Speaker, whom she knew was very unhappy with Audrey's living arrangement with the Democratic president in the White House.

"I don't want HR 1610 to become an issue at all. There are thousands of jobs at stake. The economy's already in a deep enough hole. The Lucas crowd, especially Dom Guillermo, is well aware of that. They also know my leverage is limited and that I can't veto a bill like that, which promises to create more jobs, unless I have some pretty effective ammunition, which I don't," the president said.

"Look, the 2012 election is nineteen months away. No modern president since FDR has ever been reelected with unemployment at over 9 percent," Eastwood added.

"That's the conventional wisdom and a historical fact. But you have a different set of markers," Sue added.

"You mean my so-called celebrity status as a black man. You know how much I hate that," Eastwood quickly replied.

"Again, it's a fact, Earl," Sue said, suddenly realizing that for the first time since they'd been in the White House together, she called him by his first name.

The president smiled. "I sort of like that, say it again," he chortled.

"I'll never use your first name again. It was disrespectful, and I apologize," Sue said, her eyes slightly fluttering in embarrassment. *This thing with Zbig, it's overtaking me. I can't believe I feel so casual, I've almost a sense of disregard,* she thought.

"It doesn't bother me a bit. You're my closest confidante. There's nothing we don't talk about. I'm sort of your surrogate spouse. That's good, Sue. I depend greatly on you," he added, thinking, *Incredibly, my three most reliable friends are Audrey, Sue, and Monica, all females. Kenny is too much the whimsical bachelor to rely on for any serious advice, and the rest of the guys in the cabinet, good people as they are, have their own ambitions. They'd leave me in a flash if I got in their way.* Monica Howard, a longtime political colleague and medical doctor, was now the secretary of health and human services. Kenny Edwards was the press secretary to the president. The formerly close relationship with the latter two was buried in the formalities that always surrounded their encounters with the president, usually in busy meetings, press meeting preparations, and other public and quasi-public situations. It never occurred to him that Sue too now had competing interests with the demands of her job and her very powerful boss.

I need to get this conversation back to specifics, Sue thought as she started speaking. "The bill, HR 1610, is going to pass. I don't think there's enough support to override your veto, and I wouldn't counsel nixing it anyway. But you do need a good political cover on it. The thing reeks of lobbyist influence even though, in this case, it's the members of Congress who are the lobbyists. That's a bit of a twist."

"Yeah, deregulating commodity trading even for cocoa beans in this climate has to be a form of advanced dementia. Here we're reforming banking practices, talking tax reform, threatening CEO pay, raising the debt limit, and now I'm supporting a bill that could make those moves look meaningless. It's this debt ceiling issue that's really troubling me. When I was over in the Senate, in fact it was in 2006, I made a statement on the Senate floor, saying that raising the debt limit is a sign of leadership failure, a signal that the US government can't manage its own house, pay its own bills, and has become dependent on foreign countries to finance our reckless spending habits," Eastwood mused aloud.

"The bill sponsors' motives may be worth examining," Sue added.

"I don't think I want to take that route again. I managed to cost the Democrats enough seats in the last election by threatening to expose ethical shortcomings as well as breaches of the law. This is not a time to draw lines in the sand within my own party. I have enough adversaries over there as it is," Eastwood said.

"The Iraqi situation has been settled," Sue added, looking for something positive during his tenure, now three years in the presidency.

"Is it? It's all flimflam, Sue, you know that. We've drawn down the troops to 35,000 from 150,000. But they're bottled up in their well-fortified bases, and we still take occasional casualties. I can't withdraw them, the place would collapse. Afghanistan is worse. I've committed to a drawdown by July. I'll take out a brigade or two. But our operations will continue, but much more covertly. What's coming at me like a freight train is the so-called Arab spring. Those fools over in the State Department got me to make those comments in Cairo back in January, urging more tolerance by Hosni Mubarak of the country's political opposition. I signed on to that because I was simply too ignorant of Middle Eastern politics outside of Israel. I didn't connect the dots, and the obvious happened," Eastwood said, the anger emerging in his voice.

Sue sensed it; he rarely came even close to the type of irritability he was now slipping into.

Eastwood continued. "What happened was something the so-called State Department experts never expected. The Muslim Brotherhood, and let's remember they used to be on our terrorism list, emerged, at first claiming they would never operate as a political power now and, of course, changing their minds as the race for a presidential successor in Egypt has become wide open. In the meantime, their close ties to the Hamas government in the Gaza Strip have encouraged protests against Israel, unarmed Palestinians walking across Israel's borders to reclaim their land. *I did that,* Sue. Once we suggested less support for Mubarak, his opponents saw it as an invitation for action. In much the same way, my statement signaled that we were getting soft on our Israeli commitment, and that's setting the Middle East afire. Even the Catholic Church is now campaigning, *lobbying* really, for parishioner funds to settle Palestinean Christians in the 'Holy Land,' as the church is saying, without adding that some of the land they're talking about happens to be the uncontested territory of the Jewish state of Israel, as well as the West Bank. Just watch, that'll become yet another campaign issue."

"And it's not going to help with the Jewish vote," Sue added, herself a product of a Jewish family that for generations had never wavered from strong support for the Democratic Party, a tradition she personally continued.

"But it started with Tunisia. That's still a volcano. They've toppled the president, Egypt has followed, and now the Libyans are stirring. Muammar Qadaffi is vulnerable, just watch. NATO is quietly pushing us to act, and France and Germany have their clandestine operatives firing up the opposition. They see Libyan oil as relief from growing pressures from their other sources, like Saudi, Iraq, Nigeria, and other parts of West Africa. The suppliers want more cooperation in the United Nations, to include UN resolutions supporting a separate state of Palestine. We have to vote with the Israelis against it, of course, or find a way to delay the vote. Our other NATO partners, including Italy, which opposes action against Qadaffi, by the way, agree with us that the UN can't 'recognize' and, therefore, create the Palestinean state. The UN charter doesn't bar it, it just doesn't allow it," Eastwood argued. "That's the difference between our legal cultures: The European variety is infused into the UN Charter, where something must be allowed to happen. In our political and legal culture, everything is allowed unless expressly barred. I wish my do-good buddies at State would understand that. They spend most of their lives in these countries, don't they ever learn?"

"Are we bound to engage with other NATO members in action against Libya?" Sue asked, knowing the answer.

"Of course not, at least legally. We always have the option of sovereign privilege. But from a practical perspective, not cooperating could cost us the top military position, the job of SACEUR, the Supreme Allied Commander Europe, who has always been an American.

"I don't need another war on my watch, Sue. Congressionals, especially my own Democrats, see what's coming. They're talking to NATO governments all the time during their trips, meetings with officials, and in other for arenas. And the smart guys on the Hill understand well that when you talk about NATO action, you're really talking about the US playing a lead role. Which means heavy spending, right now estimated at a billion a month for what, four to six months? Even with French and British involvement, they don't enough of the right munitions and other equipment to do the job. Keep in mind that while 16 percent of our spending goes to defense, they average about 4 to 5 percent spending for defense in their budgets. In the case of the French, that spending is mostly devoted to building arms that can be exported, sold abroad, to buyers from places like Saudi, Kuwait, and now Iraq."

"Will Congress support intervention, on balance, I mean?" Sue asked.

"Our party will be split. The Republicans will oppose it also. I will have to skirt around the War Powers Act to get us involved as others have done, my immediate predecessor, Bob Davids, Clinton, among a few. Old Jake Javits will be smiling in his grave. He warned that the act was too easily bypassed and effectively gave the president a private army," Eastwood added, referring to the late New York senator who had opposed the law's purpose in the 1970s.

"Just watch, I would not be surprised to see resolutions from House and Senate Democrats opposing use of force in Libya. But these are just a few of the dicey issues coming at me as the election closes in. Foreign policy is manageable. The economic issues are killers.

"The people want our prosperity back. Their lives are mired in uncertainty. They can't save for anything. We are a consumer economy officially. We're in the idiotic position of having to force people to spend and to discourage savings. People have jobs and their day-to-day lives to contend with. They can't become investment experts. What can they do? Passbook savings are gone. Stupidly, we've given the banks free access to near-zero interest rate monies through the Fed's open window. So why would they pay interest on saving accounts? The market collapse eviscerated 401(k) accounts. Investment advisers are telling people to forget about saving for their kid's education. 'Let them get student loans,' they're saying, and I add parenthetically that there's our next big bubble.

"We need to reinstate Glass-Steagall, fat chance of that. The banking lobbyists have everybody who counts in their hip pocket, and most of them are Democrats who see representing banking interests as a fantastic job opportunity after they depart Congress and join the bulging lobbying ranks," Eastwood said, his voice grave.

"I agree. We let that law be chipped away. There was that 1987 Chase Manhattan Bank application where the Fed allowed them to use depositor funds to underwrite stocks and bonds, provided it was only a small part of their revenue. I worked on some of these cases when I was in practice," Sue said. She had worked for a DC firm active in securities law before entering the political realm full-time as then senator Eastwood's chief of staff.

"From there, you knew it was only a matter of time before the law would be repealed, which happened in 1999. I agree, the bank lobbying was heavy and involved my own firm. There was so much movement in the investment banking community to underwriting mergers and acquisitions that Congress just caved. I spoke to many members during the period. Even those on the finance-related committees had no real understanding of the issue, believing only two things – the repeal fostered economic growth and growth helped them get reelected along with the campaign money-flow necessary to it," Sue said.

"So now we've bailed out the banking system that created its own threat and in the course of which put ourselves at severe financial risk of default on our debt. Add to that the weakened dollar, imagine $1.42-plus for one lousy Euro? And we're still urging the struggling consumer to get out there and spend more, all this at a time when the next generation is looking at a glum future of high taxes, substantially lessened medical care and Social Security program, which is and has always been the classic scam. We pay the bills from current revenues since the trust fund that was intended to support it has been borrowed from so completely that it consists of nothing more than filing cabinets of promises to pay it back. On top of all of this, Congress is asking for more legislation to gut safe and prudent investment in commodities.

"Worse, I have to support this short-term scheme to save and create jobs when, over time, we both know that these are not the real motives and purpose behind HR 1610," Eastwood concluded.

CHAPTER 12

SHOWTIME

AT EIGHT THIRTY WEDNESDAY MORNING, APRIL 28, 2011, LA PALMERAIE, THE ELEGANT BREAKFAST ROOM AT THE PALAIS MONTREUX, HAD COME ALIVE. It had been a quiet Easter weekend, some would say a typical Easter weekend in Switzerland, where families tend to congregate at church and hearth. But the somewhat rowdy, by comparison, US executive from Lucas, Brent, and Belmont who resided at the hotel had returned from long weekends just about everywhere. Most traveled back to the States, returning to the original state or district haunts that they once represented in the US Congress. Others sauntered about Europe, exploring as far east as Budapest and to the south toward Naples.

Jeff Scharfman, the former New Jersey senator and always an early riser, usually talked his way into La Palmeraie dining room before it officially opened at eight thirty. The staff was quite tolerant, providing him with his daily newspaper and a secretive cup of coffee while the breakfast buffet was being assembled. Secured in a corner away from the eyes of travelers peering through the closed etched glass doors, Scharfman conversed casually in French with the workers, taking a special interest in a rather attractive very young Swiss hostess, who returned Scharfman's sly, leering peeks over his newspaper with a polite smile, while she groaned to herself, thinking, *Cette vieux, il fait de l'oeil. Il est plus agee que mon grandpere. (This old guy, he just leers. He's older than my grandfather.)*

The doors to the restaurant had finally opened with typical Swiss precision at eight thirty sharp; Scharfman then found himself surrounded by a noisy tour, mostly Americans, readily noticeable because they always seem to scream at one another even when sitting next to one another at the tables. Then the Lucas group started to dribble in. The former California senator Nancy Lehman first, then Jane and Marc Gregoire; Marc had been a Louisiana congressman and Jane a Washington attorney, now handling US legal matters at Lucas Holdings. Scharfman's former New Jersey colleague in the senate, Andy Tantillo, strolled in along with former Mississippi congressman Bennie Thompson, their conversation animated but conducted at close range, almost in whispers. They spotted Scharfman and joined him at his table; a table with a Lucas executive at it was an open invitation to any other colleague to sit down, which the two did.

"You know, Jeff, I don't know what the hell's goin' on, but I glanced at my bank account last night after getting back. There was an incredible amount of money suddenly added to it. Bennie tells me he had the same experience," Tantillo said.

Scharfman dropped his paper. "What! I had the same thing happen to me."

"Yeah, but I found an extra fourteen million Swiss francs in my account," Thompson said, leaning across the table with a whisper.

"That's about what I got," Scharfman added.

"My increase was just under six million," Tantillo said. "I wonder if the bank has misdirected some funds."

"I think mine's a mistake, but if we're all affected, then it's our payroll bank, isn't it?" Scharfman added hesitatingly.

"Right, it's the Banque Credit d'Helvettia," Thompson interjected, his French pronunciation making much progress in the four-month period he'd spent in French-speaking Switzerland.

"Then, maybe it's intended. That'd be nice. But the amount's outrageous. It's six times my salary, more or less, and much too early for bonuses," Scharfman reasoned.

"Even if it's legitimate, it's one hell of a bonus, and paid early. It has to be some type of mistake. I just don't want the Swiss tax authorities or the Internal Revenue Service all over me because of some mistake," Thompson added to the affirmative nods of the other two.

"Let me give Dom a call. He's a late riser and often eats in his apartment," Scharfman offered, taking out his Blackberry with its international SIM card and dialing Guillermo's private access code.

As predicted, Guillermo was sitting at his dining table, looking over Lake Geneva toward the French side. A devout man, he actually awakened early but said part of the rosary before breakfast, something he hadn't disclosed to colleagues who simply considered him to be one who preferred to sleep late. The memory of his deceased wife, now gone for nearly two years, was especially stirring in the morning; he found prayer as a satisfying form of bereavement and way to honor her. As the former US ambassador to the Holy See, he had met several times with the Holy Father. The pope himself had urged Guillermo to find solace in prayer.

"Yes? Hello, Jeff. Good to have you back. I hope the trip went well. You were in New Jersey, right?" Guillermo said after seeing Scharfman's name on his caller ID.

"Good morning, Dom. Yes, we were with our family there and then spent several days in Washington at the condo. I'm at La Palmeraie having breakfast with Andy and Bennie. All three of us have noticed that our bank accounts have suddenly fattened without our feeding them. Do you have any notion why that might have happened?"

"Yes, you didn't see the e-mail? We were all paid a special bonus resulting from Brent's highly successful commodity market activity last week."

"I never got an e-mail. Hold on one second, please," Scharfman said as he leaned over to the others, saying in a loud enough voice for Guillermo to hear, "Dom says we should have received an e-mail on the subject. Apparently, we were paid a special bonus related to Brent's activity in the commodity market."

Thomson and Tantillo just grimaced, looking at each other with slightly exaggerated expressions of surprise.

"Thanks, Dom. I hope I didn't wake you."

"Nope, just having coffee and something akin to what we know as a bagel," Guillermo responded.

"Take care, see you at the office," Scharfman said, hanging up.

*   *   *

It was nearly ten as the upbeat group of American expatriates, now in the comfortable financial hug of Lucas and the vertiginous pleasures of the heady Swiss Riviera at Montreux, walked from the Montreux Palace Hotel to the railroad station, a mere block and a half away. The swarm of suits, all dressed in business attire, hardly attracted the attention of locals who busied themselves with setting up the outdoor cafés and local shops along the way.

They had become accustomed to taking the picturesque and highly efficient Swiss railcar to the Blonay-Chamby station, across from which stood the massive headquarters building of Lucas Holdings. The thirty-minute trip was a respite from the treacherous drive up twisting Alpine roads with unforgiving cliffs that ignored the shaky, rotting wooden poles originally designed to keep herded cows from the trail's edge. The local Swiss drivers, of course, had mastered the course up and down the mountains, often speeding down the one-lane roadbeds with seeming disregard for whatever may lurk at the next turn or over the approaching hill. There had been enough close calls for the expats to induce in them cautious fear along with high regard for the courage of their new neighbors.

Domenic Guillermo and former California senator Nancy Lehman sat facing Jeff Scharfman and his former New Jersey senate colleague, Andy Tantillo, as the railcar glided through the last tunnel and onto a plateau with the jagged peak, Dent de Jaman, suddenly appearing to the north.

"What a sight. Look at that, Nancy," Guillermo said, slightly nudging his right elbow into her left arm. The upright sliver of rock resembling a tooth was brilliant in the morning sun.

"I love seeing that in the morning," Nancy responded. "It reminds me parts of Northern California, near the Lake Tahoe region. I'm toying with going back to San Francisco, you know, Dom. I think I'm done with Washington and politics. I can see myself living in the Cascade Range, near Mount Shasta. I've years of experience, I'm ready to write. I'll do so-called political thrillers, dealing with the mess in Washington. But first, I want to get through my own mess . . . you know, the pardon."

"How does Steve feel about this?" Guillermo asked, referring to Steve Rubin, Lehman's longtime companion. They lived apart, and Steve remained in the Washington area, never visiting her during the four months that she'd been in Switzerland. She did see him briefly when back in the United States during their Easter break.

"We're finished. He's found a much younger woman of which there's no shortage in DC. It was expected. He's two years younger than I am. It looked bad from the start, but we had a great run, five years, more or less. I always knew I was useful to him as long as I was in the Senate. And now, he's struggling to make a living. His lobbying gigs are fewer and fewer these days. Steve had no government experience. He never worked on the Hill or in the administration. He can't compete with the hordes of former members of Congress rushing on to the lobbying scenes with clients they've already lined up before giving up their seats, or losing them," she added with a dismissive shrug to their mutual laughter. Lehman was sixty-two now and had become somewhat haggard from the scandal and the punitive aftermath when she had been avoided by so many of her close friends in Washington.

"If it hadn't been for Niko, we'd all be pretty much in the same boat," Guillermo responded. "I could never have gone back to a law practice in Hartford or New Haven even though I'm a former governor. I would've gone to Washington to work as a lobbyist to make the real money. And as you just pointed out, since I've had no federal experience, it would not have been easy. I had a few offers from Italian aerospace companies to represent them in DC. But the fees were too low and the work too difficult for me since I have absolutely no background in either the aviation industry or the defense department."

Scharfman and Tantillo had stopped chatting between them, tuning in to Guillermo's comments to Lehman. Scharfman caught Guillermo's eyes, saying, "I couldn't help hearing that, Dom. I agree. It would be tough for you. But also for me, especially with this controversial scandal rap hanging over me. Bob Castignani manages it because he was never implicated, but he still encounters barriers. Setting up the New England Industries Association as an interlocutor was a brilliant move. He gets to the people he needs to work on through the lobbying act loophole."

"Well, things are looking up for us. If we can get the pardons, we'll be in even better shape," added Tantillo, who had served several months in prison, one of the sharpest penalties handed down by the court.

"That's for sure. It'll restore my coffers after what my defense cost me. Like everyone else, when I saw the eleven million Swiss francs in my account last night, I almost fainted," Lehman said, wrapping her arms over her chest. "I can hang in for that type of money, nearly seventy times my annual Senate salary and ten times my Lucas salary."

"Let's not get too carried away," Guillermo added somberly. "That was a one-time special bonus related to a series of market trades needed to implement the rest of the strategy. There will be annual bonuses and probably even a special one now and then, but I doubt if we'll ever see the likes of this one again."

"That's okay with me," Scharfman added. "I'm not greedy. I was satisfied with the original salary arrangement."

"As was I," Lehman said, chiming in.

"Same here," said Tantillo.

The train gradually eased into the Chamby stop; the expats clamored to the doors, business cases slung over their shoulders. The train's conductors assisted them at the exit with their friendly good-byes now a daily routine between them and the very friendly American group. They enjoyed the contrast, this in a country where years of similar encounters between Swiss nationals would pass before the same level of friendliness would emerge.

They walked in pairs from the station, up the very steep hill, and to the even steeper concrete staircase in the front of the building. At four thousand feet above sea level, the air was not as much an obstacle to rigorous movement as the slope of the terrain. Yet after several months now, the hardiest of the group could manage the walk and the sixty-five-step staircase without a rest stop. The older members, along with those in less great shape, like Guillermo, whose past as a top athlete at Yale made an even more annoying difference, walked around the corner to a less severe sloping driveway that curved around the front of the building. They usually arrived at the entrance at about the same time as the stair hikers and feeling much less tired.

"Mornin', mates," said Rallis with his best American accent showing. "I thought you'd all be looking happier today, the haul up the hill notwithstanding." Rallis had just arrived himself, having driven up the hill.

"Right about that," said Anne Rathbone, the Lucas chief financial officer and former Delaware congresswoman; she had clamored up the stairs and was noted in the group as one of the better-conditioned members. She was breathing quite easily despite the trek. "Bonuses have a way of doing that to me," she said to the laughter of the others within earshot.

The group separated to their respective offices and, highly inspired, got right down to work.

Many reviewed the e-mails that had accumulated during their relatively long absence, now almost ten days. The highly protected computer system employed complex security codes that were, to the moment at least, impenetrable. Embedded software had prioritized most of the transmissions while the others could be further categorized as "business," "official-US," "other-official," and "personal." E-mails from colleagues back in the States, for example, were designated for the "official-US" category, along with whatever communications might have come from the regulatory agencies or other government entities. Swiss government matters were similarly grouped under "other-official."

Marc Gregoire, the former Louisiana congressman, who had also served a short prison term, and his wife, Jane, were doing well with the company in the short time they'd been there. Together, their salaries would bring in 1.2 million Swiss francs for 2011. Both also collected a combined 11.25 million through the special bonus payout. As he scrolled through the e-mails, his eye caught one from a former staff member who had moved over to the office of a Louisiana senator. It read as follows:

Hi, Marc. Hope you and Jane are doing well. The commodity market shrill vibrated throughout the Hill. Some folks taking it in stride. "Typical market turbulence," some said, but others, especially those on the committees of jurisdiction, are pushing for a CFTC investigation. There were a few smearing remarks about your group, which I'm sure you expected anyway. Just pure jealousy, I find. My thought (recommendation) is that Bob Castignani should get out some form of explanation to his buddies up here. They trust him and will listen. I don't know who the lobbyists are for the big confectioners here, Rose and Havens, but no one in the Massachusetts or Connecticut delegations has been complaining.

Let me know if I can be of help. Regards, Julius.

Sounds like he's angling for a change of employment, Gregoire thought to himself. *Julius is a good guy, but he's ambitious. I can't blame him. It took me too long to figure out that the smart people in that town don't work on the Hill. They make the Hill work for them. Besides, he's much more valuable to us where he is, so I better play him along.*

Gregoire returned the communication:

Thanks for the note, Julius. We're aware of the various impacts but highly confident that we've done everything properly and, therefore, have no fear of any type of inquiry, whether from the US or EU side of the pond. I always welcome your observations and appreciate your friendship. Please keep me posted on your career plans as they unfold. Jane joins me in sending our regards, Marc.

Gregoire read over the note a couple of times, making minor changes. *That should hold his attention. I'll let him think we have an interest in his services,* he reasoned to himself.

*   *   *

Even the staff among the New England delegation was picking up the shards of information disseminated by their former American colleagues, the expats, now visiting from Switzerland. Castignani had urged Lehman, Guillermo, the Gregoires, and others to talk to their former congressional colleagues, keeping it on a social basis to avoid any conflicts with the restrictions on former members lobbying Congress. That they succeeded in arousing the interest and rapture of their incumbent colleagues would be an understatement.

Following the guidelines laid out in talking points provided by Castignani, the visitors invited the congressionals participating in the New England Industrial Association to lunch, dinner, and other events and opportunities to talk shop. They discussed the plans for job expansion in the New England confections sector with infectious enthusiasm. Rose and Havens had no lobbyists, they were reminded, therefore relying on the respective members of Connecticut and Massachusetts and the other sympathetic members from other parts of New England. But the talking points suggested there would be a time as the two US confectioners expanded that new managerial, director, and other positions would have to be created to fulfill the expectations of the business strategy. It went without saying that the members, who had been so supportive of the strategy, essentially forming its lobbying base, would be the natural successors to such employment opportunities.

Upon their return to Switzerland, and the surprising receipt of substantial bonuses, the expats lost little time in communicating back to their colleagues the good fortune that their positions with Lucas continued to shower on them. The solicitous staffs became aware of the largesse prospectively awaiting their bosses upon retirement and, like Gregoire's former staffer Julius, made an effort to inculcate in the minds of the Swiss-based expats that they too would be available as distribution targets.

It unfolded exactly as Nikos Rallis had intended. He had said nothing beforehand of the bonuses, raising the element of elation among the recipients, nor did he share that part of the lobbying plan with Castignani, who was led to believe that his mission was to encourage the socializing that ultimately took place during the recess period. Rallis reasoned the smarter of the expats would figure it out in time. That didn't bother him. His objective was to implant Belmont in the US confections markets and ultimately to dominate it to the extent that US antitrust laws would tolerate. But with hundreds upon hundreds of smaller confectioners in the US, Rallis knew that calculating the actual market-share position of a rejuvenated Rose and Havens, dangled from above by himself as the master puppeteer, would be very difficult and time-consuming. He was savvy enough regarding the US judicial system to understand that few courts of equity would risk enjoining the market operations of Rose or Havens without reliable, preferably federal, government statistics on market share.

*   *   *

It took even less time than Rallis expected for the Swiss partners to discern his strategy. They had been reluctant to engage the quick-witted, scheming Greek in their own secretive thoughts regarding a takeover of Rose and Havens. But in the meantime, they certainly subscribed privately to Rallis's maneuvering and manipulation of the American expats. His moves fit their own schemata rather perfectly. From Rallis's perspective, they were thinking exactly the way he had anticipated. Rallis saw himself becoming simultaneously indispensible to the three parties: the Swiss, the American expats, and the congressional members of the New England Industrial Association. It was his "three-legged stool," as he thought about it.

The Swiss leg became more animated the next day, Friday, April 28, when Paul von Schlossen of Brent and Lutz Gorgens of Belmont conducted a three-way conference call with Frau Urs Hochdorf, the Swiss deputy minister of finance. Frau Hochdorf managed the sovereign investment fund of the Swiss government. The government investment in Belmont and Brent was substantial enough to warrant her attention and cooperation with the two companies.

"Good morning, Frau Hochdorf," von Schlossen said. The group would be speaking in German with the director of the Federal Finance Administration, or FFA, the principal job function of the deputy minister. The terms "ministry" and "minister" were often used although, formally, the official name of the government entity is the Swiss Federal Department of Finance, which in German is the Eidgenossische Finanzdepartement.

"Good morning, gentlemen," Hochdorf said, having seen on her telephone monitor screen the names and photos of the two Swiss corporate officials. "You must be enjoying the beautiful sunshine this morning. I'm sure the lake must be stunning," she added.

"It lacks only the grace of your presence, my good friend," added Gorgens.

"Lutz, you are such the smooth talker. You have never changed since our school days," Hochdorf replied to her longtime friend. They had grown up together in Zurich.

"I would not say he hasn't changed at all, Urs. Those jowls are not something he sported as a schoolboy," said von Schlossen to everyone's laughter.

Von Schlossen continued to speak. "As you no doubt know, the Brent commodity operation went very smoothly, and we will address it in more detail at our next board meeting." Frau Urs Hochdorf was a member of both boards of directors, representing the Swiss government's stake in the two companies.

"Yes, Paul. I had tried to follow it, but the coverage was very spotty. Of course, we are very pleased with the outcome nonetheless," Hochdorf replied.

"Which is what brings us to call you," von Schlossen added. "The issue is whether we are putting too much of ourselves at risk by joining with the American companies. Obviously, they are a necessary conduit into the US market, but we are providing the cash, our product line, and the essential production element, the cocoa bean. In other words, without any of those three items, the US companies not only lose much of their market but also are closed out of any export opportunities they may have, to include any offshore production they may be doing."

"I have thought about that," Hochdorf replied. "But are there not other factors at play? First, there are the WTO rules, which can limit the use of the three sources of influence that you mention, and second, both US antitrust laws and the growing role of the US Congress must be considered. Congress seems to believe it can manage, not just regulate, contrary to some rather basic principles of capitalism that here in Switzerland are rather sacred."

"Forgive me, Urs, but I'm not sure I follow your thoughts here, especially as regards the World Trade Organization," said Lutz Gorgens, Belmont's CEO. "Belmont already exports to the US as well as all of Europe and much of the rest of the world."

"I was referring to another trade matter, that dealing with Brent's control of the cocoa bean market. You see, under the US trade remedy laws, which we monitor very closely in this department, *any* foreign trade activity unfavorable to the US can be the subject of retaliation. Therefore, any evidence that Brent, which after all holds 20 percent of Belmont, is depriving the US confections market of cocoa, this can be construed as a hostile trade act," she said.

"As we speak, I am looking at the US statute, section 301 of the Trade Act of 1974. It establishes specific authority to, and I quote, 'enforce US rights to respond to actions by foreign countries inconsistent with or otherwise denying US benefits under the trade agreements.'"

"But these actions are taken under the WTO dispute settlement rules, are they not, Urs?" asked Brent CEO von Schlossen.

"Not necessarily, Paul," she replied. "Of course, the US may seek redress under the dispute settlement rules of the WTO. But section 301 is very powerful and addresses a sovereign right insisted upon by the US in the Uruguay Round negotiations that established the WTO in the 1990s. But this particular section has been argued in US courts or other tribunal venues related to foreign trade, like the US International Trade Commission. One example is the US steel industry's success in limiting steel imports by somewhat arbitrarily imposing antidumping duties, a matter decided entirely within the framework of US courts."

"But why would they place antidumping duties on cocoa beans? Wouldn't that harm themselves?" von Schlossen asked.

"Of course, and they wouldn't. They could, however, restrict Swiss confections and perhaps other of your products as well. They could simply claim that the benefits accruing to Belmont because of Brent's control of cocoa allowed for Belmont's chocolate goods to be sold in the US at a price level below that of the same products in Switzerland, therefore establishing intent to dump for purposes of getting market control," Hochdorf explained.

"Let me address my second reservation," she continued. "Would Congress accept a scheme that would cause disruption in their confections market at a time when the US is already under economic stress?"

"Actually, I have answers for you on both of the reservations that you've raised. First, our relations with Congress, thanks to Bob Castignani, whom you've met, are good enough that I don't see Congress objecting to Belmont's move into the US since Belmont will be partnering with Rose and Havens, the two largest companies. I can't imagine the Senate Finance Committee or the House Ways and Means Committee, the two parliamentary committees with oversight on trade matters, supporting an interventionist move by the US Trade Representative to seek either antidumping duties or to object to the partnering arrangement.

"In fact," von Schlossen added, "Castignani has rather conclusively captured the key members of Congress, some of whom are on the relevant committees, and persuaded them to support us, which they have done."

"That is very interesting, Paul. How has that been done?" Hochdorf asked.

"I have been at meetings with congressional people. The US system is very different. The right to petition, which is to say 'lobby,' is absolute and written into the US Constitution. Secondly, while congressional members cannot accept gifts or anything that suggests a conflict of interest between their official positions and private pursuits, they can support a legislative move that benefits a much broader group of citizens that just may happen to include a member without running afoul of the law.

"This Castignani has done this very smartly by creating an information type of council. They call it the New England Industrial Association, which brings together the legislators we're trying to influence for purposes of, if you'll excuse the term, 'educating' them on our purpose," von Schlossen remarked.

"*C'est incroyable* [unbelievable]," came Hochdorf's reply, deliberately stated in French. "So they've signed on to our endeavor?"

"I'd say rather completely, Urs," von Schlossen answered.

"But what was the purpose of this call if you have already managed to circumnavigate the official barriers?" she asked, adding, "You said something to the effect that we were *giving* too much, how so?"

"Please, let me address that, Paul," said Lutz Gorgens.

He began to speak. "Urs, you see, we think we can do better – over time, that is. What we're thinking is that we can enter into the partnership with the two US companies on two levels. First, we would license them to produce our products for which, of course, they will still need cocoa. We would provide enough cocoa at prices discounted to our favor so that the cost of producing the licensed confection would be very slightly more than the prevailing price of the item in, say, Switzerland. That certainly would remove any grounds for a dumping case against us.

"But we would be selling cocoa to them for their own production at a premium. After all, Brent is entitled to a fair market price for its sales, and Brent owns the coca bean market so to speak. That Brent has the right of discretion in selling its commodity at whatever the market will pay is an indisputable and, I would add, nonjudiciable commercial right and privilege."

"But Brent is a major shareholder of Belmont, Lutz. Isn't there a conflict?" she asked.

"Under the laws of what jurisdiction? Certainly not Swiss or American. Brent is not a speculator. It is hedging its market transactions as a part owner of a company that depends on a stable price of a critical factor of its production, cocoa beans in this case. It is allowed to, as the traders say, 'trade for its own account.' *Sind wir recht.* Isn't that right?" the Belmont CEO replied with a question of his own.

"I believe so," she said.

"In fewer words, we are convinced that we should acquire the two companies. We would operate them for a short period and then repatriate our investment gains, move production to more suitable areas offshore, and, regrettably, shut down the US facilities. What do you think?" Gorgens asked.

"To be honest, I have thought about it in that way and have even spoken to some colleagues in Bern indirectly about a greater Swiss investment in the US for a short term of, say, three to five years. The US is just too risky for anything longer. The country's finances are nearing the disaster level, in my judgment. The US debt is out of control. American consumption habits are replicated in their government. They spend on the status quo rather than the future and are even talking about eliminating R&D tax breaks. The tax code itself is a nightmare. Everyone has some type of special deduction that keeps revenues well below anticipated collection levels. The current administration spends too much on helping people remain unemployed. Imagine, ninety-nine months of unemployment. The country must be desirous of becoming another Sweden. Worse, from a Swiss perspective, saving is discouraged. The Glass-Steagall Act, which allowed commercial and investment banks to merge, means passbook savings pay less than 1 percent interest, and there are no other real savings tools opportunities available to average citizens. Everyone has to have an investment adviser now because no one understands how to save and invest, including most of the advisers, from what I've read from our embassy reports. So I would be supportive of that and willing to promote it at the highest levels in our government," she responded.

The call ended after the appropriate courtesies were extended.

Lutz Gorgens and Paul von Schlossen remained on the phone.

"Well, Lutz, there you have it. We have the government's seal of endorsement. What now? How do we approach Rallis, or should we?" asked von Schlossen. "He's obviously thinking along the same lines. It may be that the presidential pardon issue will provide the opportunity. The Americans on our staffs can use it as leverage to insist on their pardon. If the president hedges, they would probably join us in shutting down US operations. They like the money they're getting, and they would get a lot more if we closed out of the US as our exit strategy.

*　　*　　*

The weakest leg of the stool in Rallis's minds was the US political scene, Congress, and the Connecticut delegation in particular. The Massachusetts members were solidly on board. Overwhelmingly Democratic with a fellow Democrat in the governor's mansion, the potential job gains blinded them to the means to get there. Moreover, the state's economy was much more diverse and buoyant than Connecticut, which was heavily dependent on the Fairfield County slice, where New York City's financial sector dispatched many of its moneyed elites to the tax-friendly state and county. If Rallis's plan hinted collapse, the Massachusetts' delegation, angered as it would be, could cover the losses. But Connecticut was a different story. The state's first incumbent in modern history sat in the White House; indirectly, the state's political clout and reach were global. Rallis needed to reset the stage. Governor Sophia Kallias was a good place to start.

It was midmorning on Tuesday, May 3, 2011, when Nikos Rallis reached Connecticut governor Sophia Kallias in her office at the state capitol in Hartford.

"Nickey, what a surprise," the governor said as she took up the receiver.

"'Nickey,' you really know how to hurt a guy. I think you're the only one at Trinity who called me that," Rallis replied, referring to a rarely used nickname, Nickey, which few of his friends even knew about.

"I heard your mother call you that years ago when she visited you at school. She invited all the students with Greek names or heritage to a private dinner at St. A's," she said, referring to Saint Anthony's Hall, the fraternity of Delta Psi founded on the feast day of Saint Anthony. The fraternity members sometimes referred to themselves as the brothers of the Order of Saint Anthony, somewhat of a mocking portraiture of a Catholic order since the fraternity, in practice, was as exclusive as Yale's Skull and Bones. Few Catholics were among the brotherhood, which leaned heavily on legacies of some of America's oldest and most distinguished Protestant families.

"I remember that. She thought you were very attractive. But please, just call me Niko or Nikos, you know, the adult version of Nickey," Rallis said.

"Thanks, in retro, but I think there were only, what, three or four women at the dinner? I can't remember the others. By the way," Kallias said, quickly changing the subject, "I was so sorry to hear that you and Malva have decided to separate," referring to Rallis's wife, who had petitioned the Orthodox Church to end the marriage.

"I can't blame her. The Greek recreation project reached scandalous proportions in the US, as you'll recall. We did nothing wrong from a European perspective. There were no conflicts of interest like those encountered by the US congressional investors. She thought her family name was being dragged through the mud, worsened by her marriage to me. Her father and other members of her family actually encouraged her. At the same time, I have to tell you, it developed that she was seeing some other guy, a Greek businessman from Athens and a boyhood friend of mine. In fact, he was with me at the Wharton School. He and Malva seemed fairly close even then. She has since told me that she sees him from time to time, but I think it's more than that. For one thing, I believe she wants to marry again, and in the Greek Orthodox Church," Rallis explained.

"I am familiar with the Greek Orthodox beliefs and traditions even though my family was Jewish. I often get invitations from the Orthodox communities here who think I'm one of them," Kallias replied with light laughter.

"Well, you and I have a strong cultural bond anyway. You father is still very important in the minds of his fellow Thessalonians."

"In fact, I'm on the board of the Sephardic Jewish museum there and visit about once every two years. Few people realize that Thessaloniki was a scholarly center for Jews in the sixteenth century."

"That's right. The Ottomans encouraged Jewish immigration there to balance the city's growing Catholic population," Rallis replied, pleased that he was building a sturdier bridge to his target. "And Americans should know that the word 'nike,' the Greek word for victory, is the prefix in the city's name, which was named after the half sister of Alexander the Great, and means Thessalian victory."

"But the city was founded in 315 BC by King Cassander of Macedon after the Battle of Crocus," Kallias replied.

"You are amazing, Sophia. You know your Greek history very well."

"Listen, I've been to so many Greek festivals, which seem to celebrate every battle in the country's long history, during my childhood and especially when I was representing the Woodbridge area of the state in the legislature," she replied.

"We'll have to talk more about this and some other matters. My son, Lex, is a sophomore at the Loomis Chaffee School in Windsor. I'm coming to see him this month and to talk to the admissions people about my daughter, Alysa, who's just thirteen but may go there next year. Can we get together?" he asked.

The prospect thrilled Kallias. *Wonderful. I've always liked Nikos. He's divorced now, but what am I thinking? So am I. Zbig is gone. That thing with Sue is accelerating.* "Sure," Kallias responded, trying not to sound too excited. "I'll look forward to it. Call when you're here. We can either have dinner at the residence or someplace else, your choice."

"*C'est parfait* [perfect]," Rallis responded deliberately in French.

She'll be an important ally. She's also single, having gotten rid of that loser, whatever his name was. I think he's still teaching at Boston University. The bum was embezzling trust monies Sophia's father had left for her. I can lead her on. She's ripe to get remarried. That may be a good line, Rallis thought.

*   *   *

On Wednesday, May 11, about a week later, Rallis arrived at Hartford's Bradley International Airport. The Falcon 900LX, owned by Brent, the commodity trading company in Switzerland, had cut through the night sky for over eight hours while Rallis slept for virtually the entire flight. Less than an hour before the 7:15 a.m. arrival, he shaved, using a straight razor rather than his usual electric Remington, all the better to wipe away the signs of fatigue from the long flight. He was excited, not only with the prospect of seeing Lex, his fifteen-year-old son, but his planned encounter with Sophia also was foremost in mind.

As the aircraft taxied to the general aviation terminal, he saw what he assumed to be the governor's limousine, accompanied by two Connecticut State Police patrol cars standing by. Sophia was talking to one of the police officers, both standing by the car. A female aide was close by, an iPad or something like it being worked furiously.

After the aircraft engines were shut down, the door opened with a small staircase unfolding onto the tarmac. The governor and her entourage approached the plane. Rallis waved as he watched his step down the small ladderlike staircase. *No time to fall flat on my face,* he thought to himself.

"Welcome to Hartford, Niko," Sophia said as she approached him, dropping the final *s* from his first name and avoiding the use of his childhood handle, Nickey.

"Delighted to see you, Governor," Rallis replied as he embraced her, keeping his hands on her shoulders to better evidence nothing more than a friendly embrace.

As they chatted about the flight and weather, she put her hand on his left arm, guiding him to the waiting limousine; the female aide walked quickly ahead, climbing into the front seat of the vehicle. The driver opened the rear passenger side door for the governor, who slipped in, while Rallis was escorted around to the rear door on the driver's side, all in keeping with protocol.

Once seated, Rallis touched her left hand. "It was very kind of you to pick me up, Sophia. I'd hate to see you tied up in Hartford rush hour traffic because of me."

"We have an escort, as you can see. He won't use the siren, but he'll get us through it. We may have a few delays, but Jennifer's on top of my schedule and can alter arrangements if it becomes necessary," she said, nodding to the young woman in the front seat.

"I'm sorry that I'm booking you into at the Marriott, the one by the convention center. I would have preferred that you stay at the mansion. But you represent a big interest in Connecticut right now. There's a lot of buzz about the confection industry's expansion. The media would be all over me, not only for providing special treatment to a corporate big wig, but also noting that you're a single male," she said with a chuckle.

"That latter's the part they'd like the best. It's probably a bigger viewer or readership grabber than the corporate story. What smells is what sells in that business."

"And even more so when the smell is morning-fresh shaving cream," Sophia added as they both dropped their heads back with laughter. "There's even a trace of it under your right ear."

Rallis pulled out the handkerchief from his jacket pocket, dabbing at it.

"Let me help, Niko," Sophia said as she took the handkerchief from his hand, moving it around the earlobe and onto the back of his neck behind it. "What'd you try to do, shave the back of your neck as well?" she said with a smile.

"That may be a great aircraft, but the bathroom is about the same size as what you'd find on a larger commercial plane. And there was some turbulence as we came in over the Connecticut River valley, turning west to Bradley. I thought I did a pretty good job," he said with obvious doubt in his voice.

I liked touching him. He has a strong neck, Sophia sensed.

The feeling was mutual. *That was nice.* He rallied back from his thoughts quickly, saying, "So we'll get together at dinner, at the mansion, with guests?"

"Yes, I've invited the mayor, Al Gomez, a Cuban American and a Republican. He's very smart. His wife, Sydney, may be even smarter. She went to Trinity, ten years ahead of me in the class of '84. She's big in real estate, so she'll be more interested in the evening than Al since she's always trying to weasel her way into state-funded projects."

They chatted about the evening, events in Greece, the budget talks in Washington, developments in the state, and a little about Belmont's plans in the state. Sophia delivered Rallis to the hotel, the driver transferring his two suitcases to a doorman, and then left. Rallis checked in, entered the room, and quickly changed into more casual attire – khakis, Sperry boating shoes, and the usual American-style blue blazer festooned with Trinity College's brass buttons. He arranged for a rental car and within the hour was approaching the intersection of I-91 and State Route 305, which took him to his son's school in Windsor.

It was nearing ten as he entered the headmaster's office at the Loomis Chaffee School. They talked for more than an hour and were joined by an admissions' staff officer to discuss the prospects for Rallis's daughter, Alysa, who was interested in the school, where she would start as a freshman the following year, if everything worked out.

It was eleven forty-five, nearing the lunch hour, as Rallis met up with Lex at the dining commons. The fifteen-year-old was completing his second year at the school. He was popular among the other students, several intimating their desire to be part of the group that Lex had planned to invite to spend part of the summer at his mother's residence in Pireaus, the port city that served Athens.

Nikos saw his son standing at the Edwardian arch leading to the commons; he waved, feeling his emotions surge. The divorce had been painful, virtually unprecedented for this Greek family. He had always been a bit of a philanderer, but that issue and behavior were not at play here. It was the decision of his wife to insulate her family from what she, wrongfully in Rallis's mind, had perceived as shady dealings, shady even in the eyes of slick Greek business practices that her own family routinely practiced. There were other causes and motives Rallis had reason to suspect. But her decision put him in a headlock.

The children had been devastated; Lex seemed almost relieved to separate himself from both parents. Alysa, however, became more attached than ever to her mother, and both Malva and Nikos knew that her attendance so far away in Connecticut at the young age of fourteen next year could pose real difficulties. For at least two years, however, she would have the company of her brother. Both parents were in agreement that they had to be educated abroad, preferably in the United States, as they had been themselves, Nikos at Trinity and Malva at Tufts in Boston.

Lex ran over to his father; there were Greek-style hugs with kisses on their cheeks. Proudly, Nikos put his arm around Lex's shoulder as they headed to the dining hall. After lunch, the two strolled the campus until three, when Lex departed for soccer practice and Nikos for Hartford.

It was after three when Nikos returned to the hotel, quickly changing into jogging gear for a run around Bushnell Park and the Capitol, then back to the hotel for lightweight work in the fitness room, a swim, and a long nap, awaking at six to prepare for his seven thirty dinner at the governor's mansion. He would join Hartford mayor Al Gomez and his wife, Sydney, along with Sophia Kallias.

The state limousine and driver picked Rallis up at the hotel, taking him to the governor's mansion. The drive along Prospect Avenue, near the University of Hartford, is a New England delight. Tudor, colonial, and Georgian houses, the latter category including the governor's house, are elegantly aligned, their venues shaded by oaks that once included some elms that were devastated decades earlier. One side of the street paid property taxes to the city of Hartford, the other levied by West Hartford, long the preference of the metropolitan area's elite. The governor's house, situated at the intersection with Asylum Avenue, readily identifiable by its black wrought iron fencing and the state and American flags at full mast.

Two swarthy, well-built, and serious-looking security men checked the car in while another awaited the car's arrival at the entrance. Entering the foyer alone, Sophia welcomed him with a warm hug and peck on the lips, which, as if by instinct, Rallis sought to linger. Sophia was wise to the move and stepped back with a smile, placing her right arm under Rallis's left, guiding him right, through the library, and left into the sunroom. There, solid rose-colored, chintz-covered wing chairs faced an identically covered love seat. A period-perfect chandelier, once gas lit, brightened the ambience in the fading evening light, providing a soft glitter on the highly polished brass fenders fronting the nineteenth century fireplace. The house, built in 1909, escaped the Victorian dimness of the period as its residents clearly preferred earlier colonial interior decor brightened by extensive use of windows.

"Al and Sydney should be here shortly. In the meantime, let me get you a drink," Sophia said.

"I'm comfortable with a simple scotch and soda," Rallis replied as Sophia moved to a discretely concealed bar built into the wainscoted wall next to the fireplace. "Those old Connecticut puritans," Rallis said with a grin, "they knew how to hide their bad habits."

"Obviously," Sophia replied with faux sternness and a giggle, "it's an update. But they did have other bad habits that they manage to conceal."

She poured herself a glass of wine from a Bordeaux bottle sporting a label that Rallis unsuccessfully, squinting, tried to decipher. Carrying the two drinks on a tray, she joined him on the sofa.

Rather nice, I'd say, Rallis thought, *glancing at her figure and especially the shape of her hips and buttocks as she moved onto the love seat. She's actually a beautiful woman, wonderful graces, quality perfume. She dresses well. She shows her breeding. It's amazing that she's in politics.*

They toasted each other and engaged in small talk, mostly about the house, when a front door security aide announced the arrival of "Mayor and Mrs. Gomez."

Al Gomez, tall for a Cuban, angled his body between the chairs, shaking Sophia's hand.

"Thanks for the invite, Governor. You know Sydney, of course."

"Good to see you both. This is Nikos Rallis, a longtime friend now living in Switzerland and a Trinity guy. I mentioned him to you on the phone, Al."

They shook hands all around while Sydney carefully examined just about every main feature in the museum-like room. "This is a wonderful place, Sophia. You've maintained it beautifully."

"Sydney's in the real estate business. She sees things the rest of us miss," Sophia said, half turning to Rallis.

But Sydney's female instincts were also at play as her surveillance discretely included Rallis, causing her to wonder, *Well, Sophia, is this Zbig's successor?*

Sophia did not miss the expression on Sydney's face. *Amazing woman, she's already figured it out. I can't imagine what I've said or done that would have revealed it. Yeah, Syd, I do like this guy.* It was as if the two were communicating telepathically.

The two couples finished off their drinks and moved across the room to the adjacent dining room.

"I'm not doing the cooking tonight. Consider yourselves very lucky," she joked. A serving butler from a local caterer smiled at the remark. They settled themselves into the Chippendale dining chairs around a table set with silver candelabra and period sterling silver service. The chinaware, embossed with the state seal, was purchased for the house by Governor Raymond Baldwin, who also contributed the original William Hart oil, *Paysage*, that hung over the sideboard server.

"You know, the table and chairs were made by a second-generation Greek American, Nathan Margolis, sometime in the mid-1700s. His workshop was located not far from here on Albany Avenue. All of the twenty chairs that you see about the room were handmade," Sophia said.

"I didn't realize that there was Greek migration to the US that early," Gomez said.

"Nor did I," Rallis added.

"Well, my father was active in just about every major Hellenic activity in the state. He knew the history very well, especially since he was among few Jewish immigrants. Margolis was also Jewish, which fascinated Dad. It turns out his parents had been living in Spain from which they went to the Netherlands during the inquisition and made their way to America. Even in the early 1700s, the elder Margolis was determined to become as much an American as anyone else. He was a follower of Sam Adams and made coffins in his carpentry workshop, which were given to the families of men lost in the Revolutionary War. In those days, as you may recall, coffins were big business, especially among Puritan families. Families would use them for storage, mostly clothing, then get buried in them," she said to general laughter.

"Well, you're well-known in this state anyway," Gomez said, looking at Rallis. "Every mayor I know would like to get a bit of the chocolate action. The job numbers are staggering."

"It's a major and complicated production process. Our potential partner in Bridgeport, Rose confections, is ideally situated at Seaside Park in what had been a shirt factory and before that an automobile plant. I never knew they produced cars in Connecticut," Rallis added.

"They did indeed," Kallias said, joining the conversation. "It was a so-called locomobile, heavily dependent on steam. When the concept failed, the building had been abandoned for years and then was bought by a shirt company, Arrow, I think. They operated there for the several generations when Bridgeport was a major industrial center. Production moved to the South, then overseas, always tracking lower labor costs since shirt making is very manpower intensive. Rose ultimately took over the facility when the then Maryland company split up, Havens settling in Massachusetts and Rose here, in Connecticut."

"Let me ask you this, Nikos, if you don't mind," Gomez started.

"No, of course not, Al, ask me anything."

"I actually have somewhat of a family background in cocoa. My father owned a large bean plantation in Cuba and Venezuela. They had been in our family since the mid-1800s, when we sold our harvests to the UK. We produced the Criollo bean at both sites. You are familiar with the bean, I suspect?" Gomez asked.

"Certainly, it is the highest quality bean and one too expensive for the consumer products that we make in Switzerland or, as I should say, the Belmont plants in Eastern Europe. We use the Forastero cocoa bean. It is indeed inferior to the Criollo but can be treated in the chocolate production process to provide a high-quality, inexpensive, and very tasty confection. If you can provide us with Criollo beans at the same price we buy the Forastero variety from West Africa, we would be very interested."

Rallis, always the shrewd businessman, was laying down a gauntlet that stymied Gomez, who sputtered, "I wish I could. It would be a business deal that I could never pass up."

"And maybe even get us one your plants in the Hartford area," Gomez's wife Sydney enjoined as they all laughed.

"Nice try, Al. I'm glad to see you're always thinking jobs," Kallias added to yet more laughter.

"You still have to process the bean, right? And you need facilities to do it," Gomez said, his countenance recovered.

"That's what makes Bridgeport so ideal. It's on Long Island Sound. The habitual winds take the aroma out over the water where it dissipates. As you no doubt know, Al, we get the dried bean from the harvester, then converting it to the cocoa paste that's needed for all chocolate products. From the paste, we produce the butter, which, when dried and pressed into powder, gives us our basic ingredient," Rallis explained.

"But isn't the powder heavy with fat?" Sydney Gomez asked.

"Unfortunately, that is the case. However, Belmont is working on a synthetic bean that will reduce the fat content to less than 3 percent. It's our ace in the hole as far as the dietetics are concerned," Rallis answered.

"Won't that compromise taste? Your cocoa bean's synthetization, I mean," Sydney said again.

"We would still have to knead the paste, adding milk and other flavors for the milk chocolate products, which sell best in the US. Taste would be preserved, maybe even improved as our research in Switzerland is showing. And the paste has to be made palatable. That's done by conching the paste, the last step of the process," Rallis said.

"'Conch,' that's the Spanish word for shell," Gomez said.

"That's right. The ovens are like shells where we bake the paste at about 80 degrees centigrade, that's about 175 degrees Fahrenheit, more or less. We smooth out the paste, almost to a silky brown and slightly brittle cake," Rallis added.

The dinner and discussions, highly animated on many political and a few historical topics, ended about ten with coffee having been taken at the table. Gomez realized the meeting was not going to produce anything material for either his political needs or career; he had his eye on the US Senate seat of Roger Evarts, the senior senator and a Republican like Gomez. Landing more jobs in any part of Connecticut would have helped his ambitions. He and his wife, Sydney, thanked Sophia and made their farewells to Rallis, then departed.

"He drilled you hard, Niko," Sophia said. "Thanks for being so gracious. Al has his own agenda as I think you easily discerned.

"Let's move to a more comfortable place," she said as they walked back to the sunroom, now lit by a single lamp near the love seat into which they settled.

Despite the narrowness of the small sofa, the two svelte and fit bodies easily maneuvered into positions several inches apart. The talk turned to Rallis's life.

"How is Lex managing at Loomis Chaffee?" Sophia asked.

"Well enough, he makes friends easily. We were very close, we miss each other. It will be easier when his sister, Alysa, joins him there next year. As in most families where parents are apart, the kids seem to compensate by growing closer to each other.

"And you, Sophia, I'm sorry to hear that you and Zbig parted."

"It couldn't last. I always knew that. I loved him, but I was a convenience for him, in every sense of the term. He even admitted it. I was only one of his many priorities and certainly not even near the top of the list. He had his career, his family, his friends, he was always tinkering with some scientific invention. Then I came in, usually when he needed romancing," Kallias said with a somewhat forlorn tone in her voice.

Rallis was touched; when he thought about it later that night, he wasn't quite sure what made him move the way he did. He had said with genuine concern in his voice that belied his behavior, "We all need a little bit of that, Sophia." And with those words, he moved his torso alongside her, his left arm around her neck as she responded, moving her lips to receive his kiss, preceded by a single word, "Yes."

*   *   *

It was midday Thursday, May 5, when the Belmont Falcon 900 LX lifted off from Hartford's Bradley International Airport. Rallis had spent the previous night in the governor's mansion. Sophia seemed to ignore the political risk. They had breakfast alone at seven with the first staff members arriving later that day as Sophia had instructed; the staff was discrete. This was not the first tryst in the house's long history, although it might have been unprecedented in that the governor and the governor's lover in this case were both unmarried.

CHAPTER 13

LICENSE – TO LIQUIDATE?

O N MONDAY, MAY 10, 2011, NIKOS RALLIS AND DOMENIC GUILLERMO JOINED PAUL VON SCHLOSSEN, BRENT CHAIRMAN AND CEO, AND LUTZ GORGENS, BELMONT CHAIRMAN AND CEO, AND BELMONT'S OPERATING PRESIDENT, MARC SMIT. Meeting at the Belmont château, they awaited the arrival of the CEOs from the two largest chocolate manufacturers in the US, Tim Sawicki of Rose Confections in Bridgeport, Connecticut, and Kyle McMahon from Havens, headquartered in Newton Highlands, Massachusetts.

The two American executives had arrived late Sunday from Geneva and were met by Marc Smit, who flew them from the Geneva airport to the Belmont facility at Tour de Peilz, just east of Vevey, on the corporate helicopter. Smit had met Sawicki at several Harvard Business School alumni events over the past decade and had become somewhat friendly, often having drinks or dinner together, along with others, and chatting about their respective operations. Kyle McMahon, an earlier business school graduate, had met Smit briefly on a number of occasions. Their reception at the airport had been gracious, even lighthearted; all parties had well-rehearsed business strategies for the forthcoming negotiation.

After checking in at the Belmont château, Sunday afternoon found the two Americans jogging along the lake, as far as Montreux, a few miles down the lakeside drive. There, still in their jogging outfits, they sat in a café among well-dressed Swiss Sunday strollers and numerous less well-attired tourists, enjoying the spectacular lakeside climate and talking constantly about the coming meeting on Monday. They returned after a light dinner to their respective rooms in the château and slept well, arising at seven Monday morning, taking a twenty-minute walk along the perimeter trail of the ten-acre Belmont headquarters building across from the château. They returned, had breakfast, and were being escorted to the conference room in the château by two young business aides to Belmont's CEO.

An aide entered the conference room ahead of the others, announcing, "*Messieurs, nos visiteurs des Etats Unis ont arrive* [gentlemen, the visitors from the US have arrived.]"

"*Ah, bien* [fine]. *Entre, s'il vous plaît, vous etes bien invite* [come in, please, you're most welcome]," said Gorgens.

The two Americans entered, shaking hands first with their principal host, the Belmont CEO Gorgens, and then acknowledging Smit.

"Hey, Tim, how the devil are you?" said Guillermo, throwing his arm around the equally large frame of Sawicki. "Kyle, good to see you. Tim was a strong supporter when I was governor as well as one of the state's largest manufacturers," Guillermo added, talking to Kyle McMahon, with his arm still on Sawicki's shoulder.

The group chatted for about ten minutes; Guillermo and Rallis departed along with von Schlossen, leaving four business leaders to discuss Belmont's offer to Rose Confections and its large US competitor, Havens.

The four men seated themselves at a round conference table; two Belmont aides sat along the wall, holding several binders with information on markets, production costs, wholesale and retail networks worldwide, and other information that might be needed in the talks.

Kyle McMahon began. "Tim and I are delighted to be here, and we're very interested in your offer. Economic conditions in the US have hampered our growth, but our sales levels remain comparably high with other periods in our accounting and market histories. Since our two companies are by far the largest competitors among the hundreds or chocolate manufacturers in the US, we had elected to negotiate as a team, with equal interest and participation with Belmont in any possible arrangement that we might be able to conclude." McMahon's subjunctive syntax conveyed the message that nothing was presumed or foreordained; everything would be on the table for discussion as well as any reservations either side might have.

"At least three of us are victims of our Harvard training, which means we all probably have the same negotiation techniques," added Tim Sawicki, making an effort to add a lighter note.

"But I would respectfully add that I was trained at Haute Etudes Commerciales," said Gorgens, "which means as a German-speaking Swiss trained in a French business school and negotiating in English, I may easily be the greatest victim."

There was good-natured laughter that followed. They helped themselves to a fruit plate, café au lait, and expresso, chatted for another ten minutes, then settled down, with the two Americans opening their iPads and laptops. The two Swiss had no notes or other materials on the table with them.

Good show, guys, thought McMahon, a former football guard at Northeastern, where he majored in business. *Like the no-huddle plays,* he reasoned, using the football metaphor.

Gorgens started; it was clear that he would be the lead negotiator as CEO and in keeping with European corporate protocols. "We are extremely interested in the US market and wish to enter into some type of cooperative arrangement that, quite obviously, would be mutually rewarding as well as compatible with our respective interests.

"Our thought is to start at a rather modest level, then determining what our business cultures can sustain. One approach would be a licensing agreement. We, for example, produce a product line of milk chocolate items that sell well in Europe but have little place in the huge array of chocolate products in the US. This could be done, we think, in a highly profitable manner for both. The licensing agreement, which we would prefer as nonexclusive, for reasons which I will detail, would be established on the basis of our market research for our selected products in the US. We would apportion the necessary supply of cocoa from our own stocks, which are managed by Brent, the commodity trading company."

Kyle McMahon was surprised, but his expression and tone of voice were controlled. "We did consider a licensing arrangement, and our attorneys also liked the idea since it provides the obvious benefits for all parties. But we would need an exclusive agreement. Putting so many resources to work on the project could be made risky if the products of another licensee were to migrate to our markets, such as counterfeits or other items for, say, Canada or Mexico."

"That, unfortunately, is always a risk. Even our pharmaceutical companies face it. Canada sells knockoffs, some are products that are legitimate in the the countries producing them, like the counterfeit items coming from China and now Eastern Europe. But we have substantial control over the cocoa bean market and can control prices that way," Gorgens answered.

"Except that Chinese counterfeiters, for example, can use lesser quality beans from Malaysia or the Philippines and still undercut our prices," McMahon countered.

"That's not very likely, Kyle. You see, we are entering that market. And we have the assurances of the Chinese government that they will eliminate that type of injurious and illegal competition. Now, I know that such promises have been made in the past on times such as software. But chocolate is a perishable and much more visible at the production stage than someone sitting in a darkened room pirating CDs or other software media."

"A nonexclusive licensing arrangement is still a risk for us. But I might be interested if you can assure our supply of coca for our other products. As you are aware, Brent's capture of the Ivory Coast market has caused prices to rise steeply," McMahon responded, then slipping into his most dangerous oversight.

When Gorgens said that he could not speak for Brent, a separate corporate entity, he agreed to put pressure on them to assure that both Rose and Havens would have *access* to reliable supply, without emphasizing the word "access."

I can take that offer. We can't even get beans right now. The promise is not enforceable. On balance, even an exclusive agreement isn't gonna keep illicit trade out of our markets. So let him think that I've caved on exclusivity to get supply, McMahon reasoned, then said, "Tim and I need to caucus privately on this."

"Certainly, Marc and I will leave the room," Gorgens responded.

Speaking in separate venues, both parties seemed confident that the deal came down on their side.

"I think I can go with that," Sawicki said. "I'm stressed for supply. I need assured sources. Otherwise, I'm poised to lay off people, lots of them, maybe as many as seven hundred. The Bridgeport area is in bad economic straits as it is. Some of these workers will leave the area so that when I need them back, I won't have my usual skilled labor pool."

"I'm in the same barrel, Tim. I think we should do it," McMahon said to Sawicki's affirmative nod.

On the Swiss side, the two Belmont executives talked in Lutz Gorgens's office. "What if they bring up price, which, as much I can't believe, they never mentioned?"

"They're desperate, Marc. They're on the ropes, as Americans say. Their sources are far and few between and costly. They don't have many options," Gorgens replied.

"But . . . still, no discussion of price? The futures contracts and other hedging measures that they must have in place can't possibly cover all of their needs," Smit replied.

"Marc, you hold the real ace in the hole if we stalemate on price: the synthetic cocoa bean."

"But it's still in development. We couldn't deploy it for, what, about a year and a half, maybe somewhat less time. Even then, we're two years from benefiting from it," Belmont president Marc Smit replied.

"The markets won't care, Marc. If the speculators know that a substitute is nearing market readiness, they'll grab the remaining crop at bargain prices once they understand the time frame before crop production is really affected."

"I see the opposite happening, Lutz. The uncertainty of the time from deployment of the synthetic to productivity-related price reductions could be sooner. They would sell everything, driving down the price and giving the Americans better cocoa beans in ample supply at lower prices."

"You miss one very critical step in your logic, Marc. *You*, Marc, control the research and development of the synthetic bean, which means *you* can control the release date."

"Yes, I guess that I can, Lutz," Smit said with a slight grin.

Back in the conference room, the two negotiating teams returned, each with high confidence in its respective position.

"We'll accept the offer, Lutz, subject, of course, to the review of it by our attorneys and accountants and our board."

"We will have the same hill to climb on our side, Kyle," Gorgens said, standing to shake hands all around.

*   *   *

Within a few weeks, the euphoria of the agreement had begun to blur. Licensed product sales were slow to begin since both Rose and Havens needed time to make adjustments to their processing and production equipment. New computer numerical control equipment had been purchased to meet the licensee's duties, and shipments of the essential cocoa supplies had been delayed by Easter demand on the continent. The Easter period sales had been only modest for the two American chocolatiers as the declining economy reached to their markets as well. However, sales did pick up substantially by mid-May, depending on the geographical region.

On Wednesday, June 1, 2011, Havens' Kyle McMahon and Rose's Tim Sawicki were on the phone. Despite their competitive relationship, the two CEOs routinely cooperated and compared notes to the extent that they even joined the Swiss licensing agreement as a team.

"I've ten days of experience with the Swiss products, which we advertised well," McMahon said. "They're not doing too badly in the Northeast, but elsewhere it's a wash, especially in the Midwest."

"That's my record too. The Midwest still harbors the buy-American mentality, like automobiles. People who buy American cars go to church and are generally middle-class conservatives. They're my Easter market. They cut back on our US products and seem to avoid the Swiss items even though they're under our wrapper but promoted as Swiss in origin. Even that teaser didn't work," Sawicki reported.

"Yeah, it's not good. We're still on the hook for a baseline production under the terms. The bean apportionment has unused quantities at my plants. I should be using some of it for my own domestic production, but even that is down," McMahon said.

"I'll tell ya, if it weren't for the licensing arrangement, I'd be laying off about eight hundred workers here in Bridgeport. But I see something worse on the horizon. Look at the cocoa prices. They're still at their highs, and there's no futures market of any significance where I can hedge prices."

McMahon was no less worried. "When I look at our market forecasts and our capital goods costs, I see something I don't like, Tim."

"I'm on your wavelength, Kyle. I'm gonna give it another week. Then, we're gonna have to rework our business strategy. We'll talk then."

The two men ended their phone call, huddling with their senior staffs in procurement, marketing, and production. By week's end, the future was becoming clearer. Sales were not only down and cocoa prices were up, pretty much ruling out special sales promotions and related marketing gimmickry.

On June 8, exactly a week later, the two CEOs spoke again, then deciding they would contact their congressional delegation. McMahon would talk to Governor Kallias and Sawicki to Guillermo and the Washington-based Connecticut senators and representatives.

*   *   *

Thursdays in Washington may be the worst time to get through to members of Congress. Work schedules, always compressed, are hectic by week's end, which is almost always a Thursday when in session. Sawicki would avoid calling Senator Zbigniew Krakowski, who, he knew, would be contacted by Governor Kallias, who was Kyle McMahon's target. Instead, he would call Representative George Mourgos, a Democrat in the Republican-controlled House of Representatives. But this was state business and something where, as demonstrated in the New England Industrial Association meetings, one issue where nonpartisanship was less intense.

As one of Fairfield County's largest employers, Sawicki had little difficulty getting through to Mourgos as he sat in the Monocle Restaurant, on the Senate side of Capitol Hill, lunching with two lobbyists from a large defense contractor.

Seeing Sawicki on his caller ID, he answered quickly, "Hello, Tim, how are you?"

Mourgos, a former classics professor at New York University, entered politics later in life. Four years older than Sawicki, they were both born in Norwalk and went to the same high school, barely knowing each other at that time. As a state delegate from the Fairfield County region of Silvermine, where he had always had his voting residence, Mourgos was also a single-handicap golfer. Moreover, he was close to Sophia Kallias with whom he shared Greek heritage, overlooking Kallias's Jewish parentage. In the highly politically correct atmosphere of Connecticut Democratic circles, the mere breath of such religious distinctions would be career suicide. Sawicki thought, therefore, that his conversation with Mourgos would get mileage via Kallias throughout the congressional delegation and reinforce McMahon's conversation with the governor.

"I'm well, George, thanks. I do have a bit of a problem regarding the Swiss agreement, which you're obviously familiar with," Sawicki replied.

Not a good time to be with these guys, Mourgos thought, looking at his dining companions and excusing himself from the table to take the call in a former phone booth that the Monocle ownership wisely kept available for such occasions.

"Sorry to hear that, Tim. What's happening?" Mourgos asked.

"Prices are spiking. We, that is Kyle McMahon of Havens and I, can't get cocoa from the Swiss."

"Has McMahon spoken to the Massachusetts' delegation?" Mourgos asked, knowing the answer. *McMahon wants the president involved, and he doesn't want to have to kick in money to his delegation if he can freeload on Sawicki's contacts. I wonder if Sawicki is wise to that,* Mourgos was asking himself.

Sawicki was not, in fact, too skilled in dealing on the political scene. Not unlike most other business people, the tendency is to trust and believe their Washington representatives.

"No, we're both focused on the Connecticut delegation. We're convinced that presidential intervention is gonna be needed," Sawicki answered.

"The president is interested in the problem, and it's been briefed at the White House a number of times, even by Guillermo, as you know. But if Eastwood does move on the issue, he has to consider the political fallout," Mourgos replied.

Sawicki was getting impatient. "Well, let me tell ya, George, there's gonna be a damn big fallout, like the two thousand people that I might have to lay off because I can't get cocoa to operate, and the same outcome is looming in Massachusetts."

Mourgos had anticipated some job loss. He and the other members were hoping for either well-paying jobs in the reorganized US chocolate sector's two giants, Rose and Havens, or for hefty support for their costly political ambitions. As starters, they knew the two companies' boards would fire Sawicki and McMahon, opening those jobs that the Swiss would offer to delegation members retiring from Congress. Visits from the former members of Congress now with the Swiss companies during the recent Easter recess and visits by Castignani and Guillermo had suggested as much without actually making offers or even symbolic overtures. But Sawicki's numbers got his attention.

Good God, that's too many. That'll hurt all of us. I need to make them think I'm trying to save jobs, Mourgos reasoned. "That's major, Tim. I'll get moving on it right away."

McMahon did not get a hold of Governor Kallias after several tries. She was wrapped up in an endless series of budget meetings regarding Connecticut's own debt issues. But he expected that she would call him back eventually. He called Sawicki, thinking, *I'd hate to call O'Meara. All I get from him is crap about how much his campaign is costing.*

"Tim," McMahon started, getting through to his Connecticut business rival. "I couldn't get through to the governor. She's tied up. How'd you do?"

"Mourgos said he'd move on it right away, whatever the hell that means. I told him about the job losses we're facing. Believe me, it got his attention. Let's give him a day and see what happens. I'm gonna call Bob Castignani," he said as they concluded their phone conversation.

Sawicki was on the phone soon thereafter with Castignani.

"Bob, we're facing some deep unemployment if we don't get the beans," Sawicki was reporting.

"The deal was that you'd get beans expressly apportioned for the licensed Swiss products that you would produce along with access to others, right, Tim?"

"Yeah, but we're not getting them at a price we can afford," came Sawicki's lament.

"Tim, I can't manipulate the price or the market. Nor can any of the congressional guys in our delegations."

"Well, you have to do something. This could shut us down, you know. Then we could be breaching our covenants with the Swiss because, believe me, I would start using some of their funds to keep the rest of my domestic business alive, and screw those guys," Sawicki angrily replied.

"Take it easy, Tim. Belmont wants to do business with you. They're not gonna let you draw down your facilities and other resources just because the relatively small amount of licensing business that you're doin' for them," Castignani replied.

"Bob, damn it. The issue here is cocoa supply and the price. You know, we didn't hire our own lobbyist or a local law firm to lobby for us. We hired the guys in Congress. That's because you told us that no outside lobbyist could possibly have the access that they have to the various remedies we'd need. Those were the assurances of the Rallis guy and Guillermo. Well, I just spoke to George Mourgos. If he doesn't move fast, although he said he would, we may just have to get a few hired guns and fight this thing in court."

He's really heated, and threatening too. If this thing goes to court, the media will have a major story. I told those guys on the Hill that the plan to have them represent the two companies would backfire. We already have the Washington lobbying community worried that this could set a precedent, using the congressional delegations instead of outside lobbyists. It's downright stupid. The political clamor would only grow if this thing gets to court, Castignani reasoned.

"I'll call Rallis in Switzerland and tell him what's happening. I'll get back to you, Tim."

No sooner had Castignani hung up when his caller ID showed Mourgos on the line.

"Hi, George. I can't imagine why you're calling," he said, making a lame attempt at low-grade humor.

Mourgos did not mince his words. "Bob, Sawicki called me. He says he could lay off thousands, same thing in Massachusetts. He said that Brent is holdin' up his cocoa supply or charging outrageous prices, somethin' like that. Also, McMahon is trying to get to Governor Kallias."

"I heard the same thing, George. I'm about to call Niko in Switzerland while it's still during the working hours."

"What're we gonna do? The job loss issue is something we hadn't fully anticipated," Mourgos asked.

"Our position is that we offered to help the two US companies by giving them more business and that they're in the same position as all other US chocolatiers in getting cocoa supplies. The market decides the prices. We can't tell the Swiss to sell the commodity that they've bought at market prices at a price that will force them to take a loss," Castignani explained.

"The jobs, Bob, think jobs. That's what matters in the state and especially in my district," Mourgos said, deciding, *He knows what I'm sayin', but we can't talk about it. For all I know, his phone line may be tapped. I could incriminate myself. I'll just stick to the political issue of jobs.*

Castignani's thoughts were not much different. *I know only too well what those guys in Congress are thinking. They want the big-time money that they think will come if we change the companies' leadership. I'm still uneasy with all that.* "I'll call you after I've spoken to Rallis, George," Castignani said; the two men hung up.

Castignani's call was exactly what Rallis wanted. He would emerge as the mediator, keeping all sides pleased as long as possible. *Everyone will eventually trust only me*, he reasoned as he listened to Bob's pleas for some type of help.

"I'll tell you what, Bob. I'll talk to von Schlossen to see if Brent can help," he said, then called Paul von Schlossen.

The conversation got into a type of Kabuki dance, each caller knew the undisclosed motives of the other; it was a contest of coyness.

"Niko, as you know, I can't tell my board that I lost money underselling my own commodity. They have to pay the going price, and our agreement never allowed for anything else," von Schlossen was saying.

"Of course, Paul, and as one of your board members, I'd expect nothing less of our CEO. Why don't we do this, let's expand the licensing product line. That puts us in the position as trying to help."

Von Schlossen never underestimated Rallis's cleverness. "I'll talk to Gorgens. I'm sure he'll go along with that. What we're selling in the States is doing quite well, in fact better than I expected. We're making money ahead of what I had scheduled."

Within a few hours, Rallis was on the phone with Governor Kallias. Their first words, highly sentimental, even romantic, turned to business.

"So we're going to expand the Belmont segment of the US business partners. We can't change the price of cocoa until market forces adjust it. It's just not good business, and the Brent board, of which I'm part, would be very angry with von Schlossen," he explained.

"I'll call Sawicki and Sue Cohen at the White House, Niko. We're at least saving some jobs."

Kallias's calls to Sawicki and Sue Cohen had different impacts. Sawicki said he had no choice but to lay off workers, except for those jobs saved by expanded licensing business at his plants. Sue Cohen said she would tell the president that Rallis had intervened, rescued a few jobs, but that economic and market conditions, being what they are, could not avoid some losses as much as he would regret it.

*   *   *

The media was on the story before Sue had a chance to brief the president. The headlines in Bridgeport's *Connecticut Press* set the tone.

ROSE CONFECTIONS FACING STEEP JOB CUTS

Bridgeport (June 18, 2011) . . . Several unnamed sources at the city's largest employer have disclosed that Rose Confections is considering substantial job reductions. Attempts to reach Rose CEO Tim Sawicki late yesterday were unsuccessful, but others close to the problems facing the company agreed to speak off the record.

The obvious cause of lower sales this quarter is the economy itself, this newspaper was told. Moreover, Rose invested heavily in equipment required to implement a licensing agreement to produce and market in the US various types of chocolate products made by the large Swiss confectioner and competitor, Belmont, headquartered near Vevey, Switzerland.

Our own investigations have shown that major cocoa bean shortages have hampered efficient pricing of Rose products. Although the Swiss items being produced under license do not compete with Rose's confections line, under the licensing agreement, the cocoa apportioned to Rose must be used exclusively for Swiss production.

Some suggest that as many as 800 workers face release in the initial layoff scheme with as many as 200 more could be affected down the road.

A near-identical report was heard on the late-night *Team-13 News* on Boston's WBRS, channel 13, which highlighted problems at Havens in the suburb of Newton Highlands. The TV anchor's short statement read:

> "There's some breaking news regarding Havens, one of the country's two largest chocolate manufacturers. Our reporters have been informed that job cuts may be in the company's future mix.
>
> "Harry McGrath reports from the company's headquarters."
>
> "That's the story at the moment. Havens is facing severe market losses in the wake of the economic downturn with its sales down by as much as 30 percent. I'm also told that CEO Kyle McMahon, who is unavailable at this late time of day, has been talking to officials in Washington regarding the shortage of his most important ingredient, cocoa. The Ivory Coast's crop has been removed from the market for the next two years, having been bought in its entirety by speculators and hedgers. Prices for the cocoa bean have risen between 56 and 109 percent, depending on the quality of bean and its availability.

"At the moment, we have no real handle on the numbers of jobs at stake, but Havens' US competitor in Connecticut, Rose Confections, has already hinted at reductions of as many as 800 soon and another 200 to 500 at a later date."

Sunday's local press and TV news programs gave some attention to the story with statements from corporate officials in both states still lacking.

But telephone conversations between reporters and congressional representatives in Washington took place over the weekend.

The ranking minority Democrat on the House Armed Services Committee, Representative Tony Provenzano, was always a media favorite. He was spared media lampooning about a year ago when it was revealed informally among his colleagues that he had been dating Sue Cohen. Sue dumped him quickly when she learned that he was cheating on his wife from whom she thought he had separated and that he was also sleeping with Monica Howard, the current secretary of health and human services in the Eastwood administration.

Tony Pro, as his friends called the former professional hockey player, lived alone in Washington since his wife hated the capital. She remained in Providence, where she had a highly profitable law practice, the success of which leaned heavily on Tony Pro's referrals. As sometimes happens, the media knew Tony Pro was too valuable a source of scoops and other information to put him at risk of losing his seat. Tony knew well how to play the media, like most professional athletes. He was the source of many leaks regarding the politically charged Base Realignment and Closure decisions. And his closest friends in the media would reliably depend on him again.

Anne Ciano, reporter for WPRO, known as the Bay State News Channel, called Tony Pro on Monday, June 20, regarding the story on the wires and in the press throughout Southern New England over the weekend.

"I can only tell you that both companies are very important to us, especially now, Anne, with unemployment in Rhode Island well above 10 percent. We actually have Bay Staters working in Bridgeport and Newton Highlands. Some even commute daily. Others come home on weekends. I can't ignore what's goin' on," Tony Pro was saying.

"What I'm hearing is that the two companies have no hired guns in Washington, that they depend on their congressional delegations to carry the water for them in dealing on commodity matters. By that I mean the cocoa bean supply," replied Anne Ciano, trying to set Tony Pro up for a juicy printable comment.

You're not gonna get me on that one, Anne honey, Tony Pro thought. *But she has a body that I'd like to get my hands on. Maybe I can reel her in.* With that thought in mind, he said, "You know, I don't like talking about these things on the phone, and I'm sure as hell not gonna send e-mails on the subject. Next time you're down here, let's get together and talk."

Good God, this guy has no scruples. That zipper on his pants needs to be locked in place. Last time I was in his office – when was it, last year? – he turned out the lights and made a move. I got out of that one okay, but the damn guy just closed me out on any news. "Just answer this one question for me. This story is too fast moving to let me take a sojourn to DC. Besides, our budgets are pretty tight these days. The print side of our business is on its ass," she said, referring to the formerly popular paper *The Providential*, now, like many others, losing readership at an accelerating rate.

"I'll try. Go ahead, shoot," Tony Pro replied.

"What's in it for the congressional guys who are acting as the real lobbyists for the two companies?" Anne Ciano asked.

"In a word, votes," Tony Pro replied, thinking, *She's too smart to buy that answer,* and he was right.

"Tony, we've been friends a long time, and you've helped my career here very much, which I appreciate. But I need something better than that. Look, we all know that most of the former congressional guys indicted in the Lucas scandal are working for the Swiss companies involved here. It doesn't take too much brainpower to speculate that they're on the take, and I use that word intentionally."

"Like what and who are you talking about?" Tony Pro replied. *I'll let her answer her own question and get myself off the hook,* he thought.

The thinking was nearly identical. *You played into my trap, Tony – gotcha!* Ciano smiled into the end of her receiver.

"I believe we both know, let's say 'expect,' that some members of the New England delegation intend to work their way onto the payroll or into the coffers of the two companies and that the lobbying monies saved by using them, the representatives, rather than lobbyists will give them leverage in arguing for whatever it is they individually want," she said quite boldly.

"Those are your words, Anne."

"But you're not denying anything I said," she quickly retorted.

"You're entitled to speculate on anything. You're protected under the Constitution. In this case, you're suggesting motives on the part of the delegation that close on wrongdoing," Tony Pro replied, feeling the mortal outcome of the exchange.

"No, there is no wrongdoing in what I said, unless *both* parties knowingly engage in what becomes a conflict-of-interest case," she said emphatically.

I'm getting out of this one, Tony Pro thought, adding, "You'll need a lot more evidence than words, Anne. You had better start digging. I've told you everything I know, which isn't a hell of a lot. I gotta run. Nice talkin' to you," he said, hanging up.

I have enough for a story. I've got to get to Sue Cohen or Kenny Edwards, she reasoned, thinking further that the president's press secretary, Edwards, might be the route to go.

"Hi, Anne, good to hear from you, what's up?" the voice in the White House press office said.

"Just something I need to run past you. It's a regional issue, Kenny, New England stuff," Ciano replied.

"Hey, the president loves all regions, especially New England. How can I help?" Edwards answered.

"Actually, I may be helping you," she said.

"I like that. We need allies around here these days," Kenny said, slouching back in his chair. "We don't give out Grammies, but we do try to take care of our friends."

"It's the chocolate issue, Kenny. You have to ask yourself why the two US companies have not hired lobbyists. Add to that the presence of former members in very lucrative jobs with the Swiss companies and now the sudden shortage of cocoa beans needed for the US guys to survive. And what are the New England delegation members saying? 'Oh, well, that's just the market at play. We can't intervene in the markets. And moreover, if it weren't for the Swiss licensing money, there'd be much deeper job cuts.' It doesn't make sense, Kenny."

She's on to it. That's what Sue and the president have been thinking. Except, they're not accusing the delegation members of anything wrong, although Sue has always believed the New England Industrial Association was little more than a bypass around the lobbying laws, Edwards reasoned, then added, "Obviously, Anne, I can't comment on what the president is thinking. I'm not so sure he's pointing fingers at all, let alone in the direction you're suggesting."

He answered my question. The president is thinking the same way. Eastwood's much too smart not to see what's happening. The question is, why isn't he acting on it? But that's Earl Eastwood. He doesn't shoot until the target is squarely in his sights. I've done my job. Kenny will talk to Sue. She'll know that I'm snooping around on the issue and won't let the president be caught off guard. He'll have to act soon. He'll realize that. Anne felt good about the results so far, but she would have to keep the issue on everyone's front burner, including that of the president.

* * *

Kenny Edwards, the definitively slick nonjournalist, learned the media game from the streets. A product of public housing in Bridgeport, he skirted the obstacles to success in his rough-and-tumble black community through two avenues: intelligence and athletic skill. His high school football and academic records got him into Middlebury on track and football scholarships. Majoring in economics with a minor in Chinese, he joined a female classmate in Shanghai, cobbling together the first financial market reporting company. Making a substantial amount of money through the endeavor, he returned to the United States after ten years in China, ultimately hooking up with his former teammate, Earl Eastwood, then a senator, to whom Edwards became press aide.

"Sue," Edwards said into his interoffice phone line, "got a call from Ann Ciano. She's got some good poop on the chocolate deal. We need to talk."

"I'll come over to your office," Sue Cohen said, putting down the receiver and walking toward the press room, an annex to which the Eastwood press secretary had moved his office.

"Hi," Sue said, entering Edwards's cluttered workplace. "What's Ann saying?"

Edwards recited Ann's suspicions; Sue did not seem particularly surprised.

"Earl predicted just as much," she said. "The idea of members using their own offices as lobbyist-type operations had to backfire. The surprising aspect was that all of them seemed to have agreed to it."

"It's the money, Sue, in my judgment," Edwards replied.

"Yes, that's the nub of it, but it's the way their plan would unwind that amused Earl. He said the media would have a blast, and they are. Worse for them, their motives were so obvious a non-Washington based media person picked it up," she said.

"Hell, the local media isn't gonna highlight it. They depend on most of the members involved to give them the inside information that keeps their careers alive," he added. "I sometimes laugh out loud when I think of how anal these different administrations would get over corruption in China when I was working there. You know, stealing our software, counterfeiting our luxury products, pirating our movies, all those different charges, and claiming that Chinese officials were on the take and ignoring the wrongdoings.

"Forgive the pun, but it's the same old crap: the kettle calling the frying pan black. The difference here is we *legalize* our corruption, and this chocolate fiasco is no exception. The members who are also the lobbyists for Rose and Havens are obviously expecting something out of all this."

"I need to keep the president on the sidelines," Sue added.

"I would agree. Nothing he can do or say right now will work to his favor. He can't criticize his congressional colleagues, especially since the ones involved are from New England, his strong constituent base. He can't defend the Swiss initiatives, which, in my opinion, will ultimately lead to their greater position in our markets. I'll keep you alert to whatever I'm getting from the media," Edwards said.

They parted. Walking back to her office, Sue pondered it further. *Zbig, is he involved in this in the same way? He's one of the strongest proponents of the Swiss deal. But he is a Connecticut senator. Just out of curiosity, I'll tell him what Ann Ciano thinks.*

Senator Zbigniew Krakowski was at his Hartford residence when Sue called. He had just put the finishing touches on his personal blog, which he distributed to several of his best categorical supporters, those who bundled the immense amounts of funding it took to run a race in media-heavy Connecticut, and the group and organization leaders, including PACs, who were always there to help whether they were running interference for him in fending off unpleasant attacks on his positions or putting together the constituent events, including the several town meetings that he had attended over the weekend.

They exchanged their usual warm greetings before Sue opened the issue.

"Zbig, Kenny came to see me this morning. Ann Ciano, a reporter for a Providence TV news program, told him that she had had a talk with Tony Provenzano," Sue said, suddenly recalling that she had had a fling with him, which she had never discussed with Zbig. She grimaced at the thought then shook it off and continued to talk.

"Tony Pro was evasive, according to Ann, on the question of whether the New England delegation is wrapped up in some type of subtle scheme to benefit personally from what appears to be their total support for the Swiss moves on Rose and Havens. What's your take on that?"

Don't be disingenuous. Agree with her, Krakowski thought. "I think she has a good point. I'm not privy to nor do I know of any negotiations that might have taken place between any of the congressional delegations and either the Swiss or US confectioner companies. And if I did learn of something like that, I would confront the parties and remind them of the conflict-of-interest rules and further urge them to recuse themselves from any legislative involvement on the matter. I just don't think any of these guys would be that stupid," he concluded.

That's what I wanted to hear, but is he leaving something out? Sue questioned herself. "But they have to expect something. I mean something other than votes or constituent good will, or even hefty campaign help, right?"

"Yeah, and I'm in at least one of those groups. I'm breaking my tail for them, and I'd like to expect help at the max giving level for my campaign fund. Even though I'm, what, four and a half years from reelection, I have to raise almost $500 a week just to meet my anticipated expenses for 2016 race," Krakowski answered.

I'd better get to the point. He knows what I mean, he's just being a little evasive. "So you don't think any of them expect, say, lobbying jobs, maybe even positions, with any new or expanded corporate entity that the Swiss investments might lead to?"

"No, Sue honey, that's not what I think. I think just the opposite. I am certain that some of the delegation members will be leaving office either voluntarily or involuntarily in the next few years and that like just about everybody who retires from Congress, they will be seeking some connection with constituent or other entities that they once either represented or helped. That's the way the town works. You know more about that than I do." Krakowski sensed his voice tightening as he realized she was interrogating him, which he resented.

Sue picked up on it. *I'm being too accusatory. I better change tactics.* "I apologize, Zbig, if it appeared that I was accusing you personally. I sometimes assume my lawyer's mantle with you. I guess it's just the odd nature of our relationship which integrates our personal and professional lives."

Zbig was instantly receptive to the apology. "Of course, honey. I know what you do in this town. You work for a guy who wants facts and details, and you're good at getting them. To change the subject, I miss you badly. Let's get together tomorrow night. We have no votes, so there won't be a late-night session. Those will start next week as we battle over the debt ceiling issue, which has to be done before the August recess. I wish we could take off somewhere, join a CODEL to Paris," he added, referring to the "congressional delegation" trips that dominate the August recess.

Sue laughed. "That would send the media into a tizzy. Imagine the reports: 'President's chief of staff *domesticating* with senator in a luxurious Paris hotel, all at taxpayers' expense.'"

"You know, Sue, maybe something like that could be your swan song at some point, your final huzzah or last hurrah as we peel out of the White House horseshoe in my SL550, headed for Andrews Air Force Base to join yet another wasteful, meaningless CODEL boondoggle to Rome or Paris."

"Be careful, Zbig, the president might be listening." They laughed and hung up.

*   *   *

The president was listening, not to Sue's telephone conversation but to another female equally powerful in Washington: Mary Rossotti Wooley, the former Speaker of the House until the Republican capture of that chamber in the last election.

"Earl, you know how much I care about you, and I wouldn't be telling you these things if I didn't," she was saying, a woman of remarkable beauty and aplomb that her age, now seventy, never diminished.

"Your living arrangement with Audrey is an issue for the party and for your image. Haven't you two talked about marriage?" Rossotti Wooley said, her voice oozing her usual charm. The discussion was directed at Texas Republican representative Audrey Holmes, who had been in residence with the president in the White House since inauguration.

"Mary, I know you mean well, and I appreciate your frankness. And I'll reciprocate. The reality is she does not want to get married," Eastwood responded.

"Then she has to move out. It's the imagery, Earl. In this town, it's always about appearances. What if she gets pregnant? What would you do then?"

"That's a bit extreme. She's not gonna get *pregnant,* obviously," the president responded, almost exasperated with the innocence of the question. "Look, she told me that she doesn't love me enough. If she were deeply in love with me, she has said, she'd want our child and want to be married and live together. She doesn't want any of those things."

"Earl, you're also a Catholic. I've had complaints from those quarters as well."

"As I have, Mary. I try to live my faith and recognize the detractions that I create. But I remind the few church leaders who confronted me that they did nothing during or since JFK was in this job. Of course, their retort to that is as expected: they're talking about me at a very different time in our history. As for moving out, we have talked about it. Actually, I raised it. She was unemotional, which surprised me, and said that it would not be her choice. But if it worsened my emotional state over our arrangement, as well as political repercussions, she would do it."

"So you obviously love her," Rossotti Wooley replied.

"I do, and very much. It hurts me badly that she rejects me but lingers on," Eastwood replied somberly.

"Earl, you'll be better off without her. And I believe she'll be happier too. You're both too old for a meaningless relationship like this, one that's going nowhere. Can you manage the emotional trauma of a breakup?"

"Yeah, I guess so. My West Point training and army experience kicks in here. You learn to accept losses. I've so damn much on my plate, the debt ceiling issue being the most important. You've been too silent on that, Mary. You're letting the Speaker dominate the issue in the House," Eastwood replied, referring to Indiana Republican Art Flaherty.

"He's the *Speaker*, Earl," she replied emphatically.

They exchanged their usual courteous good-byes.

*   *   *

In yet another setting, the debate over the Swiss insertion into the US chocolate market was taking place. CNBC's *Squawk Box* had both Rose and Havens' CEOs on remote conferencing during their TV broadcast on Tuesday morning, June 21. Sitting in the program's guest host seat on set was Representative Frank Poole, a Massachusetts Republican, who as chairman of the most powerful committee in Congress, Ways and Means, had jurisdiction over tax policy. CNBC invited Poole on the program to comment on the debt ceiling debate, which was then dominating executive-legislative relations, as CNBC found it an opportune time to be updated on the commodity markets and the cocoa bean issue specifically.

"Congressman, we thought this might be a good chance also to address the cocoa commodity issue, especially since one of your large constituents in Massachusetts is the Havens chocolate manufacturer," the show's anchor said.

Poole was totally unprepared but unable to display anything but graciousness since, after all, he was the *guest* host on the show. But it did not preclude his thinking: *These Goddamn media bastards, they're always out to stir the pot. I sure as hell would never have consented to being here if I knew that issue would be raised.* "Of course, I see we have my good friend Kyle McMahon up on the monitor. Good morning to you, Kyle," Poole said, the smile on his face totally contrived.

"Hello, Frank, good to see you – well, sort of," came McMahon's reply, remoted from his office in Newton Highlands.

"I hope that 'sort of' comment refers to the TV conferencing," Poole said, trying to jest the scene.

"Yeah, Frank, what else could I mean?" McMahon replied. They both laughed as did the anchor staff on CNBC.

The anchor started the discussion. "Kyle, I understand that Havens is facing deep cutbacks because of the economy and the shortage of cocoa. Are you satisfied that the US commodity markets are properly regulated?"

"Let me say that the economy figures mightily into our earnings nosedive this quarter. But even if the economy were better and our sales prospects looking good, we still lack competitively priced cocoa to produce at a price point that would raise our sales. The commodity markets need better regulation in the sense that any trader or group of traders can still tie up a commodity. This is the problem with cocoa. Our largest supplier, the Ivory Coast, agreed to sell its entire two-year harvest to a Swiss commodity trading company," McMahon responded in length.

The anchor asked Massachusetts congressman Frank Poole, a Republican, to respond.

"I agree with Kyle," Poole started. "I don't have jurisdiction over the commodity markets in my committee, but I follow the issues because Havens, and Kyle and his workforce, are important constituents of mine. We just passed a bill, HR 1611, that would allow companies like Havens, and the Rose Confections company in nearby Connecticut, to hedge the future costs of cocoa without being treated as speculators, who make up the bulk of cocoa commodity traders by the way.

"Havens and Rose could not cover their needs with futures contracts because the bulk of the crop was not offered to the exchanges for trading. As Kyle mentioned, the largest cocoa source, the Ivory Coast, underwent a bloody revolution recently. The fighting stopped when the president agreed to step down after losing the election. His insistence in holding on to the seat is what had triggered the bloodletting. When a sovereign nation decides how and where it will market its agricultural commodities, US commodity exchange regulations become rather irrelevant. We can't demand or compel any nation to sell their goods to us."

McMahon listened, deeply frustrated, thinking, *What bullshit, he's just covering his own ass, damn it. I need to get back in this . . . Calm down, breathe easily, and control yourself! Taking a deep breath without doing it too visibly and forcing a softened expression.* McMahon interjected, "Frank, that's fairly accurate except that we have an embassy in Ivory Coast that is supposed to be looking after American interests there. The cocoa trade is our biggest interest there, and we were let down."

Just what I wanted. I can shift the blame to the Democrats, Poole thought, then said, "Kyle is right on my target. I was mad as all get out that the president and his state department experts were caught off guard by the outcome in Ivory Coast. The Swiss trading company that bought up the crop cut a deal with the outgoing president and his incoming successor, ensuring benefits from the deal for both of the politicians."

"But doesn't that type of behavior violate our laws regarding bribery?" the CNBC anchor asked.

"The Foreign Corrupt Practices Act of 1977 was not part of the WTO negotiations in the 1990s. Rather, our 1988 Trade Act directed the US Attorney

General to provide guidance to our government trade officials. We, that is, the US, have also tried to get universal condemnation of such practices in a series of OECD Anti-Bribery Convention talks. Excuse my officialese. OECD stands for the UN's Organization for Economic Cooperation and Development, which is headquartered in Paris. But the Ivory Coast never signed on to the agreement, and besides, we're not entirely sure that there was any type of conduct, like bribery, that occurred," Poole said.

"But let me return to Kyle's concerns. We have no jurisdiction, speaking as a nonmember of the congressional oversight committee, regarding foreign relations between third parties and a foreign sovereign nation. That's a diplomatic issue as I suggested in my earlier comment."

Watching the CNBC session in Montreux, Switzerland, at Lucas Holdings headquarters, Rallis quickly put in a call to Governor Sophia Kallias. The call was answered with Kallias on the line. After the usual formalities, Rallis said, "Sophia, we need to get the information to CNBC that Belmont is adding product to the licensing production mix at both companies starting in Bridgeport with Rose this week."

"I'm not calling CNBC. I'll let Zbig know," she said. They spoke briefly on other issues and ended the call.

Senator Zbigniew Krakowski was in the Senate TV studio, awaiting remote contact with the CNBC show, which had requested his slightly delayed appearance with McMahon. The show producers were concerned that the two congressional members were both Republicans but believed that McMahon, a strong Democrat, would adequately present the ideological balance the debate might need.

On the line with Kallias, Krakowski mentioned that he was awaiting the CNBC connection and could not talk.

"This will only take a minute, Zbig. I just got a call from Niko Rallis. He affirmed that the Swiss partner, Belmont, would be adding licensed production to both companies starting in Bridgeport this week," Kallias said with some excitement.

"Fantastic news. The timing is perfect! I'll get that news out as soon as I can do it without making it appear too prearranged," said Krakowski, taking some relief from the disclosure.

"Gentlemen," said the CNBC anchor, "we've had Senator Zbigniew Krakowski standing by in Washington and now adding him to our monitor. Good morning, Senator."

"Morning to you, and greetings to my good friends, Frank and Kyle," Krakowski said as they all exchanged greetings.

"Senator, you no doubt have been listening and watching the exchanges here, do you have anything to add?" the anchor asked.

"Yes, a couple of things," Krakowski started, thinking, *I'm gonna take a little of the heat off the president. Poole hammered him too much. We're gonna need his help along the way here. And we're still tied up with trying to get presidential pardons for the former congressional guys.*

"First, let me say that the Ivory Coast situation was settled without further bloodshed. The unfortunate aspect is that they had to sell their most important market asset, their cocoa crop, to keep their economy humming. I don't think we can blame the White House on that, unless we were planning to step in with substantial foreign assistance to replace the funds earned from the crop sale. And as everyone who's had a heartbeat for the past several months now knows, there just *ain't* that type of cash available from the US at the moment," Krakowski said emphatically.

What the hell is he doin? Poole was asking himself. *These damn guys in the Senate, you just can't rely on them. Sometimes I wonder if they just don't give a crap about getting control of the Senate or the White House in 2012.*

"Second," Krakowski continued, "I've been informed that the Swiss chocolate giant Belmont, which has already partnered with the two large chocolate manufacturer's in Frank's district and my state, will add licensed production manufacturing to the amounts they already committed."

"Kyle, does that help Havens?" asked the CNBC anchor.

What a dumbass question, but I better get back in this, McMahon thought, then replied, "Yeah, of course. I'll take anything to keep my workforce intact. No company likes layoffs. Our workers have been there forever. We have very little turnover because we cooperate with the union and take care of our people. We've never had a strike in my twenty years with Havens.

"But I'm increasingly put in a position where I'm producing more and more of a foreign-trademarked product and less of my own US product," McMahon concluded.

"Where can that take you?" the anchor asked McMahon.

Holy Mary, don't these guys know anything about business? McMahon was thinking, his temper barely controlled. Not wanting to put his growing Swiss dependency in any jeopardy, he replied cautiously, "I'm grateful for the Swiss support at this very moment. As to where it can lead, I'm hoping that as the global economy, at least Europe and the US, improves, that we can reciprocate with our product sales through their European marketing outlets." Despite his words, McMahon knew well that US chocolate items sold badly in Europe, and Asia for that matter, where Belmont was already negotiating to buy a Chinese manufacturer.

"Let me conclude," McMahon went on. "Right now, we pay $4,200 per metric ton for cocoa beans. That price is up over 55 percent from a year ago. For the best-quality bean, the price is at $15,000 a ton, up 109 percent. And I have to add, my market is down with sales of the high-quality product down nearly 50 percent and 35 percent for the regular items."

"But, Kyle, you've saved some jobs because of the Swiss support," Poole added, thinking, *I'm gonna turn this guy off right now.*

McMahon was blitzed; he had said all he could without adding problems with the Swiss to his menu. "Yeah, that's where we are now, I guess."

Krakowski was gratified that Poole's retort ended the session.

Kyle McMahon, CEO of Havens, and Tim Sawicki, CEO of Rose, spoke on the phone after the CNBC session.

"You handled it well. I don't know what more you could have said," Sawicki was saying.

"What I didn't say was what you and I are now thinking, but we can't discuss publicly without roiling our staffs and the unions. We may have to shut the doors or sell out to the Goddamned Swiss!"

CHAPTER 14

SWIRLING SCHEMES

T HE DEBATES IN THE MEDIA DID LITTLE TO SOLVE THE PROBLEM AND EVEN LESS TO INSTILL CONFIDENCE IN THE COMMODITY MARKETS. The price of cocoa continued to soar as it became more and more evident that the availability to US end users was less than what had been forecast. Speculators were back driving up the price buying higher-priced futures contracts. The growing number of "shorts," options to sell as the price fell back, pointed to even more uncertainty.

Rose's CEO, Tim Sawicki, had exhausted his appeals to politicians. Kallias was doing all she could, so he thought, and the Washington delegation seemed as detached as ever.

"It was a big mistake to depend on those guys. He should have found the best wired-in lobbyists or even gone to court," Sawicki was saying to Kyle McMahon, the CEO of competitor Havens in Newton Highlands, Massachusetts.

"I don't think there's a legal remedy, Tim," McMahon replied. If we want an exit strategy, we can't object to possible antitrust issues raised from our sale to the Swiss. And if we go to the WTO with a trade case, there's no right of private action. It's a sovereign case with the USTR handling it for us."

McMahon was referring to the World Trade Organization's dispute settlement proceedings. Under the Statement of Administrative Action implementing the WTO agreement, Congress addressed the trade treaty as a matter between sovereign states, including the resolution of trade disputes. In such cases, the US Trade Representative presents the complaint for the aggrieved US party seeking redress under the trade agreement.

"And not one of those bastards in Washington is even coming back to the state. Who the hell do we complain to? They're all gonna be hoppin' around the world on some type of junket," McMahon continued.

"Maybe we can get the president to go to Switzerland to talk turkey to the Belmont people," Sawicki suggested.

"Do we want him to do that, Tim? He, like the governor, wants jobs even if they come from direct foreign investment in the US. Think about it, we're goin' broke and the Swiss have the cash. The political outcome is a lot more favorable for all the politicians, state and national, in dealing with them rather than us. Hell, he may even accelerate our demise. And you know it, if they take over, our jobs are toast. They'll keep us in place for a while, probably even hire us as consultants, but they're gonna put their own teams in here," McMahon insisted.

"They have enough experience here and elsewhere to bring in some good people to replace us," Sawicki said glumly.

"That and the people below us who'll be kept on, you know, our mid – and upper-level managers. The Swiss will just dump us and even form their own boards. The politicians aren't gonna care about us, you and me, Tim. As long as things operate, jobs are secure, and they're gettin' credit for settling things down, the politicians will be happy."

*　　*　　*

The phone lines were also abuzz between Hartford and Switzerland with Nikos Rallis talking to Governor Sophia Kallias.

"Sophia, I want you to come to Switzerland during the July Fourth recess," Rallis was saying.

"That's hard for me to do, Niko, as much as I'd like to. I have all of these veteran activities, and I am the commander in chief, so to speak, of my state's national guard. We have guard troops from Connecticut in Iraq and Afghanistan, I have to honor them. I don't want to be out of the country on personal business. That will not look good."

"Look, the fourth is Monday. Leave the next day, coming back, say, on Saturday. That's the ninth. I'll send the jet. You can come back with my son, Lex. He's just finished his summer session at Loomis Chafee."

That seems workable. It would be good to be with him. This relationship needs a little more structure to it. I can handle Lex. He's a good kid. The flight will be fun for both of us and give us a chance to know each other better. And I'll just treat it as business anyway, letting the party know I'm trying to encourage more work from the Swiss for

Rose Confections, Kallias thought. "Okay, Niko. Let me work on that. Set up some meetings with Belmont so I can justify the time away as business. I'm saving the state money by flying free. How'll we handle the lodgings?" she asked.

"You'll stay at the corporate chalet in Chamby, in the Alps just above Vevey and Montreux and within walking distance, more or less, from the Lucas office," he replied.

"And where will you stay?" she asked in a rather enticing tone.

"Wherever my guest decides I should stay," he said to their mutual laughter.

"I'll call Tim Sawicki and let the president know that I'm making the trip," she said.

That could work out for me. They know of our personal relationship, and they have every reason to believe that whatever Sophia is doing is best for the state. Her cue will be important as to how they behave on this matter. And they'll know that I'm setting everything up for her visit and assume that I was behind her final decision, Rallis reasoned, then said, "Whatever you think is best, Sophia. You're the governor, and I'm a novice when it comes to your political wisdom."

Moments later, Kallias was on the line with Sawicki, who was not unhappy with her decision, believing that she would either argue strongly for more Swiss business to Rose and Havens or try to encourage the best possible deal for any buyout. "I know you'll have the best interests of Rose in mind, Governor, and I'll have a binder prepared for you with all the relevant information you'll need to make our case. You just need to stress to the Swiss that we're their best avenue into the sizable US market and that you can attest to how well we've been managed up to this point in our economic history. The data I give you will amply show that." *And the data will show why I should be kept on as CEO,* he added in afterthought.

Kallias's next call was to Sue Cohen, the president's chief of staff.

Sophia is not one to let fate take charge, Sue Cohen thought as she listened to the Connecticut governor explain her plans for visiting Switzerland. "There's still the risk that your intervention and the relatively small amount of licensed manufacturing that the Swiss are willing to offer will make much difference, and if you fail, Sophia, there'll be political egg on your face in the state."

Right, and you'd like me to slip up so that Zbig can take the governor's seat in the next election, Kallias was thinking as Sue spoke. *Sue has disentangled herself from the party net, pretty amazing considering she's the president's top staffer. Love can blind us all, Sue old friend. I know, I've been there twice, once locked in a miserable marriage and the other time with Zbig. The difference is that I also managed to keep my eye on the bigger goal, my political career.* "I'm not worried about that. My constituents will credit me for at least trying," Sophia was telling Sue.

This initiative could hurt Zbig. He wants to be governor, Sue was thinking. *If she pulls this off, she'll sweep the 2012 race. With Zbig in Hartford and if I can take his Senate seat, we could marry. Connecticut Republicans are traditional, like most other New England Republicans. Earl would support me. I'd be balancing things out: Zbig takes the*

Republican gubernatorial seat and I take the Democratic Senate job. I need to talk to him about this, but I'll talk to Zbig first. "Well, I wish you much luck. We're all in this together. We want to rescue our chocolate sector not only for New England, of course. I'll let the president know, Sophia, and thanks for calling."

The two women were constantly aware that Senator Zbig Krakowski had figured large in their lives. They were able to suppress their feelings, most of which were highly antagonistic toward each other, in their formal encounters.

Sue spoke to Zbig. He agreed that the Kallias trip could weaken his undisclosed plan to challenge her for the Republican gubernatorial nomination. He had been cautiously building up his relationships with the party officials in the state and had been praised by them for keeping the Democratic president's attention on his home state; so they thought anyway. He knew the party leaders in Connecticut were not happy with Kallias's party role or her policies, which included frequent battles with the Democratic legislature that ended in stalemate. She had not succeeded in feathering their favorite projects, especially the rescue of the pharmaceutical industries along Long Island Sound, often referred to now as Connecticut's pharma coast. The region had been growing so fast that some were referring to the state as Geneticut.

But change was in the wind. The largest pharma company, Rehovot-USA, headquartered near West Haven, had transferred substantial amounts of its production and research to its global headquarters near Tel Aviv. The battles with Connecticut's strong unions had overwhelmed them, and they chose to fight no longer. In suspense was the promise of high-paying life-science research jobs that the Republicans had fostered with tax-forgiveness schemes as well as subsidies to the state's universities to boost their academic strengths in related disciplines.

"It would make it easier for us to get together," Sue was saying, avoiding the use of the word "marriage," which they had discussed anyway but about which, Sue felt, Krakowski was not yet entirely on board.

She's begun pushing me. Maybe I need that. My life is pretty uneventful down here. And I like the idea of fatherhood. I'm almost ready, I think. "Geographically, it'd be awkward for us. But it might work. Let's make it our plan. You're gonna talk to the president?" he asked.

"Yes, I owe him full disclosure, Zbig. Having him discover our motives from a third source or at a later time would make him very unhappy. And we're going to need him for whatever political careers we aspire to from this point on."

"Okay, I've no reason to even question you on that score," he said as they ended their call.

*　　*　　*

The president was not in the best of moods as he spoke with Sue that afternoon, Tuesday, June 28. Still sweating from his workout at Fort McNair, Eastwood dabbed at his brow with a gym towel that was always in the opened bottom-left drawer of his desk after vigorous exercise. He was pouring over labor statistics and data provided by the National Economic Council, which at the moment was the most important cog in his Office of Policy Development, a major component of the Executive Office of the President.

Sue settled in, the two of them alone in the office to discuss political strategies regarding the positioning of the president in the economic crisis and its impact on the forthcoming 2012 reelection campaign, now sixteen months away.

"You know, the economy is killing the campaign. I'm getting money from the financial sector but mostly from traditional Democrats who wouldn't support any Republican anyway. Many of the Wall Street leaders are descended from immigrant families, Jewish and Italian mostly, who lionized Roosevelt. The other Democrats in that business sector are just ideologically locked into the party because they don't trust people with accents that suggest parts of the country they don't like, the South, for example. It always amazed me that we still have these cultural gaps in the society, gaps that they managed to close up in the army years ago!" Eastwood was saying.

"And the media has ruptured itself along the same fault lines with ideology being the tectonic plates yanking the country apart," Sue added.

"Yeah, you know, that's the problem. I respect that people get elected as representatives. As a senator from Connecticut, I was sort of the state's ambassador to Washington. But it takes moral courage to explain and act the other role you're mandated to play, that dealing with the national interest. I tried doing that in the Senate . . ."

"And you did do it, and did it well," Sue interjected.

"Thanks, as I was postulating, since I don't have a hell of a lot of reliable information on the subject, these guys in Congress are careerists. In earlier times, congressmen and senators had no official offices back in their states and districts. They would operate out of their houses or even their workplaces. You'd call your representative up on the phone, walk over to his office. Obviously, that type of structure makes no sense today. But my point remains: they see themselves running firms, companies, rather than public service offices. We're constantly hustling out there for cash, planning on what to do if we resign or lose our seats. Their focus today is on where they'll be once out of office, and it affects their behavior. What it comes down to is great admiration and respect for those who commit themselves to the public service notion of elected office and give up the temptations of big money. Those are the real heroes in public office today.

"While we're on that subject, you said that you've talked to Kallias about the Swiss deal. I hate to take time from our discussion about our national agenda, but update me if you will," Eastwood said, once again wiping his brow and apologizing. "Sorry, as you can see, it takes hours for me to cool down from a run."

"Sophia is off to Switzerland after the July Fourth break. She thinks she can negotiate more support from the Swiss chocolatier crowd," she said, adding a French accent to her statement.

"You can bet that Rallis is pushing her," Eastwood blurted out.

"You have a theory on this thing?" she asked.

"Rallis is all about himself. Let's not forget he was behind the original Lucas scandal. He then hires the members who were prosecuted and, when they demand a pardon from me, gives them the leverage to make it happen in the form of promised jobs in the US. All the while, it's Rallis who has little to nothing at risk and everything to gain regardless of what happens. The guy's a classic con man. This town's loaded with them, and he's among the best since he straddles two continents, and God only knows how many governments he's swept into his scheme."

"Other governments, I haven't found anything that makes me think there are others, other than the Swiss," Sue said.

"Why are the French and Brits so quiet? They're at risk in their large confection sectors, which, relatively speaking, are even larger than ours. They've been appeased by Rallis's commodity partners, what's the company, Brent?"

"Yes, they're the ones that seized the Ivory Coast crop. But that country's a former French colony and a member of the francophone West Africa community. Wouldn't the French be furious at the Swiss company for squeezing them out?" Sue asked.

"They are, so the European desk folks at the state department tell me. But they're also happy to take their troops out of the country now that Brent settled the dispute by bribing the outgoing and incoming presidents, which, by the way, will have safe haven residence in the case of the outgoing guy and a substantial offshore depositary for the incoming one. Brent, in the meantime, assures the French and British of dibs on its cocoa bean commodity accounts, enough to meet their production demands. The crown achievement in the eyes of French, though, was the humiliation that we endured as our own diplomatic efforts, which were competing with those of the French, became effete," Eastwood said, pausing to dab his moist brow.

He continued. "And people think Charles de Gaulle is dead. Believe me, he still personifies the Gallic spirit of letting others do your dirty work for you. Remember, it was the Allied invasion of France that cut the Germans down to surrender size, and de Gaulle who slithered back into France on the tail of the American forces. We marked the trail of his victory lap with our blood."

"But getting back to Kallias, she's the governor and plans to run for a second term. She's not going to do anything that would be disadvantageous to her state or her own ambitions," Sue added.

"Sue, you're smart enough to answer that in your mind. Love does strange things to people. Politics is mostly about ego, but money and sex can be the bonus. You're in love with Zbig. He spurned her, and now she's wrapped up with Rallis. Kallias is also an ambitious woman, like you, right?" he asked, looking straight at her with a grin just above his towel again moving about his moist neck.

He knows, the guy's psychic. Did I say too much at some point? she thought, then she spoke somewhat meekly, "I'm not that ambitious, I mean, so ambitious that I would screw the people who elected me."

"I know that, and you're in a different situation, which I hope you'll talk to me about sometime,"

Eastwood added, still grinning, as he placed the towel back to its position on his opened bottom-left drawer of his desk.

"Is this a good time?" she asked in a quiet voice.

"Of course, we're more than just colleagues. We've great affection for each other," he replied.

"I'm exhausted, Earl. Perhaps 'enervated' is a better word. I want things that my biological clock is demanding, like love, a family maybe. I don't think I can wait another few years, to the end of a second term, when I'm pushing forty," she said with a passion that aroused Eastwood's sensitivities.

"I understand," he said quietly, resting his moist arms and clasped hands on his desk and looking at her, undistracted. "This is where Zbig comes in, I suppose."

"Yes, we've talked about getting together, even marriage. But we can't do anything under the current circumstances, I mean to say, with me here, in the White House with you. I can't do what you rightfully expect of me and pursue my personal needs."

"Of course you can't. Even if you tried hard giving it all, which is your nature, resentment would develop, and it would manifest itself in your professional behavior. Tell me, Sue, what would you like to do?" the president asked.

"Our thoughts run along two lines. Zbig will challenge Sophia for the nomination, and I would run for his seat since he would give it up contingent upon winning the gubernatorial race."

"That's tough one, Sue. First, I know Connecticut Republicans. I'm not so sure they're gonna want a party race like that. Second, if Zbig loses, he keeps his seat, and where does that leave you? Third, if Zbig does win, which I frankly doubt, and you run for his seat, the two of you are still apart, with you in Washington at the Senate and Zbig back in Hartford. How does that fit with starting a family? Not that it hasn't been done before. Was it Blanche Lincoln who had the twins?" Eastwood asked.

"Right, but she had dropped out of politics when she was pregnant until her kids were four, then reentered, winning the Arkansas senate seat. On the other issues, we talked about them. We can handle the separation, even managing a child." *I may be overstating Zbig's position. I'm still not sure he's entirely with me on this plan,* Sue mulled to herself.

Eastwood looked at her with evident skepticism. *She's shaky on Krakowski. What's he up to? I wonder.* "Sue, you know what *you* want, but your plan is contingent upon someone else as well, and that someone else has an equally unpredictable plan. It's complicated enough to require a lot of sacrifice and commitment, just be very careful." *Too many escape hatches for Krakowski,* Earl thought. *He's a slick guy too. He may be exploiting Sue for access to the White House.*

"Thanks, but I've also given some thought to my replacement if I leave: Monica," she said, referring to Monica Howard, the secretary of health and human affairs in the Eastwood administration. "She's matured politically, knows Washington well, has Senate experience, is held in the highest esteem in her medical profession, understands the electoral process from working on your presidential campaign, and enjoys your confidence on some very dicey issues."

"You think Monica can handle your job as chief of staff without any White House experience?" Eastwood asked with a quizzical look.

"I did, Earl," Sue softly replied.

They stared at each other, faces softened, their eyes locked on each other, without speaking for almost a minute, as if in deep thought.

"So when does Zbig plan to start his campaign, publicly, I mean, and what's your timetable?"

"Zbig is convinced that her relationship with Rallis won't help her overcome the economic issues in Connecticut, to include the bleeding of jobs in the pharma and confection sectors. Even if she slows job losses in the latter, the economy is in a nosedive, and the financial sectors in the state, as well as the spillover from New York City, will cripple her fund-raising. He'll move for more foreign investment, direct investment, from Europe especially as Italian and Spanish monies are looking for safer venues for their companies. He's had contact with an Italian liquid natural gas manufacturer, an aviation company, and bank, as well as two Spanish wind and solar power equipment makers."

"LNG, in Connecticut, are you talking about storage or marketing or both?" the president asked.

"New London is on its back. As you know, the sub base can't justify itself much longer. The security and safety procedures already in place there are optimal. Bridgeport would be his target to establish wind and solar power sectors, and he would direct the banking interests to Hartford and New Haven."

"Those are Democratic strongholds, except, somewhat, for New London."

"Exactly, he thinks he can use his popularity gained from his Senate service to lock in enough Republican support to reach out into those areas," Sue replied.

"A lot will depend on who challenges Kallias on the Democratic side," Eastwood commented.

"Rumor has it that Sam Schlesinger may want to get his seat back."

"Schlesinger, he's finished! He was a lousy mayor of Waterbury, a worse state legislator, and involved in a corruption scheme as a US senator. Besides, now he's living in Switzerland working for Rallis. He wouldn't stand a chance," Eastwood said with a tone of ridicule in his voice. "Who else is there? Dom Guillermo sure as hell isn't coming back . . . Or is he?"

"Whoa!" Eastwood exclaimed with an expression unuttered since his childhood. "Is it possible . . . Could it be that Guillermo, who is not as enthusiastic about the pardons as Castignani and the others . . . ," he hesitated, his syntax getting garbled. "I . . . mean, this stuns me. Do you think Guillermo wants me to continue to deny pardons to get Schlesinger out of the picture so he can get back into the governor's mansion in Connecticut? Without the pardon, Schlesinger has no political future."

Sue smiled, slanting her head as she shook her head. "That's not out of the question. And we understand, of course, that you'll have to support Guillermo."

"Certainly I will, you know that. Even though he's not only the Democrat, I have no choice: I owe him something. He's been very good to me over the years even though he still foolishly believes I took his spot on the 2008 presidential ticket. I was drafted into that, as you know, and it was done principally because I'm black. I suspect that there are a lot of my supporters both in and out of government who wish I weren't black so they could dump on me," he said to their mutual laughter. "So Zbig will make his real move soon as the cocoa issue worsens New England's already teetering economy, right? And your timing is triggered when?"

"I want to get you through the State of the Union speech and the report on the economy in late January. Monica, if she's your choice, should start working with us in December while Washington's relatively quiet. Your 2012 race will be loaded with health issues as well as the economy. The agreement being cobbled together in Congress now is going to hit defense spending hard. Defense and health are two of her many strengths. Raising the debt ceiling will require some major cuts. The House Republicans will take that issue right into your presidential campaign, Earl."

"That's for sure. Even though they don't have a candidate yet, the GOP guys have me in their crosshairs, and they have real issues. The causes of our economic slowdown are deeply rooted, beyond our control. Even high economic growth, I'm saying 4 to 5 percent or higher isn't achievable in the near future and growth alone, even at those higher levels we still can't control our rate of debt growth. That's the secret we can't let out of the bag. You've sat in on those meetings with the best macroeconomists in the country. Worse, once our debt levels reach 90 percent of gross domestic product, even the growth of GDP becomes depressed.

"Worse, we don't even talk about our other obligations, those that are not in entitlement problems. I'm referring to the hidden or off-balance-sheet guarantees. When you include promises to guarantee mortgages, savings accounts in banks and credit unions, student loans, thousands of other types of small businesses, defense contractor and still more government loans, advance and progress payments, contract suspensions, and more, we're looking at a real debt load that's easily four times the $14.3 trillion of obligations that we argue about publicly.

"And then some of advisers are urging more inflation. They're nuts, and that's why I'm making major changes in that area of my office. Imagine inflation at even 6 to 7 percent. Match that with the millions on fixed incomes, such as retirees, they'll be flocking into our welfare programs as we're adjusting upward support payments, which rise with the consumer price index. And job losses, higher wages will be demanded to cope. The trigger effect is far-reaching. We'd have to jack up the minimum wage to $15 an hour with 7 percent inflation. Unemployment among black males is already at 15 to 16 percent. It'll rise more. And where are we getting the money? We're printing it, backed by the junk mortgages that the Federal Reserve bought over the past few years.

"Listen, if a Republican steps forward with a plan that'll put our economy back together, hell, *I'll vote for him*," the president said emphatically, his disgust evident in every spoken word.

*   *   *

The Fourth of July celebrations around the country seemed undaunted by the economic crisis. In Washington, the president and Representative Audrey Holmes, the first "consort" to occupy the White House, watched on TV monitors at Camp David. Sue joined Zbig in Connecticut as he made his rounds to numerous state events, his focus on Fairfield and New Haven Counties. Kallias placed a wreath on the several war memorials in the Hartford area, her mind fixed on plans for a quick departure the next day for Switzerland with Lex Rallis, son of Nikos and her houseguest for a two-day period before leaving the country. Traveling about the state with the Connecticut National Guard adjutant general, or commander, she had arranged for him to have one of his junior enlisted members escort Lex, who had every fascination with the events as expected of a sixteen-year-old.

On Tuesday afternoon, July 5, the governor's limousine and a separate security escort vehicle took the two to the general aviation terminal at Bradley International Airport. The Falcon 900LX executive jet, provided by Brent, the commodity trading firm, was already standing by. Kallias and Lex boarded the jet, which immediately departed the field, and reaching its cruising altitude of thirty-nine thousand feet within thirty minutes, headed over the pond for Geneva.

Kallias had grown attached to the young boy during their time together; the feelings were reciprocal as Lex, missing his parents, now separated from each other, welcomed the motherly attention graciously provided by Kallias. They sat side by side, Lex at the window, as they had an early supper before retiring to the seats across the aisle from each other and behind them, where they would sleep through the nighttime flight.

"I liked the guys in the guard units," Lex was saying. "I might even sign up in the state guard during my senior year at Loomis. Can I do that as a Greek national?"

"I believe so. We have many newcomers to the country who serve in the national guard as a means of getting citizenship," Kallias replied.

"Is that automatic? I mean, do you become a citizen when or because you sign up?" the boy asked.

"It helps, but one must still go through the application process. The federal government looks very favorably on persons of foreign birth who elect to serve and provide a duty or service to the country before applying for citizenship," she replied.

"That seems fair to me," Lex said, putting down his napkin as he finished a dessert of raspberry parfait with Greek yogurt. "If you'll excuse me, I'm going to the flight deck to sit with the pilots before going to sleep, if that's okay, Sophia. They have a small jump seat there. I've done it before and won't stay too long."

"Have fun. I'm just going to finish my drink and crawl into my bed, if you can call that reclining seat a bed," she said.

"It's very comfortable. Dad and I have slept on this plane a number of times. I won't disturb you," he said, smiling at her and then heading to the front of the aircraft.

A nice boy, he has good manners, like his father. The separation bothers him, I can tell. But he says nothing, too polite. If Niko and I end up together, he'd be a welcome addition, she thought, then catching herself, she added, *Why am I even thinking this way? It's too soon.*

*   *   *

On Wednesday, July 6, after Kallias and Lex arrived in Switzerland, Bob Castignani was consulting by teleconference with Domenic Guillermo and Jeff Scharfman, the former New Jersey senator, now the president of Lucas Holdings and second only to CEO Nikos Rallis.

"I think the timing is almost optimal, Dom," Castignani was saying. "Washington is totally subdued in the debt ceiling debates. Getting an agreement on the pardon would gather little media attention."

"Well, the leverage is there," added Guillermo, a seasoned politician in his own right as former Connecticut governor. "Niko has Kallias in tow, who arrived last night with his son, Lex. They're gonna talk to Belmont's Lutz Gorgens. He'll make it clear that they can only support Rose and Havens for just so long. They may have to look at a merger if Belmont is to continue in the US market. Niko will work on her, trying to convince her that a buyout is almost certain the way the two US companies are operating now and that the only options are to let them draw down employment dramatically or accept a Swiss infusion of resources that will actually boost employment."

"I think the White House sees it that way. I don't know what exactly Zbig has been saying to Sue, but I've every reason to believe he's with us on a buyout if it comes to that. He wants to be governor. Involving himself in the takeover that saves existing jobs and creates new ones can only help him," Castignani said.

"Who's fighting it," Scharfman asked, "besides the two CEOs of Rose and Havens?"

"Not very many others. Our plan was pretty well orchestrated. Everyone did the right thing, and getting Rose and Havens to use congressional delegations rather than lobbyists, which was your idea, Dom, may prove to be the final element needed for our success," Castignani remarked.

"I say let's go for the pardon now," Scharfman added.

"I agree, Bob, go ahead and make the pitch to Sue Cohen. Let her drop it on the president. I'm not sure he's gonna go along with it, but at least it's on the table for him to deal with. He'll weigh it against his other political needs," Guillermo added as the group ended the teleconference. Guillermo then thought, *Better for Sue to tell him than Castignani. Earl will feel less pressure. But I know him well. The timing will bother him. He'll want a deal before he commits himself, and he'll never give in on the pardons. At least I won't be seen as a stumbling block. It would have been better if the Swiss were moving more smartly with some type of arrangement with Rose and Havens.*

Castignani had anticipated the endorsement of his proposal and prepared the written materials to be submitted to the Justice Department's pardon attorney. He called Sue, who would prompt the president to the initiative.

He was on the phone with the White House chief of staff, Sue Cohen, within hours after his call to Switzerland and discussion with Guillermo and Scharfman.

They exchanged their usual greetings, during which Sue tried to act as controlled as possible as the debt ceiling crisis consumed her every working hour and a good part of her sleepless nights as well.

"I know this is more than a courtesy call, and you realize the weight of the debt issue that's pressing us, so how can I help you?" Sue asked in a way quite a bit more direct than customary for her.

"Thanks for the opener, Sue. Here's the deal. We want to submit the pardon petition now. The media is distracted with the debt business. The president could nudge the approval process along with minimal attention."

"I don't disagree with that, Bob, but what's the hurry on your side?" Sue replied, being merely courteous and knowing Eastwood's reluctance on the pardon issue.

"Our guys in Switzerland are getting nervous. They've been working their tails off trying to keep the US confections industry alive, and they think they're just being taken for granted. Scharfman, in particular, is asking why he's shorting his own balance sheets to bail out Rose Confections. He reminds me all the time that he wouldn't have signed on if it weren't for the promise of a fair deal on the pardon. The others in the group feel precisely the same way. They've basically expatriated themselves from friends and, in some cases, families in the US. Of course, they're doing well financially, but money is not their goal. They want their names, reputations, and, I think, in the cases of Scharfman and maybe Sam Schlesinger, their political careers restored," Castignani answered.

"Schlesinger, what's he up to?" she asked, referring to the former Connecticut senator who was appointed to a Senate seat briefly abandoned by Roger Evarts.

He wants the governor's job. Zbig would be running against him. Damn it, but I've got to support the Democrat as will Earl, but it won't be Schlesinger, that's for sure.

"You can guess. He wants Kallias's job," Castignani said.

"Yeah, I figured as much," she replied, being a bit disingenuous.

"I recognize your personal conflict, Sue, without saying anything more," he added.

"Thank you, but Zbig knows I'll put my obligations to the president first as long as I'm in this job."

"I would expect nothing less than that of you, Sue," he replied, thinking, *First hint that she's considering leaving. What would she do? She's not gonna go back to some law firm, she's too ambitious. Maybe she's interested in the governor's job . . . or Krakowski's seat if he decides to challenge Kallias. I don't know that much about Connecticut politics, but I strongly doubt the state Republican Party would support a nomination challenge between a sitting governor and senator, especially when the party already controls the two of them.* "We'll be submitting the papers to the pardon attorney at Justice later today."

As the call ended, Sue glanced at the clock. *It's almost time for Earl to leave for his workout. I'll get this to him. He can mull it over while he's running.* As was her unique privilege among all White House staffers, she signaled the president that she was en route. Earl spotted the blinking signal on his desktop special intelligence panel, an array of colored diodes for different matters. He had just changed into his workout gear and was tying his shoe when he saw the light, then he signaled back that he was available. Sue walked in two minutes later.

"I guess there's nothing that isn't urgent these days," he said. "What's up now?"

"The cocoa bean mess. Bob Castignani called me. They are submitting the pardon petition to Justice today. Something for you to think about on your run," she added with a grin.

Eastwood finished the double knot on his running shoes, lifted his head, and said, "Hey, if I have to solve every problem on my plate while I run, you won't see me back here until after my term expires.

I'll tell you what. Call Castignani back. Tell him that, at the moment, I cannot support the petition."

Sue's jaw dropped; her head ached, as if she had been suddenly afflicted with a stroke. She had not anticipated that response. Up to this point, the president had been leaning forward on the issue. It would encourage the former US congressional members in Switzerland to work that much harder for him and for expanding the US confections sector with Swiss investment funds. She was blinking hard, almost speechless, as she backed out of the door, saying, "Okay, I see. I'll do nothing until we talk again."

"No, come in," Eastwood said. "Look, I know what these guys are up to. The pardon will settle nothing, at least not at this instant. I'm not gonna be pushed into something the consequences of which are not at all clear to me, and what small part of the problem I do understand is the part I don't like. They feel like I'm over a barrel – the economy's in the toilet, New England needs jobs, they're positioning themselves as angels but with gratuitous promises to bail us out. I've thought this thing through to this point. I'm not gonna move quickly on it, and to repeat myself, I want you to tell Castignani there's no deal.

"By the way, I'm running with Monica today. I agree with your choice of your successor," he said, communicating his less-than-complete approval of the way that Sue had been behaving regarding the Swiss matter.

"Thank you, Mr. President. Have a good run and give Monica my best," Sue said, backing out of the door, thinking, *Well, I've done it to myself. I've just been fired! I can't tell Zbig. Better he find out from someone else. Earl, I hope, will trust me on that one.*

Within minutes, Sue was back to Castignani. "Bob, the president has no objection to your filing of the pardon petition today. However, he has directed me to tell you that, at this moment, he opposes the pardon for the former members of Congress and the one former administration official. I'm sorry and know that this isn't what you wanted to hear."

It was as if the line suddenly went dead. Castignani breathed hard, pulling the phone away from his face to avoid communicating the sound of his deep breaths, heaving in and out. His chest was caving as he reflected on his unusually good physical conditioning that could manage stress like this. "It . . . it is a surprise. Please give the president my regards and appreciation for his consideration. I will let the group know of his thinking on the matter."

They hung up.

Castignani slumped in his office desk chair, reaching for the urn of water that succeeded his morning coffee and was always present on his desk. Water, he reasoned, thins the blood and, like coffee, allows for the flow of blood gasses, like oxygen, to the brain to facilitate clear thought. *They're gonna go berserk. It's not that we didn't game this type of outcome. We did, as well as the consequences. They're gonna react, harm the president for revenge. The US guys will support a hostile takeover of the two US companies, I'm sure. And their Swiss counterparts will be right with them. I've gotta get this to Dom and Rallis.*

Guillermo's reaction was slightly less traumatic when Castignani told him of the president's decision. "I believe I've said all along that Earl has a good nose for fishy matters, and this one must have smelled to high heaven. I thought the timing was right, and I also believed he wouldn't buy into it. We were pushing him. He might change his mind. That'll depend on what we do. I'm worried about Scharfman and a few others who think the pardon's a slam dunk. They're gonna hit the roof," Guillermo said as they ended the call.

It was near midnight when Guillermo called Rallis at his chalet in Chamby, several miles up the steep and curving Alpine roads from the Palais Montreux, where Guillermo and the US expatriates lived.

Rallis and Kallias were spending the night together. Lex had been ferried to his mother's residence in Pireaus, near Athens, on the Brent executive jet.

Rallis and Kallias were sitting in the chalet's sparsely furnished great room. A modest wood-burning fireplace kept the evening chill at bay, which was welcome comfort as their guests for the evening departed only minutes earlier. Rallis had befriended a neighbor, a scholarly British expatriate who lived in a chalet less than a half mile away and who looked after the place during Rallis's routine absences.

"Bryan's a very charming fellow," Sophia said. "I was deeply impressed by the work he and his father and grandfather before him had done on the Oxford dictionary. Bryan's contribution was to digitize the immense etymology. What a history of a language!" The neighbor had devoted his professional life, like that of his forebears, to the advancement of English language linguistics, a subject on which Bryan made a respectable living by consulting on a global basis.

"And he liked *you*, which you must have noticed," Rallis said with a smile.

"As I said, Niko, I found him charming," she replied in a tone suggesting there was nothing more to be said on the matter. They both laughed and sipped their after-dinner sauterne as the phone rang.

"It's Dom, Niko. I'm sorry to call so late, but it's important. The president has said that he would not support the pardon petition."

"What? Incredible, did he give a reason?" Rallis raised his voice in a way that alerted Kallias to the importance of the call. "I thought it was something certain, that we could depend upon. I have to figure out how it affects our relationship. The whole move on the US confections industry was to exchange jobs for the pardons while both the US and Swiss companies made reasonable earnings. Do you think he grasped that?"

"Bob was no less disappointed or, more appropriately, I would say offended. He thought the president got the picture even though the details were spared in our discussions with Sue. When I met the president, I omitted details too. For the reason that in US politics, you don't position the people you depend upon to have to perjure themselves in an investigation. You do this by simply not sharing everything with them but using language that communicates the goal. I'm sure Bob did exactly that. He had almost eighteen years of Senate experience. He knows how the game is played."

"But it didn't work this time, did it, Dom?" Rallis said, his voice almost stern, lacking its customarily courteous tone. *Damn it, there goes the third leg of my plan. I was depending on Castignani to demonstrate my essentiality, that I was the source of resolution as well as the funds necessary to rescue the US companies. Now I have to deal with Sophia. What the evil do I tell her?*

"Few plans unfold according to their original design, Niko. We need to step back, regroup, and rethink our next steps. In the meantime, I'll have a situation here created by the expats. You may recall at our meetings in Alexandria back in December, there was a strong feeling among them that some form of revenge would be in order if the pardons were denied," Guillermo said.

"Be careful. Rash moves taken in anger seldom accomplish what is intended. Take it from a Greek who learned the works of the tragedians as a schoolboy.

The message is that anger creates contrived solutions, or deus ex machina, as the Romans later referred to the process. We Greeks have tinkered with anger in our theater and philosophies for over 2,500 years," Rallis said.

As Kallias listened, it occurred to her that the president had done something adverse to the Swiss companies' interests, but just what it was escaped her. The references to the Greek poets and playwrights were familiar to her. Young Greek Americans are generally learned much about their heritage at the Hellenic cultural centers located near their population clusters. Within that setting, she learned about Aeshylus, Sophocles, Euripedes, and even the later tragedian, Aristotle, an interest that she continued as an undergraduate at Trinity College in Hartford, where she majored in the school's strong classics curriculum.

As Rallis hung up, he turned slowly, putting his glass down on the table. "The president has denied the pardons," he said solemnly to Kallias.

That's Earl. I suspected he would. The political impact of forgiving a dozen members of Congress for conflict of interest was too obvious, she thought, then asked, "How are the petitioners taking it?"

"We don't know yet. Domenic just received the word from Sue Cohen. I suspect they're going to be very angry, and that's what worries me as you no doubt heard me cautioning Domenic about any type of irrational response. Scharfman's the leader of the expatriate group. He's the most irascible and impetuous one as well. I have doubts about him although he's done a very good job for me at Lucas, here in Switzerland. He's making good money, so there's somewhat of an outside chance that he won't much care anymore. But these guys are all politicians, they have big egos. As Domenic mentioned on the phone, when we first came together last year, they were all seeking revenge. I told them that we should get rewards rather than revenge. But I continue to sense among them a feeling that they need to be exonerated," Rallis said.

"Eastwood doesn't think they should be. In his mind, they committed punishable offenses," Kallias said.

"I understand that, but there was a matter . . . How do the American lawyers put it . . . ? In *mitigation*?

"Eastwood and the president before him had been led to believe that Iranian money was paying the dividends on their investments. I use the word 'investments' loosely since, actually, they only made pledges to invest but in the meantime collected dividends anyway, which ultimately amounted to sums ranging from hundreds of thousands of dollars to multimillions for the larger investors. The Iranian money involved was not governmental but private investment from Iranian citizens who had fled Iran or were otherwise looking for safe havens to put their money. Those funds went to Swiss banks, one of which is on the boards of Lucas Holdings, the Brent commodity trading firm, and Belmont confections."

"I didn't know those facts. I agree. They are mitigating circumstances if the actions taken against them were based on erroneous information," Kallias said, thinking, *There's more to this. Earl would recognize the injustice, if that's what it was, and he would correct it.* "I'm very reluctant to get involved unless his action adversely affects my state, Niko. Pardons are very sensitive issues, and constitutionally, they're entirely and absolutely a presidential right and privilege. The president would be offended if I inserted myself into the matter." *I have to draw the line here even though it may affect my own personal interests and my relationship with Niko,* Kallias realized.

She's not going to intervene. Sophia can get adamant, it's not worth the effort to try to persuade her otherwise. But there could be a Connecticut interest since the US guys, the expatriates, are going to be very angry, Rallis thought. "What worries me, Sophia, is that the US expatriates here in Switzerland, especially Jeff Scharfman, are going to hit the roof, maybe even seek some type of revenge against Eastwood. That could reach to the deals we're trying to fashion with the Connecticut and Massachusetts confectioners."

"What would they do? They're not likely to suddenly pull out, are they?" She asked.

"That's what we need to discuss with the Belmont and Brent CEOs when we meet tomorrow," he replied. He walked over to Sophia, sitting on a small love seat, the windows behind her slightly ajar with the cool Alpine night air chilling the room. From nearby France, a classical music station, which seemed to devote more time to talking than playing music, tempered the room's atmosphere. The wood-burning fireplace, the only source of heat in the chalet, hissed the sounds of dying flames, adding to the chill in the room. Reaching Sophia, he leaned past her, closing the windows, and then dropped beside her onto the sofa. She relaxed into his embrace; they kissed with growing passion. Pulling his head slightly back, Rallis said, "Tonight, for us, neither the pardon nor anything else in the world except each other will matter."

*   *   *

The next morning at six thirty, Thursday, July 7, Kallias and Rallis were up early. Both in their running suits, they stepped out onto the chalet's terrace. They stretched, then shifted to several yoga routines. Cowbells sounded in the valleys below them, signaling the return of some herds from their summer mountain pastures. Lake Geneva spread massively on the horizon but three thousand feet below them, with a vaporous veil of cool air hanging over the grayish water warmed by the summer temperatures. In the distance, they could see Mont Blanc, even the peaks of Chamonix across the lake, on the French side.

Straightening up, they walked down the steep staircase from the chalet to the road on which few cars passed this early. Reaching the bottom, they walked briskly up the hilly road, Kallias pumping her arms in her "power walk" style, while Rallis flexed and extended in arms to the side and up into the air, breathing methodically. Neither seemed particularly slowed from the intense passion of their first night together in several weeks. After several minutes, they began their slow jog, both breathing in an exaggerated fashion to deal with the altitude's challenge to their lungs.

They picked up the pace to a modest ten-minute mile; so they thought. Finally, Rallis spoke. "I'm hoping that we can get to Evian-les-Bains over on the French side. The spa there is as good as anything in Switzerland. It depends on how long we're at the meeting. It's less than an hour away, but the spa's hours are fixed. We need to spend at least three hours there, then we'll have dinner at one of my favorite restaurants, Brasserie la Voile. You'll love it."

"At the moment, dear Niko, I'm thinking only of a collapsed lung from this altitude," Kallias muttered out in a puffy voice.

They laughed but spoke little as they lumbered along the narrow road for nearly twenty minutes. Finally stopping and bending over to catch their breaths, they agreed to turn and take the easy downhill trek back.

"Just a sec, Niko, I need to tighten my shoe," Kallias said, walking over to a wooden post strung along a thin gauge-wire barrier marking the edge of the road. As she put one arm on the post, balancing herself as she leaned over to tie her show, the post snapped. She caught her balance as the rotted timber tumbled down a three-hundred-foot cliff, falling end over end to the roadbed below.

"Yeow!" she yelped. "*This* is a guardrail?"

Rallis laughed nervously but shared her reaction. "Thank God you caught your balance, but the wire probably would have saved you. Yes, it's a guardrail okay. The Swiss depend more on the skill of their drivers than roadside barriers."

They jogged back to the chalet, showered, and changed, then prepared for their ten o'clock meeting at the Belmont Château.

*   *   *

A different form of drama was being enacted at breakfast in the Palais Montreux, where the American expatriates lived. Guillermo had sent a message to all parties there regarding the president's decision, urging they congregate at nine for breakfast in the private back room of La Palmeraie, the hotel's breakfast restaurant.

Jeff Scharfman, the former senator from New Jersey, and California senator Nancy Lehman were already seated at the long table requested by Guillermo. Guillermo devoted his earliest morning hours to prayer and meditation, much of his thought honoring and memorializing his deceased wife for whom his bereavement seemed endless. He arrived just before nine, finding, as expected, the two former senators highly agitated.

"Goddamn it, Dom, what the hell is Earl doin'? We're breakin' our rear ends over here trying to rescue him from screwing up the economy even more while he continues to twist the knife in our backs," Scharfman said even before Guillermo could sit down.

"It's grim, folks, I admit. We have to talk about it," Guillermo said as the others started flowing into the room.

The tables now packed with the eleven expatriate Americans in residence at their Swiss business locations. All were former members of Congress except for former treasury secretary Charles Seaton, Domenic Guillermo, and Jane Gregoire, the wife of former Louisiana representative Marc Gregoire. In addition, the three Brent executives managing the New York City, London, and Toronto trading offices – former senators Sam Schlesinger and Mark Baldwin and former Michigan representative Jarrett Rodman – were on the conference line speaker, in the center of the long table set up by the management for the meeting. The door to the back meeting room was closed. Wisely, Guillermo decided to hold the session at the hotel rather than alert officials at the Lucas offices or Belmont château that a meeting for Americans only was under way.

"As you may have heard, the pardon has been denied. Whether that's a final, irrevocable move by President Eastwood or not, I have no way of discerning at this moment. But I suspect it is final based on my close friendship over many years with Earl," Guillermo started. "The question is how to proceed from here, and I have had a long chat late last night and again this morning with Nikos."

"I say screw him, Goddamn it," Scharfman said, spewing anger in his abrupt statement.

"Wait, Jeff, how the hell do we get back at the president of the United States?" asked former treasury secretary Seaton. "He's got more than just a little advantage over us."

"Yeah, of course, but he doesn't control us, and we can hurt him where he'll feel it, in New England," Scharfman replied.

"Jeff has good reason for feeling this way, as we all know. We were pressed into resigning our congressional seats because of false information regarding supposed Iranian government money in the investment scheme that we were all pledged to as sitting members. Eastwood owes us due recourse for his error," added Nancy Lehman.

"We need to get real," said former Delaware representative Anne Rathbone. "Eastwood has hedged before on the pardon, claiming we still acted in conflict of interest, merging our personal gain with our public duties as congressional members."

"Okay, but we paid the price. I should say 'you' paid the price since I was never sentenced," said Mark Baldwin, the former Virginia senator and the only one of the congressional group who was completely exonerated, having been seen by the court and the jury as an innocent investor in the Mediterranean scheme to build a massive hospitality and recreational center on the Greek island of Santorini.

Baldwin continued to speak. "That is, our resignations, the injury to our reputations, as well as the sentencing and fines were based in some part on the false information. Therefore, the pardon is, in fact, only a partial recourse and is entirely justifiable in my mind and, I believe, once explained would be acceptable to the majority of the American people."

"I sort of agree with that." It was Seaton speaking again. "I hadn't looked at it quite that way. My take on it was too political. We may have some ammo to deploy against the president after all."

"Damn right, Chuck, and it includes the survival of Rose and Havens. Those companies are going down the tubes, and fast. They're operating on the strength of Belmont's licensing arrangement. I know, I see the cable traffic from Rose and Havens," said Scharfman, always having a problem controlling his anger.

"I propose we encourage the boards at Brent and Belmont to put the screws on the two US companies, forcing them into a sellout to us, or enough of a deal to get ownership and operational control of the companies." Scharfman made his recommendation as if placing a bill before the Senate.

There was commotion and movement, private exchanges between the group at the meeting and overtalk comments from the remote conferees on the speakerphone.

"There seems to be unanimous approval. What remains now are the details. I will pass the word on to Nikos," Guillermo said in terminating the meeting.

CHAPTER 15

THE SCENT OF A DEAL

FORMER CONNECTICUT GO-VERNOR AND EX–US AMBASSA-DOR TO THE HOLY SEE, DOMENIC GUILLERMO, ALSO A DIRECTOR OF THE THREE SWISS PLAYERS – LUCAS HOLDINGS, BRENT COMMODITY TRADING COMPANY, AND BELMONT, THE GIANT CONFECTIONER – HAD HIS MARCHING ORDERS. The US expatriates, a reference to the former officials from Congress and the administration now occupying high-level posts in the Swiss companies, had decided unanimously to use their collective leverage to force the attention of the president to their pardon demands.

"That's what they want, Niko," said Guillermo, who called Rallis immediately after the morning meeting with the US expats and knowing that Rallis and Sophia Kallias, the Connecticut governor, were meeting with the two CEOs of Brent and Belmont within hours.

Rallis took the call at the chalet, where he and Sophia had been spending time together. They were getting ready to depart for their meeting with the Brent and Belmont CEOs, Lutz Gorgens and Paul von Schlossen.

Perfect, thought Rallis, as he listened to Guillermo, *fits right in with my plan. I'll get Belmont and Brent to make an offer and then work on Sophia to get a government bailout in the US, paying back the Swiss investment many times over.*

"There'll be some opposition as you might expect. The CEOs of the two US companies have political clout. Bob Castignani is telling me that they're mad as hell that they used their congressional delegations rather than lobbyists to make their case in Washington," Rallis said, referring to former Maine senator Bob Castignani, who lost his seat in the 2010 election and was, in fact, the Swiss companies' lobbyist in Washington.

"As you know, the US expats are up in arms. They're after the president's head. We need to work on that tactfully," Guillermo said.

"Do you mean with regard to the Swiss infusion of monies to the US companies?" Rallis asked.

"Right, the expats want a buyout," Guillermo replied.

"That's been a part of our longer-term strategy anyway, Dom."

"I know, but you have to get Sophia to accept that, Niko. That's not going to be easy. I'll talk to you after the meeting."

The two hung up; Rallis turned to Kallias, who was seated in the foyer, awaiting the completion of the call, parts of which she overheard but could not decipher from the comments that Rallis was making into the phone.

"Sounds serious, Niko. What's up?" she asked.

"Dom met with the expats this morning. It won't surprise you to know that they're furious. They want revenge."

Sophia's brow furled, something Niko had rarely seen – or noticed – before. She looked older, seasoned really, in her seriousness mode. *She looks different, more like my mother when she was a bit younger, more Greek. Dark-haired women show stress more than lighter-haired females.*

"I don't like those prospects. They do have some leverage over us, especially my state," she said after pondering the thought for a few moments.

"That's what we need to work out at the meeting. In many ways, the president's move, timely as it was, will make out meeting here that much more important," added Rallis.

They walked down the hill by way of an ancient Roman cobblestone path near the chalet; reaching their car, they watched the Vaud Canton bus, which traversed the Route de Villard twice a day, careen down the roadway.

"That guy is either nuts or out of control," Sophia said.

"No, that's just the way they drive. They've mastered the roads. To the newcomer, it looks like a runaway, but the driver is in full control, just watch," Niko urged, pointing at the oncoming bus.

They watched, standing on the side of the road, as the bus, downshifting, gradually slowed slightly as it reached the downhill hairpin turn without even braking and easily navigating the turn as the bus listed only slightly to the right.

"Absolutely amazing. But if a car were coming up the hill and in the turn, the bus would have overlapped the other lane just enough to collide," she observed.

"The driver is high enough in his seat that he can see over the cliff and the down side of the curve well enough in advance to begin braking or downshifting earlier. It's not uncommon to have a car exactly in the position you just described, so the driver's prepared for it," Rallis countered.

They started down the hill in Rallis's Range Rover. Sophia still felt uneasy about the scene she had just witnessed, especially in their wide SUV on roads where small European cars barely squeezed by each other.

Arriving at the Château de Belmont, they proceeded along the drive of crushed shell, parking at the rear of the building. The morning haze lifted from the lake, revealing the French Alps on the other side and the several small villages along the lakeside road toward the French resort village of Evian-les-Bains.

"I can't get over the startling beauty of this place," Sophia commented as they entered the château.

"It never gets old. The Romans felt the same way when they used Switzerland and this area in particular as their invasion route into what is now Germany. As far back as 58 BC, Julius Caesar saw the strategic value of the area when he drove out the Helvetii, the Celtic tribes that came over the Rhine from France two hundred years earlier. In many ways, the Montreux region became a type of rest-and-recreation center, like the modern R&R venues used by modern armies," Rallis explained.

"The Romans did that in Carthage too, didn't they?" she added.

"Exactly, they conquered what was known as Ancient Carthage, occupied by our ancestors, the Greeks and Phoenicians, then destroying the city in 146 BC. They rebuilt it under Caesar one hundred years later. He recognized the maritime value of the city in much the same way that the preceding occupants did – perfectly situated on a promontory controlling all traffic into the Eastern Mediterranean. The Roman army and navy pleasured themselves with bacchanalia that made the orgies of Rome seem like weddings in St. Peter's Square," he replied with a chuckle.

"As informed as you are, dear Niko, you know very little about the Vatican," she added as they both roared with laughter, surprising the greeters at the château.

"*Monsieur, mademoiselle, nous vous attendons avec plaisir* [sir, miss, we have been awaiting the pleasure of your arrival]," said one of the two young men who welcomed them at the door. They were escorted to the office of the Belmont CEO, Lutz Gorgens.

Lutz Gorgens and Paul von Schlossen were standing at the open office door as they approached; the two young men drifted away into the large foyer as the two Swiss offered their hands to the couple, shaking that of Rallis first, then gently taking Sophia's hand and bringing it to their lips, which barely touched it. Kallias's lifelong European orientation and experience welcomed the male gestures appropriately as she stood formally erect, slightly nodding her head forward to acknowledge the greeting. The two Swiss immediately sensed that this was a cultivated person in the European fashion, having experienced many American women who tend to either giggle or recoil when encountering the traditional greeting of a European male.

"May we call you Sophia, mademoiselle?" asked Gorgens in English.

"*Certainement, c'est ce-que je préfère* [of course, I would prefer it]," she replied, speaking in French as a matter of greeting propriety.

The foursome sat in a comfortable section of the office. They took their seats on the black kid-glove hand-tooled leather seats with white pine siding, supported by angled, highly polished nickel-alloy struts. Kallias looked at Rallis and smiled, then turning to her hosts, she commented, "I see you've combined your Swiss and Greek interests with your Simos Karamichalis furnishings. My father had been an investor in the Kolonaki factory in Athens, where it is still being manufactured. I still have the company in my investment portfolio." Kallias was referring to the highly desirable and ultramodern office-type furniture that blends functionality with innovative architecture. Using chrome and glass and molded polymeric compounds, the chairs and tables defy mass, fostering a sense of space, light, and freshness.

"Yes, the designs were originally Swiss with some customizing made by the Greeks as the market for the product became more popular," said von Schlossen. "Our offices at Brent are also largely furnished in Karamichalis in the executive suites since it is very expensive. I am impressed that you are so familiar with the product in which I, too, am an investor. Do you use it in your state offices in Connecticut, Madam Governor?"

Kallias and Rallis both laughed, Kallias adding, "I'm afraid not. Connecticut has an equally strong heritage, although, of course, not as old as that of Switzerland and Greece. It would be, let me say, 'politically uncomfortable' for me to contemporize the furnishings in my office or my official residence."

They all laughed as two trays of coffee and related Swiss pastries appeared, the stewards placing it on the elegant coffee table, a thin plank of Cypriote cedar atop a frame of thinly squared chromium legs.

Kallias's shapely and fit-looking body did not escape the attention of the two Swiss men. She was dressed in a close-fitting Phillip Lim draped wrap white dress, the drape feature a tribute to her Greek heritage. Her choice of apparel suited to both travel and climate at this time of year in Europe. As she leaned forward, her crossed legs tightened, accentuating her hips and buttocks. As in many parts of Europe where powerful women are still a relative rarity, the presence of attractive ones evoke a certain air of informality and even flirtation among some men, more so in business settings. Unlike politics, where such women tend to be more prominent, making jaunty comments or engaging in suggestive male behavior can become risky.

"I've invited Sophia to join us in our efforts to see what we can do to help Rose Confections, the country's largest confection company and principal consumer of the cocoa bean," Rallis said, opening the discussion.

"Yes, of course, you know that we met with both Rose's and Havens' CEOs just a little more than two months ago," Gorgens said.

"Tim Sawicki, who is the Rose CEO, as you know, did brief me on the meeting, which he thought went very well," Kallias added.

"They have been fairly successful with the licensing arrangement, have they not, Madam Governor?" Gorgens asked.

"As successful as I think the state of our economy will permit," she replied, relying on her lawyerly instincts to guide the exchange. "And that seems to be the issue. We are in a market warp, as I call it. Corporate earnings are up, but employment is in the cellar along with the rest of the economy in which our GDP is expected to grow at less than 1 percent for the annualized year."

"You say corporate earnings are up? I assume that you are referring to the blue chip firms, the big guys, like IBM, GE, Coke, and Caterpillar?" von Schlossen asked, his first comment in the discussion.

I walked into the trap, damn it, Kallias thought. *I better play it straight. I underestimated these guys.* "Yes, in part I was referring to the larger Dow Jones index companies. And I do recognize that most of them rely on heavy overseas earnings, so they don't really reflect the US economic situation," Kallias said somewhat defensively, thinking, *Not a good move, Sophia, you only evaded that stupidity by a hair.*

But von Schlossen realized that she had only tactically sidestepped the problematic response she had made for herself, thinking, *Not a bad tactic, Governor. You tried to mislead us, realized you got caught, and then dealt with the mistake honestly and openly.*

He started to speak. "You see, Sophia, we expected our US partners, especially Rose, to market our licensed products there in the US, but we do see the dilemma they're now in. Your economy is consumer dependent with, what, 70 percent of GDP growth tied to consumerism? And with employment down and jobs scarce, people are husbanding their resources, trying to save more and spend less, while paying off the immense personal debt loads that the entire country, from the individual to the state and federal levels, has burdened itself with. In that scenario, earnings that depend on foreign markets, like the companies that I mentioned a few seconds ago, become somewhat irrelevant to our particular business interests, do they not, Sophia?"

"Not entirely, I would not say they are totally 'irrelevant.' Foreign earnings still figure into our current accounts and balance of payments, and they become taxable assets when those earnings are repatriated to the US," she replied, thinking, *Damn, I've given him yet another shot at me. Too late, I'll just have to deal with it, again . . . Crap!*

What is she doing to herself? This is a skilled politician? She seems rather naïve to me, Belmont's CEO, Lutz Gorgens, was thinking.

I need to get into this. This goes beyond Paul's interest in the cocoa commodity and more into my business. "Please, Paul, allow me to comment," Gorgens said to von Schlossen.

He started, "Sophia, we Swiss have been traders for thousands of years. It is our lifeblood in our family discussions and our school curricula at all levels. We understand issues related to the balance of payments and current accounts. After all, the Bank of International Settlements was created here in Switzerland, in Basel.

"But," he continued, "in fact, there is no incentive for US companies that derive substantial foreign earnings to repatriate them. They would be taxed, and secondly, it could harm their overseas exposure by depriving them of the funds they need to expand and invest in the source of their best business prospects, here in the overseas markets."

Sophia gathered her thoughts; she was out of her league. Neither her experience nor her education at Trinity and Harvard Law had prepared her for this type of in-depth discussion of economics and trade law. *I just have to wing it*, she thought, then said, "But much of the portfolio resources, like bonds and stocks, that these companies depend upon for growth are US based and traded. So when they do well in the US and globally, the benefits migrate also to individuals and institutional investors like banks, insurance companies, hedge funds, and other financial sector components such as our pension funds."

"True, Madam Governor, but those fund-raising sources also include the German, French, Swiss, British, and even the Asian and Middle East stock exchanges. Collectively, I would suggest, lacking finite evidence to support my statement, the non-US exchanges are major, perhaps even greater, sources of capital for the US internationally oriented firms," von Schlossen said.

At last, I can end this. He made a basic debate error here. "Yes, but you are now talking hypothetically since, in your own words, Paul, you lack evidence to make that case," Kallias added.

Very good, Sophia. You struggled out of that one, and I will let you go. "Yes, sometimes discussions reach that point and lose their purpose. Let's move on to a matter more imminent," von Schlossen suggested.

Aahh, thank God, Sophia thought, taking a deep breath masked by a soft smile. "I do need your help, gentlemen. I don't see how my state can sustain Rose, nor can Massachusetts aid Havens in the current economic climate in the US. What more can we do together?" Kallias asked.

Rallis, listening closely, was thinking, *This is good. I've said nothing while Sophia herself has followed the logically fashioned path to my own objective.*

Gorgens spoke, adjusting himself ever so slightly in his seat, legs crossed, back upright as he leaned forward from his waist. "Speaking for Belmont, which is already at risk in the current arrangement with the two US companies, I can only surmise that we have two options. Ultimately, we would have to withdraw if the sales of our licensed products continue to falter. Secondly, we could be interested in taking a financial position in the two companies, if, of course, the price was right."

Sophia was unprepared for the second option. *Buyout, damn it. Have I been set up, by Niko? Keep cool, act as if you expected that . . . which is the only two routes a discussion on this topic could have gone anyway.*

She masked her slight dip in composure with the coffee cup, held slightly longer at her lips while she constructed her argument. Blinking slightly and watching Niko in her peripheral vision, she said, "Of course, those are the two logical options at the moment. I can't speak for the companies and lack sufficient familiarity with their business models or balance sheets. They are private entities, as you know, and I'm unable to offer any useful guidance regarding your business decision."

She noticed that Rallis's countenance remained unchanged; his facial muscles softened, and his body relaxed. *I was right. He did expect the buyout question. Otherwise, he would have reacted as I did, with some surprise rather than contrived self-control. Am I being used?* she thought as she awaited a response.

"But you do have a political interest, of course, in Rose Confections. There are jobs at stake. Your tax base at the state and county levels could be affected and your own political future placed in some doubt if the company were to fail," Gorgens replied.

He continued. "Connecticut is a very rich state, is it not?"

"The state has a very solid tax base, but it does not cover all of our costs and we face a $10 billion budget deficit, which is about 25 percent of our expenditures. Therefore, I am forced to cut spending and have been battling with our public service unions. I am also making cuts to our Medicaid program, which covers lower-income citizens, by reducing their dental plan benefits. Other cuts will involve salary, retirement benefits, and working days for public employees. I'll be laying off 6,500 state employees and not filling another 1,000 current jobs. These are very stressful times for us," she replied.

"The loss of Rose would cost another 5,000 jobs, maybe more, would it not, Governor?" Gorgens asked.

"Yes, the state could lose as many as 25,000 jobs in both the public and private sector over the next two years. Adding the consequences of a Rose company collapse to the losses already being absorbed by our failing pharmaceutical sector would not paint a pretty picture. The New Haven, Hartford, and Waterbury metropolitan areas and Bridgeport, along with the rest of Fairfield County, are our employment centers. Hartford faces significant losses as defense spending will be cut. The New Haven area's pharma sector that I already mentioned is looking bleak. In Bridgeport, Rose's job losses could add amount to 10 percent of the total public and private workforce of just fewer than 60,000.

"The rising job loss numbers mean heavy strains on our human resources budget with unemployment along with Medicaid, housing, and other offsetting assistance efforts going through the roof and adding to our deficit and state debt," Kallias concluded, thinking, *He's going to demand tax and other benefits from the state to sustain Rose if they make a bid for the company. That places still a heavier burden on me. Damn it, I should never have come here. If we weren't face-to-face, I could keep them guessing.*

"If Rose and Havens, on which I understand you cannot comment since it's in Massachusetts, were to be buyout targets for us, our offer would be affected by whatever assistance we could expect from the state. From the review you've just given me, I can see that there would be very little. Under those circumstances, we would be offering a price reduced by the baseline costs of renewing or upgrading Rose's productivity, markets, and workforce," Gorgens said, totally poised and very obviously a highly skilled business negotiator.

"Business expansion, and these days even sustaining an ongoing business in a souring economy, depends on markets. With personal spending down, any investment by us in Rose or any other US company for the most part could face what I would consider unmanageable risks. Foreign direct business investment in the US is already down, with some exceptions, of course, like automobiles. So both us, Madam Governor, you and us, must ask ourselves what is the best conciliatory arrangement than can be carved from these depressing economic scenarios."

"May I make a suggestion?" asked Rallis.

"Of course," Gorgens said to the joining nods of Kallias and von Schlossen.

What in hell could Niko add to this discussion, especially as it relates to Connecticut? Kallias wondered.

"The pharmaceutical industry in Connecticut is in the doldrums, as Sophia has said. However, in building the sector, just less than a decade ago, much funding was provided to Yale and other institutions to train the scientific workforce required by the pharma sector. With employment down, the federal monies for those programs, that the sector's lobbyists and state delegation worked into the permanent budget structure, continue to flow. Let's adjust the use of those monies to research on the health benefits of chocolate," Rallis said.

Wonderful, and I doubted you, Niko! Kallias then spoke calmly and with confidence, "Yes, that could work out very well. Moreover, this would be a form of in-kind assistance that would be budget neutral and would not involve the state legislature, which is controlled by my opposition party, the Democrats."

The discussion then centered around Rallis's proposal as the collective minds began running numbers on their respective gains from the arrangement. The foursome then concluded that a successful research program, federally funded at a distinguished, globally reputable institution, like Yale, could find economies in chocolate production that would lower prices and help make the product inelastic in demand despite the state of the economy and consumer wallets.

The group had negotiated for several hours, which included a working lunch. By 4:00 p.m., they had concluded that, as Rose and Havens' sales continued to decline, the only workable option would be a buyout. Each sensed the benefits.

Kallias would speak to both CEOs of the US companies. They would acknowledge the outcome and realize their own jobs would be lost. Kallias would promise to work with the president in finding them ambassadorial posts in countries where their business skills, now buttressed by the contacts from their political appointments, would create new opportunities for them. Also, she knew that Eastwood needed a deputy commerce secretary; McMahon, a strong Democrat, might fit the bill.

The two Swiss CEOs, Gorgens and von Schlossen, guilefully heaped silent praise on themselves, feeling they had outmaneuvered the young, innocent Connecticut governor.

But both Kallias and the two Swiss CEOs were unanimous in their assumption that Rallis had played his hand in *their* favor.

CHAPTER 16

THE OFFER

A T 6:24 AM, ON FRIDAY, JULY 8, 2011, THE SUN ROSE OVER LAKE GENEVA, CASTING THE CHALET IN A QUALITY OF LIGHT UNIQUE TO THE ALPINE REGION OF MONTREUX-VEVEY. Nikos Rallis and Sophia Kallias emerged from the chalet, stretching to prepare for their now customary jog along the Route de Villard, a rugged road that bound the mountainside with its sinuous hairpin turns and treacherous dips. The glare of the sun on the lake caused them to blink as they negotiated their way down the sixty-five-stair, seventeen-degree slope to the roadbed. Once there, they started their slow jog, grunting and aching a bit after a second night of intense passion.

"I will miss this beauty. It surpasses anything I could have imagined before coming here," Sophia said.

"And I will miss you, dear Sophia," Nikos said, his voice laboring from the uphill start of their jog. "What can we do? We understand our feelings for each other."

Rallis was concealing his real motives, thinking, *I have to keep her attention. If she falls out of the deal any time soon, everything collapses.*

Sophia, in somewhat better shape than Nikos, spoke in a steady voice, seemingly unaffected by the physical exertion at the high altitude. "We managed everything, didn't we, Niko? The meeting started as a disaster in my mind and then unfolded into an outcome I honestly hadn't expected, in two ways. First, the arrangement with the US confection giants and, second, us – both rather complex issues," she said as they both laughed.

"We're probably better off keeping things as they are now. Seeing each other can be made easier since you'll be coming to the States more often, I assume. Is it possible that you'll move to the US? Wouldn't that be optimal, Niko?"

"It may come to that. The start-up phase . . . it will be a challenge," Niko replied, pausing and puffing after each cluster of words as he struggled to get a more relaxed pace. *I have to be careful. Too much proximity will not be good. My life is in Switzerland, not the US . . . Connecticut's an awful place to live for me. Too isolated, I need access to regulators and policy people and financial institutions in places like Washington and New York and Zurich,* he thought as his pace picked up with the leveling off of the road.

After a few quiet minutes, Sophia spoke again. "It might be a problem if you lived in Hartford, or even Bridgeport. The media would be all over us."

I certainly will not live in either of those places, but for reasons quite apart from what she's thinking, he reasoned before speaking. "Yes, I agree, the American paparazzi are little different from their colleagues in Europe. But just about anyplace I stay in the US will be more convenient than the arrangement we have now," he replied, thinking, *Perfect, that opens the door for a place in Washington, if I have to make a temporary, short-term move.*

They ran for about two kilometers, then reversed direction back to the chalet, where they would prepare for Sophia's departure and return flight to the United States. They descended two hours later along the Alpine route to Vevey, where Belmont's slick Italian-made Agusta AW 139 executive helicopter met them on the landing zone within the plant's perimeter. They had kissed tenderly in Rallis's Range Rover before walking together to the aircraft. Within minutes, the Paninfarina-designed, medium-twin-turbine-powered aircraft was rising, slightly angled downward at the nose as it climbed over the lake, and then turning to its west-southwest flight path to Geneva's international airport. Seated on the starboard side of the chopper, she waved back to Rallis standing with his hand in motion. She settled into her seat as the aircraft climbed through ten thousand feet and leveled at thirteen thousand feet, its assigned altitude, where it cruised westward at 160 miles per hour.

Three hours later, Sophia was passing over the English Channel on Belmont's Falcon 900LX executive jet. Comfortably seated and having a light lunch, she prepared her notes for the calls that she would make. First, to the presidential chief of staff, Sue Cohen, to explain the deal and to encourage her to seek the president's assistance in placing Rose's Tim Sawicki and Havens' Kyle McMahon in meaningful government assignments to ease the pain from the planned takeover of their companies. She wanted that promise, however gratuitous at the moment, to be in place before talking to the two executives.

It was now 2:00 p.m. Swiss time and 8:00 p.m. Washington time as the Falcon raced over Scotland's Sea of Hebrides, just short of the Western Isles in the initial phase of the transatlantic leg of its flight to Hartford. *Sue will be in the office by now, probably preparing Earl for his weekend at Martha's Vineyard. I know he had stayed in Washington for July Fourth events.* She called Sue's office on a closely held private number. Dialing in the communications codes assigned to her by the copilot, she reached 202-456-7256, which was answered by Sue's assistant who immediately got Sue on the line.

"Sophia, this is a surprise. Are you calling from the air?" she asked, knowing from the information on the phone's monitor screen exactly what Sue's location was, including the geographical coordinates.

"Good morning, Sue. Yes, I'm en route back to Hartford. The meeting went well, I think," she said, laughing lightly, adding, "Only teasing. Actually, it went quite well. But I may need some help."

Of course, why else would she be calling, to remind me that she used to sleep with Zbig? Sue thought, getting some amusement from her reaction to Sophia's call. "Tell me more," Sue said.

Over the next five minutes, Kallias explained the meeting and its decision to acquire and merge with the two US companies. Lacking details as to the exact offer price, she explained, she could not provide anything more concrete on that important aspect of the deal. She emphasized that the two US companies' margins were shrinking along with their domestic markets, and even the licensing arrangement – a bailout really, she said, of the two companies – was not producing desired results, leaving the Swiss with two options: cut bait and leave or make a move toward acquisition. Sue listened closely, turning on the phone's recorder to assure that she had all the details, as flimsy as they were at the moment.

"But here's where I need your help. Obviously, the Swiss will install their own management at the two companies. This means that Sawicki and McMahon will lose their jobs, not that they won't walk away pretty handsomely rewarded. Their compensation packages and other parts of their employment contracts will leave them in good shape," Sophia explained. "Can we provide any type of job at the federal level for them?"

"Offhand, I don't know. Of course, McMahon has always been a heavy bundler of campaign funds for our presidential campaign and our planning for the 2012 election. The president is indebted to him. As for Sawicki, he *is* a Republican, so as you know well, it's hard to accommodate someone from the other party. We have all these hardworking Democratic hopefuls around the country who get upset when they see us rewarding the opposition. Right now, I think we can help McMahon. Sawicki will take a little longer," Sue related from her out-loud thinking.

"How about an ambassadorship somewhere? Switzerland might be ideal since Tim has much global business experience and this is the headquarters of the World Trade Organization," Sophia asked.

"That could be a possibility. There are some drawbacks. He could conflict with the US Trade Representative's office or the USTR director himself. Even with his substantial business experience, trade policy implementation in this country has become heavily bureaucratized, too often, in the president's mind, with people having no real experience in international business. Tim could ease that difference and the problems that it's caused. On the negative side, again, he doesn't understand how the political or bureaucratic processes work. Political agencies can't easily be managed as if they were corporate entities. The authority rights of bureaucrats don't match those of a corporate CEO, for example. But USTR is as close to a business-type organization as one could expect to find in government, so it might work. Otherwise, the embassy in Bern is like any other elsewhere, and our political appointments to them usually work out, with some exceptions, of course," Sue responded in a lengthy dissertation.

"I think Sawicki could handle it, Sue. As for McMahon, I know there's a vacancy at the deputy secretary level at commerce. He'll have the Massachusetts delegation behind him, and it might be a good payback for that state's strong support of Earl in 2008, as well as help him next year."

"Yes, I hear you. Politically, both might be possible. Needless to say, the president will decide. I'll be seeing him in a few hours. He'll be leaving for several days at Martha's Vineyard. As you may have heard, Audrey has moved out of the White House. The president is devastated, not depressed, but highly discouraged over the change. The media hasn't gone ape over it yet, but they will. A few media people know about it, but Kenny Edwards, you know him, the president's press secretary, has warned them that if it leaks out prematurely, they would find themselves starved for news about this place," Sue said, laughing.

"Sounds like Kenny!" Sophia responded with a chuckle.

"These media guys know their careers hinge on our hot poop. They'll hump a keyhole for a peek at a possible scoop," Sue said.

"I have my own platoon of humpers in Connecticut. The difference is that I sometimes feel I'm more than just their media target when it comes to humping." They both roared at Sophia's comment.

"Thanks again, Sue. I assume you'll tell the president. I have no objections if you folks decide to call either Sawicki or McMahon. If you get to them before me, you can tell them that I'll be calling to fill them in with details."

So that Sophia's ploy. Get the president to give them the bad news and then alert them that she, Sophia, will ride to the rescue with good news on their future, Sue thought. *I don't think Earl will let you sit easily in the saddle on that one.* "Talk to you later, Sophia."

They hung up. Sophia was pleased with the call and convinced that she could accommodate both Sawicki and McMahon. But should she call them now? That question bothered her. She knew the White House would protect what she was just told until the president acted. Sue would be talking to him before noon. Maybe, therefore, she should wait until then, when she would be back in her office.

*   *   *

Within an hour after Rallis said good-bye to Sophia at the Belmont helipad, he was back at the château to talk to von Schlossen and Gorgens.

"Wonderful move, Nikos," Belmont CEO Lutz Gorgens was saying as the three seated themselves in the château conference room. "Belmont will still be at risk, but it will be controllable if they accept our offer."

"They would be fools not to," commented Brent CEO von Schlossen. "What are their options? Very few I believe."

"Their best hope at this juncture would have been a government assist, maybe even a bailout of their debt," Rallis offered.

"The federal government bails out private companies?" Gorgens asked. "I thought the beacon light of capitalism passed over the dark corners of the market where deals are made."

"It used to be that way, but the US has changed. It's been bailing out the big guys for years. You remember Lee Iacocca? He asked Congress for a loan to save Chrysler, a loan like the railroads and airlines were getting. Congress offered him loan guarantees, which were good enough at the moment, which was 1979, when the economy was on its back. Today, you see General Motors getting indirect cash infusions through stock purchases," Rallis replied.

"It would be more difficult with a privately held company, which brings me to my next point. We will want to take Rose and Havens public through an initial public offering once we're in full control. That will give us two options. If we can't raise sufficient funds, we seek government help," he added.

"Why haven't the two US companies done that?" Gorgens asked.

"They're too far in debt. Their balance sheets are garbage, and the investment banking community, where I have excellent contacts, would never take a client in that poor fiscal state. In our case, with the solid financial shape Belmont is in, the bankers will salivate over the chance to do a deal with us.

"My years at Wharton were well spent. I made contacts that brought US investment into Greece when I was the finance minister there, and I got the investors out, with profits, before the public service workers brought down the economy.

"We can do the same in the US. Anyone can see the future of the US economy. The public service unions have such immense power over most members of Congress, not to mention other lobbyists, that neither the Simpson-Bowles commission nor any other special task force set up to cut government spending can get these guys to make badly needed reforms. Every day you look at the crisis there, you have the president and Congress offering tax credits, payroll tax exemptions, and other special tax treatments at a time when everyone knows that the tax code needs reform. That's yet another example of how unlikely any type of real reform or spending cut program can be fashioned.

"It's not clear how we can navigate through that mess for our own benefit," von Schlossen said perceptively.

"It won't be easy. I'm working on the assumption that the emphasis on job creation will compel help for us if we need it. By that I mean if the IPO doesn't produce a satisfactory amount of investor interest. There's a big caveat staring us in the face because the same consumer restraints that are jabbing the Rose and Havens balance sheets could persist. That could weaken investor interest, and I'm including that prospect in my plan.

"Our first approach would be to create more market. I'm thinking, and I hope Lutz would agree, that we could take some of our high-luxury confection products, modify them along American lines, and sell high-end items for which demand still seems to be fairly buoyant. Something like a Swiss Rosette, a play on both the Swiss ownership in Rose Confections and the Rose trademark," Rallis said to the rapt attention of the two Swiss executives.

"*Bien entendu* [certainly], we can do that," responded Belmont CEO Gorgens. "But what if 'sellers' remorse' sets in and other parties in the US, perhaps even the ousted CEOs, decide they want the company back?"

"And now, my friend, you get to the other part of my plan. In our contract, we agree to a first-refusal-option clause for Rose and Havens to accept or reject our offer to sell the company, but at 200 percent of the price we paid for whatever share of the companies that we have bought. In the meantime, we could have Belmont's entity in China, Belmont-China, make an offer, if needed. That would send the government into a tizzy and, I suspect, allow Rose and Havens to 'find' the funds needed to recover their companies from us," Rallis explained.

"Actually, Nikos, that's not a bad early-exit strategy. We won't need to do an IPO. We'll try for a market surge along luxury lines and then trigger the Belmont-China *faux* offer to get prospective US buyers to start thinking about recovering the two companies. We could double our investment within a year and still market our high-end items in the US since we'd never agree to a noncompete clause in the sales contract," Gorgens said pensively, jotting down his thoughts on Rallis's plan.

"One more thing, Nikos," von Schlossen offered. "We need to do something with the US expats who are here. Aside from Bennie Thompson, who brilliantly maneuvered our buy of the Ivory Coast cocoa, the others are mere figureheads. With a few exceptions, they know little to nothing about business and seem to think that there's a political solution to every market issue."

"That's the type of person that they have in the US Congress. Few have any business or finance background, even in academic economics, nor do they have the mental aptitudes to learn it. What are you thinking, Paul?"

"I'd suggest we send them to the US under the pretense that they will manage our operations there. They'll be glad to be back, I'm sure, and with their current compensation levels, believe themselves secure for the rest of their working days," von Schlossen replied.

"What about Guillermo, Nikos? He's on the board of Lucas Holdings, Brent, and Belmont. Will he go along with this?" Gorgens asked.

"I've considered that. Here's my thought. He's in his midsixties, he loves politics more than business, he's made a lot of money here, and he's not wild about living in Switzerland. It's too removed from the high-visibility, high-activity life that he relishes.

He's ready to go, I think. Let him negotiate the deal with Rose and Havens. We'll pay him a premium for this added task. We'll make him chairman of Belmont–North America or put him on the board there if we doesn't want that type of role. We can take care of him in a way that we can plan without his sensing our incentives and goals, I believe. Nor would I be surprised if the president wouldn't welcome him back with some type of assignment in government, such as roving ambassador or special diplomatic envoy. He'll always be a politician first," Rallis answered.

They agreed on Guillermo's role. Rallis would explain both offers to Guillermo, the first regarding the purchase, the second his role in it and, if he chooses, to direct North American operations for the combined Swiss-American company.

Not surprisingly, Guillermo welcomed the offer enthusiastically. Rallis would call Connecticut governor Sophia Kallias advising her of Guillermo's role.

At seven thirty Saturday morning, July 9, 2011, Rallis was on the line with Sophia.

"I miss you, dearest one," Rallis was saying. "I can't pass the chalet without thinking of the wonderful two days we spent there."

"Leaving you was more difficult than I thought, Niko. But it motivated me to move quickly in talking to the White House and getting this deal done," she said as she read the *Hartford Courant*, sipping her coffee in the brightly sunlit garden room off the kitchen in the governor's mansion.

"I've more news on that score. I had a meeting yesterday with Gorgens and von Schlossen. We decided to have Domenic make the offer on our behalf. He knows the political landscape and is on the boards of Belmont and Brent and can speak for them. More importantly, it may be better to have the offer coming from an American rather than the two Swiss executives or, God forbid, a crazy Greek like myself," Rallis said with a chuckle.

"You're not *that* crazy, but yes, I agree. Also, the White House trusts Dom, he's a Democrat and closer to the president than most people," she said.

They talked about themselves, making rather fuzzy plans as to their joint future. On her side, Sophia was reluctant to push too hard in getting Rallis into a tighter and more permanent relationship. For Rallis, everything was business first.

*   *   *

Later that morning, Sue was assisting the president with the materials he would need at Camp David. She would not be going, having made plans to spend what remained of the weekend with Zbig.

"The last item regards that pesky cocoa bean saga," Sue said, summing up her weekend-departure briefing.

"What in hell is happening now? I'll tell ya, it's getting tiresome. I've got my campaign to worry about, not to mention ten thousand other pressing issues needing my immediate attention," Eastwood said with obvious annoyance.

"Sophia called. The Swiss will do a buyout of Connecticut's Rose Confections and the Havens company in Massachusetts," she said quickly.

"That surprises no one. So what's that got to do with us? I have no mood . . . or money to bail out either one," the president said, unprompted.

"Kyle McMahon is a heavy bundler for us, and Kyle Sawicki has never hesitated to support you as a senator or in the 2008 campaign, offending many of his fellow Republicans," Sue said.

"You're tellin' me their losin' their jobs and I should help them," the president said, typically astute despite his added burden and distress over losing Audrey Holmes, the woman he had been living with in the White House for nearly three years. Sue knew it was the cause of his sudden short-tempered behavior.

"Yes," Sue responded quietly.

"Okay, tell me, what's available in the plum book? I'm more concerned about McMahon," he replied, referring to a patronage job list with a plum-colored cover.

"My recommendation, McMahon fills the deputy commerce job and we nominate Sawicki as ambassador to Switzerland," she replied.

Earl pondered the choices for less than a minute while he put *The Hope*, a book by Herman Wouk regarding the Israeli wars of the 1960s and '70s, into his weekend bag. He then smiled. "Get McMahon on the phone," he said, aggressively zipping up a section of his bag.

Sue picked up the phone near her, getting Marge, the president's favorite administrative assistant on the line. For the next five minutes, she explained to Eastwood what Kallias had told her about the offer. Guillermo would make the presentation, she said, omitting any mention of Sophia's anticipated call to Sawicki and McMahon.

The president's desk phone buzzed. "I have Kyle McMahon, sir. He's at his house in Sconset on Nantucket," Marge said. Marge Davidson had been with Earl since his days as a senator; she was totally reliable and, as this particular request demonstrated, masterful in her ability to find someone at any time of the day or night.

"Thanks, Marge," the president said with the complete admiration and respect he held for the woman.

"Hello, Kyle. How the hell are you? You must be sitting at your house on the Brotherhood of Thieves," the president said, recalling with sudden precision the name of the street on which McMahon's summerhouse was located and which Earl had visited four years ago when he was reportedly involved with Monica Howard, now his secretary of health and human services.

"A pleasure to hear from you, Mr. President. You need to be here, away from all that claptrap in DC," McMahon replied.

"Hey, if I could, I'd be there within the hour. This town's in bad enough shape. I'm afraid if I left for the Cape, they'd think I was abdicating, which might not be such a bad idea, by the way," Eastwood replied to their mutual laughter, then continued.

"Kyle, I've some bad news. The Swiss are planning to make an offer for your company and for Rose as well."

"Well, I sort of expected it, and by the way, it's not altogether bad. We're on our back, I can barely make payroll, and Tim's in the same boat," McMahon said, referring to Tim Sawicki. "We know we're toast."

"If there's anything good to it, it's that you're gonna be available, and I need help in a major way. I want you to be my deputy commerce secretary. Harry Samski, who you know, is the secretary. He wants to get back to the pharmaceutical industry if I'm reelected. I'd move you up to the cabinet seat. The issue is trade. I need someone who understands business and can get our export markets open and who can work with the USTR. Along those same lines, I'm gonna offer Tim the embassy job in Bern. He'll be a great ambassador there," the president said.

"Mr. President, I am deeply honored as I know Tim will be. I hadn't thought of a successor job like that, but I will accept your nomination, and I'm doing it with commitment and not because I'm about to be thrown out on the street," McMahon replied.

"Good man, we'll work well together. Of course, I'm gonna need your help on my campaign. Round up some of those summer guys on Nantucket if you can. I'll be making the nomination next week. In the meantime, give my best to your family," Eastwood said as they said good-bye to each other.

"Next," Eastwood said.

"I have Sawicki holding," Sue said, anticipating precisely what the president's next move would have been. "Marge found him at the Black Rock Yacht Club. He's on his boat headed into the Sound."

"Tim, Earl here. How's the fishing?"

"Good to hear from you, sir," Sawicki replied, adding, "I haven't dropped a line yet. I'm waitin' for you. How soon can you be here?"

"I wouldn't wait any longer, Tim. When the blues are runnin' and mating, they don't wait around for someone to catch them," Eastwood replied. "Listen, I need your help. As you may have guessed, and I just spoke to Kyle, the Swiss are about to make an offer for both of your companies. That's gonna take your job from under your feet, I understand," Eastwood continued.

"Yes, sir. We've been expecting it, and as I'm sure Kyle told you, we've run out of string. We can't tie and patch any longer. I'd have to drop nearly two thousand workers and maybe even close down for good. My credit lines are exhausted, and no one's renewing them during these economic times," Sawicki replied.

"Tim, I'd like to nominate you as US ambassador to Switzerland. I need a good leader there, one with your business background and high comfort level with trade issues. What's your take on that?" the president asked.

"First, my gratitude that you would even consider me. Second, I would be privileged to serve in your administration in just about any capacity. So I guess that's an indirect way of saying 'hell yes.'

I accept the honor of your offer with profound appreciation. There's some work to do beforehand in getting Rose settled, but I'll be ready," Sawicki said as the two hung up.

Turning to Sue, the president looked at his watch. "There, that took less than ten minutes. Let's get on with the real business. Call the key people in the Massachusetts and Connecticut delegations and tell them what's goin' on in the unlikely event that most don't already know. They may be a little peeved that I called McMahon and Sawicki before them. Tell them I wanted to spare them the political pain of delivering the bad news."

The two finished the exchange of information as Sue brought in the Secret Service agents to escort the president to the waiting Marine One helicopter. As the aircraft lifted from the West Lawn, Sue thought, *There goes my Saturday plans. By the time I finish calling the two delegations, and bickering with them, I'll be here until midnight.*

*   *   *

As was the case, her first call was to the senior Massachusetts senator Kevin O'Meara, chairman of the Senate Armed Services Committee.

After explaining that the president asked her to call him since he was en route to Camp David, she explained the pending offer from the Swiss and the call that Eastwood had made, including his job offers to both McMahon and Sawicki. O'Meara's response was somewhat unexpected.

"Why in hell are we letting the Swiss buy out Havens without even trying to save them ourselves?" he asked.

"We've been through this before, Kevin. Think about it, Democrats bailing out corporations when we're facing cuts to Medicare, Medicaid, and maybe some Social Security programs?" she answered.

"C'mon, Sue, you've worked up here. You don't think we couldn't have slipped that into one of the major bills comin' up after the August recess. We'd save the president's neck by puttin' it in the defense bill. Hell, I can do that, I'm the damn committee chairman. He can't veto a defense bill, and he would have emerged unscathed."

"We all know that, but the president's position is, why spend our money when we can bring in foreign investment?" she replied.

"Why? I'll tell ya why, because we would have kept it as an American company and kept the top jobs there in US hands," O'Meara said, getting a bit testy.

Sue knew that congressional leaders know that she spoke for the president and they could only push so far.

"I have two answers to that, Kevin. First, he offered them good jobs in the commerce department and an ambassadorship. They'll be able to use their business acumen to rebuild second and probably even more prosperous careers.

"Second, and in all due respect, *Mr. Chairman*," she said with emphatic formality, "you haven't exactly been a 'buy American' stalwart yourself. You've authorized appropriated monies to buy Swiss Pilatus aircraft for Air Force flight training programs, Italian helicopters for Coast Guard's Homeland Security accounts, German biological and chemical warfare vehicles for the army, British-made gas masks, and many other items."

As she spoke, O'Meara was thinking, *Okay, I've made a stab at pretending I'm disappointed. Actually, the Swiss are gonna need a lot of us around here to run and represent their investment. There are guys in this delegation lusting for those big-paying jobs with the company or as lobbyists and the rest of us for PAC monies. I'll just cool it.*

"Yeah, you're right, but those were needed defense items. That's a little different," he said as if conceding. "Listen, I'm the dean of the States' congressional delegation, I'll let the others know. Tell the president I agree with the way he handled this. Have a good weekend, Sue."

Good weekend! Good grief, I'm up to my eyeballs in work here. I'm surprised he gave in so easily, that's not like him, Sue thought. *I hit him hard on the offshore spending on defense. But I know these guys on the Hill, even at the Pentagon, they love these overseas buys so they can justify trips to their contractors all over Europe, especially France, England, and Germany.*

Her instinct was to call Zbigniew Krakowski, but he was the *junior* senator from Connecticut, as well as, of course, her more intimate friend. *I better stick to protocol, Zbig will understand,* she thought as she told Marge to get the senior senator, Roger Evarts, on the line. Marge found him at home in Stamford when the Republican came to the line.

"Good morning, Sue. It's always good to hear from you, what's up?" Sue looked at her annotated file on her computer screen. *Oh, it's his birthday tomorrow. That'll work well,* she thought.

"Happy birthday, Roger, even though I'm a day early," she said.

"Thank you, fifty-nine is a momentous time, a year away from elderly status and, in my case, with one leg in the simply advanced adult camp," he said as they both laughed.

She explained as she had with Senator Kevin O'Meara that Earl had asked her to call him as the senior member of the state of Connecticut's congressional delegation. She explained the impending Swiss offer and the proposal of the president to recruit the two men for positions in his administration.

Evarts listened, thinking, *It had to happen. They were going down fast. All of Fairfield County and beyond would have been affected by those job losses if we lost the company to bankruptcy, either in Chapter 7 or 11 for that matter.*

Evarts was also fully aware that many of the delegation members from the two New England states were expecting to gain personally from the Swiss takeover. He had openly resented and rejected those notions in several discussions with his colleagues from the region, all to no avail. Their plans were a form of conflict of interest, he had told them, warnings that fell on deaf ears as did his further admonition that the president was no slouch; he would learn of their scheme and turn on them. He's done it before, he reminded them.

He said little to Sue, thanking her for the call.

*   *   *

On Monday, July 11, 2011, following his usual morning prayer routine, Domenic Guillermo, the former Connecticut governor and US ambassador to the Holy See, had arrived at the Château de Belmont. He would receive the details regarding the offer that he was to proffer to the two US companies on behalf of his Swiss business partners.

It was nearly noon as they wrapped up the discussion.

"I'm comfortable with the details, and I think the offer is fair. From a sentimental point of view, I like what we're doing for Connecticut. There are no alternatives. The state's employment picture is as bleak as that of Mississippi. You know, we Yankees like to compare ourselves to certain Deep South states. In fact, they're doing much better than most of New England, certainly better than Maine and Vermont in bringing in foreign investment. I love the unions, and my father was a union leader in New Haven, but they've overreached, and the states with right-to-work laws are the places where the money is going," Guillermo was saying.

"Does not Mississippi have a heavy black population?" Belmont CEO Lutz Gorgens asked.

"Yes, which is exactly why we use that and the other Deep South states as strawmen. They've long been yoked by traditions of slavery, tenant agriculture, and indigence that we in the North never experienced – well, almost never experienced. Rhode Island started its existence as plantation. Newport was the center of the New England slave trade and launched over a thousand trade voyages that brought about sixty thousand slaves into the colony by the time of the American Revolution," Guillermo explained.

"That is something we don't learn in Europe when we study American history. We associate slavery only with the Southern states," Gorgens added.

"Sorry to have let our discussion get off track. To get back on topic, I agree with the purpose and the details of the deal. We will acquire 51 percent of both companies. Together those two companies control 40 percent of the US confections market. That figure has always surprised me because I think the market share is even greater, closer to 60 percent, but deliberately suppressed to avoid our antitrust laws.

"Rose has about 60 percent of the $800 million slice held between the two, and Havens has 40 percent. That gives us the market value of Rose to be about $480 million," Guillermo said, as if pondering out loud, "which is fairly close to what we think is the company's book value."

"That is what our research shows, and our analysts are very good in getting details on even the most closely held private companies," Gorgens interjected.

"Likewise, Havens, as I understand from what we've covered here, is valued at $320 million, a reflection of its 40 percent share. So our offers will look like this," Guillermo said, stepping up the white board to sketch out his numbers as talking bullets.

"We will offer Rose $72 million in stock and cash for 51 percent control. That is 30 percent of $240 million, which is half the book and market value of the company. As for Havens, the comparable figures are an offer of $48 million, representing 30 percent of half its market and book value, or $160 million.

"If the companies' cash demands are greater, we will assume full control at a premium of 50 percent above the offer price, or $108 million for Rose and $72 million for Havens.

"We should probably use another term besides 'premium,'" Guillermo suggested.

"I would use the word 'premium,' it's more in keeping with business language. Technically, we are after all paying something above our offer price, although no doubt well below whatever their asking price will be," Gorgens explained.

"We need to be careful, Lutz," Brent CEO Paul von Schlossen said. "The word 'premium' in my commodity trading world means we're paying above the asking price."

"Actually, I agree with Lutz, Paul. The word gives the impression that we're above our original offer even though we're buying more of the company. I believe they'll accept it, based on what the analysts have found. Their market is evaporating except for a few high-end items, and most of those are our licensed products anyway. Moreover, their book value is highly dubious and, after all, is heavily weighted with real estate. I know that real estate, at least in Connecticut. Their principal facility is a run-down automobile plant. It's at least one hundred years old. I can easily argue that point in the negotiation. They may see it as a great chance to unload the old building," Guillermo added.

The two Swiss executives nodded in agreement with Guillermo's suggestion. "Okay," Gorgens said, "let's negotiate along those lines. Do we all agreed?" he asked, seeking final confirmation among the three of them.

They all nodded affirmatively.

"I will inform Niko of our decision. He wisely left it to us to work out since we are a private company and can tell our other investors, the Swiss government, and the bank in particular that we made the decision based entirely on offers that will draw on our Swiss resources," Gorgens said.

"One more thing, Lutz," von Schlossen said. "Niko wanted a buyback clause. If within two years, the previous owners elect the option of a preferential offer for the return of the two companies, we will sell it back to them at 200 percent of our purchase price under a right of first refusal. Are we still agreed on the contract language in that regard?"

Once more, all three members of the buyers' council agreed.

The next day, Tuesday, July 12, 2011, Domenic Guillermo, accompanied by Marc Smit, the Belmont president, flew by corporate helicopter to Geneva's international airport. The pilot flew at six thousand feet along the coast of Lac Leman, the French name for Lake Geneva. They passed the legendary Swiss vineyards, Lausanne, Morges, and other small cities and villages as the morning traffic along Swiss Autoroute One intensified as they passed over Nyon, now on a slight south-southeast heading for Geneva.

Smit had been entirely read into the deal that Guillermo was to negotiate. He understood also the scheme to transplant Guillermo to the United States as part of the overall effort to remove all but a few of the US expatriate managers and executives from the three companies that had brought them there. Smit would be the eyes and ears of the three principal plotters: von Schlossen, Gorgens, and Rallis. The pretext for his joining Guillermo would be his alumni status at the negotiation site, the Harvard Business School, near Cambridge, and his long-standing friendship with Kyle McMahon, also a B-school alumnus.

At the juncture of Collonge-Bellerive, the pilot received instructions from the airport controller to turn west, crossing over the French village of Ferney-Voltaire and then turning south on to the flight's final leg to the airport's helipad. The position of the airport, overlapping two countries at their border at the foot of the Jura Mountains, posed no real communication issues for the two French-speaking entities as flights unavoidably drifted into the airspace of both.

It was now 9:00 a.m. as the two men disembarked from Belmont's Paninfarina Agusta chopper. They walked across the tarmac to the waiting Belmont corporate jet, the sleek Falcon 900LX. Within forty minutes, they were airborne heading west-northwest over France, beginning the six-hour flight to Boston's Logan International Airport.

"Forgive me if I snooze, Marc," Guillermo said to his flight companion. He lifted his large frame from the backward-facing seat, the preferred position for passengers as small jets of this nature were known to lose an engine from time to time on takeoff.

"I plan to so likewise, Dom," Smit said as he too moved to the center of the aircraft, his seat already elongated for him by the cabin crew and equipped with a pillow and fleece blanket.

Four hours later, as the small three-engine jet sped at five hundred miles per hour over Iceland, cruising at thirty-eight thousand feet, the two awoke, almost simultaneously. They moved to the front section of the aircraft, where a table between them sported a light breakfast of croissants and fruits.

"Are you encouraged by this move, Marc?" asked Guillermo as he sipped his café au lait, rejecting the harsh expresso that always irritated his esophagus.

"*Bien entendu* [of course], we will all profit, including the US companies, I might add," said Smit, thinking, *Avoid talk of the synthetic bean. We've been able to keep it out of the discussions, but Dom lacks the background to understand it anyway. McMahon's a different story. He's been trying to get a research program together for Havens for years. I don't see how we can avoid the subject coming up in the negotiation. I'll just remind Dom that it's not on the table in this deal.*

"I am too," Guillermo added as he chewed easily on a small croissant section that he had carved out with his knife and fork, European style. "You know, I miss the US. A big part of this for me, quite frankly, as I told Paul, is getting back to the US," he said, referring to conversation with von Schlossen and Gorgens regarding his expected role in the United States with the newly created Swiss-American confections giant; he would be its CEO for North American operations.

"It is your fate, you're a natural for the job, and I congratulate you. In our business sector, I can't think of a better person in that role. In your country, business and politics are too convergent. You bring skills from both sectors to the table now that you've been a big part of our business for several years."

"Thank you, Marc," Guillermo said as he glanced out the right side of the aircraft. "Looks like Iceland down there. We'll be off the Greenland coast shortly and then head over Nova Scotia and into Boston. You've done this flight many times, I gather, Marc?"

"Yes, I was at *the* business school, as you know, for two years but have flown to Boston a number of times."

Guillermo laughed, adding, "I get a kick out of you Harvard Business School guys. You always say '*the* business school,' as if there were no others, when you refer to Harvard."

"Are there others?" Smit replied with a wry smile.

They both laughed. They chatted casually, almost entirely about the business model and implementation plan for the new company that they were taking the first steps to create. But their orientation and goals were quite different. Smit saw himself ultimately replacing Lutz Gorgens as CEO of the massively expanded Belmont, one leg in the immense US market, the other tucked in the more friendly and familiar Alpine pocket of Europe. Guillermo imagined himself two to three years down the road, well into his seventies, ready for a retirement with several compensation sources allowing personal freedom along political influence as a graybeard adviser to business and government. Gone were his plans for a real political recovery, like recovering the governor's job in Connecticut.

Guillermo was beginning to feel his age. His bereavement for a his late wife, the strain of travel back and forth across the Atlantic, the other stresses of his work, and his general lack of systematic exercise, so long a part of his daily routine.

Guillermo's morning workouts were replaced with prayer; his afternoons filled with lunch, snacks, heavy coffee consumption, and endless meetings. His evenings demanded social events almost nightly as the gregarious, prominent, and "available" American became a favorite among the highly visible elites of the Swiss Riviera. He would be happy in many ways to be leaving Switzerland; he had formed a number of intimate relationships with too many women with lives that overlapped. And he was now using Viagara on a daily basis despite a history of heart disease.

Belmont's Falcon jet landed at Logan before noon on Tuesday. The two passengers had lunched on board. A limousine met them at the general aviation terminal, the car navigated through Sumner Tunnel, having chosen to avoid the more heavily trafficked Ted Williams Tunnel at this hour, then headed west up Storrow Drive, past the Harvard Bridge leading to the MIT campus across the Charles River.

Smit mused over the "hybrid cocoa bean" project that Belmont had been financing at MIT but refrained from discussing it. Instead, he directed Guillermo's attention to Boston University as they passed the campus.

"My daughter has applied to BU," Smit said. "She is very interested in the arts and communications, two highly reputable areas in the university's curriculum."

"That's true, Marc. It's a very good school, but like too many others here, it lives in the shadow of MIT and Harvard, especially the latter. As a foreign student, would she not have been a good candidate for Harvard, which is always eager to expand its enrollment of foreign students?"

"Actually, I took her for an interview at both places about a year ago. She definitely preferred BU, especially when she saw the living accommodations. Our tour was conducted by a French student, a young woman who was critical of Harvard and said she had found BU to be more agreeable for foreign students who wanted to experience a more typical slice of American college life. I'm sure she meant the social life." They both laughed.

The limo crossed the Charles at Boston University Bridge into Cambridge, continuing up Massachusetts Avenue toward Harvard Square.

"You know, I think the driver is taking us to the other Harvard rather than the business school. We need to be back on the other side of the river," Smit commented.

"You're right," Guillermo said, leaning forward over the front seat, saying, "Driver, we're going to the Baker Library at the Harvard Business School."

"Oh, excuse me," the driver said. "I thought you were going to the Widener Library on the main campus. No problem, I'll cross back over at Western Avenue. My dispatcher must have gotten the destinations confused."

The car turned west again and headed to the business school campus, parking to the rear of the Baker Library. The two got out.

"I selected the library because we're less likely to be recognized here. Also, the technology here is terrific, and we can get just about any type of economic or finance information we need in real time or instantaneously," Smit said. "The dean agreed to have a student assistant standing by to guide and help as needed."

"Very smart, I've been to social events at the Dean's House, as they call it now, which, I gather, had been the former residence of deans but which is a very pleasant setting for business banquets," Guillermo replied as they walked to the front of the building, already finding the weather insufferably hot and humid.

"I decided to avoid the place, too many visitors mulling around. Likewise, I rejected Morgan Hall, the faculty offices, since many of them are consultants to our sector and might recognize us or our American counterparts," Smit replied.

As they approached the columned redbrick building, a young man and woman appeared, walking toward them.

"Excuse me, are you the Belmont delegation?" the young man asked.

"Yes, thank you, I'm Domenic Guillermo and this is Marc Smit."

The foursome shook hands, the young man adding, "Mr. McMahon and Mr. Sawicki are awaiting us in the conference room. Please, follow us."

As they walked, the young woman spoke up. "We are equipped to retrieve whatever information you may need to support your discussions," she said. "Our Center for Research in Security Prices, which we refer to as CRSP, is already on line on my laptop, and I will be positioned outside the door, where we've set up a desk. We can also get any data on commodities or even corporate histories in very short measure."

"Thank you, I believe that we're well equipped with what we'll need for our talks, but having you there as a contingency is very comforting," Guillermo added.

"Of course, Governor. We'll be standing by," she said, surprising Guillermo by her reference to his title as former Connecticut governor.

"You're from Connecticut?" he asked.

"Yes, I grew up in New Canaan and was in the pharmaceutical sector in West Haven before coming to the business school. I'm in the second and final year here. Also, our paths have crossed before. I was the health assistant to the senator Tom Felice before he died. My name is Liz Sachs."

Guillermo stopped in his path. He told Smit and the young man to continue and he would catch up. Then turning to the young woman, he said, "By chance, are you Sid Sachs's daughter?"

"I am indeed," she replied.

"I'll be darned. How is he?"

"Not well, he has had Parkinson's for some years and is quite feeble although he's only sixty-five," she replied.

"I am so sorry to hear that. And what are your plans after graduation?" Guillermo asked.

"Like everyone else here, I'll be out on the auction block."

"Listen, take my card," Guillermo said, reaching into his jacket pocket. "I'll be looking for an executive assistant. Your training here and experience on the Hill as well as your Connecticut background could be critical to my decision."

Just as I had hoped, the young woman was thinking. *And I didn't have to push too hard either. I know exactly why they're here today and what Guillermo will be doing. This is a great break for me.* "Thank you, Governor. We had better catch up. The others are waiting."

As they scurried along, the young woman explained that she had worked for Earl Eastwood when he was a senator, before joining the Rehovot-USA staff as a marketing director for the US subsidiary of the large Israeli pharmaceutical firm headquartered near West Haven, Connecticut.

Guillermo was escorted into the conference room, where the other three were chatting, having made their welcomes. He shook hands first with Sawicki, patting him on the back as an old lost friend, Guillermo the politician emerging from his persona. Then he greeted Kyle McMahon, whom he had met only briefly in the past.

*   *   *

The meeting got under way almost immediately, all parties well prepared on the purpose and various outcomes the session could produce.

As McMahon summarized the disappointing sales data for the two companies, he thanked Smit for his help in accelerating the licensing arrangement and expanding its product coverage.

"But it's not enough," McMahon added.

"Yes, Kyle, we know that. We're prepared to make an offer for both companies. We are interested in either controlling interest, which is to say 51 percent more or less, or an acquisition, which would merge our companies," Guillermo said, initiating the first talk of the real purpose for the session.

McMahon and Sawicki were prepared, having even rehearsed their response. "We can go either way, Dom," Sawicki said.

"Yes, we still have substantial market value," McMahon added.

"It's not so much your market value as it is your book value that concerns us," Guillermo responded. "Our analysts in Europe and Switzerland have done a fairly intensive audit of your facilities and other parts of the organization of your two companies."

I was afraid of that, McMahon was thinking. *Even private companies can't keep their balance sheets secret anymore.* "We were sure that you would have done more than customary diligence, Dom," he replied to the light laughter of all.

"Well, we all understand your market value, based largely on earnings, and we had fashioned our offer accordingly. But when we did a facilities audit, we found that much of your intrinsic value, such as your real estate assets, we were forced to recalculate your operating leverage, examine your break-even points, and do other discounting analyses," Guillermo said, deliberately softening the muscles on his face.

Yeah, damn it, he's got us by the gonads. Our plant and equipment costs are out of whack, McMahon was thinking.

"Your operation is a maintenance nightmare by the standards of your own sector, especially that part of it that includes our facilities in Switzerland and the other foreign competitors' facilities in England, France, and even South America," Guillermo responded, adding, "These margins are so extreme that I'm not sure that we could be competitive if we invested in your companies, unless we made substantial upgrades, all of which would add to our costs."

Very smooth, Dom, Smit was thinking.

"So let's talk resources, Dom. What's on the table?" Sawicki asked.

"As I said at the outset, it depends on how we proceed. Do we talk control or acquisition and merger?" Guillermo responded.

"Let's start with control," McMahon quickly inserted.

Guillermo walked the two US executives through the Belmont analysis. He discussed the market earnings and the state of the economy in the United States and the prospects not only for growth but for weathering the recessionary storm for the next two years. "I don't want to walk into this thing and then find a Chapter 11 or Chapter 7 situation facing us after one or two years. We do know that you probably can't survive the next six months, right?" Guillermo asked.

"We could do that if we sold assets . . . ," Sawicki said.

Guillermo interrupted him, "Or defaulted on your debt in which case your creditors, perhaps even us, would be pressing you toward involuntary bankruptcy under Chapter 11."

McMahon was getting impatient, thinking, *Let's stop the crap, guys. We both know we won't be around four months, maybe even two months, from now. We can't get rid of any more people without collapsing our production. We're up the damn creek.*

McMahon then made a conscious effort to settle his countenance and, speaking softly, said, "Let's talk about your offer, Dom."

Smart move, Kyle. He knows we're right, and he's not fighting it. The situation may be even more desperate than we had figured, Guillermo thought. Guillermo also realized that he was getting tired. *I can't let Smit sense that I'm exhausted. I'm just beat. My thinking is getting sloppy. I had just better get it out and settle it. Be careful, don't do anything in haste.*

Like McMahon, Guillermo tried to calm himself while keeping his focus. He realized that the long trip, his run-down body, and too little sleep were getting to him. He spoke. "Gentlemen, we'll pay, in cash and stock, the proportions of which to be worked out, $72 million for Rose and $48 million for Havens, giving us 51 percent control."

The figure was fairly close to what the two US CEOs had expected. But both realized it would not save them; it was not enough if they were to remain in control, as CEOs, that is.

"Unfortunately, Dom, we'd still be limping toward the grave with that amount, especially since the stock could be used as very little leverage in increasing our debt load, which we must do. Banks and other lenders or investors won't place much credibility on our equity values in this market," McMahon replied.

That's a surprise! He wants to get out completely, a buyout, Guillermo was thinking, knowing that Smit's reaction was along the same lines but avoiding looking at him.

The four men stared across the table at one another for about a minute, then looked down at their yellow pads and other materials in front of them, as if to discover new troves of data to bolster their arguments in the negotiation.

Finally, McMahon spoke. "And the offers for full acquisition, lock, stock, and barrel?" he asked.

"We'll pay a 50 percent premium over the earlier offer price," Guillermo quickly responded.

McMahon and Sawicki quickly calculated the new offers in their heads as Guillermo prepared to elaborate.

"That comes to $108 million for Rose and $72 million for Havens," Guillermo said finally.

"How is that a premium?" Sawicki asked. "You're not paying more than market value."

"But we are being very generous when it comes to your book value. We both know your maintenance and replacement costs. The IRS would never give us a reasonable depreciation period for the run-down properties that your companies hold. Some of them, like Rose's production facility at Seaside Park in Bridgeport, are well over one hundred years old. We'd face terrific resistance to any upgrades and would be monitored constantly by the historic building trusts at the federal, state, and even local levels. Facilities like these keep productivity down when we compare costs to output," Guillermo explained.

As he spoke, Guillermo recalled the thought that had occurred to him during his research and the planning talks in Switzerland with Lutz Gorgens and Paul von Schlossen. They had planned to hammer the facilities issue into the talks. But Guillermo began to wonder about his own role after the buyout. If the production facilities were inadequate, the work would have to be moved. He was assuming that new locations would be found in Connecticut and Massachusetts or even that new facilities could be constructed. He resisted discussing it with Gorgens and von Schlossen because of the deadlines being imposed on him in completing the buy.

"I believe we have a deal, in principle that is, pending the language of the final agreement. Tim and I assume that we will be replaced and that you'll bring in your own management team?" McMahon said quietly, recalling that both he and Sawicki had important political appointments from the president to fall back on.

"You've made the right decision," Guillermo added with a soft voice that seemed odd to a man of his size. "New England will prosper in this sector again, and your pioneering work in building this market for our region will be memorialized, I can assure you."

They all stood up, reaching their hands across the table, all of them solemn in mood. Even Smit, little more than a fly on the wall during the talks, respected the impact that the decision had on the two men who had given so much of their careers to companies that were now on the ropes, and for reasons beyond their control.

As they sat back down, Guillermo walked to the door, advising Liz Sachs that they were ready for upgrades to their coffee, fruit and pastry trays, and that he would further appreciate her help in cancelling the reservations he had asked her to make for the foursome at his favorite Boston eatery, Faneuil Hall. "I will be in touch with you, soon," Guillermo said to her.

The atmosphere had suddenly become more relaxed.

"So what's the management plan, Dom?" Sawicki asked.

"We're not settled on it yet. I'll be the interim director of the combined Swiss-American company's North American operations. I expect my office will be here in Boston or in southern Connecticut, maybe Greenwich or Stamford.

"We also plan to, if you'll excuse the terminology, 'repatriate' the former members of Congress that our three companies in Switzerland now employ. They'll all assume new roles in expanding markets here and in other parts of Asia and South America," Guillermo added, noticing surprise on the faces of Sawicki and McMahon.

"I'd reconsider that part of the plan, if I were you. This is a highly technical, cash-intensive, market-driven business. It's a model that demands experienced hands manipulating it. Those guys, as best I know, have no real expertise. They're all politicians!" Sawicki added.

"I think you're nuts to bring them back here, putting them in major management jobs in these companies," McMahon said with unabashed bluntness. "Some of them are pariahs. They're too controversial. It can only hurt your business."

"They've done rather well for us, and in a very short time," Smits interjected.

"Hey, it's your show. Don't say I didn't warn you," McMahon grunted out, his displeasure very evident.

We were right, Smits thought. *The US expats are not good for us either here or in Europe. It will be to our advantage to get rid of them by shipping them back and then letting them go as we close down operations. McMahon and Sawicki are highly respected in the global confection sector. Their judgments were immediate and direct, no-nonsense as they say here.*

CHAPTER 17

THE EXPECTATIONS SPECTRUM

"LET'S GET THE HELL OUT OF HERE, CANCEL THE HOTEL RESERVATIONS," DOMENIC GUILLERMO WAS TELLING MARC SMIT AS THE TWO LEFT THE BAKER LIBRARY AT THE HARVARD BUSINESS SCHOOL.

"I agree, there's too much to be done back in Vevey," Smit replied as he pulled out his cell phone, calling the crew of the Belmont corporate jet, now parked at Logan International Airport. The crew responded favorably, telling Smit, in answer to his question, that under Swiss law, there were no flying-time restrictions requiring rest time for private commercial aviators between flights.

The rented limousine pulled up just as Smit was calling Switzerland, advising the company travel coordinator that they would be returning within several hours and to cancel the balance of the US itinerary.

"It's almost four. If we can get off the ground within an hour, we'll be there by morning," Guillermo was saying. "I did this often when I was at the Holy See. The legation there hated it because they goofed off when I was gone. Italians take many holidays, more when you work at the Vatican," he added as they both laughed.

The limousine sped through Ted Williams Tunnel to Logan International Airport, finding that at this time of day, the traffic was less congested. The Falcon was ready, fueled, and provisioned; they boarded quickly, having whisked through customs and ordered the chief steward to ready the communications suite. The plane taxied as Guillermo was reporting to Rallis that the deal was done. At the same time, Smit was on the phone to his boss, Belmont CEO Lutz Gorgens. Guillermo was not intentionally listening to Smit since he was answering Rallis's many rapid-fire questions, but the German words *die Vollendung . . . völlig* riddled through Smit's discussion. Trying to search his limited German vocabulary for their meaning while listing to and managing Rallis's excited comments, Guillermo finally figured out their meaning: "Completed . . . *fully* completed," Smit was saying as if the words were a code.

Guillermo hung up as did Smit soon thereafter. The two retreated to their respective reclined seats on opposite sides of the aircraft and two rows apart, with Guillermo to Smit's rear. Both men admitted to complete fatigue and the desire to sleep through the flight back. But Guillermo's mind was not ready to retire: *What the hell did he mean by that? "Fully completed," he must have said that five or six times?* Finally, he drifted off to sleep as the small jet winged toward Labrador, now over the open Atlantic side of Nova Scotia, with Cape Race in Newfoundland in sight from the cockpit's perch at forty-42,000 feet.

Rallis and Gorgens had spoken to the two around midnight, Swiss time. Both slept badly. Gorgens was concerned about the size of the investment he had committed to. And Rallis moved uneasily about his large chalet in Chamby. After getting up several times, reigniting a temperamental fire that seemed to reject the crispy synthetic kindling, he made a cup of chocolate. The drink in his hand, he gazed over the moonless night onto Lake Geneva 2,600 feet below. The ambient light that always seems to be present in the Swiss Alpine regions cast a faint glow on the water. He sometimes did his best thinking at three in the morning, especially when at the chalet, looking toward the French side of the lake.

Now comes the tough part – Sophia. How do I extract myself? Too soon, the deal's still fragile. It could fall apart if all of the components aren't orchestrated, which only I can do at this juncture. First step, I'll encourage consolidation of the two US companies at the Connecticut site. That'll please her.

I'll let Castignani battle it out with the Massachusetts delegation. They'll be enraged, as Bob will be. But that's his job.

Then, we'll get an initial public offering drafted up. As the market recovers, we'll offer the company back to the US investors, maybe even McMahon and Sawicki. They'll miss the money. What are they making in their government jobs, $175,000, maybe $180,000? That's chump change compared to what those two guys were paying themselves with Rose and Havens. We'll clean up. The public offering will bring in maybe $200 million, and we're selling the company back with 100 percent profit, all in less than a year. I'll put that money to good use. I'll be free of the US expats, including Guillermo . . . Hate to do that, he's a good man . . . But this is business. Lucas Holdings could take as much as $80 million from the deal, maybe a lot more, and I'll have total control over all of it.

Satisfied that he now had a plan, Rallis jotted down several pages of notes on his ever-present yellow legal pad, tucked the materials in his desk drawer. He returned to the bedroom as the fire fizzled out. He opened the French windows of the bedroom to let in the brisk Alpine air, then stepping out on the small balcony, he took a deep, cleansing breath as he had learned from yoga. It cleared his mind as he let out the air, flowing upward from his thighs to his abdomen, through the sternum into the glottal zones of his throat, then exhaled. He would sleep soundly until 6:00 a.m.

*   *   *

It was nine when Guillermo and Smits got back to Vevey on Belmont's Agusta helicopter, which had met them at Geneva International Airport. They went to their respective residences, with Guillermo passing up his usual morning prayer hour to prepare for the ten thirty breakfast meeting that he had arranged from the aircraft. He would break the news to the US expats in a very upbeat way, he decided, since he was not entirely sure how they would take it. There would be different reactions, of that he was sure. But he too was experiencing some doubt: what did Smit mean when he emphasized the words "fully completed" in his conversation with Gorgens from the aircraft?

The management of La Palmeraie, the elegant breakfast room of the Palais Montreux in which the entire expat contingent lived, had become accustomed to the use of its facility for the group's breakfast meetings. A recently remodeled room of the main dining area had been expensively furnished and expanded to include several business amenities such as Wi-Fi, a translator booth, and an enclosed area with desktop computers, fax transmission equipment, and printers. A separate door to the kitchen was also installed, not only to allow for better service but, as had already occurred in the several weeks of the meeting room's renovation, as a discrete entrance and exit for important business personages and even government officials whose presence could spark rumors.

The group had gathered at the large round table and was awaiting Guillermo's appearance. Discussion was lively, much of it with undertones of lingering anger regarding what they considered to be the "uncooperative" attitude of President Earl Eastwood, many sounding as if the pardon had been a presumed feature of the entire undertaking to expand the Swiss chocolate market into farther global reaches.

Former New Jersey senator Jeff Scharfman, always the angriest at any moment, continued his usual harangue, this time complaining that the Swiss takeover of the two US companies was as much a favor for Eastwood as for the company, Belmont.

"What the hell," Scharfman was saying, "Eastwood gets thousands of jobs at our expense, and we get screwed by the guy. We're making big-time sacrifices for his reelection in 2012."

Sitting next to him, listening to the tirade, former Connecticut senator Sam Schlesinger, now the commodity trading chief at Brent's US office in New York City, calmly sipped his coffee. "It's not a total loss, Jeff. We've made a lot of money in the short time we've been in these jobs. There was nothing else on the employment horizon that most of could have matched."

"You've gotta be kiddin' me, Sam. We all had our Senate contacts and could have lobbied for dozens of clients. You could've had the entire Connecticut pharmaceutical and insurance base in your pocket. I could have lobbied for oil, telecom, transportation, and other manufacturing and R&D firms in my state. That would have meant big bucks, maybe not of the magnitude we're sitting on here, but substantial enough."

"Jeff, look, the fact is we're pariahs. We're controversial. The premium clients aren't gonna deal with us, we're tainted."

"C'mon, you don't think there are former members out there with other types of stains on their ties?" Scharfman added rhetorically as he listed five or six of them who had actually served prison sentences then self-birthed into lobbying careers.

"Here's Dom. Let's see what happened in Boston," Schlesinger said, knowing that Guillermo had met at the Harvard Business School with the CEOs from Rose Confections and Havens.

As Guillermo entered the room, the talk quieted somewhat with several standing to greet him, exchanging a few words as he walked to what appeared to be a reserved place for him at the round table. The group was almost silent as he sat down.

"I believe we have a deal," Guillermo started. "They accepted our offer for a full buyout. We had done our due diligence, and it paid off. Our analysts had put together the perfect book. We could and did anticipate their arguments and counteroffers and were able to pretty much dismiss them with hard facts. Our lawyers and accountants will meet with their staff and finalize the contract language.

"It was awkward for me, at first anyway. Tim Sawicki was one of my strong supporters when I was governor. His Bridgeport operation is one of the largest employers in Fairfield County, over 7,500 jobs, although that number is highly fluid with market changes. But he was agreeable. He has a good exit package, a pension, health coverage, limited use of the company's executive jet, and even some of its facilities for several years. Moreover, the president will nominate him as ambassador to Switzerland," Guillermo added, prompting murmurs in the room.

"What about Havens, in the Boston area?" asked David Ford, the former New York congressman. "Did the president take care of Kyle McMahon?"

"He did, Dave, and I think Kyle got the better job. He'll be nominated as deputy secretary of commerce," Guillermo replied.

Jeff Scharfman was visibly agitated. "I'm still not exactly sure who got the better deal. We bail out the US confection industry, saving thousands of jobs, many in the president's own backyard of Connecticut, and we get screwed when he denies us our pardons," Scharfman ranted on, his endless whining always expected but tolerated among his colleagues, many feeling the same way but satisfied with their high incomes and rather agreeable lifestyles.

Nikos Rallis had entered late, taking a seat almost unnoticeably, thinking, *Scharfman will fit perfectly into the new role we've designed for him. When we pull out of the states, he'll be condemning the president for his lack of cooperation, reminding the White House that they could've saved the two companies. As the congressional members learn that they're not getting windfall jobs in the new Swiss-American company, Jeff will slam them for not putting more pressure on the president, the perfect pretext. Maybe Greek tragedies are in my blood. What a play this could be! He'll distract any attention from me. Keep yelling, Jeff.* Rallis laughed to himself.

Guillermo had seen Rallis enter and glanced at him while listening to Scharfman and thought, *Why is Niko smiling? He doesn't seem too upset over Scharfman's charges. Jeff is right in many ways. The expats have paid a big price despite the handsome compensation arrangements. I'm still pondering Smit's attitude change after the deal with Sawicki and McMahon. Is there somethin' goin' on here that I'm missing? I better pull Niko into this.*

Guillermo put up his hand, looking at Scharfman, who by this time was pouting with frustration. "Jeff, let's hear from Niko. We all need to know how the next planning stage is to be implemented," he said, looking at Rallis.

Rallis leaned forward in his seat, sipping from then putting down the coffee cup that had been placed in front of him by a very attentive waiter at La Palmeraie.

"Sorry I'm late folks. There was some trouble coming down from Haut Montreux. Some guy missed a turn, the front of his car sticking over the cliff, dangling there while some people who had stopped were lashing the rear of the car to a large truck before trying to extract him from the car. In the year we've been here, there've been, what, four fatalities on Route de Villard? I'm amazed there haven't been many more than that," he said to an audience well aware of the treacherous Alpine roads that some of them navigated several times a week.

Rallis's English was impeccable, in great part because he was raised by an English-born mother but also because he was educated in the United States, at places like Trinity College and the Wharton School at the University of Pennsylvania. He seemed more American than Greek, which might have been the main reason that so many of his American friends accepted him at face value, especially the expats.

"Let me get right to Dom's question. What's the next step, and how does it affect the people in this room? First, there will be some necessary changes in your roles. This is the most important issue for all of us. Belmont's CEO and I, at a recent board meeting, which, regrettably, did not include Dom since he was in the US negotiating the takeover, although we were in constant touch, made some amendments to the original plan. This happened in great part because Dom had succeeded brilliantly beyond our expectations. We had not really expected to buy the totality of the two companies. This outcome required some quick adjustments," Rallis said.

What's he talkin' about? We planned on reaching for full control and even worked out the purchase prices and negotiation strategy, Guillermo wondered, then recalled that Rallis had actually said that the board had not "really expected" that result. *Okay, maybe I'm gettin' too suspicious here. But it's still a mere play on words.*

Rallis continued to speak. "The plan from the outset would install Dom as North American CEO, as well we know. But in light of the outcome, we need to get much more involved, quite obviously. We now own the entire show. It's our baby. That means *all* of us have to get involved."

The expats expected something salutary; Rallis was too upbeat to deliver bad news, most thought.

"Here's what we think is the best approach. Our plan is well anchored in the good work that *all* of you have done in your tenures here. We are very much aware of how far we've come, and the rewards for everyone have been substantial, and they can be even greater. We need to put the US operation in the best hands we have, and they're yours. We want to move most of you to manage the US operations, in the US," Rallis said, pausing and looking around the table.

What is this all about? Guillermo wondered. *The management staffs of Rose and Havens are good people and know the markets better than our bunch. We're putting them out of work to bring back our guys? Is this the "best" plan?*

Generally, the reactions were favorable. No one thought Rallis was the type who would falsely burnish a business situation; he had successfully taken them through a couple of very complicated but highly rewarding ventures.

He's not the type of guy who makes rosy assumptions, Scharfman was thinking. Scharfman had been president of Lucas Holdings, working more closely with Rallis than any of the other expats, with the exception possibly of Guillermo.

Rallis continued to speak. "Jeff will shift to the presidency of the North American operation, working with and reporting to Dom. Everyone else will assume jobs in the new structure somewhat akin to what you've been doing here in Switzerland. David Ford, for example, will manage futures contracts for our commodity needs and organize within the company our own trading platform. Mark Koerner will be the manager of North American marketing. Sam Schlesinger will direct operations at the Connecticut plant, and Mark Baldwin will be his counterpart for the former Havens' company in Newton Highlands. Sticking a Virginian like Mark in Massachusetts made us think that through again, but Mark, as the former senator from Virginia, seemed to handle the integration of liberal Northern Virginia with traditional Southern Virginia with enough poise to convince us that he could easily handle that part of the job," Rallis said to some laughter and emerging high spirits in the room.

"I'm not going through all the new jobs, which will be posted on our closed corporate website today. But I don't anticipate any really strong objections," Rallis said. "Bennie will be invited to remain with the trading company, Brent, taking over the entire US operation with the option of staying in Switzerland or relocating."

All heads turned to former Mississippi representative Bennie Thompson. His role in negotiating the acquisition of the Ivory Coast cocoa crop had become legendary. It was clear that he had special importance in the minds of the boards of the three Swiss companies.

"Niko, there are some major logistical issues as well, as I'm sure you're aware. We're now residing here. Aside from Mark and Sam, in Massachusetts and Connecticut, where do the rest of us land up?" asked former New Jersey senator Andy Tantillo.

"Swiss-American Confections Corporation will be headquartered in Greenwich, Connecticut, which, of course, is where Dom will be located as well as most of the rest of you. We've been in touch with several relocation realtors and are taking bids on a company to represent us in finding housing and other facilities. As for your condos at Palais Montreux, they're all rentals, as you know, so we'll be able to phase out of here at a more leisurely pace," Rallis said.

There was much talk among the group as the meeting wound down.

"I could get back into politics, I miss it," said former Connecticut senator Sam Schlesinger.

"I feel the same way, but getting the pardon will make a big difference. Otherwise, I don't have that type of appeal to overcome the stain," said former New Jersey senator Andy Tantillo.

As he listened to the chatter, his coffee now cold, Guillermo answered as many questions as he could, always watching Rallis, who, in his mind, seemed too comfortable and confident, smug really when one examined the work that Guillermo knew would be rigorous with outcomes that could hardly be easily anticipated any time soon.

*   *   *

On Thursday, July 14, Bob Castignani called for a meeting of the New England Industrial Association, a legitimate cover for lobbyist-type access to congressional principals. Castignani knew it was a bad time. The debate in Congress over raising the national debt limit cut into every member's favored programs, with a deal emerging that could lead to a 10 percent reduction across the board. That would happen if Congress reneged a plan to cut spending by nearly $4 trillion over ten years. Castignani had spent nearly twenty-four years in the US Senate, so he knew better; they would never do it. The Joint Select Committee on Deficit Reduction, the so-called super committee, would consist of twelve members from both houses. They would choose the programs to be cut. Castignani laughed to himself and sometimes aloud as he read reports on committee progress and, especially, the member selections. The house minority leader and Speaker would designate members for the super committee as would their respective party counterparts in the upper chamber. He read the names as they leaked out; it was apparent that extremists on both sides of the aisle would constitute the panel. It was at that point Castignani, seated at breakfast in the Dirksen Senate Office Building cafeteria, laughed aloud, catching the attention of some Capitol Police officers.

"C'mon, Senator, share the joke," one officer said. They all knew Castignani well from his many years in the Senate.

"The joke is the super committee," Castignani replied, still laughing. "But hey, guys, I know you can't comment on it . . . But I know what you're thinking," he said to the light laughter of the four officers at the adjoining table. "I'll tell ya, this place never changes – well, almost. It seems my successors have found yet another way to befuddle the poor American taxpayer into believing that Congress is in control and things are going well."

The Capitol Police are accustomed to partisan comments and generally take them in stride. Members are cautioned about trying to influence them politically, so both sides tend to make and treat such chatter respectfully but without any sign of endorsement. The four officers turned their heads back to the center of their table, looking at one another from their slightly bowed heads and rolling their eyes as they resumed eating.

Castignani finished breakfast, delivering his copy of the *Boston Globe* to Bettie, a longtime cook at the cafeteria whose chipped beef on a bun had been seducing Castignani's palate for years. A former Bostonian, the two would chat almost daily.

"Thanks, Senator," Bettie said as he handed over the newspaper to her. "Will I see you tomorrow? Oh, it's Friday, that's right. You don't hang around here for weekends."

"I do now. I'd rather be in Maine, skulling my boat on the Darmiscotta, too much to be done here. I thought it would be better after the Senate, but no such luck. You enjoy your weekend. See you next week," Castignani said to her.

It was after 8:00 a.m. as he headed to his parking spot a block away on Delaware Avenue, just in front of Senate Park and on the west side of the Russell Senate Office Building. It was a typical mid-July morning in Washington. The temperature was already at 80 degrees and the humidity defying any chance of relief. Castignani removed and tucked his blazer under his arm as he went to his car. Former senators are granted parking privileges in certain designated areas on Capitol Hill. The parking perk and privileged access to the Senate floor were welcome features of their retirement benefit package.

Castignani had organized the NEIA meeting at eleven to be held in his Watergate suite's conference room. There would be groans among some of the members because of the tightness of voting schedules in both houses and the distance they'd travel from the Hill. He mentioned this to Ben Ochs and Don Tranh, his two junior law partners and former top staffers in the Senate, both of whom retired when Castignani lost his seat.

"They're going to get a lot hotter when they hear about Rallis's staffing of the North American company," Ochs said as they discussed the agenda.

"Yeah, I know. They were planning on big jobs for themselves. Some of these guys had already made plans to retire with those opportunities in mind," Castignani replied. "I'll have to find some way to accommodate them. Otherwise, they could make life difficult for the Rallis reorganization, something which I don't think Niko fully understands."

"I'm sure he doesn't get it," Tranh replied. "He probably thinks that the Connecticut governor can manage everything he needs, you know, the thought that she and the president are from the same state."

"Are they still together, Rallis and Kallias?" Ochs asked.

Tranh and Castignani both looked at Ochs. "Why would you say that, Ben?" Castignani asked. "Do you know something the rest of us don't?"

"Al Gomez, the Hartford mayor, his wife, and Shirley went to Trinity together and have been close friends. They talk all the time," Ochs said, referring to his wife, Shirley. "Gomez's wife, Sydney, is also friendly with Kallias, also a Trinity person, and over the past few months have been talking together a lot, even having dinner. For Sydney, it's probably all business since she's always hustlin' some favor for her real estate development projects."

"What's Sydney saying?" Castignani asked.

"In a few words, she's uneasy with the Rallis relationship. She thinks he may be more interested in her politics than her person," Ochs replied.

"Yup, she's got Rallis pegged okay. That guy can be ruthless," Castignani added. "Amazing that she would say something like that to a third party, but you said they're good friends, right?"

"Right, it makes sense, women share things like that," Ochs added.

"That's good to know. We need to keep abreast of that. It may help us figure out just what the Swiss are up to. To be honest, I'm really not sure, which makes our lobbying work risky. If something goes awry, you know who's gonna take the heat," Castignani warned.

It was minutes before eleven when two members of the Senate delegation arrived. Senator Mike Lampert, the Maine Republican, walked in with Senator Paul Rienzi, a Rhode Island Democrat.

"Paul, I hear your son's gonna start as quarterback at UMass this season," Castignani said in shaking his hand. "I hope to hell he doesn't have *all* of your genes," he added laughingly.

"You and me both, babes, but the kid's doin' too well academically. He doesn't fit his old man's mold, not that I'm disappointed," Rienzi replied

Castignani then turned to Senator Lampert. "I was just tellin' Bettie in the Dirksen eatery this mornin' that I'd rather be paddling my boat on the Darmiscotta. How the hell are ya?"

"You know, this damn debt ceiling issue. Maine can only suffer more with the deal that's brewin' up there," Lampert replied. "I'll tell you, Bob. The right opportunity comes along for me, I'd hang it up. It just isn't fulfilling, and it sure as hell ain't fun anymore."

That's a lead. He's already letting me know he's available, Castignani thought.

The door had barely closed when two other Senate participants in the NDIA arrived, Senators Kevin O'Meara, a Massachusetts Democrat, and Roger Evarts, a Connecticut Republican. They shook hands, greeting each other warmly in this type of quasisocial setting where surprising comity generally prevails regardless of partisanship.

"Have you seen Zbig?" Castignani asked Connecticut's senior senator, Roger Evarts, regarding Zbigniew Krakowski, his junior counterpart.

"He's on his way, probably had to stop off at the White House for a quickie," Evarts said, discretely talking quietly toward Castignani's right ear, scoffing Krakowski's rakish behavior with women, most recently with Sue Cohen, the president's chief of staff.

They both laughed as Castignani added, "Yeah, I hear that part of the Clinton legacy is a condom dispensing machine in the office's private bathroom." They both roared with laughter.

In hysterics, Evarts added to the humor, "That's why Earl moved Audrey in with him. It was cheaper than paying a buck for condoms from the machine." They were both bent over with laughter.

The five House members of the NEIA arrived in tandem: Democratic representatives George Mourgos of Connecticut and Tony Provenzano of Rhode Island and Republican representatives Frank Poole of Massachusetts, Paul Treadway of Connecticut, and Brendan McNeal of New Hampshire.

As they gathered around the conference table, having helped themselves to various beverages, there was an evident air of high expectations, which was uncomfortably felt by Castignani, Tranh, and Ochs.

"Gentlemen," Castignani began, "the Swiss have acquired both Rose and Havens and will consolidate them into a single US entity with various production and marketing offices. The two US companies, as some of you have heard from your constituent CEOs, agreed to the buyout. The immediate change will be the removal of Tim Sawicki of Rose Confections and Kyle McMahon of Havens, who will receive appointments in the Eastwood administration. McMahon will be nominated to fill the currently vacant deputy commerce secretary's job, and Sawicki will be nominated as US ambassador to Switzerland."

"Good deals," said Tony Provenzano, known to all as Tony Pro. There were head shaking and thumbs-up gestures among the group.

"The employment levels will be sustained, nearly twelve thousand jobs between the two locations, and it can be expected to improve as the economy does," Castignani said, adding, "If and when it does."

There were heads shaking, arms raised in frustration, and other such gestures of frustration and even futility. Little doubt pervaded the thoughts of those present that an economic turnaround was not likely any time soon.

"By the way, we'll have a fact sheet distributed. You can get it in your wires, Facebook, Tweeter, newsletters, whatever other means you use for constituent communication," Castignani added.

"There was something related to the buyout in the *Wall Street Journal* online pages this morning, Bob," said Representative Paul Treadway of Connecticut.

"Yeah, who the hell released that?" asked Representative George Mourgos, whose district included the Bridgeport plant.

"I saw the online report," answered Don Tranh. "There was nothing in it that made sense, only that a deal was brewing. My bet is they got the news from the *Financial Times,* which has good contacts in the Swiss government. The information we're providing to you today is a positive scoop for your favorite media freaks."

"And we all have them," yelled Massachusetts representative Frank Poole, whose district included the Havens plant in Newton Highlands.

Before Castignani could even get to the topic of management and structure and organization of the new company, the question was raised by Maine senator Mike Lampert, who had earlier hinted to Castignani that he could be available.

"How're they planning to staff the new company, Bob?" Lampert asked.

"For the time being, according to what I was told by Nikos Rallis and Dom Guillermo, who I spoke to last night, the Belmont CEO, Lutz Gorgens, has designated Dom to be CEO of the Swiss-American Confections Corporation. Dom will be headquartered in Greenwich and has hired his executive assistant, a young woman by the name of Liz Sachs, who once worked for former Connecticut senators as Tom Felice, Bill Rice, and even Earl Eastwood," Castignani said, sensing some solemnity in the mention of the late senators Felice and Rice, the former having died in the midst of a 2008 scandal and the latter having been assassinated in a terrorist attack on Washington in 2009.

"What about the operations management, you know, the lower-level CEOs, presidents, and other senior managers?" asked George Mourgos.

Castignani decided he would try to appear as if it was a routine response to the specific question of management staffing at the two US companies acquired by Belmont. *Keep cool, there's gonna be a reaction. They'll be furious,* he thought to himself, avoiding too much delay in getting to the question as he shuffled a few papers, thinking further, *Bad move, they're not gonna be fooled into thinking you're looking for information. They're aware you're right on top of the story.*

Castignani spoke. "Jeff Scharfman will be dispatched back from Switzerland as corporate president."

There was a numbing silence. There was no movement among the group, no grimaces or other facial gestures, hand wringing or covert signals, just quiet. So quiet that the message was as unmistakable as expected: deep disappointment.

"They're sending *Jeff Scharfman?* The damn guy's an ex-con. What are they, Goddamn nuts?" said angered Connecticut representative Paul Treadway. "Who the hell is gonna run the Bridgeport plant, an exhumed Jimmy Hoffa?"

"Yeah, who are the others, Bob?" asked George Mourgos, the House member representing Fairfield County and the Bridgeport plant of Rose Confections.

"That's what I'd like to know too," asked Massachusetts representative Frank Poole, whose House district included Newtown Highlands' Havens plant.

Hell, here it comes. This could get ugly, Castignani thought as he started to speak.

"Sam Schlesinger will be the president of the Bridgeport operation, and Dave Baldwin will run the former Havens facility in Massachusetts," Castignani answered.

"Bob, this is crazy," Poole reacted. "Dave's from Virginia, an old Virginia family, whatta ya call it? FFV or somethin' like that, meaning famous first families, or whatever. No one coordinated this with me. You gotta be kiddin', the media will go nuts. Many Massachusetts people still think they have slavery in the South. He's replacin' Kyle McMahon, a guy with strong Boston roots from a well-respected Irish family."

"Frank, this is a business decision, not a political nomination," Castignani said, trying, albeit weakly, to defend the decision.

"C'mon, Bob. It's more than a business decision. The company can't thrive without our help. They're gonna need regulatory relief, maybe even exemptions from some of the antitrust restrictions. They may even need a bailout, although there's a fat chance of getting that past the president. If it came to that, we may even have to override a presidential veto. Think of the work and the payoff in political chips that would require, but it would also mean saving over ten thousand jobs," said an angered Kevin O'Meara, the Massachusetts Democrat and chairman of the Senate Armed Services Committee in the Democratically controlled Senate. "Hell, the only place that type of bailout money can come from is defense spending. And that could only mean two things: we cut personnel, or we cut someone's generally useless weapons project somewhere in the US, maybe even our own backyards in this group."

"He's right, Bob," added the generally moderate Tony Pro, the Rhode Island Democrat and now ranking minority member of the House Armed Service Committee. "And not just right regarding debiting the defense budget for a bailout but also Kevin's comment regarding a business versus political decision. The two sectors are now too tightly linked. The banking crisis did that, or I should say the bankers did it to themselves. They got greedy, they didn't police themselves, and they got their rears caught in a crack. I guess I could've found a better hockey metaphor, but you know what I mean," the former professional hockey player said.

Tony Pro continued to speak. "Why do you think Washington has become such a hot place to be? We're now the show, guys. No serious business sector can any longer ignore us. As one of my colleagues in the House said after the government took over Citibank, 'we own the banks.' Look at what the banking sector is spending on lobbying, over $1.2 billion, just to keep the Dodd-Frank law from being implemented.

"Look, I'm on the defense committee," Tony Pro continued. "I understand well what it's like to be lobbied. And it's what makes me, like the rest of us in the room, laugh when we talk about finding $4 trillion in cuts and tax savings over ten years. Hell, remember when Earl became president, he couldn't cut $1.5 *million* from spending when he submitted his first budget, and now we're talkin' trillions. I don't wanna get off topic here and apologize for ranting a bit as I have. But the Swiss guys just don't understand how this place is now working. It's a very different show from how it was even five years ago."

"So who else is comin' over from Switzerland to run things, Bob?" It was the voice of Connecticut senator Zbigniew Krakowski, who had slipped in and taken a seat while the discussion was under way.

Crap! The reaction is even worse than I thought. But I gotta lay it all out. It's my task, thought Castignani as he started to speak. "Just about all the expats: Dave Ford will manage futures contracts since the new company will have its own commodity trading platform. Anne Rathbone will be the new finance chief for the company. Marc and Jane Gregoire will handle legal matters. Andy Tantillo will coordinate production. Mark Koerner will direct development of North American markets."

As he spoke, the group became highly agitated, some pushing their coffee cups away from them, others furiously taking notes on the fact sheet that had been distributed, and still others, with their chairs away from the table, poised as if to leave. Few would stay for the planned lunch. They quickly realized there would be little personal gain from the reorganization. No jobs, maybe even reduced contributions to their ever-gaping campaign and PAC coffers – nothing but frustration as, they sensed, the job-sustainment effort could only falter along with the increasingly dismal economy.

The final comments came from Tony Pro. "Bob, it's a damn disaster. I can only say that the Swiss had better be prepared to pump a lot of money into this endeavor and to protect these jobs. Otherwise, they're gonna suffer big time. The Swiss government has a stake in Belmont, so that makes them liable for the outcome in no small part. I'm on the Armed Services Committee. Kevin chairs the Senate committee. The Swiss economy depends quite a lot on the heavy spending we provide for their Pilatus pilot training aircraft. If they screw with us, they're gonna suffer some big hits in their own economy."

The entire group from Congress left, leaving luncheon plans in turmoil.

*   *   *

August was a hyperactive month. The expats gradually swept into their new positions in Rose and Havens while lawyers on both sides of the Atlantic aligned sales and postsales contracts to the respective demands of the EU, Switzerland, and the United States. The new corporate structure quickly emerged in principle while their cultures reluctantly surrendered to the global nature of the new company.

In Washington, however, August was a month of recess. The president had nominated Tim Sawicki as ambassador to Switzerland and Kyle McMahon as deputy commerce secretary as promised. However, with Congress in recess, the nominations would have to await their turns on the already-overcrowded committee and floor schedules in the Senate.

Using the authority available to him, Eastwood made "recess appointments" of the two men to their new offices, meaning they could temporarily assume their duties while awaiting confirmation in the Senate. Wasting little time, McMahon and his family found a condominium in Alexandria's Montebello, an elegant four-tower, thirty-two-acre complex on Mount Eagle, which is the highest elevation in Fairfax County, Virginia. Their sixteenth-floor unit overlooked the Potomac and had a northeastern orientation, giving them a sweeping view of the nearby Washington skyline.

Tim Sawicki and his wife, Allie, were at the ambassador's residence in Bern, the Bundesstadt, or capital city of Switzerland, within ten days after getting the presidential nod. The ambassadorial position had been vacant for nearly three years and managed by the chargé d'affaires, a type of "deputy ambassador" title, and always a very savvy career officer from the State Department. The urgency was noted by the Swiss government, which had complained that the recipients of several musical awards from the Montreux jazz festival that had ended in July still awaited acknowledgment of their accomplishments. Allie quickly arranged a ceremony for the male bassist and female vocalist, both from Connecticut, as it turned out. The two had stayed in Switzerland after the festival and were easily located at Geneva hotel. The third recipient was a Swiss saxophone player from Lugano; the Swiss government's anxiety regarding the recognition of the young man was tied to its determination to build a national reputation for its own musicians.

Sawicki had a hidden agenda. He was determined to learn more about the deal that had cost him his career, although it was only a brief respite from it. His first official priorities after getting his temporary credentials accepted by the Swiss were to rapidly involve himself in trade and finance issues within the Swiss government.

*   *   *

Guillermo, now situated in Greenwich, had established the US headquarters for the Swiss-American Confections Corporation in a recently abandoned corporate office building at the corner of West Putnam Avenue and Pemberton Road, minutes from the heart of Greenwich as well as the New York border. His executive assistant, Liz Sachs, originally from the Stamford-New Canaan area, excelled in managing the nightmarish logistical gyrations in establishing the company's presence in one of the country's highest-per-capita-income cities.

On Monday, September 5, 2011, after just six weeks of SACC's formal presence in the United States, Guillermo was teleconferencing with Nikos Rallis, Belmont's

Lutz Gorgens, and Brent's Paul von Schlossen at the Belmont Château in Vevey, Switzerland.

"It's not a slam dunk, guys," Guillermo was saying. "Our production and productivity are both up, but our sales are lagging, and we're swimming with inventory."

"That's because we made this foolish commitment to keep employment high, Domenic," Gorgens was saying. "Eventually, the curves will cross and your productivity will diminish and revenues lag. The productivity number is artificial since it relies heavily on the cash we've been putting into the company rather than earnings. Your auditors will quickly see this when they analyze the balance sheets and assess the US company's financial position."

Guillermo was getting uneasy. In many ways, he felt somewhat over his head. He was trained as a lawyer, worked most of his life as a career politician, and had very little business experience until he left the Connecticut governor's job and his succeeding ambassadorial post at the Holy See to work briefly for an Italian company. His time in Switzerland, for nearly two years, was the extent of any real managerial responsibility. Now he depended on two equally inexperienced subordinates, David Baldwin at the Massachusetts location and Sam Schlesinger in Bridgeport, to manage day-to-day manufacturing and related operations. Both of these men also came from political careers, except for their brief time in Switzerland.

Guillermo struggled for an answer; looking at the data compiled by his assistant, Liz Sachs, he could find nothing relevant. Clearly, earnings were flagging. Markets were still down and taking sales with them. Cash reserves were getting thinner, and even fixed assets, like plant and equipment, were in serious straits when marked to market.

"It's still the general economy, gentlemen, and I can't do much about that," he said finally.

Rallis intervened. "Dom, you might want to move to a single-shift production schedule in both facilities and then start thinning out the ranks. Just don't fill vacancies as they occur."

"But you know, I'll take heat from the media. The *Wall Street Journal* has been all over me, for example. They're wondering how we can succeed in this economy, especially with the luxury product line we're offering. Thanks to Liz, my assistant, you've met Liz Sachs," he added, "our corporate gift business is the best margin line that we have right now."

"Keep on that, Dom. It's a very small part of our market, but we might be able to grow there," Rallis said, adding, "We'll talk to you on Wednesday."

The session ended. Guillermo looked at Liz. "You've saved our chestnuts, thanks."

"Dom, to tell you the truth, I'm not sure what I'm doing. I was just following a recommendation from one of the production managers, who urged me to look at that market slice, the corporate gift business having been a sector that the former Rose Confections actually abandoned a decade ago. We just got lucky," she replied.

Guillermo worried more. *Good God, she's as much an amateur as I am. This is a hell of a mess. I need real business people, but how do I get rid of the others?*

Liz Sachs had the same thought as she stared at Guillermo. *We're in deep shit. No one knows what's goin' on. Schlesinger is using his Bridgeport perch to get back into politics, and Baldwin is already cavorting around, spending more time with his new girlfriend than with the company. He's urging that we open a production facility in his state of Virginia, the guy's nuts! We're bleeding here.*

*　　*　　*

Back in Switzerland, the three men looked grimly at one another as the teleconference ended.

"We have to act, and soon," von Schlossen said. "I'm supplying US operations from our cocoa storage at NYMEX warehouses. The usage rate is far below what was forecast. That product is perishable even in the best storage facilities."

"Yes, and he will have to start cutting inventories and production fairly soon, worsening the bean's shelf life. We don't have many options," Gorgens added. "I could send some of my best Swiss managers to the US to trim operations and bring things into better balance."

"There's a problem with that, Lutz," Rallis said. "We'd have to lay off the US managers. That would create an image issue."

"Why should we care about what the media thinks? We'd be engaging in good business practices," von Schlossen asked.

"We should always do that, use sensible business approaches to business problems, Paul. But I'm thinking that we need a public offering. We can't do that at a time when our balance sheets are in bad shape," Rallis replied. "The bankers managing the initial public offering and even the Securities and Exchange Commission will insist on lower-bid asking prices. The IPO could implode on us."

"That could be our answer, but we have to prepare. We can take sort-term measures to strengthen the balance sheet," Gorgens said. Of the two Swiss, Gorgens was the more experienced business manager, while von Schlossen's strength rested with commodity market analysis.

"What did you have in mind, Lutz?" von Schlossen asked.

"As a start, do what any good business would do. Start consolidating operations, reducing duplicative functions and tasks," Gorgens replied. "We may have to consolidate the Bridgeport and Newton Highlands plants. There would be modest increases in transportation costs related to both the production inputs as well as finished-product shipping."

"That could work, Lutz," Rallis said. "And we could emphasize that it's a short-term measure until the economy recovers. Our potential investors in the IPO will welcome a move like that, one that shows a willingness to bite the bullet, as the Americans say."

"Also, we could seek bailout monies, as you had mentioned, Niko, during our last conversation on the topic," von Schlossen added.

"Yes, we could seek a bailout quietly through political channels, promising to pay it back with monies raised from the IPO. What worries me is that anything political tends to leak to the press in the US," Rallis said.

They looked at one another, their expressions reflecting deep thought. Rallis was thinking, *Sophia could talk to the White House as could Dom. Zbig would be on board . . . if, if . . . I've got it: consolidate at the Bridgeport plant. That'll frost the Massachusetts people, but we'll keep a skeletal crew there, promising to reopen.*

"I think that could work," Rallis said finally, explaining his reasoning for consolidation in Bridgeport with a gratuitous promise to the Massachusetts workforce. "We'll hire an investment banking firm for the IPO and explain that the consolidation is under way and would be completed before the IPO is released."

CHAPTER 18

A POCKET-PADDING EXIT STRATEGY

THE MOMENTUM TO FASHION AN INTERIM STRATEGY STUDDED WITH DECEPTIONS AND DISTRACTIONS TO MASK THE ULTIMATE OBJECTIVE TO DEPART THE US MARKET BECAME VERTIGINOUS FOR THE SWISS. Their principal ally and coconspirator, Nikos Rallis, the cunning Greek financier, was the phalanx that would open the avenues of attack. His first step was to promote the consolidation of the two US production facilities, formerly Rose Confections and Havens, both failing badly in an economy inebriated by its own excesses. Next, he would solicit financial help, pleading further losses despite the cost-cutting disposal of the Havens facility in Newton Highlands. He would promise redemption for the Massachusetts facility as the economy recovered to leverage government support. Lastly, he would take the company public with an offering that would be expected to repay the government loan. Of course, this was his immediate business plan; the last steps would be withdrawal by selling the US operation back to the original owners at a 200 percent premium over the purchase price. That failing, the Swiss and Rallis would strip US assets from the company, exporting them to meet corporate demands in Europe, and then declare bankruptcy.

The day after the conference between the Swiss and Guillermo, the CEO of the new company's North American units, Rallis was in touch with Connecticut governor Sophia Kallias. The two were still enraptured by a romance that might have rested more on infatuation, but for Sophia, it was an escape from the imponderable nightmares of satisfying constituents whose dislike of taxes was matched only by their demand for more government services.

It was ten in the morning of September 6, 2011, in Hartford and five in the afternoon at the Chamby headquarters of Lucas Holdings from which Rallis was calling.

"When am I going to see you again, Niko? It's been, what, six or seven weeks now," Kallias was asking.

"I have to return Lex to school at Loomis, so we'll be flying over this week," he replied. "I've missed you terribly. Our time at the chalet was magnificent."

"Yes," she added, thinking, *This isn't working as I had thought. I understood that he would be here, living here, at least part-time. Why isn't that happening? I won't raise that question now, too pushy.* "Plan to stay here in the governor's mansion. I'll make arrangements."

"Okay, I like that. I have to spend some time with Dom in Greenwich, at the office. Would you like to accompany me?"

He just doesn't understand my job. I'm the governor of this state, not some always-available housewife or free spirit that can react to his every need. She then caught herself in the middle of her thought, relenting somewhat. *That was stupid. Of course he knows the pressures I face.* "As you might expect, Niko, I'm overwhelmed. We've just entered the new fiscal year, and I'm taking a lot of heat from the budget cuts I've had to make. The teachers' unions are even talking about a recall. That's not going to happen, but the threat alone is prompting the media," Kallias replied.

Better that she stay there anyway. I don't want her too allied with Guillermo, who's going to oppose the consolidation, maybe even fight it openly. I need his help, but I will fire him if necessary. I have no real choice on that matter, Rallis reasoned.

"I've something very important to share with you. Please don't take any action until I talk to Guillermo, which will be right after this call. I'll tell you exactly what I need," Rallis said cautiously.

"What . . . what is it? Don't tell me you're closing down the Bridgeport plant. I've read they've been suffering, but Sam has never called me," Kallias said, referring to Sam Schlesinger, the former Connecticut senator and a colleague of Kallias when she was in the state legislature, although they were on opposite sides of the aisle.

"We're going to expand in Bridgeport . . . But we must close down in Newton Highlands." Rallis was relaxed as he spoke, knowing the first part would please her but that she would be well aware of the political consequences.

"Jesus!" she blurted out, somewhat amused that she, as a Jew, had let the word fly with an epithetic quality to her tone of voice. "I didn't realize things had gone *that* badly. The Massachusetts delegation is not likely to be pleased."

"No kidding, but I'm also asking for federal help. If I can get it, I should be able to keep the lights on in Newton Highlands until the economy improves a bit. In the meantime, I'll offer jobs at the Bridgeport plant to about half the workforce in Newton. Few will take them, I realize that."

"Bridgeport has high unemployment, so it depends on the skill level you'll need. Also, we have hundreds out of work in the other coastal counties, and they're relatively close by. How many jobs are we adding?" Kallias asked, suddenly thinking, *This could get me reelected. I've brought in foreign investment and expanded the Bridgeport workforce by, what, maybe 50 percent?*

"At least 1,200, maybe more. We still need to refine the numbers, which we're doing in Switzerland. But I'll need your help. Please, talk to the White House and then Zbig. Obviously, you can determine the best political strategy. We will need $200 million, federal loans preferably, or guarantees if we have to turn to the private markets. If we can get our plan moving to find improvements in the cocoa bean, we may even qualify for R&D grants." Rallis provided few further details and correctly assumed that Kallias was sufficiently familiar with the company's operations to sense the urgency of the need and the reason for the amounts requested.

"I'm glad I spent that time with the Swiss CEOs. I've a good sense of what needs to be done. What type of terms are you looking for?" she asked.

"Maybe two years, or less, 1 percent below the LIBOR rate or the Fed's open window rate," he replied, referring to the London Interbank Offered Rate, a benchmark for short-term loan rates, as is the Federal Reserve's "window."

"I think you'll find higher rates, especially if you go private, even with a federal guarantee. I'll talk to Krakowski first and then call the White House. Zbig will have to do the dirty work on the Hill. As a freshman senator, and a Republican at that, I can only wish him luck," she said with evident sarcasm. The junior Connecticut senator had been her former partner in romance before taking up now with Sue Cohen, the president's chief of staff. "I'll have to do that tomorrow, if things can wait, because I'm in the midst of some very heavy budget negotiations with the legislature. In fact, I'm meeting this afternoon for what I hope will be the final settlement on the matter."

"Of course, I understand the priority of your own matters. But thanks, dearest one. We'll get through this and then focus on something important . . . us!" Rallis said with as much sincerity as he could muster, but they were words that Kallias welcomed, her own feelings about Rallis reverberating in her brain.

They hung up.

Rallis's next call was to Guillermo. It would be eruptive, to be sure; at least that's what he anticipated.

*   *   *

Domenic Guillermo, CEO of Swiss-American Confections' North American operations, had just finished lunch with his new assistant, Liz Sachs. Sipping their cappuccinos and seated on the comfortable bar stools at Jean-Louis, an unpretentious French bistro with much ambience, the two chatted easily about whichever subject came to mind. They had become close friends; the sixty-nine-year-old Guillermo and the thirty-two-year-old Liz Sachs. Liz had been schooled in both politics and business long before enrolling in the Harvard Business School, where she happened to meet Guillermo during his visit there to discuss the takeover of the two US confection companies. She had served on Senate staffs as a health legislative assistant and then worked for Rehovot-USA, the Connecticut-based subsidiary of a large Israeli pharmaceutical company.

Her marketing record at Rehovot was exceptional, easing her entry to Harvard, where the business school prefers students with prior working records and great potential. But her training was letting her down at SACC; she had not been able to find the right solutions to the deepening marketing slump that was threatening earnings and corporate survival, the subject of their noontime lunch.

"Despite my political and legal training and my short stint in Switzerland," Guillermo was saying, "I have to confess to being without answers. People are saving and conserving. Consumer habits are changing. The dual effect is that they're not spending on high-discretion items, like confections."

"Except for the luxury items, you mean," Liz added.

"Yes, they'll do okay. But they're special event items: birthdays, anniversaries, promotions, and occasions like that. And all of those items are largely Swiss made with the few licensed exceptions. I don't see how we can avoid layoffs, Liz."

"But you know, that's what many buyouts are all about. You try to turn around the organization to sell it to a buyer at an appreciated price. Of course, that sometimes includes debt being transferred to the new owners," she said. "People know that our type of takeover can include job losses as well as job creation. That's the way these things work."

"That's a Harvard case study answer, Liz. But in the real world, we're talking about people with families, expenses like mortgages, saving for their kids' educations and their own retirements, and the like," Guillermo added. "Damn it, every time I think of the way I supported college loan legislation. Little did I realize then how much debt it would create, drowning people. It's now the second-biggest consumer debt load after credit cards. Even these financial advisers are telling their clients to worry about their own retirement and to let their kids borrow for education. I helped create one of the country's worst nightmares.

"I have an obligation to our employees. Having been the former governor of this state makes it worse for me. I see these people as my family, Liz. That's impossible for those hard-ass Swiss guys to grasp," Guillermo continued.

"It's all about business, Dom. Investors put up their hard-earned money to support an idea, one that will create wealth for them as well as jobs and other benefits for employees and society alike. And our style of capitalism does best at it. I know the system has bleeding wounds in places, but the hearts of people who've never met a payroll bleed for right and wrong reasons. It's right, obviously, to care about the people who make up the corporation, employees and investors both. But it's wrong to expect investors and management to sacrifice their hard-earned gains to provide extravagant benefits for those who lack the same skill, ambition, and acceptance of risk."

"You're a Democrat, Liz. You've always worked for Democratic principles. Tell me, what's extravagant about Medicaid for poor people?"

"That's not my point, in all due respect. There's nothing extravagant if it's properly administered. I've been involved in the program for years, on the Hill and with my pharmaceutical company. Many in the program never contributed to it. We've loaded it with cases of people who have no stake in American society, like tens of thousands of refugees, and even more who have never paid taxes and probably never will. But how did they get there? I'll tell you from personal experience.

"First, there are the absurdly loose and open-ended immigration standards or no standards at all. Second, the public education system is a disaster. No one you know sends his or her kids to public schools, right? Do your own children send your grandchildren to public schools, even in New Canaan where they live? Of course not, not today. The result is a demographic cohort of untrained, uneducated, and unskilled people with meaningless high school diplomas that amount to nothing. Look at our own company. The human resources folks tell me that 60 percent of the takers flunk our basic math and English test they administered to employee prospects. They can't get jobs and end up on Medicaid when they should be well enough trained to work, pay taxes, and build a society. Third, the system is abused by Congress, which recklessly adds new categories of Medicaid and Medicare eligibility to gain political favor. The health system is abused by many providers, ranging from badly trained so-called 'mental hygiene' clinics staffed with practitioners as inept as teachers who pursue those frivolous graduate education degrees to a few of those shady medical offices that fake patient rosters, illnesses, and treatments.

"It's the poor people who get screwed, Dom, and Medicaid is just another way of apologizing for letting them down," Liz concluded.

Guillermo chuckled slightly as he commented, "It's a good thing you weren't at the business school for another two years. You'd probably be organizing a new extremist wing of the Republican Party."

"I guess I did get carried away," she said, noticing that others sitting at the Chef's Bar at Jean-Louis had been eavesdropping. She sensed the looks she had been receiving were less than friendly.

They were finishing their coffee when Guillermo's Blackberry stirred in his jacket pocket. Turning away from the bar, he answered the call, seeing that it was Rallis in Switzerland.

"Hello, Niko. How are you?"

"Fine, thank you. Where are you at the moment? I have some serious business matters to discuss," Rallis asked.

"I'm at Jean-Louis, the French place on Lewis Street. You know, it's not far from the office. We were here last month."

"Please, call me when you're back in the office. We are going to consolidate the two US plants, putting everything together at the Bridgeport facility. We need to figure out how to do that with minimal disruption regarding personnel and production," Rallis said.

Guillermo's jaw dropped, lowering his head slightly forward.

Liz was alarmed. "Dom, are you okay?"

With one arm slightly elevated, he signaled affirmatively, lowering it and turning back to his call, his breathing now erratic.

"I see, right off, it sounds bad, but we'll talk later," he said, ending the call and breathing hard.

He put the phone back in the left breast pocket of his jacket; straightening up and turning toward the worried-looking Liz, he said, "Very bad news, we've got to get back and call Rallis in Switzerland. We have to close the Massachusetts plant. We'll consolidate here in Connecticut, in Bridgeport." His voice was solemn and his face strangely ashen in color.

"You don't look well, Dom. May we should walk back. It's a beautiful day, the air is fresh, and it'll probably do you good."

Guillermo felt heavy, his left arm weakening as he used it to lift himself from his stool. As he tried to stand up, his head tilted to the left; the room seemed to swirl about him and darken. He started falling to the left side as his legs seemed unable to support his weight.

"I . . . I think I'm passing out. I feel like I gotta throw up . . . Must've been the coffee," he said, turning back to the stool, trying to hold it as he slumped toward the floor, slipping down onto his buttocks as Liz grabbed his shoulders, easing him onto the floor, flat on is back.

Two male patrons at the Chef's Bar leapt from their stools, coming to assist Liz, one removing a pillow from the bar stool to place under Guillermo's head, now awash in cold sweat. "Get 911, quick!" he yelled.

Guillermo lay on the floor, his eyes fluttering; he was gasping for breath. Finally his head jolted back, eyes slightly open, his lower jaw dropping. He stopped breathing.

"CPR," Liz yelled, "can anyone do CPR?"

No one answered; patrons stood around the bar, watching, motioning to others, nodding. "Who knows CPR?" someone yelled in earnest. Again, there were no volunteers, no answers.

The sous-chef, racing around to the front of the Chef's Bar, which faced the small kitchen, carried a defibrillator with the cover off. He bent over Guillermo, tearing open his shirt.

"Does he have a pulse?" he yelled.

The male patron from the other bar stool put his hand on Guillermo's wrist artery, then his other on the external carotid artery on the right side of his neck. "I'm not getting anything," he said.

"No pulse, probably ventricular tachycardia. The defib might help," he said as he sluiced a conductive gel onto Guillermo's now-bared chest, rubbing it into its hairy mass. He skillfully placed the electrode paddles across the chest, one above the heart, just at the pericardium, and the other just below the right clavicle. The electrode pads were properly placed to the left of the sternum and its posterior partner to the left of the spine. He triggered the charge button, sending a two-hundred-joule shock intended to connect the paddles and pads, now "sandwiching" the heart, with an electronic wave that would depolarize the mass of heart muscle, ending the arrhythmia and encouraging the normal sinus heart rhythm. There was no response; again he shocked Guillermo, his bodily spasms quickly settling and ending.

"It's not working, damn it," the sous-chef said. "I've done this many times, I've never lost anyone."

The EMT team arrived, entering the restaurant, as patrons cleared a path for them, their own defibrillator equipment both hand carried and on a wheeled carrier. The team captain swept in alongside the sous-chef, the two discussing the procedure and commending the sous-chef for his timely and impeccably correct use of the equipment. Both concluded that Guillermo was beyond recovery.

A gurney was wheeling into the restaurant as Liz stood up, making room for them. She winced as the gurney was lowered to the floor level, carefully rolling and lifting Guillermo's massive frame onto it. There was complete silence in the room, no tinkling ice cubes in water glasses, no hissing from the sautéed items in the close-by kitchen, everyone's breathing heavy but quiet. Guillermo was covered with a dense white sheet, the gurney raised; the EMT team moved quickly but carefully toward the door, the rubber wheels soundless as they passed over the tiled floor.

Liz followed the EMTs to the waiting ambulance, making arrangements to travel with them in the front seat vacated by one of the team members now attending Guillermo's remains. She felt ill, but her emotions were under control. Her training in her pharmaceutical career had included encounters with persons who were dying and, in a few instances, some who had died in her presence.

It's all about change, she thought. Nothing is forever and we mortals the best example. Her simple philosophy only momentarily interrupted her thoughts as to what was the next chapter in the very brief history of the Swiss-American Confections Corporation.

The ride to Greenwich Hospital on Perryridge Road, less than two miles away, took mere minutes. The hospital was prepared for the arrival and quickly took Guillermo's body to the emergency room, then, she was advised, to the hospital morgue. She sat in the waiting room for about two hours, wrestling with her thoughts, knowing that she would have to call Rallis soon since it was now close to 10:00 p.m. in Vevey, Switzerland, not far from the Palais Montreux into which Rallis had only recently relocated, giving up his house on an Alpine ridge overlooking Montreux.

*　　*　　*

It was almost eleven local time when Liz reached Rallis at home. He was reading in his comfortable chair, which looked out over Lake Geneva, which reflected the starlit sky and natural ambient light of the Alpine night. The phone rang; it was Liz Sachs.

"Liz, thanks for returning my call. I must say I expected an earlier response, from Dom. But I further assumed the news was rather shattering to him and that he needed time to collect his thoughts," Rallis said in opening the call.

"Nikos, I have some very sad news. Domenic died shortly after receiving your call," she said solemnly.

Rallis's mouth opened; speechless, he tried to think before speaking but, as if by rote, delivered a genuinely sympathetic response. "I . . . I am so sorry. I admired that man just about more than anyone else I know. What caused his death?"

"At this moment, without the autopsy having been performed, it was very likely a heart attack," Liz replied.

Guillermo dead, I never foresaw that. Everything must be on hold. We must honor the man, Rallis concluded before speaking. "Liz, I'm sure he told you of the purpose of my call. I believe it's in everyone's interest to defer any action. So please, if you've alerted anyone else, please let them know there will be no change. I did speak earlier to Governor Kallias and will call her." *Thankfully, Sophia was planning to defer her call to Krakowski and Sue Cohen until tomorrow. So the news of the consolidation has not yet been disseminated.* The thought dominated his senses as he called the governor's residence in Connecticut.

Kallias answered the private line, having seen on the early-evening news minutes earlier the news of Guillermo's death. "Hello, Niko. You've no doubt heard that Domenic has died. I am devastated. He was as honest a politician and decent a person as I've ever known."

"Yes, Sophia, I had just been called by Liz Sachs. Dom died soon after I had advised him that we would be consolidating in Connecticut. I am hoping that the call didn't contribute to his collapse."

"I doubt it. He was under doctor's care for some time. He was aware of a lightly damaged artery, but it didn't seem that serious, so he told me. He had even decided that since he was having no pain, he didn't need the medications prescribed by his doctor. Apparently, it was more serious than he thought," she said.

"I assume that you've not notified Senator Krakowski or Sue Cohen of the planned consolidation?" he asked cautiously and hopefully.

He breathed easily when Kallias replied no, adding that her meeting with the legislature had been too hectic for her to engage in discussing any other serious topic.

"I'm sorry for you. I hope you're recovering," he responded.

"Oh, of course. I'm used to it. But it is disturbing. This is a very ugly game these days. We've been so generous to our public servants that they've come to expect an endless flow of increased pay and retirement benefits, free health care and other advantages not available in the private sector, which, I might add, is even madder at the civil service for their gains at the expense of the taxpayers. All in a day's work, Niko," Kallias said as her tone lightened.

"As regards poor Domenic, my first thought is to have him lie in state in the capitol, which he's entitled to as former governor. I'll have to check with his children, who I suspect will be calling me anyway with the same request. I'll call the capitol custodian's office and start things in motion tonight so I can assure the kids that we were thinking alike. The Joint Committee on Legislative Management is responsible for funding special events, like funerals in the building. I have no doubts whatsoever we will all agree. I'll keep you posted," she added.

"I'll plan to arrive this week with Lex and get him up to Loomis for the school year. My daughter, Alysa, will be with us, entering the school this year," he added as they exchanged tender good-byes.

CHAPTER 19

A PROGRESSIVE DIRGE

THE CONNECTICUT AIR NA-
TIONAL GUARD'S ALENIA
C-27J SPARTAN SWEPT INTO BRAINARD AIRPORT IN HARTFORD.
ON BOARD WAS THE BODY OF FORMER GOVERNOR DOMENIC
GUILLERMO, WHO HAD DIED LESS THAN TWENTY-FOUR HOURS
EARLIER. As the airlift taxied to the military terminal, the governor, lieutenant
governor, and state adjutant general stood in the sunbaked tarmac, cooled by the
aircraft's twin turbopropellers prop wash as it turned to allow the rear cargo door
to open facing the greeting party.

Air Force and Army National Guard members in dress uniforms entered the ramp
of the aircraft, minutes later emerging with the coffin carrying the former governor.
With great formality, a bugler sounded a mournful version of taps while the coffin was
carried to a commercial hearse. There, it was transported in convoy up Wethersfield
Avenue, passing crowds in front of the city hall and turning on to Capitol Avenue,
headed for the capitol rotunda, where Guillermo would lie in state for two days.

The white marble-and-slate flooring of the rotunda, with occasional swatches of
colored marble from Italy, laid between 1872 and 1879, glistened from the overhead
spotlights in the rotunda dome, while the sounds of feet, especially the clicking
high-heeled shoes, broke the sullen space and silence of the setting. Centered on an
elevated pedestal lay the unopened coffin draped in the American flag, while four
Connecticut state flags stood at each corner of the funereal arrangement. The State
Capitol Police estimated that during the two-day period, 1,500 hundred visitors paid

their last respects to the popular governor, who had also spent two decades in the state legislature, including a term as Senate majority leader and president pro tem.

On the third day, Friday, September 8, 2011, a funeral procession was led by the troopers of the Governor's First Horse Guard Company mounting, with their summer-brown uniforms and cavalry hats on their trim, chestnut-colored American Bred horses. The Governor's Foot Guard, which, like the horse guard, are state militia units dating back to 1671. These units exist largely for ceremonial purposes and are staffed with aging volunteers, which in the case of the foot guard are dressed in the attire of their founding period: thigh-length bright-red coats over skinny legs enveloped in white stockings, giving the appearance of a parade of Easter eggs on toothpicks. The ceremonial units preceded the governor's car, behind the caisson carrying Guillermo's coffin. The procession moved slowly toward the Cathedral of St. Joseph, the church at which the very Catholic Guillermo family worshipped during their years in the state's capital city.

The congregation filled every imaginable sitting and standing space within the modern cathedral of the Archdiocese of Hartford. Standing at the entrance with the archbishop of Hartford was Earl Eastwood, president of the United States and himself a former US senator from Connecticut, and Governor Sophia Kallias. As the procession stopped in front of the entrance, the military coffin bearers, led by a color guard carrying the American and Connecticut official flags, entered the elegantly majestic setting of the cathedral to the sounds of Mozart's *Requiem* from Guillermo's favorite opera, *The Marriage of Figaro*. The pulsating opening of the piece followed by the voices of the combined St. Joseph Cathedral choir and Hartford Chorale added to the stately character of the moment.

The archbishop opened the funeral mass with somewhat awkward but well-understood references to the nobility of public service from the scriptures. Eulogy after eulogy followed with the final one delivered by the president of the United States immediately after a version of *Ave Maria*. Sung by a talented young alto soprano, the music stirred emotions with many eyes dampened as President Eastwood stood to speak after the music.

"No man in my lifetime who has had my well-being, indeed my soul, in his hands as well as his thoughts could have influenced me any more than our beloved Domenic. No man in my lifetime has better served this state, where he was raised and nourished, and which he rewarded with his inimitable abilities to bring parties together toward righteous outcomes that benefited our citizens. And no man in my lifetime has left this life with so much undone, so much awaiting his magical touch and deft hand in removing the clutter that buries the good will of people who yearn for the type of leadership that has been lost with his demise," Eastwood said with an intensity that caused his own eyes to well, but it never affected the steadiness and firmness of his voice. He ended his eulogy with thin but noticeable tears streaming down his brown face, falling onto the lectern on which sat no notes, none needed by a president who knew his subject too well to be anchored to a text.

The mass over, the sounds of Beethoven's *Moonlight Sonata* filled the cathedral as the coffin was escorted out to the waiting caisson. It would be transferred to a hearse and flown to New Haven, Connecticut, for burial in the Guillermo family plot. Guillermo would be placed alongside his wife, who preceded him in death by two years.

The archbishop escorted Eastwood and Sue Cohen to the rectory, where a room was set aside for him to meet with Governor Sophia Kallias and Senators Zbigniew Krakowski and Roger Evarts. He had met earlier, upon arrival, with several representatives from the state legislature as well as leaders from both of the state's Republican and Democratic Party organizations. The conversation here would deal with the prospect of major employment changes in the state caused by the reorganization of the US confection industry. Kallias had, despite her call earlier in the week, mentioned the planned consolidation when talking to Sue Cohen regarding the Guillermo funeral arrangements. Sue, of course, had informed the president but said nothing to Krakowski, as requested by Kallias.

They gathered in the rectory conference room after using the bathroom facilities and refreshing themselves somewhat. Coffee and light beverages were served by a rectory assistant.

"This is one of the saddest days of my life," Eastwood started. "I don't think I've felt this way since my time in the Gulf War or when we lost some of our best special operations soldiers in the aborted attempt to capture Senator Bill Rice's assassin in Canada," he said in reference to an unofficial entry into Canadian territory to extract a Canadian citizen known to have been a terrorist. The event happened before Eastwood became president but involved military personnel who had been his classmates at West Point.

"The worst part of the reason we're getting together here is that Dom himself was involved in the consolidation plan as I understand it," he added, looking askew at the expression on Krakowski's face, now with a furled brow.

Sue was straight with me. She really didn't tell Zbig about the plan, he thought as he watched Krakowski looking over at Sue. *That'll put a crimp in that relationship.* He smiled inwardly as he glanced over at Sue, who was expressionless.

"So, Sophia, tell us what you know about this," the president said.

"Let me first say, Mr. President, how much we all appreciate your direct interest and involvement in this matter, which is critical to Connecticut as well as New England. Over twelve thousand jobs are generated by these companies," Kallias started.

"Sophia, are you the new CEO?" Eastwood jokingly asked. But the irony behind the remark was not lost. All knew of her relationship to Rallis.

Cool, Sophia, you've locked Niko into the scene, thought Krakowski, uneasy with Sophia's connection to the Swiss through her new lover and Krakowski's successor in her life.

Kallias was, if anything, a seasoned politician. She dismissed Eastwood's remark almost immediately, determined not to let it interfere with her gains from the planned consolidation, especially since Krakowski was trying to persuade the leading state Republicans to assist him in taking her job in the next election.

"The current market can't sustain the two companies. I was told of this threat when I went to Switzerland to meet with the Belmont CEO. The initial help from Belmont saved over five thousand jobs in Connecticut. Their investment, by my calculations, has almost self-amortized because of the bad market and the effect it's had on both the Massachusetts and Bridgeport operations," she said.

"So they're gonna consolidate their operations, which seems like a smart move to me if the alternative is shutting everything down and departing. But they're not gonna walk away from their investment, is that what you're saying, Sophia?" the president asked.

"Yes," she replied, thinking, *Sue did brief him somewhat. He won't be overwhelmed with my next statement.* "And the business focus would be in Bridgeport."

"What happens to the Newton Highlands facility?" Eastwood questioned.

"I don't have all the answers on that issue just yet. My understanding is that the facilities there are old and run-down with huge maintenance costs," she replied.

"And the Bridgeport facility isn't?" Eastwood asked further with evident irony in his voice.

"Comparatively, it's better. Obviously, Mr. President, I'm not going to argue differently," she said with a smile.

"Of course not, Governor, but I have to answer to the Massachusetts delegation in Congress. They're gonna suspect my collusion in picking Bridgeport," Eastwood replied. "The next thing you know, they'll be pestering me for bailout monies to either keep both plants operating or recover the companies from the Swiss, right, Sophia?"

"I would not be surprised at all if that happens. If the situations were reversed and Massachusetts plant selected, you can be sure I'd be on your doorstep," Kallias replied with a tone of directness that surprised Eastwood.

You're not intimidated, Sophia. I like that, Eastwood thought. "I'm even surer I'll be hearing from the Massachusetts folks, and probably sooner rather than later," he said with a smile. "I hope they'll come up with some offsets to other spending to find whatever amount they'll be asking for."

The meeting lasted barely fifteen minutes. The two senators and governor accompanied the president and his chief of staff to his waiting limo as Secret Service agents flocked to their convoy SUVs.

Sue waved knowingly to Kallias as she entered the limo on the driver's side, sitting alongside the president.

She knows something I don't, Kallias thought. *That expression on her face, what was that all about?*

Inside the rolling limo, Eastwood, looking straight ahead, said, "There's more to this, isn't there? Wanna bet that Rallis shows up and takes Dom's job?"

"I think it's a foregone conclusion," she replied.

"And Sophia, what does she do next? I'm not even convinced she'll run for a second term," he added.

I hope not, Sue reflected, thinking that her departure would give life to her hope to settle down with Zbigniew Krakowski in the governor's mansion. She knew she couldn't deceive Earl, saying, "Well, you know, Mr. President, many women reach a point in their lives when they might like to embellish it with a partner."

They both laughed.

CHAPTER 20

A ROMANTIC INTERLUDE

NIKOS RALLIS HAD FLOWN IN FOR THE FUNERAL OF DOMENIC GUILLERMO, STAYING IN THE BACKGROUND AT THE FUNERAL MASS AND AVOIDING ANY DIRECT CONTACT WITH THE PRESIDENT OR THE TWO CONNECTICUT SENATORS. He was convinced that Governor Sophia Kallias was fully on board with the consolidation plan, and he had briefed her extensively before the meeting with the president and the two senators.

Rallis spent much of the time with his two children, Lex, a third-year student at Loomis Chaffee, and Alysa, who would be entering as a freshman. Rallis's wife, Malva, heiress to a Greek shipping fortune, had spent her childhood in both the United States, where she went to high school and college, and Greece, where she spent her summers with her American-born mother and Greek father. Nikos and Malva met in Philadelphia. Nikos was a student at the Wharton School pursuing his MBA, and Malva an undergraduate at Tufts in Boston. Her roommate was from Philadelphia, where she often spent holidays rather than returning to Greece. Malva was pleased with Alysa's decision to attend Loomis Chaffee, knowing that both children would need a solid education as well as mastery of the English language to pursue the global business careers that almost certainly would await them.

On Monday, September 11, 2011, Nikos and Sophia were at breakfast at the governor's mansion, where he and his two children had spent the night. Niko's relationship with Sophia was becoming more open and the inhibitions of being seen together breaking down everywhere, among the public as well as between them. In fact, that Saturday evening, after the funeral and Sophia's meeting with the president, the foursome went to dinner, and delivered the two Rallis children to Loomis the next day.

"The issue of Dom's successor remains unsettled. It's likely that I'll have to fill the role, at least temporarily," Nikos was saying.

"That will help me," Sophia said, "and the president. It'll lessen the image that Dom was favoring Connecticut in making consolidation decisions. And at least, we'll both be on the same continent for a change." They laughed.

"Liz Sachs, I don't know her, but I've spoken to her a couple of times on the phone. She sounds very efficient and has already taken steps with the Guillermo children to clear out his condominium. So I'll have that residence if I need to stay there. That will make it less awkward for us since I won't even be living in Hartford," Rallis said.

"Yes, on Liz, I know her slightly," Sophia said, putting down her coffee cup and looking as if she were trying to recall the past. "Her family has always been active in the Democratic Party in Fairfield County. They have a very small footprint on politics at the state level. She had worked for the former senator Tom Felice and is the niece of his first wife, who is Jewish. There was a nasty rumor that Felice and young Liz, who must have been in her midtwenties at the time, were very close, maybe too close. I'm convinced it was just a rumor. But Connecticut's a small state, and news like that flies far and fast."

"I seem to recall that Dom said she was a Harvard Business School graduate and had compiled an impressive record in the pharmaceutical industry before going to Harvard, and that was after she had worked on the Hill as a legislative assistant on health matters. As a Democrat, though. That's not going to be a problem for you, is it?" Nikos asked.

"I doubt it. Her orientation is business, not politics, I'm sure. Dom would have seen to that. After all, he made the same transition. She is well wired into the Connecticut political scene, knows all the key congressional players, as well as her way around Washington. She and Sue Cohen have been together socially from time to time as well. I think it'll work out well," Sophia concluded.

"Okay, so I'll keep her in place as my executive assistant, maybe change her title. But for the time being, she should be okay," Nikos said thoughtfully as he took a final sip of coffee, folded his napkin and then his copy of the *Wall Street Journal*, which he never opened at breakfast, and started to rise, as did Sophia.

She sidled over and embraced him. "We have a good relationship, Niko," she started, dropping the *s* from his name, preferring the abbreviated nickname. "We both have heavy lifting to do in our jobs, and that keeps us apart, but I hope the separations won't become fatal," she added with a smile.

"I feel the same way, Sophia," Nikos said, tightening his arms around her and kissing her.

Rallis took a limousine provided by his Marquis Jet Card service to Bradley International Airport, where Lucas Holdings had bought a fractional interest in a Hawkerbeechcraft 400XP. One of the lighter corporate jets, the aircraft seemed perfectly suited for the New England–New York–Washington flight demands of the Swiss-American Confections Corporation. The arrangement included options for larger Hawker aircraft for overseas jaunts back to Switzerland.

Within the hour, the small jet was airborne, making the thirty-minute flight to White Plains Westchester County Airport. Rallis was on the phone to his colleagues in Switzerland, where it was now near closing time at Belmont.

With Lutz Gorgens on the line, the Belmont CEO, Rallis was commenting on the funeral and the meeting with the president on the consolidation. "Governor Kallias managed the meeting very well. The president seems to have accepted not only its inevitability but also the business rationale behind it," Rallis reported.

"Very good, now we have the Newton Highlands staff to deal with. What's your thought there, Niko?" Gorgens asked.

"Along the lines that we discussed, we'll keep a skeletal crew at the plant to keep the lights on, so to speak, to avoid any impression that we're shutting it for good. I'll move Mark Baldwin to Greenwich and make him executive vice president at the corporate level. I'll assume the title of CEO and president for the time being. The rest of the old Havens company middle management, which is still in place, will be laid off indefinitely along with the greater part of the employment force. We'll be offering them jobs at the Bridgeport facility, but few will relocate, I'm sure," Rallis answered, referring to former Virginia senator Mark Baldwin, who had been serving as the president of the Massachusetts operation.

They concluded their talk as the plane made its final approach into White Plains. As the plane taxied to the general aviation terminal, Nikos could see the black limousine awaiting him on the ground, an older Lincoln alongside of which stood Liz Sachs. Seeing her, he stretched and twisted his neck to get a better glance, thinking, *Very nice, a good-looking young woman.*

Nikos disembarked from the aircraft while Liz stood at the bottom of the rolling staircase.

"Good morning, Mr. Rallis," she said; even from those few words, Rallis could detect that unique Fairfield County accent, a blend of southern New England and metropolitan New York City.

"Hello, Liz? I assume, yes?" he added awkwardly, trying to avoid overreacting to the sight of this rather beautiful young woman.

"Yes, of course," she said, smiling broadly and behaving with aplomb and an air of self-confidence that Rallis found so charming in European women but too often lacking among their American sisters. *First impressions, Niko, first impressions, be careful. Let's see if the mind matches the body,* he thought.

"We're only a short drive from the office. Have you been to Greenwich before?" Liz asked.

Before he could respond, she spoke again, "Luggage, is there any luggage?"

"Yes . . . it's in the plane," he stammered out.

"I'll take care of it," she said matter-of-factly as she approached the limo driver, instructing him to work with the cabin steward in retrieving Rallis's bags.

He watched her as she turned to walk away, his dark glasses concealing his eyes as they meandered toward her: *Nice hair, strong legs, good buttocks . . . very nice. I'll enjoy having her around.*

His thoughts were interrupted as she turned abruptly. Fortunately behind his sunglasses, he happily avoided the appearance of glaring at her.

Liz never noticed the way he looked at her or that he looked at her at all. She had formed no real opinion of him and, besides, knew only too well that he was involved with Sophia Kallias, Connecticut's most powerful female politician and someone who could be very valuable to her own ambitions.

The late-morning air was a comfortable seventy-two degrees, with the sun perfectly angled on them. They stood outside the limo, talking casually as the driver fetched Rallis's large suitcase and a second bag, a combined laptop and briefcase.

"Okay, I believe we're ready to go," Liz said, taking full charge of the arrival.

"Was arrival protocol part of your business school curriculum?" Rallis asked with a slight smile.

"Oh, yes, it was one of the more difficult parts of the program. We really had to crunch numbers

In that course, you know, two, three bags; times of arrival; rate of speed in making it to the airport before the plane arrived. I'm glad I had done well in my college calculus course at Tufts. Otherwise, I might have been the only Harvard Business School student to flunk out in the past fifty years," she replied, her humor impressing Rallis and putting him at ease. She crossed her legs so as to lean over, as if confiding some great secret to him regarding the business school program. He sensed her closeness, even feeling the heat of her body and welcoming her odor of freshness.

He wanted to touch her, thinking, *This is insane. I'm already attracted to this woman. And I just got out of bed this morning with Sophia. This could be a problem.*

* * *

Within a few hours, Rallis was settled in. He called in a number of the former expats, now installed in SACC's Greenwich headquarters. They conferred for several hours, with lunch having been brought in by the ever-attentive Liz. She had culled key data on operations, arranging it in a binder and on a disc, which she installed on a corporate laptop available to Rallis and prepositioned for him at his place at the conference table.

The meetings adjourned at five thirty. The expats were still rearranging their lives in Fairfield County, with some living over the nearby state line in New York.

Traffic issues, something rarely, if ever, faced in the Vevey-Montreux region of Switzerland, now figured in their lives, although the roads were graciously more forgiving than the treacherous Alpine hairpins. Rallis was exhausted also, trying to mask it with an infectious charm that emerged from the very sight of Liz.

"We need to get some dinner, Liz. Where can you take me?" he asked as she whisked around the table, ensuring that all the papers were secure and the wastepaper baskets free of notes, documents, or other materials that could reveal trade secrets or corporate strategies.

Darn, I had made plans. But he's still feeling his way around here. I better be available, she thought, vocalizing no hint of her conflicting prior arrangements. "There's no shortage of great restaurants in Greenwich. I'll drop you off and pick you up, say, seven thirty? Or you can meet me somewhere, your call."

Rallis contemplated the options for less than three seconds. "Great plan, let's do exactly that. As soon as you've secured the room, we'll leave. Come back for me at seven thirty. That'll give me time for a quick jog or a visit to the fitness room in the condo complex."

Less than twenty minutes later, Liz had dropped Rallis off at Guillermo's condo residence. She was on her Blackberry explaining to a female friend living in her condo building that she would be unavailable tonight because of the management changes and the arrival of the new CEO. There was mutual understanding and plans made for the coming weekend. Liz loved being in Greenwich, but she did notice a shortage of suitable men as most of the more desirables appeared to have families that they deemed to dote upon.

A combination of duty, loneliness, and her strong social orientation caused her to become close to Guillermo, despite the age difference of more than thirty-five years. She had found him to be rather sophisticated, admired his linguistic talents and the ease with which he managed relations with his Swiss partners. She recognized the value in this since business had become so globalized that she needed a mentor, a service which Guillermo was pleased to provide. Harvard had not prepared her well for international business, nor did she seek any particular type of specialization in her business school curriculum other than acquiring strengths in international finance with much attention to currency-based corporate investment management. Companies with substantial overseas operations were always tasked heavily with keeping working capital at levels that facilitated good day-to-day requirements, and suddenly changing currency values could upset even the best business plans. SACC needed working capital at a ratio of 25 percent to sales in Europe, but in the US dismal sales had the ratio at 50 percent; Liz had wisely urged Guillermo to use the excess of US capital to buy Swiss francs, which, as it turned out, had risen 20 percent against the dollar as the currency was, next to gold, a preferred haven for investors.

As the relationship with Guillermo became closer, they often kissed at the end of the day, sometimes in the office or after their almost nightly dinners together.

The kissing gradually migrated to other physical activities, stopping short anything extremely intimate or sleeping together. The autopsy had revealed that Guillermo, however, had taken Cialis medication a day earlier and that traces of the drug were evident in the blood tests. In pondering the report, she realized that he had been unusually warm at dinner the previous evening. She recalled also that he had long been on heart medications for a modestly irregular heartbeat. The death certificate even reported hypertrophic cardiomyopathy as the cause of death. The coroner had explained that this was very uncommon for a man his age but that he had been an athlete through his college years and very active in fitness programs ever since. In Switzerland, he would run the heights above Montreux several times a week after work, returning back to the Palais Montreux, where he lived, in a state of such utter exhaustion that he would collapse, taking short naps, but rising soon thereafter for a dizzying round of social events, his colleagues had told her.

Liz had concluded that he took Cialis planning to encourage sex between them. What bothered her now was the appearance that she was the cause of his demise, sort of a latter-day Nelson Rockefeller choice of departure. Managing this image would be difficult, for they had been seen together by many colleagues in various settings: dancing, outings on weekends, late-night dinners, the high-demand social events that compelled attendance locally and even in nearby New York City by the well-known CEO of SACC, and many other places and times. The difference in their age naturally generated glances and stares and, of course, the presumptions behind them. She gradually concluded that, somehow, she would have to explain all this to Rallis, bringing him in on the matter as an ally.

Liz raced back to her own residence on Riverdale Avenue, checked the mail, cleaned up, and returned to gather Rallis, who was waiting for her in the lobby at Delamar Harbor House. Situated on the harbor, the condo was also an extraordinary boutique hotel, where its preciously few available rooms started at $800 a night. The 2,600-square-foot corporate suite faced the harbor, with a private terrace and hot tub squeezed into its imported Umbrian marble deck. A conservatory shared half the deck and had been transformed into a private fitness room.

I need to figure out a way to get her back here, Rallis thought, watching Liz as she emerged from the car, a S550 Mercedes leased to SACC. *She's a beauty.*

Rallis stepped out to meet her halfway. "You look terrific," he said, glancing at her summery linen dress, which accentuated her athletic, well-proportioned body.

"Thanks, and you look a lot better than you did when I dropped you off. Must have been the fitness room. That's quite a place, isn't it?" she added, then thought, *Dumb, dumb, Liz. He'll know you've been in the place when Dom was living there.*

So she's been in Dom's house. If they were having a fling, it sure as hell must have put a smile on his face when he died, Rallis thought to himself, controlling even the hint of a knowing smirk. "You've seen the place?" he asked.

"Sure, I cleaned it out after poor Dom died and tried to make it ready for you. I hope everything was satisfactory," she said, thinking, *Okay, I squeaked out of that one.*

"Of course, it's in wonderful condition and very welcoming," he said as he moved around to the driver's side of the car to open the door for Liz.

"You can drive, if you'd like?" she said.

"No, you drive. I'm not American enough that I'm uncomfortable having a woman drive me around," he said as they both laughed. "Where are we going, by the way?"

"To the Homestead Inn, less than a mile from here," Liz said.

"Right, I jogged by it. Rather than stay inside and use the treadmill, I thought it would be better to be out in the air, especially along the harbor here. I notice there's a park across the harbor from me. Can you jog there?"

"Yes, Roger Sherman Baldwin Park. It's small but a good place to run and easy for you to get to. And right now, they're doing so-called Septemberfest, which is a big deal here," she answered.

"And who was this fellow, Roger Sherman Baldwin?" Rallis asked.

"Coming from this part of Connecticut, I'm happy to say I can answer your question. He was a governor and US senator in the early 1800s. He was probably best known as the lawyer for the *Amistad* case, where mutinous African slaves took over the slave ship and landed in the US. Baldwin freed them and went on to lead a number of other efforts to end slavery in the US. His descendants became major players in American history, governors, a New York supreme court justice, professors at Princeton and Harvard, clergymen, and other distinctions. He was a descendant himself of Roger Sherman, who signed the Declaration of Independence," she said.

"Where was Roger Sherman from?" Rallis asked.

"Actually, he was born in Newton, Massachusetts. The only reason I know that is I did my undergraduate work at Tufts and met some of his family that was living there at the time. They're linked to the Greene family into which his daughter married. They were medical missionaries in Japan and spawned many generations of doctors and other scholars at schools like Vassar, Harvard, Princeton, and Columbia," she said, recalling this detailed history as she drove the few blocks to the Homestead Inn.

"You have an amazing grasp of history. Is that what you studied at Tufts, which, by the way, is where my former wife went to college?"

"I was biology major, but I picked up my MPH from Harvard afterward. Sorry, it's strictly an American degree, meaning master of public health. It's a rather useless degree unless you're a physician involved in some type of policy-making role. There's no real science in the degree course, which makes the title of the degree very misleading," she said.

"So what did you do with the training?"

"I went to work in the Senate. My family had good connections with a Connecticut senator in Washington. I say with regret that that's the only way you get real jobs on the staffs of major New England politicians. I was the health legislative assistant to two senators, Tom Felice and Bill Rice," she explained.

"Oh, yes, Rice. Wasn't he the fellow killed in the terrorist raid on Washington?" Rallis asked.

They pulled up to the valet parking position, and Liz answered the question. "Yes, a very sad day. He was a wonderful man," she said, adding, "Here we are. I'm sure you're starved by now."

As they entered, Rallis was struck by the decor. "This is an amazing amelioration of cultures and time periods. It's so eclectic as to defy any easy description," he said as he gazed at the furnishings and works of art from such cultural hiatuses and China, Bali, India, and even Morocco. "I'm having trouble figuring out where I am," he added.

A very sensitive man, very few like that in my life, Liz smiled inwardly, then said, "I'm very impressed that you could identify the origins of these pieces so quickly."

"I'm Greek, remember? My family has had a global shipping business for over three hundred years. I've worked on our ships and in our warehouses and other facilities since I was twelve," he said, then took her hand, leading her to a solid cherry-framed chair, the brocade seat and back cushions bringing life to its presence in the overfurnished room.

And gentle too, she thought, firming her hand somewhat in his, which he released when they crossed the room, and he began to speak.

"This chair, it's from the firm Achilles-Brunswig. It's now called Brunswig et fils, a French company in Aubusson and Bohain, French cities where they've been producing fabric, like what you see here, for well over one hundred years. This print on the seat and back panel is a replica of works of Louis XV and are found in the Palais de Versailles. The chair is a masterpiece and may be the best example of the company's works. I'm quite amazed to find it here since much of the rest of this stuff is rather conventional," Rallis said with a tone of confidence and authority that altered still further Liz's impression of the man.

As she listened to him, she thought, *He's as good-looking as he is informed. Very definitely an alpha male, but one comfortable with the opinions and even the leadership of others, as I noticed at today's meeting. He had made his mind up on several issues regarding the consolidation but invited others' comments and especially their ideas regarding the implementation of the plan. I never sensed that he saw himself as challenged, and when there were several somewhat hostile statements regarding job security, he put everyone at ease with a statement of assurance that fair treatment of all was a high priority in the company. I need to be careful. I could get involved with him. That would not be good. Sophia Kallias didn't get to where she is today as a woman without dispensing of competitors like myself.*

They took their table among the timber-and-mortar ceiling and walls in the main dining room. It was clear that Rallis was influenced by the setting as he continually referred to different aspects of the decor: "Normandian here, Bauhaus over there, and, oh, look at this, hand-tooled Moroccan leather," he would say.

Both ordered crepe-wrapped Long Island crab; Rallis picked a bottle of 1962 Château d'Yquem.

"Connoisseurs say that this wine tastes like 'pure gold,' if you can imagine what gold would taste like," he said as they drank the last few drops. As the sommelier approached to drain the bottle, Rallis lightly tapped his hand, a signal that well-trained and experienced maîtres d'hôtel and sommeliers immediately understand as a gentleman's seductive "intention." By pouring the last drop of a great wine into the glass of the most beautiful woman present, the gentleman would convey his desire for her. She would respond by sipping from the wineglass held only by two fingers and her thumb. Four fingers and the thumb would say, "Thanks, but no, thanks."

Liz had no idea what Rallis was up to. In fact, she actually cupped the upper part of the wineglass, as if holding a brandy sniffer, and simply smiled, assuming that the ritual she had witnessed between the sommelier and Rallis was merely a polite gesture by Rallis.

The sommelier smirked, and Rallis almost laughed, thinking, *So much to learn, my beauty, but I am such a good teacher, and you will be my student.*

Liz had consumed a before-dinner Cosmos and half a bottle of wine. She was feeling it; fatigue was inching into her body, and her mind was too much at ease to fight back. It was now ten thirty. Rallis suggested that they leave since both had early-morning workouts.

As Rallis paid the bill, he said, "You know, today, at the meetings, you raised the issue regarding the health benefits of chocolate. What's the status of that?"

Surprised by the question, Liz rallied her thoughts. "Right now . . . the Yale labs are doing research," she replied.

"And where are they on the matter? Is there something we can use in our marketing?" he asked.

"Dom didn't give much attention to it. He said that Belmont was hoping for a breakthrough, but all seemed to agree that it couldn't happen any time soon."

"You're a clever woman, Liz. Do you think we can move it along?" Rallis asked.

Liz's fatigue slowed her thought process, but she was now alert enough to see the drift of his question and was somewhat disappointed that she hadn't considered it first. "I can see that it could help us, especially with an IPO. I've done enough case studies at Harvard to grasp the value of a major new product or process breakthrough that, if verified, can have the investor community doing cartwheels.

"If they haven't made progress at Yale, I could take the research to my former company, Rehovot-USA. That's the company that Monica Howard directed before the president tapped her to be his health secretary. Both Rehovot and Yale are, of course, in Connecticut, so it won't offend Sophia or the state's congressional delegation. In fact, it could help us with any possible interim operating loans that we may need from the Feds," she said.

"Let's go back to the office and bat this around. I think we're on to something," Rallis said, thinking, *Could be a doubleheader in the making – work and love, a great mix.*

"O-okay, but you know, Niko, I've had quite a bit to drink. I'm not sure my thinking is too cogent at the moment."

"Don't worry, a little bit of Dom's Italian expresso and you'll be flying. I had some of that today. It was as if I had received a shot of adrenaline," he replied to their joint laughter.

As they rose to walk to the car, he said, "Do you have this information online, or is it in hard copy documents?"

"Both," Liz replied.

"Then let's go to the condo. I'm cabled to the office network there. You're a little shaky, Liz, running around the office for an hour or so might do you in," he said.

Thank you, I'm beat, the thought of sitting at my desk or in the conference room under those awful fluorescents would be agonizing. "That's a much better plan, thank you," she replied, then thought again, *No chance of a move by him. He's too involved with Kallias, although* . . . She refused to let the thought emerge.

Rallis drove as they headed back down the road along the harbor to Delamar. The moon reflected on the channel, as if a sheet of frost had settled on the water. The September air was surprisingly mild, although cool. She opened the car window a bit more, hoping the fresh air would clear her mind.

They parked in the garage, walking to the first-floor condo, toward the terrace entrance. She took his hand as they navigated the fieldstone steps, her high-heeled shoes striking them irregularly and somewhat loudly. She liked the feel of his hand; it was strong, cool, and like Rallis himself, confident as he led her to the terrace.

"What a night!" Rallis exclaimed as he stopped, releasing her hand and pointing to several yachts in their slips at the marina next to the hotel. "I've spent many nights in marinas throughout the Mediterranean on boats like those. I have to say this is as beautiful a spot as I've ever seen."

"I understand those slips sell for nearly a million with a long waiting list," she added.

"I can certainly see their value," he replied. "I may even get a boat if I stay here."

They entered the great room. "We'll work in the den, where the computer is set up," he said. "I'll see you there in five minutes."

Liz activated the corporate computer network, coding in the access information, and within a few minutes was into the appropriate file. Seated at the desk, Rallis saw only her upper back exposed at the top of her dress. Her short blond hair that sculpted her face allowed only the lobe of her left ear to be seen as she tilted her head to the right to jot down some notes. He weakened, thinking, *I'd love to nibble on her ear and kiss the back of her neck.*

He moved alongside her, then knelt beside her on his right knee. "What do we have?"

Liz was moved; like most European men, his cologne identified him and its odor unavoidably present. She nudged her shoulder against him as if to suggest that the information was important, but in fact, it was her surrender to a reflexive impulse to touch him. Rallis moved in to the nudge, his face close and on the same plane as hers as he looked at the data on the monitor.

"Here," Liz said, "is the last report. As you can see, the researchers have concluded that cocoa has high flavonoid levels, which, of course, we've known for years. But the chemical epicatechin, they say, may have a favorable effect on cardiovascular health. That would help our adult market."

She strolled down the page. "But this is what really interests me. In all ages, flavonoids may modify allergens and viruses, as well as carcinogens. And get this, the powdered form may have benefits that extend to the brain and, to quote, 'have important implications for learning and memory for persons under thirty.'

"Imagine, it's September, kids are going back to school. We need to be in their lunch boxes as well as on their breakfast tables," Liz concluded.

Rallis's predatory sexual instincts suddenly folded. He was less entranced by the messenger at that moment than he was the message. "My God, how do we advance the research? This could be incredibly positive for us. Before we got into this, we were searching for a genome to breed disease-free beans."

Liz was equally excited. "We need to take the research out of Yale's hands and redirect it to a private source. My former employer, Rehovot, would be a good place. The Weizmann Institute of Science near Tel Aviv is affiliated with Rehovot's main pharmaceutical plant there."

"Tomorrow, I want you to fly to Belmont, explain the finding to Lutz Gorgens, then get to Israel with the database from the Yale lab," Rallis said, making an instantaneous decision.

"We have the database. It's in the SACC vault and was part of this report," she responded.

Like bounding lambs, the two stood. "Fantastic work, Liz. You're wonderful," Rallis said as he awkwardly embraced her as she stood in front of the chair.

His strong hug, his masculine and decisive decorum, and his obvious desire influenced her response as she moved away from the chair, facing and submitting readily to the movement of his arms synchronized with his kisses. The amorous beginnings escalated as they walked, arms about each other, to a love seat, flinging themselves onto it with growing passion; the end result was already a matter of mutual eagerness and need.

CHAPTER 21

THE BAILOUT PLAN

*W*HAT IN HELL HAVE I DONE? LIZ SACHS WONDERED TO HERSELF AS LUFTHANSA FLIGHT LH405 SOARED FROM THE RUNWAY AT JFK INTERNATIONAL AIRPORT EN ROUTE TO GENEVA. *I can't believe I let it happen. It has to have an adverse effect. Sophia's a Republican, but her influence has long tentacles across party lines.*

Liz was already ruminating over her new relationship with Nikos Rallis, the CEO of Lucas Holdings, a major investor in both Brent, the commodity trading company, and Belmont, the huge Swiss confectioner. Rallis, on the board of Belmont, was also the major strategist in the takeover of the two US confection companies, now merged into the US giant Swiss-American Confection Corporation. Rallis stepped in as the acting CEO after the sudden death of his predecessor, Domenic Guillermo, the former Connecticut governor and US ambassador to the Holy See.

Cunningly, Rallis, the former Greek finance minister before returning to the business world, had started a running romance with the current Connecticut governor, Sophia Kallias. Kallias, from a Jewish-Greek family that had immigrated to the United States as World War II broke out, had inherited a fortune from her entrepreneurial father, who made millions selling combat clothing to the military during the war. Kallias became thoroughly Americanized. A graduate of Trinity College and the Harvard Law School, she served short terms in both houses of the Connecticut legislature. Ridding herself of a marriage during which her former husband, a Boston University economics professor, had embezzled funds from her trust, she developed a relationship with a fellow legislator, Zbigniew Krakowski. The two ultimately ran successfully on the gubernatorial ticket, Kallias topping it. She appointed Krakowski to fill the seat of former senator Earl Eastwood, who was elected president of the United States in 2008.

Krakowski's Washington presence and extended separations from Kallias put a damper on the relationship after which Republican Krakowski took up with Sue Cohen, the chief of staff to the president.

Now, Liz Sachs saw herself involved with Rallis, who had spent a night with her only one day after leaving the governor's mansion in Hartford, where he had been staying with Kallias following the Guillermo funeral in that city. Sachs feared Kallias's revenge, knowing she would soon learn of Rallis's treachery. The blade of revenge was double-edged: Kallias could destroy Sachs's business or future political career, and she could undo the progress that SACC hoped to make in consolidating the badly outdated Massachusetts-based confection company with its former US competitor into a location in Bridgeport, Connecticut.

But would Sophia do that? She needs jobs, but she's taking them from Massachusetts. That could hurt her relations with other members of the New England congressional delegation. My job is even more important. I have to get the market moving so we can save both plants. Her thoughts dominated the first leg of the flight. She stared out the window as the plane cruised past Provincetown below her; she decided that she must sleep. She summoned the cabin attendant, ordered and quickly consumed a light dinner, washed away with a watery, disappointing Swiss wine, and had the seat transformed into her bunk for the nighttime flight.

Liz slept surprisingly soundly, not even waking as the flight made a routine stop in Frankfurt. It was noon European time when the attendant woke her up. The plane was still on the ground and awaiting the last leg to Geneva, only an hour or so away. She used the opportunity to call Rallis, who raised her level of confidence in her mission to "rescue," as he put it, the future of SACC by using Israeli research on the health benefits of the cocoa bean as a dynamic tool for a major product promotion in the United States.

"I know it all happened so suddenly, Liz dear. But we are two of a kind, even though I'm, what, twelve years older than you?" Rallis said to the thirty-two-year-old Liz Sachs. "Think of what the two of us can do for this company, and for us."

He's right. I'll never have another opportunity like this fall into my lap, but there's Sophia . . ." I agree. We have a terrific opportunity staring us in the face. But frankly, Niko, what do we do about Sophia?"

"Sophia is a very mature, smart, and ambitious woman. She has been through romances before. She cannot blame me for becoming attracted to you," Rallis said, thinking his own intentions to be more salacious, perhaps, than romantic. "I will talk to you when the time is right."

"She'll destroy me, Niko," Liz added ruefully.

"Nonsense. She'll no more destroy or harm you than she would me. What, is she to persecute either of us because we suddenly found ourselves attracted to each other?" he countered, trying to avoid using the word "love."

Rallis continued to speak. "She has no power over either one of us. She won't let the Connecticut operation fail. That could mean almost ten thousand actual and potential jobs. It would doom her political career in that state forever. She's in a tough race with Krakowski, who's determined to take the nomination from her, and she believes the state's Republican Party is increasingly leaning toward him. So she could be out of the political picture anyway.

"And even if the whole SACC project fails, you can work in Switzerland with me. You'll have more responsibility in a global operation and, I add, make much more money than most of your business school classmates. But this mission is critical to that goal, Liz. So we need to focus on the immediate."

He makes sense. I'm too immersed in a political scene that is not static, and I'm too worried about a threat from Sophia that is highly speculative. "Thanks, Niko. That helps. As planned, I'll be meeting the helicopter at the airport and spending several hours with Lutz Gorgens and Paul von Schlossen before leaving for Israel."

"Yes, I hope you managed to get some rest. But you'll be flying from Geneva to Tel Aviv on the Belmont corporate jet. It's a short hop of about three hours. You'll lose an hour for the time change."

"I'm quite at home there, having spent much time at the Rehovot headquarters when I was with their US subsidiary. I'll be at the Melody Hotel, great fitness room and pool and a wonderful rooftop bar looking out over the Mediterranean, especially at night, which it will be when I arrive. I'll be ready for the next day's work at the Weizmann Institute," she said.

*　　*　　*

On Thursday, Liz was met at the Geneva terminal by a crew member from the Belmont corporate helicopter, who quickly escorted her through customs and to the waiting aircraft. Within the hour, they were over Lake Geneva and passing Morges, its floral displays pleasingly visible from two thousand feet as they descended into their final approach to the landing pad at the Belmont plant in Vevey. Liz left her baggage on the chopper since she would be embarking again at 6:00 p.m. local time for the three-hour hop to Tel Aviv.

Von Schlossen met the chopper as it landed. It was his first encounter with Liz, which he had highly anticipated having heard much good reports about her work from both Guillermo and Rallis.

As the pilot shut down the engine, the centrifugal force of the aircraft's rotor blades gradually surrendered to gravity, slowing to a stop. The crew chief opened the passenger door, giving von Schlossen his first glance at the attractive young woman as she stepped down onto the telescoping staircase that had unfolded from the door frame.

Very nice, von Schlossen mused, his expertly concealed leer taking in the whole image of Liz.

Moving cautiously to the landing pad, von Schlossen noticed her short well-coiffed blond hair and her traveling outfit, looking as if it had been pressed only moments earlier. The breeze from the lake blew Liz's hair only slightly but enough to encourage a pert, almost instinctive shift of her head to reassemble its strands; the highly feminine gesture brought a quiet smile to von Schlossen's face.

"Welcome, mademoiselle. I am Paul von Schlossen. Can I help you?" von Schlossen said, offering to take the bulky briefcase Liz was toting.

"Nice to see you," Liz said, adding, "Yes, please, this thing is squeezing the blood from my hand."

Von Schlossen, oh yes, the Brent CEO. I wasn't told he would be here, but it shouldn't matter, she thought. "Thank you for meeting me. This is an incredibly beautiful country, and the flight up the lake was breathtaking. I wish I could spend more time here."

I too wish that, von Schlossen reacted in his mind, saying, "That can be arranged. Sometime, you will need to see our operations, mine at Brent and the Belmont facilities."

They walked across the road from the Belmont landing pad to the Château de Belmont, where the meeting would be held. The short distance revived Liz as she breathed in deeply, sensing, *Aahh, yes, the cleansing breath of yoga, it is like rebirth.*

They entered the château; von Schlossen took Liz to the reception room, there motioning to a young woman who acted as a type of concierge for guests. "Marie," he said in English, "would you kindly assist Mademoiselle Sachs, who, I am certain, would like to freshen up before our meeting."

"*Bien entendu, Monsieur von Schlossen.* Of course, sir. Mademoiselle, would you please come with me," she said, guiding Liz to a large ladies' restroom adjoining the reception area.

Liz had welcomed the relief. Twenty minutes later, she emerged looking relaxed and fresh. Marie guided her to the second-floor conference room, walking up the Italian marble staircase that fronted the entrance. Lutz Gorgens, the Belmont CEO, and von Schlossen stood at the conference room entrance as the two women approached. Von Schlossen introduced her to Gorgens, whose impressions easily matched those of von Schlossen, who had described the "highly talented and stunning" assistant to the late Guillermo and now acting in that capacity for Rallis.

Gorgens guided her to an armchair at the center point of the round conference table, pulling out her chair for her. He and von Schlossen then took their seats on either side of her. The arrangement was preplanned so that Gorgens and von Schlossen could give any needed facial signals to each other.

"We are very interested in the health benefits that you have identified for some of our products, Liz, if you'll allow me to address you by your first name," Gorgens started.

"Of course, please. We Americans routinely use first names. We're very informal as you no doubt know," Liz said to the light laughter of all. "I'd like to review what our findings are to date and provide a road map with benchmarks to our objective as well as our anticipated outcomes. I've also prepared a budget along with the market projections. Rather than do a PowerPoint presentation, I've had charts printed," she said, reaching into the large briefcase conveniently placed at her side by von Schlossen.

She distributed the materials and brought out both an iPad and Toshiba laptop, placing them on the table in front of her. "I can immediately access any additional information we might need if I cannot answer, to your satisfaction, any questions that might arise in our discussion."

"This looks fine. Niko has briefed us rather extensively on the marketing aspects, which, along with the project costs, are important matters for us, of course," Gorgens said.

Liz explained the status of the research and the preliminary findings regarding the variable benefits for age demographics. She emphasized that, from a marketing perspective, the area where she felt strongest, especially after her two-year program at the Harvard Business School, she was recommending that they provide every appropriate incentive to the Israeli researchers to quickly identify child-related benefits. This would allow a major marketing effort to get the amended products into school lunches and on home breakfast tables.

"So the flavonol-rich cocoa powder is the principal and immediate goal," Gorgens commented.

"Yes, the research at Yale showed that the bean processed into the powder would improve the brain, especially memory and learning abilities, and without any adverse effect, provided the consumption levels were scaled to reasonable amounts, of course. Also, we face the usual US Food and Drug Administration regulatory scrutiny, but this product is little more than a food supplement that would replace many existing powders that are routinely stirred into milk, for example. The food supplement rules are much less rigid, as you may know," Liz said in concluding her remarks.

"Will the Israelis be able to get this past the US FDA authorities quickly?" Gorgens asked.

"In 1993, the US and Israelis established the US-Israeli Science and Technology Commission, or USISFT, as we call it," Liz responded. "Within that framework, there is the Task Force on Food Standards Harmonization, the objectives of which include the cooperation and collaboration to remove barriers between the two countries. There is also a task force on FDA matters. But by agreement, food supplements are addressed in the food task force. If the Israelis agree with the findings we're hoping for, it is highly possible that the approval by US authorities would mirror that of the Israelis."

"You sound very confident on that matter, Liz. What allows you to conclude that the FDA approval would follow the Israeli recommendation?" von Schlossen asked.

"I spent two years with the large Israeli subsidiary Rehovot-USA before going to the business school. I had been dealing with the Israeli research organizations at the Weizmann Institute almost weekly. We've had many Israeli-developed products move quickly into the US market through this process," she replied. "Weizmann and Rehovot of Tel Aviv are colocated and work very closely."

The two men looked at each other; they seemed to gesture their approval, almost simultaneously, their heads shaking affirmatively.

"We will do it then. I gather you'll be leaving in another hour or so. We're flying you to Tel Aviv on our airplane. Good luck," Gorgens said as both men stood. They helped her reload her briefcase. Marie appeared, and the foursome walked back to the reception area.

"I've called a car to take mademoiselle to the helipad," Marie said to Gorgens as Liz retreated to the restroom to relax momentarily after the intense one-hour session with the two Swiss CEOs.

*   *   *

While Liz was negotiating in Switzerland, Nikos Rallis was meeting with the investment community in New York City regarding a prospective initial public offering, or IPO, for SACC. The plan was that the Banque Credit d'Helvetia, which had a substantial interest in all three Swiss companies – Lucas, Brent, and Belmont – along with a presence on each of the companies' boards, would manage the IPO through its long-established New York City office. BCH was new to this expanded area of investment banking; in fact, the SACC transaction would be its first major IPO.

Leading the discussion was Henri Baptiste, also the Swiss bank's representative on each of the Swiss company boards. He had flown to New York for the meeting and to work with Rallis, who arrived at the Ten Broad Street office at about ten.

"*Bonjour, Henri, comment tu vas, j'espere que tu as voyage bien* [hello, Henri, how are you? I hope that your trip went well]," Rallis said in greeting his colleague from Switzerland.

"Very well, thank you, Niko," Baptiste replied in English. "Of course, I'm never prepared for the Wall Street scene, which seems to be in a perpetual state of chaos. You know, protesters, street vendors, thousands scurrying along to work. It's more like the Shanghai financial scene, without the protestors, of course."

They laughed as Rallis responded, "So true, the Chinese would never allow that."

"Back in Switzerland, we're all very excited about the Belmont venture in the States. I spoke at length to the finance ministry, which seems totally on board with the idea of a public offering," Baptiste added.

"That's a good endorsement," Rallis added as the two walked into the conference room. Occupying the entire thirty-fourth floor, the room looked out onto Wall Street and up the Broad Street canyon. The new investment department of the US BCH branch had recently moved to the thirty-fifth floor, with an interior staircase now connecting the two levels.

The two were joined by two of the BCH investment banking staff, an American and a Swiss. The discussion began almost immediately, with the American banker reviewing and summarizing the highly complex US banking laws, explaining that both the Securities Act of 1933 and the Securities Exchange Act of 1934 were tightly regulated by the Securities Exchange Commission, the SEC.

"The SEC has come under fire of late," he said. "It seems that they've been destroying documents pertaining to the Madoff and other highly visible securities fraud cases over the past two years. Some insider collusion with some of the scam artists is being widely predicted in the media as well as among others on the Street and in Washington," he emphasized, using Street as the common reference to Wall Street.

"This will raise our visibility as will any other IPO proposals since the SEC knows that Congress will be like a fly on the wall," the American added.

"But we will endeavor, of course, to comply in full with the statutes," the Swiss investment banker at BCH added.

"And those of Switzerland," Baptiste interjected.

"Of course," the Swiss banker said, somewhat irritated by Baptiste's comment. "Here, however, Monsieur Baptiste, we are obliged to follow US banking laws. They tend to be much more rigorous than our own."

The tension between the two Swiss became immediately evident. "What I am saying," Baptiste added, making it clear that he was the senior BCH authority present, "is that we will apply Swiss accounting and accountability procedures wherever there is uncertainty with the US regulations and negotiate with the SEC over the differences."

"I don't think that would go over too well, sir," said the American banker.

"*Et pourquoi pas*, and why not? There are always differences between nations over sovereign rights," replied Baptiste in a controlled but stern tone of voice.

"True, sir, especially where there are no agreements, such as tax treaties between the nations. That's not the case here, as I'm sure you know from your long experience. There are many such deals before the SEC, but there are many litigation issues as well between Switzerland and the US. So we have to navigate through the statutes, case law, and regulations, especially those that are in play or being challenged," the young American said in a very respectful way.

Listening to the exchange, Rallis thought, *Just another typical Swiss encounter. They can't accept expertise and knowledge among younger colleagues. Baptiste is making a fool of himself. Worse, these younger guys will make an issue of it if something goes wrong and they end up testifying before the SEC or, God forbid, in court.*

"Let me suggest that we move forward and consider the US regulations at each step of the way. Where we have a conflict, we can have our attorneys advise us or get their guidance from the SEC," Rallis suggested.

Sensing the futility of the prior argumentative climate, the younger Swiss banker, in a highly respectful voice, speaking to Baptiste, added, "Is that agreeable with you, monsieur?"

Baptiste was satisfied that he had now established his authority, replying, "Of course, a very wise and prudent approach."

The foursome went through the existing licensing and acquisition materials, then addressed the balance sheet.

"From my experience in dealing with the SEC," the young American banker said, "we need a stronger balance sheet. More specifically, we need to lower maintenance costs and raise cash levels."

"We can take care of that. The bank will make a cash infusion," Baptiste said.

The two young bankers gave knowing glances to each other; Rallis remained quiet, his face relaxed. He knew the moment would be tense.

The American banker spoke. "That adds debt, sir, and since an IPO is all about debt, we're doing debt on debt. The SEC examiners will get suspicious."

I need to get in here. Baptiste might end up firing the younger colleague for insubordination, but he was right. Too much debt in play here, Rallis thought, then said, "I need to talk to Lutz, Henri. The only real alternative is to sell assets. That'll bring in cash without debt and could lessen some of our heavy operation and maintenance costs."

Baptiste's neck stiffened. Referring the matter to Lutz Gorgens, the Belmont CEO and chairman of the board on which Baptiste sat, was something he could not oppose. Gorgens could easily remove him from Belmont's board, even destroy him at BCH. He did not like the direction the meeting was taking because it was *away* from him, his prestige being slighted in his mind. Struggling to regain a leg up, he spoke. "Yes, Niko, that would be fine. I will coordinate with the Swiss Finance Ministry any decision that Lutz decides upon."

Rallis smiled inwardly. *Good move, Baptiste. You'd be well advised to keep your damn mouth shut and put your ego on hold, or Lutz and I will remove you from both of our boards.* Baptiste was also the bank's representative on the board of Lucas Holdings of which Rallis was chairman. Finally speaking, Rallis said, "Let's take a break. I might be able to get Lutz on the phone since it's only about six in Vevey."

The other three got the message and cleared the room. Rallis readily got through to Gorgens, explaining the slight hiccup in the proceedings. "We're not stalemated. It just makes a stronger case for us and will raise greater interest in our shares if we can capitalize at a higher level and without adding debt."

"As I see it, we have two ways of addressing it. First, we transfer our licensed product line to SACC. And we can sell the Havens' plant in Massachusetts," Gorgens reasoned.

"I like the first part of that, Lutz. The licensing component is a good asset. As for the Havens' plant, its value is dubious. I don't know who would buy it. It's a maintenance nightmare. Moreover, most of these former production facilities in New England are being converted to retail malls, art studios, and other nonproductive activities like that. It seems as though the US has just given up on manufacturing. Instead of making something substantive and building industry, they prefer these frivolous, self-satisfying enterprises that end up in bankruptcy in short term. What I'm saying is that unless the local government has money to buy and remodel these white elephants, there's no real buyer in sight. And these Massachusetts municipalities are just as broke as the rest of the state and local governments in this country."

"I have an idea, Niko. As you know, Marc Smit is still committed to his cocoa bean genome project. He's not too happy with the shift in emphasis to finding the health benefits of the bean, especially since it's being paid for from his research budget. I can make Marc happy, and the SEC people, if we made an offer for the Havens' place. It would be a new research facility for Marc's genome work. We'll pay a premium price for it and then repay ourselves from the IPO proceeds," Gorgens said.

Excited, Rallis replied, "Great thinking, Lutz. We'll need a side agreement on that."

"Do we have to disclose the side agreement?" Gorgens asked.

"I would think that we do if it's material to the value of our offer," Rallis replied.

"Then maybe we should execute the agreement in Switzerland. We would leave the Havens' buy as a pending deal or maybe just keep the agreement as a Swiss issue and not disclose it," Gorgens replied.

"Well, I'm not a lawyer and certainly not familiar in detail with all of the US banking laws," Rallis started, adding, "I'd like a legal opinion on this, but I don't want to disclose too much by even asking the question. Offhand, I'd say let's go with making an offer without reference to the repayment from IPO earnings."

"Try that, Niko, good luck," Gorgens said as they hung up.

Rallis left the conference room, finding the threesome seated in the cavernous lobby outside of it, looking out through massive ceiling-to-floor windows at the ever-hectic Wall Street scene below.

"Gentlemen, we may have a plan. Can we resume our talks?" Rallis asked.

They returned to the room, taking their seats, as the door opened again. A catering group arrived with several trays of sandwiches, salad selections, a variety of wine, soft drinks and water, and small fruit tarts for dessert. The three took another few moments to gather their choices, taking them to the table, as Baptiste summoned one of the servers, asking for *un biere Belge*.

Back at the table, Rallis relayed the offer from Gorgens. The licensing activity would be transferred to SACC, thereby becoming a cost-free asset. And the Havens' facility would be bought by Belmont and transformed into a modern R&D facility.

The spirits of the bankers were uplifted, at first. The American banker started the quest for details by urging that the deals be put in place as soon as possible so as to facilitate the quick preparation of the SEC offer documentation, which lawyers tend to drag out.

"Once we have the value of the licensing deal, we can recalculate the balance sheet," the American said, then asked, "Do we have a number for the Massachusetts deal?"

"Lutz said he would pay a premium. We would execute an agreement to purchase," Rallis said, trying to avoid a direct answer.

"As long as it's at fair market value, I think intent to buy would work. But the price is important. Without it, we would still have to delay submitting the SEC documentation," the young American insisted.

"Let's go with $300 million," Rallis said, barely taking time to blink.

All heads looked up. Baptiste's mouth opened, but he knew better than to say anything. This was clearly a matter above his pay grade. The young Swiss banker looked grimly at his American colleague, who spoke.

"I . . . I haven't seen the plant, but boy, in that town, that's a hell of a lot of money."

"Let's get the paperwork moving. Get with the lawyers as soon as possible, and let me know by the weekend what the prognoses and schedules are," Rallis replied, acting the CEO that he was in fact but of the company that he now intended to exit.

*   *   *

On Friday, September 16, 2011, Rallis decided to inform Sophia Kallias of the progress made in forming up the consolidation plan. He knew she would be pleased to hear about the plan to sell Havens, converting it to an R&D facility with good-paying jobs that would lessen any political tension between the two states. He was preparing to call her soon after he arrived at the office and had the usual daily business strategy session with the senior directors, many of whom were among the former expat group now relocated to the Greenwich-based North American headquarters of SACC. His private line flashed, and the phone's monitor screen showed that Liz Sachs was calling from Israel.

"Good morning, Liz. How are things going there?" he said as he reminded himself it was midafternoon in Tel Aviv.

"Swimmingly, I would say. The Rehovot folks took the database into the lab almost immediately and started running preliminaries on the flavonoid compounds. They said they've done work like that before on some of their post-op cardiac drugs and had a very good in-depth genome file. They were quick to point out some of the lapses in the work done at Yale. For example, the cocoa genome for species that are called eukaryotes, which includes most plants, has only chromosomal DNA.

Rehovot, however, points out that the bean also has chloroplasts, which have their own genome. The Yale guys missed that. This opens the door to ratifying the effects on health that we're looking for. I've simplified this, of course, but you get the point. The more important one being that we'll have a quick answer as we had hoped," Liz said, complementing her already-lengthy explanation.

"The timing couldn't be better. I'm impressed that you know enough about this stuff to explain it so succinctly," Rallis responded; he was ecstatic over the good news.

"You forget I was biology major at Tufts," she added.

"Right, forgive me. I should have remembered that. By the way, the meeting with the bankers went well, and we're putting the offering documentation for the IPO together over the weekend. I should say, we're starting the work this weekend. IPOs take time, but we're trying to minimize it as best we can," Rallis said.

"Be careful, Niko. I worked on many IPO case studies while at the business school. There are always blips on the radar screen, you know, bad math in doing the forecasting, shaky risk analysis, underestimating the competition, and the like. Are there any major obstacles?"

"This is my first IPO in this country, and the rules I found are very much more rigorous here than in Greece or Switzerland. The American guy at the bank did raise good questions regarding debt and capitalization, which I think we were able to resolve," Rallis answered. "I am a bit concerned that the Swiss banker wants Henri Baptiste to stay in the US to further develop the IPO business. This will put him in charge of our deal. He can be reckless, and he is the senior guy. This means the two younger guys, who are much more knowledgeable bankers, will have to follow his lead. That worries me, but I think I can stay on top of it."

"Worries like what, if I can ask?"

"Well, the big issue was capitalization. Baptiste had no real understanding of balance sheet credibility in the eyes of the SEC. He bugged me to the point that I recessed the meeting, then discussing the capitalization issue with Lutz. We decided that we would sell the Newton Highlands plant, the former Havens operation, to Belmont, which would then become an R&D facility for a disease-resistant cocoa bean. This is Marc Smit's lifetime endeavor, as you may recall, and would substitute for the work that's being done at MIT for Belmont. Baptiste simply wanted to dress up the sheet with a cash infusion from the Swiss bank, but it would have added to the sheet's debt. He backed off with Lutz's intervention. After all, he knew well that Lutz could and would destroy him if he botched things up." Rallis was uneasy about saying too much more.

But Liz understood balance sheets and knew that the SEC would be reviewing every aspect of it with a magnifying glass. "That sounds like the seller, Belmont, putting more money into SACC to facilitate the IPO. Better be careful on that one, Niko."

Bloody damn, she picked up on it too easily. Maybe we need to be a little more circumspect. The American guy at the bank was also dubious, Rallis thought. "Well, it's still in proposal stage. The other alternative is to boost asset value by transferring the entire licensing operation from Belmont to SACC," he answered cautiously. He was not surprised with Liz's response. It was the same as that from the two young bankers in New York.

"But that adds to debt, and you did say a minute ago that debt was an issue." *I need to end this discussion, especially on the phone.* Rallis was on the defensive; she was much too savvy on the subject. "We have a plan to avoid it by a lowball sale. This is something we should not be discussing on the phone, Liz. I'll talk to you when you're back, which will be when?" he asked, further thinking, *She has a telephone personality that is much less inviting than her physical presence.*

"Oh, you didn't know. You haven't checked your e-mail. It's Friday, Sabbath begins in Israel at sundown, so I'm leaving at six this evening and should be there in time for a late dinner . . . and bed," she added with a chuckle, which Rallis readily acknowledged.

"And I will be very eager to join you in those endeavors," he replied.

They hung up; Rallis was momentarily distracted at the thought of having Liz back in his arms. *I've got to get to Sophia. I almost forgot.*

He reached the Connecticut governor at her office. She was preparing to visit the fitness room and take a short jog in Bushnell Park near the Capitol grounds, a date that she had made with Sydney Gomez, the wife of Hartford mayor Al Gomez.

"Good to hear from you, Niko. I was just about leaving to work out," she said, thinking, *He's been busy with the IPO meeting and consolidation. But I haven't heard from him in days.* "How have developments been going?"

"With some caution, I have to say much better than I had expected. We've had a real breakthrough on the health benefits issue, and the IPO has taken baby steps. The meeting in New York yesterday was exhausting but promising. One thing you'll be glad to hear . . . I hope," he add with a slight pause.

"I hope so too. I like surprises, provided they're good ones," she said with a slight laugh.

"We, that is, Belmont, are going to buy the Massachusetts facility and transform it into an R&D center. That will put more cash on the SACC balance sheet and make the IPO process easier to get through the SEC. This will mean some job gains for Massachusetts, jobs that might have gone to Connecticut, but at least it should help your political relationships with the Massachusetts state and federal officials."

"I'd have loved to get the work since they would be good-paying technical jobs. But I'm happy enough with the gains from the consolidation. And you're right. I have to get along with the rest of the New England delegation. I've already been taking heat from the Massachusetts Republican Party. They accuse me of undermining their electoral efforts by taking Havens' jobs to Connecticut. I told them it was a business decision," she said, adding, "If it's okay with you folks, I'd like to tell them about the R&D plan at the Havens facility."

That's just a gratuitous promise. It'll be kept in offer form and may never occur. It's just part of our IPO . . . approach. Good God, he thought, catching himself. *I almost said "scam." But she needs some help here.* "Be careful because there remains a lot to be done to finalize it, and we are in the midst of developing our IPO offer."

"Oh, yes, maybe prudence is the better option," Kallias replied. "The SEC is very zealous these days. They're all over my corporate regulators here at the state level. Telling the Republicans anything could be used for their political advantage and our job losses. It would soon be leaked out, and the SEC would be furious."

I ducked that arrow, Rallis thought. "Let's do this. We definitely can use bailout monies. Tell the Massachusetts folks that, with these funds, we can keep a skeletal crew and modest production in Massachusetts, and as a fallback position, there is consideration of a buyout and conversion of the facility into an R&D center."

"Excellent," said Kallias quite enthusiastically. "I'll do it right after my run. And when do we get together? I can be in Greenwich tomorrow if you'd like."

I'm going to have to deal with this. I'm not sure this is the right time. Let her get the bailout process going first. "This weekend is madness. We're starting our first weekend shift work, I have the IPO numbers to work out, and we have the Israeli report on cocoa health benefits to work into a market promotion as well as the IPO. There's just too much going on."

"I understand. Will Rehovot-USA get any of the health research?" she asked, referring to the Israeli company's Connecticut-based plant, and always with an eye on political benefits for herself.

"Absolutely," Rallis responded with utter abandon of reality and truth. In fact, the plan called for two bailouts: one from the US government and the other totally different, Belmont bailing out of the US entirely with a massive, almost obscene profit in an equally remarkably short time.

*　　*　　*

Connecticut governor Sophia Kallias returned from her run, joined by her close friend and increasingly becoming her confidante Sydney Gomez, wife of the Hartford mayor. Kallias had offered to help SACC get a bailout to avoid a loss of thousands of jobs, most in Massachusetts, but some also in Connecticut, she would tell the Washington folks. Her first thought was to contact the junior Connecticut senator, Zbigniew Krakowski. His involvement with the president's chief of staff, Sue Cohen, Sophia reasoned, would get the matter before the president.

In a quick call to Krakowski, Kallias explained the need for financial assistance, both to keep the Massachusetts plant operating, although on a much-reduced schedule, and the plan for its transformation into an R&D center, as well as the interim nature of the bailout monies since the pending IPO would ensure paying the funds back. Krakowski was immediately in sync with the idea and called the Senate Armed Services Committee chairman, Kevin O'Meara, the Massachusetts Democrat. It was Friday, and O'Meara was enjoying an unusually pleasant day and, hopefully, the weekend at his Marblehead summerhouse.

"Zbig, what the hell are you doing in Washington? You gotta grab this weather before it changes and enjoy New England," O'Meara asked, thinking, *Sue Cohen, almost forgot. That's why he's there over the weekend.*

"Too much to do here, Kevin. Listen, the New England delegation needs your help, it's a regional issue. We've gotta find monies to help the Swiss-American Confections Corporation. The Massachusetts plant, as you probably know, has been rumored for closure, and even the Connecticut operation is laying off workers. The economy is pulling us down with it." Krakowski then explained his call with Kallias and the reasons for the bailout and the plan to transform the Newton Highlands plant into a first-rate research center. The government funds would be repaid with proceeds from an IPO.

"That's a bailout, Zbig, clear and simple. I'd have to get the president on board. You're asking me to find monies in the defense budget and shift them to a nondefense purpose. It's crazy." O'Meara was not pleased that the burden was being placed on his shoulders. With a very safe Senate seat and strong state support among the Democratic Party leadership as well as his constituents, he could be very independent and resistant to colleagues' pressure.

"But hell, I can't let that Newton Highlands plant go. It's been a major employer in that small suburb for years. You've got me by the gonads, Zbig. Can you get your Republican buddies in the House to help?" O'Meara asked.

"The only reasonably available source of funds is defense. It's most of the discretionary money in the budget. So my thought was you could talk to Tony Pro. He's a member of the New England Industries Association too," Krakowski replied, referring to "discretionary" budget funds, meaning those that are authorized annually. Although a relatively small amount in the budget, 70 percent of discretionary spending is in the Defense Department budget. This has made defense a perennial favorite for last-minute money searches.

Krakowski could sense that O'Meara was weakening.

"Aw hell, okay, I'll call Tony Pro," O'Meara said finally. "Do you happen to know where he is? I should ask who he's with. I'm sure it's not his wife. With that guy's hormonal surges, we don't even need nuclear weapons."

They both laughed huskily.

"He's in town," Krakowski replied. "I'm sure you have his private Blackberry line."

"Yeah, okay, buddy, I'll take care of it. But let me tell you. You gotta help in a major way. And you know what I'm talking about," O'Meara said in hanging up.

Damn it. Sue, yeah, I've got to let her know. This is gonna add some stress to our relationship. Krakowski decided to call Sue, knowing that she was assisting the president, who was preparing his speech before the United Nations, urging the Palestinians to hold off on their appeal to the General Assembly and Security Council to become a nation.

Sue was sitting in the White House press room with Kenny Edwards, the press secretary, and other officials from the National Security Council and State Department. All were assisting the president with the final touches on the UN speech. Her Blackberry vibrated in her hand; she glanced at it, seeing the call was from Krakowski.

Zbig, he knows I'm busy. It must be important. She quietly stepped out into the corridor; no privacy, but answering the phone in the room with the president was unthinkable.

"Zbig, everything okay?" she asked.

"I apologize and just want to make a one-minute heads-up comment. Sophia and Rallis want a bailout for the confection folks. I just spoke to Kevin O'Meara who'll be looking at the defense budget for funding. You need to know that since O'Meara will obviously have to deal with the president and defense secretary on the request," Krakowski said.

"Ouch, not a good time, Zbig, I mean for the request from defense. I'll see you tonight, and we can talk. Gotta get back, bye." Sue hung up, thinking about a subject that had begun to consume her. *This job, is it worth it? I've aged ten years in three. And Zbig, I hope you know what you're doing, Sue. I need a life before it's too late to do anything about it.*

*   *   *

The Senate Armed Service Committee chairman, Kevin O'Meara, reached his counterpart among the House Armed Service Committee's minority Democrats, Tony Pro, now the ranking minority member, having lost the chairmanship when the House went Republican in the 2010 election.

Tony Provenzano, or Tony Pro as he was known among friends and colleagues, was a mercurial, somewhat flashy, but very smart and reliable Rhode Island representative. And he was solidly supportive of New England. O'Meara knew him also to be very creative when it came to the defense budget and believed that they could work something out to rescue one of New England's few remaining industries that did not depend on government spending, until now.

O'Meara had laid out the problem, and they talked about where funding could be found. O'Meara did not get an exact figure from Krakowski, but from their discussion and their joint diligence regarding the information on SACC available from Bob Castignani's NEIA, he estimated the request would be at $150 million.

"That's a hell of chunk of change, Kevin. I have the navy setting up 'bins' of programs that they can scale down, and the air force has organized so-called tiger teams to find reductions. It would be easier if we could find something they could do and award them a contract, any ideas?" Tony Pro asked.

"Hell, I don't know squat about chocolate. I don't even like the stuff," O'Meara replied, clearly disgusted. "I don't usually pay much attention at those NEIA get-togethers. I just attend to show my interest and do a little politicking on other issues, to tell ya the truth."

"I know, and I respect that. It's always a toss-up between the interests of my district and committee business, and I try to combine them wherever I can, but this is a weird one. I'll tell ya what, let me talk to DOD. I'll call ya back," Tony Pro said, referring to DOD, or the Department of Defense.

"Liam, Tony Pro here. How ya doin', buddy?" Tony Pro was on the line with Liam Donnelly, the newly appointed assistant secretary of the army for acquisition, logistics, and technology. Donnelly and Tony Pro played hockey in high school and college. A great player, Donnelly chose a PhD program in physics while Tony Pro went professional. They had remained friends.

"Congressman, it's funny calling you that, and if you give me a hard time, I'll tell the world about a couple of your college girlfriends," Donnelly joked as they both laughed.

"Forget it, they're all mothers now with growing families," Tony Pro replied.

"That's the point, whose kids are they?" They both roared.

They settled down, still laughing lightly. Tony pro spoke first.

"Liam, a bit of a problem. I have to find $150 million. Lots of congressional even presidential support behind this since it's a New England company. I'm very uneasy about a bailout but more inclined toward a contract for some useful purpose."

"What's the company, and what do they do, Tony?" Donnelly asked. Donnelly had spent three years as an army engineer before launching a highly successful career in the night vision sector. He developed the first use of gallium arsenide to replace silicon in night vision tubes, accelerating the flow of electrons that captured ambient light. His inventions opened the way for the army's dominance in night operations and earned Donnelly a small fortune in licensed use of his patents. He retired early and was appointed by President Earl Eastwood to his current public service position in the Pentagon. Tony Pro had appeared as his witness and supporter at his nomination hearings in the Senate, strengthening their friendship.

"That's the problem, they make chocolate products," Tony responded uneasily.

"You mean like Rose Confections and Havens?" Donnelly asked.

"Precisely, well almost. They were taken over by a Swiss outfit and are now consolidated into a company called Swiss-American Confections Corporation, headquartered in Connecticut with plants here and in Massachusetts," Tony answered.

"Yeah, I read about that. I also was told by the defense attaché at the US Embassy in Israel that SACC is developing a product with the Israelis that will boost energy and mental capacity levels over a short term," Donnelly said.

"Right, that's the outfit. There's an Israeli company, Rehovot-USA, which is using its Tel Aviv labs to work out the product. You've got a good intelligence network, Liam."

"It's my job, really. Our attachés spend a lot of time looking for new technologies in all sectors, even foods. But let me try to help you out. If the Israelis are on to something for the Israeli Defense Force, we want to be in on it. Who owns the property rights, I hope it's us, or SACC?"

"I'm quite sure but not certain that's the case. But tell me, Liam, what're you thinkin' about in terms of some type of army interest in the product?"

"Obviously, I know next to nothing about the development but will find out, pronto. Best-casing it, if there's a valid scientific value to the use of flavonoid compounds for the purposes stated earlier, we'd have a big-time interest in it, as would some of the other services in DOD, as well as the Homeland Security Department, I would think. I have thirty thousand troops on the ground in Iraq and another seventy thousand in Afghanistan. I could put a good chemical booster product in the MREs – sorry, I mean 'meals ready to eat.' Forgive me, I forgot who I was talking to. You know what MRE means. In any case, yeah, I could have an interest in it."

Donnelly's short explanation encouraged Tony Pro. "That's the way to go. I'll get the latest on the Israeli findings and get the information to you. I'll be talkin' to Kevin O'Meara, by the way. So he might call you. Take care and stay away from the windows in that building," Tony Pro joked.

"Hey, they're all bulletproof now, I hope. But you know me. I'm a hard-ass anyway. Bullets won't hurt me." They laughed as the call ended.

*   *   *

Senator Zbigniew Krakowski had been informed of the developments under way in the House and Senate Armed Service Committees. He coordinated the information back to Kallias. She, in turn, talked to Rallis, who excitedly directed Liz Sachs to get formal endorsements from the US-Israeli Science and Technology Commission. By Tuesday, September 27, 2011, Liz had managed, almost miraculously, to get clearance from USISTC. This step included approval from the US FDA, which, under the charter, fulfilled the terms of the USISTC joint agreement in accelerating and transferring technology developments into high-demand products.

It had now been two weeks since Rallis had seen Governor Sophia Kallias. Their calls were fewer and too often plugged with work-related talk that involved the recurring name of Liz Sachs. Rallis was spending full time with Liz, their nights together mixed business and romance, two soul mates with fully integrated lives, so it seemed.

Increasingly, their work together would bring in conference calls and teleconferencing with Lutz Gorgens and Paul von Schlossen in Switzerland. Rallis and his two Swiss partners remained fixed on their exit strategy, now heightened in value with a pending defense contract well in excess of the $150 million expected for the original bailout plan. Now the plan would take a different direction. They would secure the contract, then triple, maybe even quadruple the selling price of the company. On top of that and after which they would launch an IPO, the share value of which would skyrocket with the announcement of the DOD contract.

One particular call alerted Liz to what was unfolding. Sitting in the conference room, Gorgens was on speaker with Rallis and Liz.

"We will need a new timetable, Niko," Gorgens was saying, fully aware of Liz's presence but assuming that she was wired into the exit plan, something that Rallis, in fact, had avoided discussing with her.

Liz looked askance at Rallis as Gorgens spoke. Rallis just smiled, making a facial and hand gesture that he would explain it to her later after the conference call.

"Recovering our assets is a high priority, Niko," Gorgens continued, "but we can't lose sight of the IPO gains either."

"All is on track, Lutz, let me assure you," Rallis responded.

"Of course, you've as much, if not more than any of us, to gain . . . or to lose if this falls apart. We will talk later. Good-bye to you and Liz," Gorgens said as they hung up.

"Am I missing something, Niko? This business about the new timetable and asset recovery, what is he talking about?" Liz asked.

Rallis pretended to be jotting something down as she spoke, creating a casual air of interest but not real concern. He dropped his pen, smiling softly as he looked up.

"Every good deal has an exit strategy, Liz. I'm sure that Dom covered this with you," he said.

"Of course, but circumstances were very different. We were almost flat, needing a bailout or taking down the company if we didn't get it. The exit strategy then would have been bankruptcy," she replied with confidence. "Now, we're on top of the world, looking at a major contract and market that could moot even the plan to shut down the Massachusetts plant."

"Liz, dear, we still have to plan in the event that all this doesn't work out and have a plan even if it does," Rallis said. "I have a concept in place that will allow me to exit Lucas Holdings, Brent, and even Belmont even though all three companies are doing well. In business, everything is *potentially* for sale," he added with emphasis.

For the moment, Liz seemed satisfied with his answer, saying, "Yes, right. I can see the need. I guess I'm still too much of a novice in this matter to realize that even though it was something we did give attention to in my business training. My focus seems to be too great on the success of this operation, and it's going so well that I don't want to think of the alternatives."

"That's where your focus belongs. Keep in mind, Liz, this is *your* doing. You have brought this company back to life and negotiated its rescue through the health-benefit strategy. Your future is very secure and not only with our organization since there will be many businesses out there eager to have someone like you guiding them. You've skipped through the middle management ranks and have proven yourself, with a little more experience, ready for major leadership roles," Rallis said, walking over to her, leaning down, and kissing her as she eagerly turned her face to receive his affection.

CHAPTER 22

SURGING MARKETS . . . AND EMOTIONS

T HE CONNECTICUT AND MA-
SSACHUSETTS DELEGATIONS
IN CONGRESS ELECTED TO STEP INTO THE CONFECTIONS MARKET
BY ASSISTING THE SWISS-AMERICAN CONFECTIONS CORPORATION
WITH A SUBSTANTIAL $200 MILLION CONTRACT. The flavonoid-rich
properties of the cocoa bean and the products that it spawned for popular use
could be further refined to meet the demanding stress faced by troops in combat
and even first responders in civil crises at home, Congress determined.

Nikos Rallis and his Swiss colleagues, specifically the CEOs at Brent, Paul von
Schlossen, and Belmont, Lutz Gorgens, would rethink their exit strategies now
that SACC would benefit from a substantial government award. There would be
no bailout in the form of a grant or even a loan on which they had planned to
default anyway by declaring bankruptcy after milking the assets from the two US
companies that Belmont had acquired, Rose Confections and Havens, now merged
as SACC.

The new strategy would allow them to profit even more greatly. First, they
would begin taking progress payments from the Defense Department grant
to start up production and issue the first prototype flavonoid products for field
and garrison meals. Second, they would let the IPO run, its share price certain
to open high because of the new government contract. Third, they would allow
token production to continue at the Bridgeport, Connecticut, plant while gradually
shifting production to offshore locations. Fourth, they would counter any objections

from the government, including Congress, regarding offshore production, arguing that the Bridgeport facility's maintenance costs would force SACC to operate unprofitably, unless they raised the unit price of the new flavonoid product. Finally, Belmont would declare the US-based SACC facilities to have too little marginal value to keep and offer them for sale. The sale price would now well exceed even the 100 percent profit baseline that they had built into the original purchase agreement, allowing the former owners of the US companies to rebuy them at 200 percent of the original purchase price. Since the company would be worth far more than the 200 percent resale agreement, they would hold SACC for the full two-year period in which the buyers could exercise their option, allowing the right to expire.

Everyone seemed to be in a self-congratulatory mood: Rallis and his Swiss partners, Connecticut governor Sophia Kallias, and several members of Congress who were leading the effort to lock in the government contract, which would be managed by the Department of Defense. The list also included the expats, former members of Congress who had been scandalized from their offices before taking prominent management positions with the Swiss companies and were now the senior managers at SACC.

But there were important exceptions to this euphoria; President Earl Eastwood – consumed with budgetary woes; a collapsing economy; foreign policy nightmares, especially in the Middle East; and a very unhappy chief of staff, Sue Cohen – had too little time to involve himself more directly. Then, on the same side of the skeptics was Liz Sachs. She was increasingly uneasy with the behavior of Rallis and his Swiss counterparts and had even become suspicious of their long-term motives regarding the future of SACC.

During the months of September and October, Congress is usually overwhelmed with budgetary matters, making their usually futile effort to have a budget in place for the coming fiscal year, which started on October 1, 2011, for fiscal year 2012, and by which date Congress rarely passes a budget. The budget approval battle routinely runs over into the next session of Congress and sometimes a new Congress. To keep the government functioning during this hiatus after October 1, in the absence of a budget, Congress will employ so-called continuing resolutions, which allow spending at the previous budget year's level. In the meantime, the one budget that does seem to make it through first is that for defense. Pleading the needs of troops, Congress does seem to be able to rally. But the defense authorization and appropriation bills begin to look like a room covered with a thousand different swatches of wallpaper.

The SACC contract would be inserted into the defense bill, although, as it turns out, there was a legitimated requirement for the company's flavonoid products. The problem was not so much the substance of the $200 million insertion into the budget but the way it was done. The money was amended into defense bill as it was being debated on the floor of the Senate. As the text of the *Congressional Record* reported,

AN AMENDMENT TO S.981
NATIONAL DEFENSE AUTHORIZATION ACT FOR FISCAL YEAR 2012
(INTRODUCED IN THE SENATE – IS)

SA 4376. Mr. O'Meara (for himself, Mr. Greene, Mrs. Okimoto, Mr. Hickey, Mr. Evarts, Mr. Krakowski, Mrs. Cummings, Mr. Lampert, Mr. Gonzales, Mr. Tulic, Mr. Stewart, Mr. Mathews, Mr. Mulligan, Mr. Welles, Mr. Rienzi, Mr. Kemp) proposed an amendment to S.981, the National Defense Authorization Act for Fiscal Year 2012, to provide for food products critical to the health, mission functionality, and well-being of combat and combat support forces of all military services engaged in the defense of the United States of America.

After **SEC. 1307. DEFENSE HEALTH PROGRAM**, strike all of subsection (d) and insert the following subsection:

(d) $632,518,000 is for procurement, of which $200,000,000 is designated for the procurement of flavonoid derivative food products to be incorporated into field and garrison food and health programs on a high priority, accelerated basis.

At 8:00 p.m., Tuesday, October 11, 2011, the Senate reconvened after adjourning for the dinner hour, which lasted three hours. The National Defense Authorization Act for Fiscal Year 2012 had been called up in accordance with the Senate calendar. Kevin O'Meara, chairman of the Senate Armed Services Committee, which has jurisdiction over defense authorizations, was temporarily acting as the floor manager for the bill, S.981. Chairmen rarely manage their own committee bills, and O'Meara had arranged with another member of the committee to assume his duties as floor manager for this particular bill because of its importance to him.

The Senate debated various parts of the bill for nearly two hours, the chamber practically empty as many retreated to their offices or their hideaways in the Capitol building. The hideaways are privileged rooms set aside for senior senators and greatly lessen the hassle of taking the subway back and forth from and to their personal offices.

At 10:15 p.m., O'Meara decided to call up the amendment to S.981, which was being introduced by him and with the evident cosponsorship of most of the key Republican and Democratic chairmen, ranking minority members, and other leaders of the Senate. Moreover, the amendment would be in the "chairman's letter" that would transmit the completed bill to the House for its action on the defense authorization act. The combined effect of this support made its priority and importance clear, so clear that few would dare offend the chairman and put defense spending in their states at risk.

The *Congressional Record* would report the amendment and debate, which could be summarized along the following lines.

"Mr. President," O'Meara started, addressing the chair, occupied by a presiding officer and referred to as the president. "I call to the floor amendment number SA 4376."

The presiding officer would respond, "The clerk will report the amendment."

Mr. O'Meara: "I ask that the reading of the amendment be suspended."

Presiding officer: "Are there objections? Without objection, the reading of the amendment will be suspended."

The reading having been suspended, the Senate had signaled that there were no real obstacles to the adoption of the amendment, which, in this case, the senator introducing it could debate with himself or simply refer his remarks on the measure for the record. O'Meara would make short perfunctory remarks and submit a statement for the record.

Mr. O'Meara: "Thank you, Mr. President. Mr. President, I am introducing this amendment, which has been cleared with both sides of the aisle. The amendment signifies this country's ability to find, validate, and field new technologies that will have a direct benefit for our men and women in the trenches. This amendment recognizes a recent breakthrough in the health food sector that will enable our troops to improve and sustain their physical and mental prowess in fulfilling their dangerous missions. I thank my colleagues for their support and submit the balance of my remarks for the record."

Presiding officer: "Without objection, the balance of the senator's remarks is accepted for the record."

With this seemingly simple procedure played out, the extensive coordination that underscored it was never in the public eye.

*   *   *

It was 6:00 a.m. on Wednesday, October 5, in Vevey, Switzerland. Lutz Gorgens and Paul von Schlossen had been at the Château de Belmont since 4:00 a.m., watching the procedures on C-Span via their satellite connection.

"*C'était incroyable, c'est tout a fait simple, ce déroulement parlementaire. Quelque minutes, sans débat et voila, deux cent millions de dollars.* It was incredible, just too easy, this parliamentary process. Several minutes, no debate, and there you are, $200 million. Little wonder the country's in such bad financial straits. Their Congress just throws money at people," Gorgens was saying.

"Happily, we are the recipients," added von Schlossen. "I too cannot believe it was so easy. And it was all televised. Who did this anyway, Bob Castignani?"

"No, he's pretty much withdrawn. He didn't like what we were doing, and I think he began to suspect that we would ultimately leverage out the US operation and shut it down," Gorgens said. "Also, Guillermo was his good friend, and he was devastated by his death. It's not a great loss for us, as you can see. But in answer to your question, it was Niko. He got the Connecticut governor on board. He had been sleeping with her, as you know. We helped to convince her when she was with us in Switzerland in July. Kallias complained to the congressional delegations that SACC needed to be saved. One of the smarter congressional guys decided a defense contract would be better than a loan. That part of the deal was helped by Liz Sachs, who conjured up the health-benefit idea."

"The whole deal couldn't be going better. The IPO is pending, and the money will start flowing into the SACC coffers from the government contract. I figure, we can start slowing things down by December, transferring funds as they come into SACC, and gradually compel the US operations to realize the need for us to offshore production back to our European operations. Our plant in Slovakia can produce the product for DOD at one-fifth the cost of the Connecticut plant, and that includes the transportation costs," Gorgens added.

Gorgens continued. "We'll just hold on to the US operation after we've stripped it until we either dump it in a bankruptcy or let the former buyers take it at twice our purchase price, one hell of a lot more than what the stripped-down place will be worth over the next two years."

* * *

Nor was there much enthusiasm that same morning in the Oval Office. It was eleven when Sue found the right time to raise the issue with the president.

"The debate on the defense bill which was briefed to you earlier, they left out a minor issue that you should know about," Sue said. "O'Meara earmarked $200 million from the defense-wide health accounts for the Connecticut confection company, SACC."

President Earl Eastwood, the compulsive note taker, had been compiling thoughts from the morning's briefings. He looked up, a look of disgust on his face. "Did you say 'earmark,' Sue?"

"Yes."

"They know the purpose of that account. I worked defense budgets for years in the Senate. They're Title 13 monies, to be used for health programs directed at the troops and their families. The amount is usually somewhere in the $650 million ballpark. You're telling me that they *earmarked* $200 million, which is, what, nearly a third of the account? That's downright shameless, especially since there's little chance to transferring money from other defense accounts to replace the earmarked losses. The defense budget is already as austere as it's ever been in my time in this town. So what do we shut down, prenatal care for young mothers at army posts and air force bases? I'm sickened by it," Eastwood said, his anger substantial, but controlled.

"They just don't care. It's all about their own constituencies," Sue replied.

"Yeah, but the troops *are* our constituents," Eastwood added. "I suppose they expect me to go along with this?"

"Yes, sir."

"Well, I have a few darts in my quiver too. For one thing, you can pass the word that I'm still out on pardons. Second, the initial public offering that SACC is planning, as you had been telling me, I want the SEC to scrub every damn word in that application. They can call in the Justice Department if they find something's not kosher. They don't even have to tell me beforehand . . . But they should keep you informed," the president said, his anger more evident as he flipped the chair around, looking out over the Rose Garden. The room was momentarily quiet.

"I'll call O'Meara first and let him know you're not pleased," Sue said.

"No, I'll call him. Get him on the line," Eastwood said as Sue rose and left. Minutes later, the president's phone monitor showed that Senator Kevin O'Meara was on the line.

"Kevin, old buddy, I missed your TV show last night. I suspect that you didn't exactly have a full house," Eastwood joked, knowing the Senate chamber is always empty except for votes.

"Mornin', Mr. President. Yeah, I guess they found a more comfortable place to catch up on their sleep."

"You know, you didn't exactly do me a favor on that bill, and I'm referrin' to the family health budget."

"Well, you know there was total support. It was a real nonpartisan issue that confection amendment."

"Is that right? You mean "Chocobrain" or whatever the hell they call that crap is more important to the United States Senate than the health of our soldiers' families?"

"Mr. President, it's all about that four-letter word we love up here, called J-O-B-S," O'Meara replied, struggling to find a politically reasonable basis for the amendment.

"Well, it's about time that we started thinking about P-E-O-P-L-E, especially those who are sick, disadvantaged, and without their spouses, who are putting their lives on the line to protect all the people. Kevin, we've been friends forever, but that was a damn stupid thing to have done," Eastwood replied.

Kevin O'Meara was a man with a tough skin and a quick reaction; he rarely, if ever, tolerated being berated by anyone, including occasional constituents who could expect a harangue no less severe than the one they might be directing to him.

But this was the president of the United States and the leader of his party. *And he's calling me damn stupid,* O'Meara mused. Yet O'Meara would be respectful.

"I am sorry, sir. I'll try to replace the funds, take something from the personnel accounts in the navy, for example. That service is barely in the picture except for a few medical corpsmen that deploy with the Marines," O'Meara replied.

"Do that, Kevin. I know the value of SACC to New England, and my heart is always there. But I have others to worry about. The defense accounts are going to be cut in my next budget, so be prepared for it. We both know that I'm not gonna veto a defense bill, so I'm screwed this time. By the way, who put you up to this?" the president asked.

"Well, Tony Pro and I spoke. The House is fully on board also, I have to tell you," O'Meara said, his self-confidence surging. "But Tony had been talking to Zbig Krakowski, who was instructed by Kallias to get the ball rolling in Congress."

Zbig? So Sue may have known about this . . . or maybe not. She would have told me if it had been discussed beforehand. But if she had mentioned it to me earlier, she knew I would try to stop it. No, Sue would never do that to me, even for Zbig, Eastwood thought, then said, "Sounds like Sophia, always going through channels. I'm not surprised that she didn't call you, or me, directly. She's a very savvy politician."

"Except in her personal life," O'Meara added.

"Yeah, I know she's been divorced, but her husband had been stealing from her trust fund," Eastwood added.

"You don't know, do you, sir?" O'Meara asked.

"Know what? I've no idea where you're goin' on this, Kevin."

"Her lover boy, that Greek guy Rallis, he's been sleepin' with her and Liz Sachs as well."

"My anecdotal antenna is very weak, especially on personal matters. I've a few of my own in that area since Audrey abandoned me," the president replied. "Rallis has always been a bit two-faced in my mind. I'm not surprised. How did you find out?"

"George Mourgos mentioned it to Tony Pro. SACC is in Mourgos's district, which includes Greenwich. The owner of the corporate condo that Rallis uses is his cousin, another Greek guy. Rallis told the owner, in Greek, to keep quiet regarding the time that Liz spends at the condo. Greeks can't keep secrets, I guess," O'Meara replied with a laugh.

The two hung up. Eastwood immediately asked Sue to come in; she was there in less than a minute.

"Sue, did Zbig tell you the Senate amendment would come to the floor last night?" Eastwood asked.

"No, I knew nothing about it," she replied with utter and demonstrative commitment to her statement.

Eastwood smiled, saying, "I didn't think you did."

"And it's a matter that I would have discussed with you if he had told me," she added.

"Of course, that's why I can't do without you. But you're not keeping up with the gossip, I'm very disappointed," he said with a grin.

"There's some that gets past my earshot from time to time, but not much. What do you think I've missed?"

"Our friend Liz, she's having a high time with Rallis, who's also sharing himself with Sophia, so I'm told by a very reliable source," he said, still grinning.

Sophia will have Liz for lunch, but Rallis will be on her menu also, Sue thought. *I need to help Liz out. I'll figure out something.*

* * *

Congress wrapped up business early on Thursday, October 13, leaving the budget deficit gaping, the economy tottering and their constituents clamoring for jobs as the real unemployment rate was clobbering job expectations, especially for those who had abandoned hope of finding another job. The president prepared to embark on a campaign trip to rally his core supporters, especially among the black community where unemployment was as high as 25 percent among young African American males. Sue would not be joining him, the president endeavoring to keep her tending fires in the already-overheated executive offices of the president.

She took the opportunity to call Liz, reaching her on her cell at seven thirty that evening.

"Sue, hi, this is a surprise," Liz said in answering her Blackberry.

"We never seem to talk much anymore, especially since you left the Hill. We think . . . and worry . . . about you," Sue replied.

"I'm honored to hear that I could occupy any space in your incredibly busy thoughts, but thank you."

"Liz, the president had a very testy call with Kevin O'Meara. There are several things you should know. First, he hasn't changed his mind on the pardons, and I doubt if they'll ever materialize, by the way."

"That was Dom's feeling," she said, referring to Domenic Guillermo, who suffered a fatal heart attack several weeks earlier.

"Also," Sue continued, "he is very unhappy about the contract to SACC for $200 million. The monies came from a part of the defense budget of high importance to him: the health of military families. But as you no doubt recall from your own experience in Congress, you can't veto a defense bill."

"The next matter is something in confidence. You would do serious harm to the president and the Democratic Party if you talk about it," Sue cautioned. "The president will have the SEC scrutinize very carefully the IPO offering of SACC. The Justice Department may also be invited in on the review."

My God, Liz reacted, almost shaking. *What do they suspect? There might be something in those calls between Niko and the Swiss partners.*

"I'm telling you this for two reasons," Sue started. "First, we care about you personally. But secondly, we know, as everyone does, that you and Rallis have become closer. That's your personal business, except there are two major complications: you could be seriously harmed if Rallis is in any way implicated during the IPO review, and as I'm sure you're aware, he's still seeing Sophia Kallias. That has to have you worried."

Liz mulled her responses. *I have to get out from under this. If I cooperate with Sue, informally, I could avoid getting messed up in a Justice Department inquiry.* The answer then occurred to her.

"Thanks, Sue. I am of course aware of everything you've mentioned. And there are some happenings here that trouble me, I mean about the IPO and even the future of the Swiss investment in the US confections industry. I have to tell you, also asking your confidence, I believe they're planning to take the money and run, to put it very crudely," Liz said.

"That wouldn't surprise the president. He's never trusted Rallis. So tell me, what's your plan?" Sue asked.

"I plan to resign immediately. But I need a pretext, and with it I can cooperate better with you," Liz said.

"I see," Sue replied, knowing exactly where Liz was going with the thought, which Sue decided to preempt. "If that's what you decided, I'll help. I can put you in a position here, not in the White House, but over in the executive office, you know, the Eisenhower Building. We need a good person in the regulatory affairs office. It's a high-visibility item in the house these days since the Republicans are hell bent on lessening what they see as regulatory overload, and the president tends to agree with them. Your Harvard background will be a real help. Most of the appointees there are wild-eyed liberals who have no understanding of or experience in business."

Terrific! Liz thought. *It's the perfect excuse. My experience at SACC, I can tell Rallis, has made me realize my shortcomings. This position will put me on top of a major issue that affects almost all of the US business community. I'll get some more background on what the Swiss . . . and Niko . . . are up to and share it with the administration. They can insulate me from Kallias.* "That is just what I need. It's a solid pretext for leaving the job. I'll talk to Niko as soon as I get a bit more insight as to what they're up to, I mean in terms of the future of the Swiss venture in the US."

*   *   *

Liz decided she would go back to the office. Rallis was staying in New York to have dinner with the bankers and discuss the progress of the IPO again on Friday. In fact, they were trying to get tickets to the New York Rangers and Islanders hockey game on Saturday in which case he would be in New York for the next three nights. Just to be sure, she called him on his Blackberry.

Rallis had just left the New York Athletic Club on Central Park South and was en route to the Ritz-Carlton at 60 CPS, a block away, to meet with his dinner partners. He answered his phone after seeing Liz's name on his screen and moved up against a building to buffer the din of traffic and pedestrian noise.

"Liz, hi. How're things at the ranch?"

"Fine, I just wanted to make sure you have everything you need for tomorrow's meeting with the bankers. I can go over to the office to gather any last-minute items and get them to you," she replied.

This woman is terrific. She anticipates problems, Rallis thought, saying, "Thanks for doing my thinking for me. In fact, I would like to have a copy of the amendment that legislated the $200 million award. I'm not too familiar with those confusing congressional documents, but I'm sure you can scratch it up. That should be a key item in the offering documentation. Just fax it to me at the bank."

"Sure, I can do that. I'll get it from the *Congressional Record* tonight and have it for you when you arrive tomorrow. The SEC would probably like a more formal copy, which I'll get from the Armed Services Committee. But you'll have enough information to evidence the award. Have a good dinner. I miss you."

"I miss you too. Talk to you later," Rallis said, hanging up and thinking, *I need to accelerate my own exit from here. Sophia is bound to learn of my relationship with Liz, if she doesn't know already. I can head back to Switzerland and put Dave Baldwin from the Massachusetts plant in my place as temporary CEO. It would be better if I'm out of the country when it hits the fan as we start transferring assets and ultimately declare ourselves unable to operate profitably.*

Liz went over to SACC headquarters; it was 8:15 p.m., and the place was empty, except for the security staff, which quickly processed her in, offering to provide whatever assistance she might need. She went to her office, adjoining that of the CEO, now Rallis. Logging on, she skillfully navigated to the computer's registry, where she coded in an error message that would give the appearance of a keyboard mistake that kept her from getting into the corporate net. This she did in the event that it was later learned that she used Rallis's computer when her own was out of service.

Moving to Rallis's computer table to the rear of his desk, she was able to get into Senate records in their public website and bring up the *Congressional Record* copy of the defense bill amendment and timed it to transmit by fax to Rallis at about ten. This would give her adequate time to search his e-mail file and would happen before she signed out at the security desk.

Deftly, and equipped with Rallis's password, which he had entrusted to her, she was into his e-mail files within a very short time. Rallis was a parvenu in the information technology world. Intelligent and entrepreneurial as he was, he never bothered to master the IT tools that dominated today's business world, relying instead on technicians, as he called them, to help him whenever needed. Even his early MBA program in the 1970s at the distinguished Wharton School preceded the IT revolution.

In the file labeled "Gorgens.strat," she reviewed e-mail summaries of meetings and conversations dating back to early July. Rallis tended to prepare a summary of important events and then send it back to whatever key party he had met with as a way of confirming understandings that might have been made.

The July 5–6 meeting, which was attended by Sophia Kallias, was especially enlightening. It was clear that Rallis had enticed Sophia into a relationship that was persuading her to accept the likely eventuality that the Swiss buyout of Rose and Havens would not go well. Rallis told his Swiss partners that Kallias was "fully on board with that prospect, would recognize it as inevitable, and that could expect to be useful to the three Swiss companies, Lucas, Brent, and Belmont, in many different capacities, either in the US or in Switzerland, regardless of whether she succeeded in staying in the governor's position."

So, Sophia, Liz thought, *Niko had misled you the way he probably is misleading me now. But you succumbed. That's the difference.*

Then there was the e-mail dated September 8 in which Rallis reminded his Swiss partners that "Guillermo's death facilitates our plan to remove him and the other expats from our companies when we exit the US."

Bingo! The first real statement and evidence that the strategy is to abandon the US venture. Liz was both angered and saddened by the realization that business can be brutal. But she thought further, *There's nothing here that's illegal. It's just their way of doing business. I'm not so sure I'd be doing it any differently. Even with the IPO, there'll be real difficulties in characterizing all revenues into the earnings column. Worse, it means that we'll be doing quarterly guidance reports to the market place, adding real pressures for short-term gains.*

As Liz continued to review the e-mails, she came to a recent one, dated just a few days earlier on Tuesday, October 11, 2011. Her fingertips were trembling on the keyboard as she scrolled through it. *It's the revised strategy that Niko was talking about on the phone earlier in the week.*

She read further; the new strategy had five principles, Gorgens had written.

The leading principle read: "First, endeavor to take progress payments to the point of shipping product to the government, then making de minimis deliveries, arguing that the typical new product R&D, manufacturing, and administration milestones were being prematurely compressed by market demand."

My God . . . that's fraud, deliberately taking payments without delivering the product! Liz thought.

The rest of the e-mail was equally disturbing to her; she could feel her body heat rising, even her heart racing faster than usual in her very fit physique.

The second principle urged appropriate patience and waiting time to let the IPO opening share price rise. The third objective was to continue token production in the United States, some at the Massachusetts facility. "All the better to ensure continuing support of the politicians there," the text read, but to increase the flow of production work back to Belmont plants in Slovakia, where labor cost differentials would amplify balance sheet earnings. The last two seemed to seal the strategic package. SACC would plead that too little marginal value remained in the two US plants, which were being stressed from the high demand for the new product and the items produced under the Belmont licensing arrangement. The plants were failing, with restoration costs exceeding the financial capabilities of SACC, compelling the company to either sell or declare bankruptcy.

There's the fatal flaw in the plan, Liz thought in a eureka moment. *They can't claim that the Massachusetts plant has the high value that would justify Marc Smit's pricey purchase and intent to convert the plant into a state-of-the-art R&D facility, unless he was planning substantial rehabilitation costs, which he isn't. That has to be misleading the SEC into accepting a higher capitalization of the SACC than intended.*

Finally, there was the footnote that Rallis should ensure that the company's disposition negotiations included a side agreement that a first claim on future revenues would go to the repayment for the value of the products being made and sold in the United States and abroad by SACC under the licenses that Belmont had retitled to SACC. *The Smits purchase and the licensing deals – frauds to bolster the balance sheet,* Liz quickly concluded.

She forwarded copies of the relevant e-mails to her computer. Then, closing down Rallis's system, she went back to her desk, logged on, entering her system's registry to remove the coded obstacle to going online. Closing the program, she signed on to her personal account, directing it to print out the e-mails on the printer at her residence. Then, reentering her system registry, she coded back in the error message that would deny access. Believing she had covered all possible traces of her detective work, she shut down her computer, and glancing at the clock, which now read 10:32 p.m., she congratulated herself on the timing of her intrusion and prepared to leave.

She went into the private bathroom that adjoined her office. There she kept a complete array of cosmetics for daytime use. Adjusting her eye shadow and other makeup, she stepped back, looking at herself in the mirror. She knew that on the way out, she would encounter Tad, a security guard who was exactly Liz's age and who had grown up with her during the years the two attended grammar school in nearby Larchmont, where her family had lived before moving to Fairfield County.

Tad had been a student at Tufts, where she encountered him again and years later. They did not date or even socialize except for an occasional run-in at fraternity parties or college events. He was a political science major and graduated in the bottom half of his class. Returning to Larchmont after graduation, his family found him a position with a Wall Street bank specializing in corporate trust management. Tad was weak in math and tried fitfully to endure a rigorous evening MBA program at NYU's Stern School of Business; it was a condition for continuing work at the bank. Eventually, he was let go, dallied in PR with a Rockefeller Center firm, and lacked the writing skills the new endeavor demanded. Over the decade, he fell further from the upper-middle-class position into which he was born, hitting a level where any type of work would be satisfactory, including that as security guard, the job that Liz had gotten him.

"Hi, Tad. How're you doing?" Liz said as she entered the lobby from the elevator.

Tad was strikingly different from his security colleagues. Well over six feet and athletic in build, he retained the good looks of his younger days. Liz knew he had few girlfriends but that he was not gay: he simply wasn't competitive in that particular female market. She also suspected that he was fully aware of her relationship with Rallis, having seen Rallis's arm around her waist one evening as he made in rounds in their office suite. Rallis waved it off, calling to Tad to join them in celebrating the completion of another licensing deal, as he offered him a glass of the light red Bordeaux wine he and Liz had been sipping. Tad thanked Rallis, saying that his supervisor would not accept his late return with that excuse, and left, tossing a knowing grin toward Liz.

"Good to see you, Liz. I saw that you had signed in. Everything okay up there?" he asked.

"Yes, I had to fax some materials to the New York bank that's handling one of our corporate deals tomorrow," she said truthfully, knowing that, if questioned, Tad would be fully aware of Liz's purpose in the building that late in the night. "They were congressional documents, but I had a heck of a job finding them online. It took hours," she added, thinking, *That's enough. Don't overdo it, or he'll begin to wonder why I'm telling him all this.*

He escorted her out of the building. Walking her to her car, he said, "You know, I'm pretty good on the computer. If something opens upstairs, please, let me know. I'd like to shake out of the security stuff, you know what I mean."

"Sure, the company always needs good, reliable people in many different areas where computer skills count. And I'm always eager to help you, Tad," Liz said, putting her hand up to his shoulder, squeezing his deltoid.

"Thanks, Liz. See you later," Tad said and left.

Terrible, I'm feel embarrassed. Poor Tad, here's the place going to hell, and I'm promising him a promotion. But who knows, things may work out after all. And I need to keep Tad quiet about Rallis and me and my presence here at night with him. Her thoughts returned to the company. *I need to understand the consequences of the Swiss attempts to dump the company.* Liz had just begun to think through the possible outcomes, especially for herself.

*   *   *

On Friday, October 14, 2011, while Rallis was in New York developing the IPO offering materials, Liz was on the phone with Sue Cohen.

"I was stunned at what I found, which I'm about to e-mail to you, if you can give me your secure fax line number," Liz was saying. Faxing the materials was safer than e-mailing them.

"Yes, it's 202-456-6279. That'll send them to the White House counsel's office. I want them reviewed there before giving them to the SEC. It sounds just awful, Liz. I'm sorry that you stepped into a situation like that. When do you plan to resign?" Sue asked.

"I'm planning to call Rallis this afternoon after I clear out my personal belongings in the office and turn in my security badge," Liz replied.

"Well, you can check in here on Monday. I've alerted Dina Fritz, the presidential personnel office chief, that you'll be joining us in regulatory affairs. Come to the EOB entrance on Seventeenth Street and ask for her. What about your living arrangements?" Sue asked.

"I'll stay with Monica at her condo near Old Town," Liz replied, referring to Dr. Monica Howard, now the secretary of health and human services. "It's a funny thing, when Monica joined the Senate staff years ago, she actually took over my condominium when I left the Hill and went to work for Rehovot-USA, where Monica later became the CEO."

They laughed and hung up.

What a pickle. I have to tell Zbig. But will he talk to Kallias? They're both Republicans, but Zbig could take her seat if the SACC deal falls apart. Kallias has to be told. On the other hand, the IPO documents haven't been submitted yet. Everything is just speculative until that happens. I'm sure that's what counsel will say anyway.

Liz hustled to clear herself out of the company and the office. She called security to ask for help in loading her boxed materials in her car, now in the garage below the building. She then advised the human resources people that she had resigned and that the personal items she had taken were inspected by security. She would be closing down her computer and signing off the corporate system, and they should change accessibility protocols to her computer.

She then called Rallis on his personal line. It was 3:00 p.m., and the team of bankers, lawyers, and financial advisers in the Banque Credit d'Helvetia were wrapping up the IPO offering, which was finally settled.

"Liz," Rallis answered, "listen, I'm with the IPO team. Can I call you back?"

"There's no need to, Niko. With apologies and regret, I am resigning, immediately," she said crisply.

Rallis laughed. "Liz, that's funny, but I just can't talk now."

"I'm serious, Niko. I've been nominated for a job in the White House, which I cannot afford to pass up."

"What? Hold on, I'm leaving the room," Rallis said, putting the phone on hold as he motioned to the group that he needed to take the call.

"What's going on here? We're on the edge of an incredible deal, and you've been a key player. What could a government appointment offer that's better?" he asked quizzically.

"I have to look down the road much further than a career at SACC. The government job in regulatory policy, which is a major issue in government-business relationships. With the expertise I could get from this work, I'd be able to write my own ticket in the future," Liz answered.

"You can do that now, Liz. Nothing beats success, and you've achieved that already, less than one year out of the Harvard Business School," Rallis replied, sounding anxious and thinking, *There has to be more to this. Who the hell is our competition? Who would make her an offer? On the other hand, she may be very helpful in the future depending on how our exit strategy works out. She said the job's in the White House.*

"It's my decision, Niko. It's an opportunity and one that I have to grab or lose the benefit forever, to my disadvantage."

Rallis calmed himself after reasoning some of the possible outcomes. "Well, this is not the time to discuss this. Can we talk later? I can come back to Greenwich tomorrow."

"I will be moving to Washington. I've cleared the office, had security verify the removal of my personal items, and signed off the corporate Internet system. Personnel has eliminated my access. Let me settle into the new job, then we might to be able to reminisce," Liz said.

"What about us, Liz? We have a very special relationship now," Rallis added.

"It was special. Thank you. You were there when I needed help, and I'll always be grateful for that. It could never have worked out, Niko. I think we both knew that at the outset," Liz answered.

"I disagree. We have everything going for us. There are no obstacles, only an open road to a great life together," he added.

This is getting too emotional for me. He's a fraud. As much as I like him, I can't get that out of my mind. "Someday we'll talk about our differing views on that, Niko. But I'm firm in my decisions, affecting both SACC and us."

They hung up after wishing each other the best.

CHAPTER 23

BAILOUT BLIPS

O N MONDAY, OCTOBER 17, 2011, THE IPO OFFERING WAS PROVIDED TO THE SECURITIES AND EXCHANGE COMMISSION VIA SPECIAL MESSENGER FROM THE NEW YORK BANQUE D'HELVETIA. The SEC counsel's office advised the White House counsel that the review would begin immediately. However, the SEC would consider but could not depend upon the separate review by the White House counsel of the evidence that had been provided by Liz to them. The SEC counsel advised that the evidence in question should be transmitted directly to the SEC by its source, namely Liz.

The White House counsel apprised Sue of the telephone conversation with the SEC. Counsel told Sue to contact Liz and have her follow the SEC's instructions. That was done by noon, and after, the White House counsel had informed Sue of its preliminary review and findings related to Liz's evidence.

At two, President Earl Eastwood had returned from his run at Fort McNair, the well-guarded peninsula separating the Washington Channel from the Anacostia River. The president was drinking from a liter-size bottle of Evian water and munching on Hershey's Kisses as Sue entered.

Still moist from the muggy, unusually warm fall day, the president was dabbing his forehead as he spoke. "I ran with Monica," he said, referring to Dr. Monica Howard, his secretary of health and human services. I can't believe she's in such great shape and only a few years younger than I am. Maybe she isn't spending as much time in the office as she should. I'll just pile more projects on her so she can't work out as often," he said jokingly.

"Be careful, Monica always finds a way to get everything done, and done right," Sue added lightly.

"How well I know that. Listen, she mentioned Liz Sachs, who left the Connecticut confection outfit and will start with us today in the regulatory affairs office. Good move, Sue. We need to protect her from that Swiss mob and from the Republicans, and you know who I mean," the president added.

"I've no idea how much Sophia knows about Liz and Rallis," Sue answered.

"Sounds like a job for Zbig. I'm sure both of you will figure out how to inform her," he said with a grin. "Back to serious stuff, what's our counsel's take on the IPO?" the president asked.

"As expected, major criminal content in the offering materials. Right off, at least four Title 18 violations," she replied, referring to the federal criminal statutes. Glancing at her yellow legal pad, she recited the suspected offenses: "Fraud against the US, section 1031; falsification of assets, section 1032; materially false statements, section 1035; and intent to deceive, section 514. Counsel said that he anticipated other issues, both civil and criminal."

"Good night! Who are the Swiss parties?"

"It's very complicated, they include the senior management of at least three Swiss companies, a Swiss bank, and, this is significant, the Swiss government itself, which had major holdings and board seats at all three Swiss companies," Sue replied.

The two looked at each other; both with legal backgrounds, their thinking ran along the same lines. "Yeah, a settlement," the president said. "They've already been burned over the secret bank accounts. They're not gonna fight too hard over the peanuts involved here. The government will want this thing off their books and away from the media. Money is pouring into the Swiss franc as it is, raising the franc's value and crippling their exports. With this bit of humiliation, they could put their tourism market in further jeopardy and, I must add, suddenly find their products very unwelcome here, especially in the defense sector. By the way, where's this scoundrel Rallis?"

"I'm not sure. He was in New York City over the weekend. I wouldn't be surprised if he skipped the country, or is about to now that Liz has blown the whistle on him."

"Does he *know* that Liz hijacked the evidence?"

"I doubt it," Sue replied.

"Then he may still be here, but we can't touch him. We have no charges, yet, and I sure as hell don't want a fiasco like that Kahn-Strauss arrest on my books." The president stared at Sue. He started to speak. "You know, maybe his disappearance should be encouraged. Think about it. We could spare Kallias a bit of embarrassment and facilitate a settlement with the Swiss government as we would not be holding a key suspect. Dom Guillermo is dead, and the rest of the conspirators are outside the US."

"How do we do that?" Sue asked.

"Easily, let him know we've got the goods on him. Have the Justice Department send a letter to the Swiss bank that's managing the IPO offering that the bank is a party of interest or, better, an object of an investigation. See what you can do on that, yesterday or sooner, if you get my drift," the president concluded.

Sue was frantically busy. First, she advised Zbig that the IPO would almost certainly never materialize and that Kallias needed to be prepared for whatever consequences would result. And he should advise her of the Liz's relationship with Nikos Rallis.

Second, she consulted with the SEC counsel, who agreed with the White House's initial perceptions to call in the Justice Department, which issued a letter of notice to Banque Credit d'Helvetia's New York office.

The letter was opened at 9:30 a.m. on Wednesday, October 19, by Henri Baptiste, the new merger-and-acquisition manager who had transferred from Switzerland. The language was not clear to him, and he contacted his American coworker who became alarmed enough to call in the bank's counsel, a New York law firm. Two lawyers were at the Wall Street office of BCH within an hour. They examined the letter, then directed the bank to ensure that all materials related to the offering were not tampered with and should be arranged for submission to any federal investigators that might have an authoritative need to examine them.

Baptiste immediately called Rallis after the two lawyers had examined the Justice Department letter.

Rallis had returned to Greenwich on Monday. He was planning to transfer his duties to David Baldwin, the former Virginia senator and one of the so-called expats who had been working in Switzerland before returning to the United States as part of the Guillermo team to manage the newly formed SACC. Baldwin, in charge of the Massachusetts facility acquired by SACC in the deal, welcomed the opportunity to leave Newton Highlands for the more cosmopolitan setting of Greenwich and the metropolitan New York City region. That decision was made on Tuesday as Rallis advised Baldwin that he would transfer duties formally to him sometime before his anticipated Christmas departure but that Baldwin should discuss the change of duties with no one until given the green light by Rallis.

The same day, Tuesday, October 18, Rallis decided that he would have to talk to Kallias. He reached her at 3:15 p.m. as she was winding up a meeting with a delegation from New London, expressing their ever-festering objections to the further erosion of defense work at the navy submarine base.

"Niko, let me put you on hold. I have some constituents who are in the process of leaving. It'll only take a minute," Kallias said as she muted her Blackberry and shook the hand of the last departing member of the delegation.

Closing the door, dismissing her staff, and returning to Rallis's call, she said, "Niko, I've heard about the IPO. I understand there may be some issues. And I want to be frank and direct, I was also informed that you've been seeing Liz Sachs, and I mean seeing a *lot* of her," she emphasized with indisputable conviction in the tone of her voice.

Rallis was taken aback, but he knew it was inevitable. He would deal with the IPO first. "Yes, I've been seeing Liz. Allow me to address the IPO first though. I don't know of any problems, or at least haven't heard anything yet. The materials were delivered only, when, Monday morning of this week. I'd be surprised if the SEC had even opened the envelope yet."

"Not when there's heavy White House interest, Niko. You need to figure out what's going on," Kallias responded.

"Yes, this is serious. Without the IPO funds, we can't possibly make it here, even with the new contract," Rallis said, thinking, *What could be wrong? They may have some questions about the capitalization. I think we've covered that scheme.* "I'll look into it."

"As regards Liz, I have taken a liking to her. Regrettably, that does affect our relationship. I am very sorry," he said.

"As am I, more sorry than angry actually since we could have had something very wonderful." She could feel her eyes welling, but her voice remained firm. "We never used the word 'love' even in our most intimate moments. It should have been a signal, a red flag actually."

"Precisely my thoughts," he lied. "The whole arrangement was hectic, sporadic, and too thin. We never had the time we needed to spend with each other." Rallis was distracted. *It's going better than I thought. If I can rescue the IPO from any problems, everything should proceed as planned,* he thought while attempting to keep a serious and sympathetic voice.

They hung up, agreeing to be friends and to work in behalf of each other. Privately, Rallis was reveling in the outcome. *But there still remains the problem with Liz. I'm out of that in one way, but she may be trying to interfere with the IPO. She's at the White House now. But she doesn't know that much, and I haven't heard anything from the SEC or the bankers. Sometimes it's better to leave things alone when you don't know the answers to your own questions,* Rallis decided.

*   *   *

It wasn't until Wednesday, the next day, that Rallis got a call from Baptiste.

"Nikos, *c'est Henri ici* [it's Henri]. We received a letter today from the US Justice Department regarding the IPO. I immediately called our lawyers. The attorneys looked it over and directed that we secure our evidence and prepare to make available to federal investigators if necessary." Baptiste's tone of voice was on edge. He read the letter in its entirety to Rallis.

As Baptiste read, Rallis was nursing another line of reasoning. *It's happened. They've discovered some of our side deals. The letter is just advising us that we're a possible target of investigation. I need to depart, the sooner the better. They can't touch me in Switzerland, and the Swiss won't extradite me. Or I can go back to Greece and manage Lucas Holdings from there. That might be better if the whole deal falls through and Belmont loses its investment. I won't be very welcome in Switzerland under those conditions. I need to appear calm.*

"Henri, there are always issues with any IPO, I'm told, as I'm sure your attorneys have also advised you. This is just a letter putting us on notice," Rallis said in a subdued, controlled tone of voice.

"But . . . but during our planning sessions. There were those capitalization deals that you and Lutz arranged. You don't think they were improper, do you?" Baptiste nervously asked, thinking, *I knew they should have gone along with my plan to capitalize the company with new loans from our Swiss bank. It would have added to debt, but so what? It would have been entirely legal.*

"Nothing has been finalized on that score, Henri, so we've done nothing wrong."

"But is not the attempt to do wrong also a tortious act?" Baptiste asked, using the terminology of the attorneys who had reviewed the letter.

"I'm not that familiar with American law or its common law principles. I suspect it could be a wrong, but certainly not something as serious as a crime," he answered, adding, "If it's a civil offense, there might be a delay, maybe even a small fine, but I can't imagine anything serious enough to delay the IPO." Rallis thought, *This is serious. I need to leave, ASAP.*

"I see, the lawyers didn't raise that side of the outcome. Maybe we're okay, with a fine I mean," Baptiste replied, seeming more relaxed.

"Let's just keep focused on the outcome, Henri. I'll deal with any major issues that arise," Rallis lied.

They hung up. Rallis immediately went into his files, selecting the folders with e-mails discussing plans with his Swiss coconspirators. He sent them to his Vevey computer via the corporate intranet, then destroyed his files, unaware that he was adding a new criminal charge to those that were also emerging: the destruction of material evidence. The destroyed files had already been copied by Liz and were in the hands of the Justice Department. The charge of unlawful tampering of evidence would almost certainly have been upheld.

He then called Gorgens in Switzerland, saying that he could not go into detail and that there were some problems but that he was very confident that "we would come out okay." He said that he would be returning to Switzerland using the private Marquis Jet service.

His next call was to David Baldwin in Newton Highlands.

"Good morning, boss," Baldwin said in seeing Rallis on his phone monitor.

With less formality, Rallis got to the point. "I need you to get in place as soon as possible, Dave. What's your status at the moment?"

"I've appointed my deputy as acting general manager at the plant and have already found a condo in Greenwich. I can start there tomorrow," Baldwin replied.

"Wonderful, Jeff Scharfman will remain president and will orient you since I need to be in Switzerland. I'll be leaving on a Swiss Air flight from JFK this evening," Rallis said, choosing to conceal his departure by private jet in the event a last-minute attempt was made to detain him.

Baldwin was reluctant to inquire as to the rush, but he was elated with his promotion and decided to ask no further questions. "Not a problem," he said. "Jeff and I have always worked together."

"Well, everything's on track. We have a few questions on the IPO, which the bank and the lawyers can pretty much deal with. Your job will be to ensure that production continues and that we implement the huge defense contract for our products. Jeff will manage the day-to-day details of that, but you will have to ensure that he has the financial resources he needs to meet demand," Rallis explained.

"I welcome the challenge and understand the duties of the CEO, Niko. You can depend on me," Baldwin replied.

"Wonderful, we'll be in constant touch when I get situated back in place in Vevey and Montreux. SAC C can operate without my constant attention, thanks to you and the other expats. You've all been well-trained and have performed beyond our expectations. You're ready to take flight with your new wings," Rallis said as they hung up.

Within the hour, Rallis was on his way to JFK, not on board a Swiss Air flight but to flee the United States in the private jet, which had been dispatched to take him to Geneva.

CHAPTER 24

SWEET REVENGE

ON THURSDAY, OCTOBER 20, 2011, FORMER VIRGINIA SENATOR DAVID BALDWIN, THE NEWLY APPOINTED CEO OF THE SWISS-AMERICAN CONFECTIONS CORPORATION, ARRIVED AT THE COMPANY'S HEADQUARTERS IN GREENWICH, CONNECTICUT. Baldwin's high expectations and enthusiasm would fade into anger as he met with the SACC counsel Marc Gregoire, the former Louisiana congressman, and SACC president Jeff Scharfman.

"What the hell are you talking about?" Baldwin said, clearly irritated after Gregoire had advised him of the Justice Department letter to the Banque d'Helvetia, which was managing the IPO. "Rallis said there were some minor glitches, which, as we all know, are common to just about every IPO application. That's part of the negotiation process between the bankers and the SEC. They'll work it out. Look, I was a lawyer a long time before I went to the Senate and was on the Senate Judiciary Committee, I understand damn well what the Justice Department notice is all about."

Gregoire reiterated the nature of the threat to SACC as he saw it while Scharfman was unusually quiet as he sat there, listening, but clearly upset.

"What I'm sayin', Dave, is that there appears to be evidence that side deals were being cut between Rallis and his Swiss partners to falsify the capitalization of the company, which would have raised the share price bids to unaccountably high levels. This would have allowed the Swiss guys to unwind their equity holdings at very high prices before the true value of the company was disclosed and the share price nosedived, which it almost certainly would have."

"The bankers could have prevented that. That's their job, to fairly assess and to appropriately represent the company's book and market values," Baldwin countered. "It seems to me at this point, and I admit I haven't seen the evidence you're talkin' about, that the bankers are on the hook. Have you talked to Niko, by the way?" Baldwin asked.

Scharfman spoke, for the first time entering the discussion. "I tried to get him this morning on all of his phone lines. He's not responding, nor is Gorgens or von Schlossen, who I also tried to call. They're probably advised by counsel to say nothing."

"What! They own the damn company for the most part. They have to respond to *us*," Baldwin said angrily. "We're running the show in their interest. I'll try Rallis after we speak. Tell me, Jeff, what's to keep us from operating as usual while this flap unwinds?"

"I'll defer to Marc on that question. We've already discussed it," Scharfman said.

"Well, I think we should continue to operate," said Gregoire, the SACC vice president and general counsel. "The worst thing is the IPO's failure. As Jeff and I had discussed, that would mean some loss of resources available to our expansion and production infrastructure, but we can limp along even in this bad market with the big government contract and our other sales holding us together."

"The IPO proceeds were the icing on the cake, as Marc suggested," Scharfman added. "We're sort of strapped, but we can manage on a day-to-day basis, provided we can continue lines of credit with local banks. That's something you'll have to work out, Dave."

"Yeah, that's my job, damn it. But from my experience, I can't see too many banks enthusiastically supporting our cash needs while we're the target of a federal investigation. Unless," he said, pausing, "it's the bankers who are under duress to answer the charges, as Marc suggested."

"Let me clarify that, Dave. Rallis provided the information to the bankers. It's the bankers' source of their information that will become the essence of their defense. So the ball will be hit back onto our side of the net," Marc Gregoire said, using a tennis analogy.

"And without guidance from Rallis as to what the hell he was thinking, I've little chance of slamming it back into the bankers' court," Baldwin said, the gloom on his face and in his voice very evident. "Okay, let's do as you both suggest, keep the company operating as best we can. I'll start pulling some political levers as well. We need help from any prospective source we can conjure up, so give me any ideas that come into your heads in the meantime. And let's get the expat group involved in this as well. How is their mood, by the way?"

"We're all worried, Dave," Scharfman added. "We've been clinging on Rallis's tail as a rising star in our eyes, at least. Fortunately, everyone has made substantial amounts of money. At least three guys are even thinking of getting back into politics, maybe running for their old seats. I'm not in that category, by the way. They still want the pardons, but Dom Guillermo and Bob Castignani were pretty much convinced it would never happen. Castignani, by the way, is now out of the picture. He was devastated by the loss of Dom, his close friend, and by Rallis's tactics in buying out of the two US companies. I'm convinced that he saw Rallis as a bit of a con man, a vision that eluded the rest of us."

"That doesn't surprise me. Bob was much too straight to tolerate the Swiss maneuvers in the takeover. But I could use him in dealing with the political challenges that face us. I'm gonna start with Governor Kallias. We're both Republicans, and she has the most to lose if this thing goes under, including her statehouse job. I'll call her right after I get an update from the bankers and the attorneys representing us on the matter." Baldwin ended the meeting, settling into his desk and sketching out on his ever-present yellow legal pad the strategy he would pursue to keep the company operating until the IPO could either be executed, or cancelled. He knew even at this point that it could go either way.

By noon, Baldwin had covered the groundwork with the bankers and their attorneys, all now convinced that the charges were very serious and that the IPO was at risk. The attorneys advised Baldwin that even if it were withdrawn, the issue of attempted fraud remained and criminal charges could be brought and, they added, probably sustained.

Too agitated to either have lunch or work out, Baldwin remained at his desk; there were no return calls from the Swiss or Rallis or any e-mails. He knew they would be avoiding any type of communication and that their counsel was advising them accordingly. Baldwin also realized they could avoid appearing in a US hearing or court if it came to that and that the Swiss do not extradite their citizens or, generally, legal residents. If it came to that, Rallis would easily attain asylum since he was very well connected in the country and a longtime resident running a very profitable business. Besides, when it came to business, the Swiss followed their own rules, which were much too flexible to be reined in by membership in the European Union, for example.

Looking at his clock, as he wrote out his plan, he decided that he could call Kallias since it would be just after any lunch break that she might have taken. As expected, she was in her office and took Baldwin's call.

"Hello, Dave, good to hear from you. I see you're calling from Greenwich, so I assume you've replaced Niko," she said.

"I hope you're well, Sophia, and I appreciate your taking my call," Baldwin replied.

"Oh, I suspect I know only too well why you're calling and am very glad that you are. I would have been getting to you in a few days anyway. I've been kept abreast by the Connecticut delegation in Washington regarding SACC's IPO and the pending Justice Department probe. Normally, I'd write it off as a fishing expedition by Democrats trying to embarrass a Republican governor. But Eastwood isn't the type to grovel for dirt. If he thought he had something, he'd confront me directly. That's what made him a great attorney general in this state when he had that job. What's your take on all this?" she asked finally.

"I'm taking it very seriously. We need to call up the heavy artillery, maybe even get the president involved," he replied.

"He *is* involved, Dave. But he's not going to allow his image to be damaged by something that is not of his making and, in fact, resulted in an outcome that he foresaw and warned us accordingly," she said.

"How is he involved?"

"I've talked to Sue, and let me explain. As you may know, Sue and Zbig Krakowski are now together. Zbig and I had a relationship for several years. You might say I've undergone a double jilt after Rallis decided to pursue Liz Sachs," Kallias added with a sardonic-sounding laugh.

"That aside," she continued, "Sue thinks we might be able to cut a deal with the Swiss. She says the president is convinced the Swiss government will not risk another flap on top of the secret-bank-account scandal. Earl would try for a settlement with them, she told me."

"What type of leverage do we have? Won't we still face the same financial issues with SACC?" Baldwin asked.

"I haven't been able to think that one through. I had met with the Swiss partners in Switzerland in July. I and Liz Sachs, according to Sue, separately realized the Swiss were hoping for a quick exit from their US venture with a very high exit price. The new finding of flavonoid health benefits in chocolate slowed their departure schedule, we think, and gave them a chance to get still more out of the venture here. But the outcome was to be the same: that is, bailing out of the US *after* they collected bailout monies in the form of a government contract with SACC. Sort of a double meaning to 'bailout,'" Kallias said.

As Kallias spoke, Baldwin's mind began to clear. *So the president would prevail on the Swiss government to do, what, withdraw from the venture? Well, the government is a big investor in Belmont, so there is so-called sovereign interest, making the government itself a passive partner in the venture, which would be potentially embarrassing for them. I need to talk to the president. This might work.*

"I see where this could go, Sophia. I want to save this company. With the right type of federal intervention, we could recover. We'd install new management, as either a private or public company. We're talkin' about ten thousand jobs, maybe even more, in the New England area. It's worth every option we can play. Do you think Eastwood would see me?" Baldwin asked.

"He's overwhelmed. You were in the Senate for many years. You know what the budget period is like. It's even much worse now. I'd suggest you talk to Sue Cohen. When you call, tell her assistant that you're calling at my recommendation. She'll take your call if she's available," Kallias added as they said good-byes and hung up.

Baldwin did exactly that, and indeed, the president's chief of staff was on the line in short measure.

After exchanging greetings, Baldwin mentioned his talk with the Connecticut governor and said that they both agreed with the president that some type of deal with the Swiss could be fashioned, but Baldwin added, "I'm not clear how we manage after the financial umbilical cord with both the IPO and the Swiss partners is severed."

"That's something for us to figure out, Dave. I'm trying to get the matter on the president's schedule. Right now, he's on the phone day and night with the German and Greek finance ministers trying to work out a survival plan for Greece. That, in addition to getting Congress to approve a jobs plan that calls for a little more restructuring of the economy. I shouldn't say this to you, but you're a dormant Republican, if I can use the word without offending you, but the Dems want only short-term fixes, Band-Aids when you consider the gaping wound the economy represents to our survival. The president's acting almost heretically in the eyes of the party, suggesting that everyone who has to file a tax return pay something, even if it's only $10, making them feel that they have a stake in the country and as well as some type of duty. He's focused also on ensuring that we pick industries with a future rather than throwing money at sectors based on labor union demands, like the public service sector, or frivolous alternative energy projects that have no real possibility of meeting US energy demands. Just how SACC fits in remains to be seen. You do have some advantage if we can keep government intervention budget neutral. That's the goal we're stretching toward," Sue said.

They exchanged courteous, if not rather warm, farewells and hung up.

*   *   *

Over the weekend, Sue had managed to set up a meeting at 11:15 a.m. in the Oval Office on Monday, October 24, 2011, to discuss the strategy in dealing with the Swiss. She had spoken several times to the president, who was at Camp David and who was resisting several aspects of an interventionist move that he disliked. Sue knew that Eastwood was with Monica Howard that weekend. Although she knew there was no real romantic connection, the two were very close friends and the appearance of such linkages could become a media issue, she worried.

By Sunday night, following the president's instructions, she had arranged the session, trying to ensure that the forty-five minutes the president allotted to the discussion would be fully exploited within that short time. US ambassador Tim Sawicki, the former Rose Confections CEO and newly appointed envoy to Switzerland, would lead the talks with the Swiss and was called back for the White House session. But he would be buttressed well: Attorney General Jack Hammond and Treasury Secretary Louis Dubin would be in tow. Despite their much-higher status as cabinet members, Sawicki would take the lead and bring them into the discussion as it demanded their particular expertise, especially on the issues of forfeiture and other legal actions.

En route back to Washington early Monday morning, Eastwood chatted with Monica as they passed over the Maryland Catoctin Mountains in the purplish dawn at 6:00 a.m. He touched her hand as he urged her to look across his chest as the barely rising sun cast an ambient light across the exposed granite faces of some of the cliffs.

"Look, I'll bet that's why they call them the Blue Ridge part of the Appalachians," he said as their heads closed in, looking out the small port of the modified UH-60 Black Hawk helicopter, now redesignated as HMX-1.

"Absolutely awesome," said Monica. She squeezed his hand and turned her head slightly as she pulled back to her side of the seat, discretely kissing Eastwood's cheek. "It was a wonderful weekend. We behaved ourselves, which was amazing," she added to their light laughter. "I'm so sorry Audrey decided to move on. I understand the pain it's causing you. After all, we went through the same thing together before you went to the White House."

"Yeah, I missed you. It's not that I simply want female companionship, quite naturally, but it's yours that is especially helpful. If I weren't a black guy in a sensitive job, we'd be together, you know that," Eastwood said to which Monica gave an affirmative nod, now upright on her own side of the seat, hands apart.

"And you're in one hell of a sensitive job, Earl, that's for sure."

The two had been together briefly during Eastwood's time in the Senate. It was less of a problem until the campaign raised questions, even among Democrats, about an unmarried president. Eastwood's social soul mate, Texas representative Audrey Holmes, a Republican, gradually eased on to a higher relationship plane as his live-in lady friend. That arrangement troubled the party even more while, simultaneously, Holmes lost interest in the arrangement and moved out.

Almost instantaneously, Eastwood resumed his relationship with Monica but endeavored to keep it at a noninvolvement level, which he had succeeded in doing for the past few months. They were seen together many times during the week. They often ran together, dined in the White House, and were openly on display at social events in Washington and, once, on an official trip to Canada. The media quip on the trip was lessened by Monica's meetings with health officials there at a time when Eastwood's health plan was facing challenges in the court system, some at the appellate level. Moreover, there were two collateral issues that inhibited too much media attention. First, presumptuous reporting regarding a high-ranking female official traveling with the president would offend women's groups, and pointed nuances regarding a mixed-race relationship would put the media in perilous territory.

Monica Howard, the West Pointer whose high class standing allowed direct entry into Harvard Medical School after graduation, emerged after several years of training as a hematologist. After completing mandatory army service, which included time on the Hill as a Senate medical fellow, she rose through the corporate ranks to become medical director and general manager of the Rehovot-USA pharmaceutical company near West Haven, Connecticut. From there, she was selected by Eastwood to take over the Department of Health and Human Services as secretary and a member of the president's cabinet.

The Marine One chopper swept down onto the Anacostia Naval Station airbase, home of Marine One. There, Monica would be let off and driven to her Washington office. This could be managed without any media attention, avoiding yet another rumor, although their weekends together at Camp David had now become routine. They kissed good-bye as she disembarked from the chopper, the assembled Marine crew stiffly looking on but seeing nothing at all.

Marine One deposited the president moments later on the West Lawn of the White House, where the approaching aircraft caught the attention of both early-riser tourists and ever-present media representatives.

After a morning of heavy briefings, Eastwood retreated into his private bathroom and locker facility, changing into his running suit while awaiting the 11:15 a.m. meeting as Sue entered several minutes earlier.

"Mr. President, you can't receive cabinet members dressed that way," she said boldly.

Not at all offended, Eastwood meekly replied, "I was hoping you wouldn't notice." They both laughed, and he quickly retreated back to his closet, changing into khakis and a blazer, but tieless.

Returning to the office, he could see from Sue's expression that she was not pleased. "Well, they're here, so we'll have to go with the way you are," she said as Eastwood smirked.

The two cabinet members and the US ambassador to Switzerland entered in order of precedence, the treasury secretary followed by the attorney general. They shook hands, exchanged short greetings, and seated themselves in the conversation pit around a coffee table with a tray of watercress canapés, water, coffee, and soft drinks, which none touched.

"Here's my thought. The Swiss government has played a big role in this matter. Therefore, I'm putting the issue on a sovereign plane. Which is to say, Tim," – Eastwood looked at the ambassador – "I want the government to know that I am intervening because my constituent, an American corporation, has been the target of a plot in which the Swiss were a sovereign coconspirator. Sue, does State go along with this?" Eastwood said, turning to his chief of staff, who had been told to coordinate with Secretary of State Harry Scott, himself a former scholar at UVa Law.

"Yes, sir. He mentioned that, of course, the career types were having a snit fit," she replied to the general laughter of all.

"Yeah, I knew they would. But I can't blame them. They have to live with our decisions, and our stupid ones don't make their lives any easier," the president said.

Turning to the treasury secretary, he said, "Lou, in the negotiations, remind the Swiss of our tax treaty and the agreement regarding the secret-bank-account holders. Our relationships have been pretty good. It is in our obvious mutual interest to keep them that way. But we are still going to pursue several issues under your jurisdiction that are of high interest to us, I'm referring to their devaluation of the Swiss franc to lower the price of their exports. Remind them that the Bank of International Settlements is after all located in Basel. Also, if needed, you can say our effort to recover Jewish property reposed in Swiss banks by Nazi victims will continue. It's unimaginable that they're not shamed by this anyway. You can mention other issues, like our preference for the relocation of the World Trade Organization's headquarters and dispute settlement tribunals from Geneva to venues like Brussels, or The Hague." Eastwood detailed his plan, speaking without notes.

"Jack," he said, addressing Attorney General Jack Hammond, "lay it on them. We have five solid counts that any US court will easily uphold on the strength of the evidence, which you can share with them. They're all violations of the US criminal code. The Swiss government is both directly and indirectly involved as a coconspirator in the Belmont plan, of which, as a board member, the government must have had foreknowledge. Indirectly, they are harboring the perpetrators and abetting their crimes. I'm referring here to the awkward situation they're in because of their nonextradition laws.

"Tim, our goal is to get them to accept the forfeiture of Belmont's material interest. All assets can be seized under our laws based on the fraudulent statements and misrepresentations in the IPO application. Attempted fraud is a crime. We want to settle without too much visibility on either side. In other words, *we want them to prevail upon the Swiss parties to walk away from their investment,*" Eastwood said with strong emphasis. "They may want a cost analysis as well, so be prepared. It shouldn't be too difficult to put those numbers together. This is not an easy mission, so I'm sure you'll be prepared, certainly they will be. When and where will we hold the talks?" the president asked.

"We'll be at their Justice Department. Our counterparts will be the federal councillor for justice and police, Chantal Matthey, and the foreign affairs councillor, Karl Stehlin. There'll be no representation from the finance department. So as you can see, they are going to make it a legal and diplomatic issue, or try to. That surprised me," Ambassador Sawicki replied. "We'll leave this evening for Berne and meet with them on Wednesday morning."

"Okay, I'll call President Ruth Maurer and thank her for her cooperation and express my hopes that we can resolve this in a mutually satisfactory way. She's been very receptive so far. We'll see what really happens," the president added.

Eastwood, who never wore a wristwatch when running or preparing to, glanced at the clock on his desk, which had been turned to allow him to see it from his seated position on the side of the room. It was just about noon, the analog hands read.

Great, they were all prepared and ready to go. Sue did good work, as usual, Eastwood thought, then said, "I apologize for my attire. I was actually in my running suit ready to jump into the car for Fort McNair. I had a busy weekend at Camp David. It rained a lot, so I had to work out on the inside equipment, which I hate. Sue made me change. I didn't have time for a tie, so I guess I'm an anathema to the office, as the historians will no doubt note."

They all laughed, rising, and shook hands.

The US delegation arrived at Andrews AFB, at 4:00 p.m., Monday, October 24, 2011. They boarded the C-37A, the military designation of the Gulfstream V twin-engine, turbo-fan aircraft operated by the Eighty-Ninth Airlift Wing, the special mission unit dedicated to travel for high-ranking administration officials and members of Congress. They were airborne by 5:15 p.m., and by 7:00 p.m., they had dinner and talked over several aspects of the anticipated meeting before settling back in their reclining seats for some sleep as the aircraft cruised at forty-two thousand feet and an airspeed of 525 miles per hour across the Atlantic.

Flying just over six hours, the plane touched down at Bern-Belp International Airport shortly after 8:00 a.m. on Tuesday, October 25, where they were met by two US Embassy vehicles. The convoy drove along the Aare River to Berne in the morning traffic, arriving at the US Embassy on Sulgenstrasse.

At the suggestion of the ambassador, the two cabinet members retreated to their rooms in the ambassador's residence for some rest while Sawicki went to his office in the embassy building to make final arrangements. That evening, a reception for the two cabinet members was held in the embassy foyer, with several councillor-level officials from the Swiss government present, including Madame Maurer, the president of the Swiss Confederation, and the two counterparts with whom the meeting would be held the next day. The reception, kept brief at two hours as a courtesy to the transatlantic travelers, provided an opportunity to chat amicably among the parties who would soon face each other at the negotiation table.

At 9:15 a.m., after breakfasting at the residence with Sawicki and his wife, the three men drove in a convoy escorted by a Berne police motorcycle to the Federal Palace at the Bundesplaatz in the center of the city for their 10:00 a.m. meeting. The one-hundred-year-old Bundeshaus, which hosts the two parliamentary chambers and offices of the elected deputies and senators, is famously Swiss: unpretentious, informally open, and somewhat austere by standards that describe the Swiss' European cousins. The group was greeted by the two councillors they would be meeting with as they entered the grand foyer: Karl Stehlin, the foreign affairs councillor, the equivalent of the secretary of state in the United States, and Chantal Matthey, the justice councillor, both of whom had been at the embassy reception the previous evening. The greetings were mutually cheerful as the crisp morning air seemed to follow the US delegation into the unheated foyer.

With an aide in the lead, the group walked up the grand marble staircase; the US members were awed by the impressive stained glass array of cantonal coats of arms encircling the one-hundred-foot interior of the dome, at the center of which was the red-background Swiss national emblem with the white cross.

"Glad to get my morning workout in," said Treasury Secretary Louis Dubin to Foreign Affairs Councillor Karl Stehlin. "We depend too much on elevators in the US. A walk like this would build character and help keep waistlines under control."

"It does build one's appetite," Stehlin replied, "and Swiss food is very rich. So we too must be careful. Here, we walk, ride our bicycles, and hike during the weekends for relaxation. It helps somewhat, but we are also facing an obesity crisis in this country," he added in grammatically excellent English.

They arrived in the West Wing, at the office of the federal councillor of justice and police, Madame Matthey's office. Entering the conference room, they took assigned places opposite one another at the conference table. A glass-enclosed translator booth was situated at the back of the room. The US delegation faced large windows, two of which were open, letting in cool but refreshing air. Three male aides were aligned along the wall behind the seated Swiss officials. Within seconds after they were seated, liveried waiters arrived with beverages for the guests, the US Embassy having advised the Swiss hosts in advance of the coffee preferences of the two US cabinet members and Ambassador Sawicki.

Madame Matthey appeared to be the more senior of the two Swiss councillors and welcomed the group, saying, "We are pleased and honored by your visit. I was informed by Her Excellency Madame Ruth Maurer, the president of the Swiss Confederation, that President Eastwood spoke to her just yesterday. She has told me further that both presidents are very eager to resolve this matter in an agreeable and efficient manner, which, I am certain, are also our objectives as we open our discussions. On our side, we are fairly fluent in English and can use that language. However, we have interpreters standing by in the event there is any need for clarification of statements or terms."

Ambassador Sawicki spoke first. "Madame Councillor, we extend further President Eastwood's regards to you and appreciate your kind hospitality. In the few months I've been here as my country's representative, I've experienced nothing but the highest form of welcome and cooperation.

"The matter before us is complicated," Sawicki continued. "But its importance is evidenced by the presence of two cabinet secretaries. And we appreciate the presence of their equivalents from your government.

"Since the embassy and the state department have provided advance information describing the history and outcome of Belmont's acquisition of the two US confection companies, I suggest we dispense with that part of the discussion and move into the more troubling consequences of the transaction, if there is no objection," Sawicki said, looking up from his prepared remarks. Coming from a business background in the confection industry, Sawicki was fully familiar with the operational nature of the companies, but still waddling in his ability to manage a diplomatic negotiation.

"There is no objection, Ambassador," Madame Matthey replied.

"Thank you. The most critical element of our case is the criminal nature of certain actions taken by Belmont and the management of their US-based company, the Swiss-American Confections Corporation, which I will refer to as S-A-C-C. Here, I am pointing to misrepresentations made in documentation material to SACC's application to take the company public."

Making an attempt to soften somewhat what was to follow, Sawicki prefaced his next comments with this statement: "Now, as anyone involved in the investments sector in Europe or the US knows only too well, our laws, regulations, and rules governing public company formation, capitalization, and trading on investment exchanges are very rigorous, so much so that many companies, including some from Switzerland, have chosen to use other exchanges, such as those in England, France, Germany, and even the Nikkei in Japan. This has led to a loss of business for US exchanges and is a matter that our Congress has begun to look at very closely.

"But we must operate under current laws, those that are on the books. Regrettably, that is what has brought us here since there have been violations, which we have listed and explained in the materials provided to you and your legal staffs. The sanctions have also been listed, and they are rather severe. I will ask Treasury Secretary Dubin to address the sanction that now emerges as the most likely outcome of this matter," Sawicki said, turning his attention to Dubin, seated to his right.

"Let me add my thanks, Madame Matthey and Councillor Stehlin, to you for hosting our discussion. I also want to say how much we all enjoyed our social visit last night. It was a perfect introduction to this magnificent country. I add that my daughter had spent a semester at the University of Geneva two years ago. She was deeply inspired by the Swiss people and is pursuing a graduate business degree back at Stanford in anticipation of working with an international organization," Dubin said to the friendly nods and smiles of the two Swiss officials at the table.

The smiles would soon fade as Dubin continued to speak. "The severity of the offenses has many precedents. Our Congress seems to have decided that white-collar crime can be as destabilizing to society as other offenses, especially where such crime weakens our economic and social structures and allows unfair enrichment and other advantages. In the particular case before us, our guidelines are fairly straight forward. We must deprive wrongdoers of the unearned fruits of their misdeeds. This policy leads us to the seizure of SACC's assets under our forfeiture laws. This, my friends, is where we stand at the moment."

One of the aides to the justice councillor, most likely a young attorney, slipped a document to her. Matthey began to speak. "Thank you, Secretary Dubin. There are indeed obvious differences in the rules that bring public offerings to the market place in the US and in Switzerland. Your generally agreed accounting practices, for example, disallow revenue categories and characterizations that our rules find to be quite acceptable additions to balance sheets. And we allow certain prospective transactions to be treated as settled events for accounting and tax purposes. The investment bank managing the IPO, as it's called in the US, is Swiss, its investment manager Swiss trained, and the SACC principal, the CEO, Mr. Rallis, a Greek national who is a Swiss resident with many business interests in this country.

"Why do I mention this panoply of players? First, the Swiss bank in New York operates under US rules. Second, although Swiss trained, the investment manager, Monsieur Henri Baptiste, is expected to comply with US banking laws and is guided by an American counterpart at the bank, as well as a US law firm on retention. But Mr. Nikos Rallis is Greek, as I had mentioned a moment ago, and has been trained in the US, at no less a distinguished institution than the University of Pennsylvania's Wharton School from which he received his MBA.

"In our discussion with Baptiste and his American counterpart at the bank, the two insisted that they repeatedly warned Mr. Rallis that the planned purchase of the Massachusetts facility by a Belmont executive, for a price not even close to its market value, could raise 'red flags' at the SEC, as his statement says.

"Moreover," Matthey continued, "we have interviewed the CEOs of the two Swiss companies most involved in effecting the US venture, Herr Paul von Schlossen of Brent, the commodity trading firm, and Herr Lutz Gorgens, the CEO of Belmont, the principal in the acquisition. Both of these business leaders say that Mr. Rallis was not their agent in his capacity as CEO of SACC, a position that he assumed, as an investor, and without their advance or prior consent. While Mr. Rallis did coordinate with Messieurs von Schlossen and Gorgens, the two Swiss officials expected that he, Mr. Rallis, as a US-trained businessman, would act in a manner in full compliance with US laws and that any advice the two Swiss gentlemen gave to Mr. Rallis could not possibly be a binding instruction by a principal or higher authority and that all such decisions deriving from this advice were the full responsibility of Mr. Rallis alone."

The three Americans had been taken by surprise. Nothing had prepared them for the Swiss response to the charges and proposed sanction. Attorney General Jack Hammond's thinking was largely synchronized with the others as they surreptitiously glanced at each other, trying to avoid appearing as having been surprised. *So they're making Rallis the fall guy. He takes the heat, but he's holed up in Switzerland, so they're still abetting him.*

Treasury Secretary Dubin was thinking somewhat along the same lines. *Rallis! The Greek, the noncitizen, pretty cool move, but what becomes of Rallis? And will they accept forfeiture? We'll need to work something out to make the Swiss company, Belmont, somewhat whole. It may be that they'll be happy just recovering some of their investment.*

Ambassador Sawicki had suspected Rallis would be the scapegoat from the outset. *Amazing these Swiss, they can shamelessly shield foreigners from tax obligations, provide secret bank accounts, steal Holocaust victims' property, provide a platform for just about every corrupt operation managed by foreigners on their soil, sell their arms and other defense items to anyone despite their neutral status, and yet never feel any moral stigma. So now it's that nasty Greek guy that misled these innocent Swiss partners and bankers into a fraudulent situation. I'm the discussion leader. The president wants me to make a decision, and I will.*

The stare down ended as Ambassador Sawicki spoke. "Madame Councillor, Herr Councillor Stehlin, my president would be very pleased to come to some settlement, which I think is very possible."

"Yes, we were very much hoping that we could resolve this matter in a mutually satisfactory way," Foreign Affairs Councillor Stehlin said. "And we have taken the first steps by nullifying Mr. Rallis's visa and directing him to leave Switzerland within thirty days."

I hope to hell they don't think that's the settlement, Attorney General Hammond was thinking. He was relieved when Louis Dubin spoke next.

"Ambassador Sawicki and Councillor Stehlin have set the stage, I believe, for a settlement. Regrettably, there still remain the violations of federal law to be resolved, and we treat the corporation in our legal system, as you do in yours, as a legal personality. I don't see how we can avoid the forfeiture sanction under these circumstances," Dubin said.

Another aide slipped yet another document to the justice councillor, Madame Matthey, as if the question had been anticipated. She spoke. "We do agree that there are innocent parties on either side who have been legally injured by the actual and prospective behavior of Mr. Rallis," she said, glancing at but not reciting from the paper in front of her. "We want the reputation of our Swiss companies to be protected as they must continue to operate globally, including in the US."

Dumb move, Hammond thought. *She's admitting to an act involving Belmont that could have resulted in harm. I better get in here.*

"Yes, Madame Councillor. It concerns the president greatly that the Swiss gentlemen and the Swiss government itself, which is on the boards of both Brent and Belmont, had sufficient foreknowledge of these events, enough knowledge to get expert advice from your ministry as to the legality of the actions that were increasingly sweeping them into the wrongs that have occurred."

The Swiss officials smiled uncomfortably. They knew now that they were defending their government as well as the two Swiss companies and their management.

Hammond continued. "Even more regrettably is that the case is now a sovereign matter. If we take the matter to our court system, the evidence will be wide open to our very aggressive media. This could harm your national image: tourism, banking, international commerce, other sectors will suffer economically. We very likely would have to reconsider even our defense contracts with you since our Congress is certain to react."

Foreign Affairs Councillor Stehlin knew he was on the hot seat. "Our countries have a long and harmonious history of working out differences, as the recent tax treaty and secret-bank-account disclosures have shown. Of course, we want to protect our reputation, which is why we have directed the removal of Mr. Rallis from Switzerland," he said.

Hammond was getting their drift. *Let him talk, he'll walk right into our plan.* He discretely nudged Sawicki's elbow, signaling his thoughts, which Sawicki immediately sensed.

Stehlin continued to speak. "Our president cares greatly about the Swiss national image and an event like this happening under, as you might say, her 'watch.' And we have an investment in Belmont, which is now at risk also."

Another stupidity, Hammond thought, *admitting to the government's financial-driven consent to the Belmont charade. Your move, Lou, give them the deal.* He turned, looking directly at Treasury Secretary Dubin, furling his brow as he nodded, as if to say, "Speak up, Lou."

Dubin knew exactly how to react; the teamwork and planning that went into the meeting, along with the president's grant of rights to act to his cabinet members, was working well. Their spontaneity and skilled negotiation tactics would make the difference. "I believe that we can come to an arrangement that's in everyone's interest," Dubin started.

He continued to speak. "I can't prevent the forfeiture since it's a crime to conceal a crime. And my position offers no immunity from commission of a crime. But let me suggest the following:

"First, the IPO is ended. There is nothing to be gained by Belmont or any other Swiss investors in the company from a public offering.

"Second, the assets have been forfeited to the United States government, which holds SACC as its trustee since the government has no interest in running a confections company.

"Third, subject to the approval of my colleague Attorney General Jack Hammond," Dubin said, turning his head toward Hammond, "we can avoid a court action on the charges since the principal suspect, Mr. Rallis, is not likely to be extradited from Greece or Switzerland." Dubin looked at the Swiss justice councillor, who nodded affirmatively.

"And finally, we can compensate you, the government and the company, Belmont," Dubin said, making it evident in mentioning the 'government' that they would not escape an appearance, at least, of complicity, "by imposing on SACC, in whatever form it revives from this arrangement, other than bankruptcy, the obligation to repay Belmont an amount no less than its original purchase price, despite the current purchase contract clause that calls for resale back to original ownership at double the purchase price."

The Swiss aides were writing furiously, adjusting the recording devices in their hands to ensure they had captured the precise language of the settlement. The two Swiss councillors' faces softened; once more, it appeared that even this outcome had been anticipated by them.

Madame Matthey stretched her hand across the table, followed by that of Foreign Affairs Councillor Stehlin, first to Treasury Secretary Dubin, then to Attorney General Hammond, and finally to Ambassador Sawicki, in precise order of official precedence of which the canny Swiss had also been apprised.

The parties agreed to write up their own impressions of the agreement and exchange them with officials at the US Departments of Justice and Treasury for corrections and any other mutually acceptable amendments.

EPILOGUE 1

THE PARTIES AVENGED were many and broadly interconnected. SACC would be revived under the restored leadership of co-CEOs Tim Sawicki and Kyle McMahon, the former chiefs of the two bought-out US confection companies in Connecticut and Massachusetts. Connecticut governor Sophia Kallias would get more jobs for her state as the government contract for the "Chocobrain" product spread from defense to Homeland Security and FEMA and into kids' lunch boxes and school cafeterias. These outcomes evened out scores with Nikos Rallis, who had exploited her. Senator Zbig Krakowski dropped his pursuit of his party's nomination for governor but picked up Sue Cohen in a matrimonial coup. The expats lost their bid for pardons when the unimpeachably straight Earl Eastwood refused to set aside their egregious conflict of interests as members of Congress who had put their own interests ahead of their public duties. Liz Sachs returned to the Harvard Business School, pursuing a doctorate in business administration and a teaching career, which would exude a commitment to business ethics that current business school curricula seem to treat with laughing disregard.

Finally, the inimitable Earl Eastwood provided yet another case study of a politician whose commitment to the rule of law, right over convenience, duty over self, and compromise over confounding conflict can give new meaning to "sweet revenge."

EPILOGUE 2

TOO OFTEN, SEEMINGLY innocent policy changes mask the intensive negotiation and deal making that is customary to the American political culture. Government intervention in the private sector has carried the custom forward and intensified. The Dodd-Frank banking legislation is in many ways a watermark imprinted on future transactions as a reminder of government scrutiny. Excessive as it may appear, this and other recent regulatory impulses respond to the troublesome inadequacy of yet another custom of the American political culture: the failure of certain business sectors to sufficiently police themselves.

But other surprises can be found at the intersection of business and government. Regulatory agencies can turn a blind eye, as seen in the inept oversight of the Madoff scam by the US Securities and Exchange Commission. This story resides at this borderline. Congressional pressure, legislation that bypasses safeguards, and the self-serving motives of members themselves can upset even the most carefully sculpted obstacles to wrongdoing. Nor is this style of exceptionalism uncommon to other democracies.

The details underscoring this internationally contrived scheme to capture a major business sector in the US marketplace are complex. The rate of global marketplace growth has dramatically outpaced every convention, treaty, and agreement to regulate it. Transactions occur somewhat frenetically on the very edge of current regulatory frameworks. The dispute settlement venues of the World Trade Organization gasp in the race to ensure normalcy, equitable treatment, and stability. Sovereign nations suspend private rights of action when their companies file grievances, insisting that governments plead outcomes. Sovereign action is always politically nuanced, the endless delay of Mexican truck entry into the United States under the terms of the North American Free Trade Agreement, NAFTA, a major case in point.

Skimming under the regulatory radars has become more common as this story attempts to explain.

19488552R00209

Made in the USA
San Bernardino, CA
28 February 2015